Lilian Jackson Braun composed her first poem at the age of two. She began writing her *Cat Who...* mysteries when one of her own Siamese cats mysteriously fell to its death from her apartment block. Since then, seventeen *Cat Who...* novels have been published, all featuring the very talented Koko and Yum Yum, Siamese cats with a bent for detection. She is currently working on the next novel in this internationally bestselling series. There are now over three million *Cat Who...* mysteries in print around the world.

Lilian Jackson Braun and her husband, Earl, live with their two Siamese cats, Koko III and Pitti Sing, in the mountains of North Carolina.

D1589967

Also by Lilian Jackson Braun

The Cat Who Ate Danish Modern

headline

Copyright © 19967 Lilian Jackson Braun

The right of Lilian Jackson Braun to be identified as the Author of
the Work has been asserted by her in accordance with the
Copyright, Designs and Patents Act 1988.

First published in paperback in Great Britain in 1995
by HEADLINE BOOK PUBLISHING

7 9 10 8 6

ISBN 978 0 7472 5035 7

Printed and bound by
CPI Group (UK) Ltd, Croydon, CR0 4YY

Reproduced from a previously printed copy

HEADLINE BOOK PUBLISHING
A division of Hodder Headline PLC
338 Euston Road
London NW1 3BH

www.headline.co.uk
www.hodderheadline.com

The Cat Who Ate Danish Modern

headline

One

Jim Qwilleran prepared his bachelor breakfast with a look of boredom and distaste, accentuated by the down-curve of his bushy moustache. Using hot water from the tap, he made a cup of instant coffee with brown lumps floating on the surface. He dredged a doughnut from a crumb-filled canister that was beginning to smell musty. Then he spread a paper napkin on a table in a side window where the urban sun, filtered through smog, emphasized the bleakness of the furnished apartment.

Here Qwilleran ate his breakfast without tasting it, and considered his four problems:

At the moment he was womanless. He had received an eviction notice, and in three weeks he would be homeless. At the rate the moths were feeding on his neckwear, he would soon be tieless. And if he said the wrong thing to the managing editor today, he might very well be jobless. Over forty-five and jobless. It was not a cheerful prospect.

Fortunately, he was not friendless. On his breakfast table – along with a large unabridged dictionary, a stack of paperback books, a pipe rack with a single pipe, and a can of tobacco – there was a Siamese cat.

Qwilleran scratched his friend behind the ears, and said, 'I'll bet you weren't allowed to sit on the breakfast table when you lived upstairs.'

The cat, whose name was Koko, gave a satisfied wiggle, tilted his whiskers upward, and said, 'YOW!'

He had lived with the newsman for six months, following the unfortunate demise of the man on the second floor. Qwilleran fed him well, conversed sensibly, and invented games to play – unusual pastimes that appealed to the cat's extraordinary intelligence.

Every morning Koko occupied one small corner of the breakfast table, arranging himself in a compact bundle, brown feet and tail tucked fastidiously under his white-breasted fawn body. In the mild sunshine Koko's slanted eyes were a brilliant blue, and his silky fur, like the newly spun spider web that spanned the window, glistened with a rainbow of iridescence.

'You make this apartment look like a dump,' Qwilleran told him.

Koko squeezed his eyes and breathed faster. With each breath his nose changed from black velvet to black satin, then back to velvet.

Qwilleran lapsed again into deep thought, absently running a spoon handle through his moustache. This was the day he had promised himself to confront the managing editor and request a change of assignment. It was a risky move. *The Daily Fluxion* was known as a tight ship. Percy preached teamwork, team spirit, team discipline. Shoulder to shoulder, play the game, one for all. Ours not to question why. A long pull, a strong pull, a pull all together. We happy few!

'It's like this,' Qwilleran told the cat. 'If I walk into Percy's office and flatly request a change of assignment, I'm apt to land out in the street. That's the way he operates. And I can't afford to be unemployed – not right now – not till I build up a cash reserve.'

Koko was listening to every word.

'If the worst came to the worst, I suppose I could get a job at the *Morning Rampage*, but I'd hate to work for that stuffy sheet.'

Koko's eyes were large and full of understanding. 'Yow,' he said softly.

'I wish I could have a heart-to-heart talk with Percy, but it's impossible to get through to him. He's programmed, like a computer. His smile – very sincere. His handshake – very strong. His compliments – very gratifying. Then the next time you meet him on the elevator, he doesn't know you. You're not on his schedule for the day.'

Koko shifted his position uneasily.

'He doesn't even look like a managing editor. He dresses like an advertising man. Makes me feel like a slob.' Qwilleran passed a hand over the back of his neck. 'Guess I should get a haircut.'

Koko gurgled something in his throat, and Qwilleran recognized the cue. 'Okay, we'll play the game. But only a few innings this morning. I've got to go to work.'

He opened the big dictionary, which was remarkable

for its tattered condition, and he and Koko played their word game. The way it worked, the cat dug his claws into the pages, and Qwilleran opened the book where he indicated, reading aloud the catchwords – the two boldface entries at the top of the columns. He read the right-hand page if Koko used his right paw, but usually it was the left-hand page. Koko was inclined to be a southpaw.

'*Design* and *desk*,' Qwilleran read. 'Those are easy. Score two points for me . . . Go ahead, try again.'

Koko cocked his brown ears forward and dug in with his claws.

'*Dictyogenous* and *Diegueños*. You sneaky rascal! You've stumped me!' Qwilleran had to look up both definitions, and that counted two points for the cat.

The final score was 7 to 5 in Qwilleran's favor. Then he proceeded to shower and dress, after preparing Koko's breakfast – fresh beef, diced and heated with a little canned mushroom gravy. The cat showed no interest in food, however. He followed the man around, yowling for attention in his clarion Siamese voice, tugging at the bath towel, leaping into dresser drawers as they were opened.

'What tie shall I wear?' Qwilleran asked him. There were only a few neckties in his collection – for the most part Scotch plaids with a predominance of red. They hung about the apartment on door handles and chairbacks. 'Maybe I should wear something funereal to impress Percy favorably. These days we all conform. You cats are the only real independents left.'

Koko blinked his acknowledgment.

Qwilleran reached for a narrow strip of navy-blue wool draped over the swing-arm of a floor lamp. 'Damn those moths!' he said. 'Another tie ruined!'

Koko uttered a small squeak that sounded like sympathy, and Qwilleran, examining the nibbled edge of the necktie, decided to wear it anyway.

'If you want to make yourself useful,' he told the cat, 'why don't you go to work on the moths and quit wasting your time on spider webs?'

Koko had developed a curious aberration since coming to live with Qwilleran. In this dank old building spiders were plentiful, and as fast as they spun their webs, Koko devoured the glistening strands.

Qwilleran tucked the ragged end of the navy-blue tie into his shirt and pocketed his pipe, a quarter-bend bulldog. Then he tousled Koko's head in a rough farewell and left the apartment on Blenheim Place.

When he eventually arrived in the lobby of the *Daily Fluxion*, his hair was cut, his moustache was lightly trimmed, and his shoes rivaled the polish on the black marble walls. He caught a reflection of his profile in the marble and pulled in his waistline; it was beginning to show a slight convexity.

More than a few eyes turned his way. Since his arrival at the *Fluxion* seven months before – with his ample moustache, picturesque pipe, and unexplained past – Qwilleran had been a subject for conjecture. Everyone knew he had had a notable career as a crime reporter in New York and Chicago. After that, he had disappeared for a few years, and now he was holding down a quiet desk on a Midwestern newspaper, and writing, of all things, features on art!

The elevator door opened, and Qwilleran stepped aside while several members of the Women's Department filed out on their way to morning assignments or coffee breaks.

As they passed, he checked them off with a calculating eye. One was too old. One was too homely. The fashion writer was too formidable. The society writer was married.

The married one looked at him with mock reproach. 'You lucky dog!' she said. 'Some people get all the breaks. I hate you!'

Qwilleran watched her sail across the lobby, and then he jumped on the elevator just before the automatic doors closed.

'I wonder what *that* was all about,' he mumbled.

There was one other passenger on the car – a blonde clerk from the Advertising Department. 'I just heard the news,' she said. 'Congratulations!' and she stepped off the elevator at the next floor.

A great hope was rising under Qwilleran's frayed tie as he walked into the Feature Department with its rows of green metal desks, green typewriters, and green telephones.

Arch Riker beckoned to him. 'Stick around,' the feature editor said. 'Percy's calling a meeting at ten thirty. Probably wants to discuss that ridiculous *w* in your name. Have you seen the first edition?' He pushed a newspaper across the desk and pointed to a major headline: *Judge Qwits Bench After Graft Qwiz.*

Riker said: 'No one caught the error until the papers were on the street. You've got the whole staff confused.'

'It's a good Scottish name,' Qwilleran said in defense. Then he leaned over Riker's desk, and said: 'I've been getting some interesting vibrations this morning. I think Percy's giving me a new assignment.'

'If he is, it's news to me.'

'For six months I've been journalism's most ludicrous figure – a crime writer assigned to the art beat.'

'You didn't have to take the job if it didn't appeal to you.'

'I needed the money. *You* know that. And I was promised a desk in the City Room as soon as there was an opening.'

'Lots of luck,' Riker said in a minor key.

'I think something's about to break. And whatever it is, everyone knows it but you and me.'

The feature editor leaned back in his chair and folded his arms. 'It's axiomatic in the communications industry,' he said, 'that the persons most directly concerned are the last ones to know.'

When the signal came from the City Room, Riker and Qwilleran filed into the managing editor's office, saying, 'Morning, Harold.' The boss was called Percy only behind his back.

The advertising director was there, shooting his cuffs. The photo chief was there, looking bored. The women's editor was there, wearing a brave hat of zebra fur and giving Qwilleran a prolonged friendly stare that embarrassed him. Fran Unger had a syrupy charm that he distrusted. He was wary of women executives. He had been married to one once.

Someone closed the door, and the managing editor swiveled his chair to face Qwilleran.

'Qwill, I owe you an apology,' he said. 'I should have discussed this with you ten days ago. You've probably been hearing rumors, and it was unfair of me to leave you in the dark. I'm sorry. I've been involved with the mayor's

Civilian Committee on Crime, but that is no excuse per se.'

He's really not a bad guy, Qwilleran thought, as he wriggled anxiously in his chair.

'We promised you another assignment when the right opportunity presented itself,' the editor went on, 'and now we have a real challenge for you! We are about to launch a project of significance to the entire newspaper industry and, I might add, a bonanza for the *Daily Fluxion* per se.'

Qwilleran began to realize why everyone called the boss Percy.

The editor continued: 'This city has been selected for an experiment to determine if national advertising ordinarily carried in magazines can be diverted to daily papers in major cities.'

The advertising director said, 'If it works, our linage will double. The revenue for the experimental year alone will be upward of a million dollars.'

'The *Morning Rampage* also will be making a bid for this plum,' said the editor, 'but with our new presses and our color reproduction process, we can produce a superior product.'

Qwilleran stroked his moustache nervously.

'It will be your job, Qwill, to produce a special Sunday supplement for fifty-two weeks – in magazine format, with plenty of color!'

Qwilleran's mind raced ahead to the possibilities. He pictured great court trials, election campaigns, political exposés, sports spectaculars, perhaps overseas coverage. He cleared his throat, and said, 'This new magazine – I suppose it will be general interest?'

'General interest in its approach,' said Percy, 'but specific in content. We want you to publish a weekly magazine on interior design.'

'On *what*?' Qwilleran said in an unintended falsetto.

'On interior decorating. The experiment is being conducted by the home-furnishings industry.'

'Interior decorating!' Qwilleran felt a chill in the roots of his moustache. 'I should think you'd want a woman to handle it.'

Fran Unger spoke up sweetly. 'The Women's Department wanted the assignment very badly, Qwill, but Harold feels a great many *men* are interested in the home today. He wants to avoid the women's slant and attract general readership to the *Gracious Abodes* magazine.'

Qwilleran's throat felt as if it had swallowed his moustache. '*Gracious Abodes?* Is that the name of the thing?'

Percy nodded. 'I think it conveys the right message: charm, livability, taste! You can do stories on luxury homes, high-rent apartments, residential status symbols and the Upper Ten Percent and how they live.'

Qwilleran fingered his frayed tie.

'You'll love this assignment, Qwill,' the women's editor assured him. 'You'll be working with decorators, and they're delightful people.'

Qwilleran leaned toward the managing editor earnestly. 'Harold, are you sure you want me for this beat? You know my background! I don't know the first thing about decorating.'

'You did an outstanding job on the art beat without knowing the first thing about art,' said Percy. 'In our business, expertise can be a drawback. What this new job needs is nothing more nor less than a seasoned newsman, creative and resourceful. If you have any trouble at the start, Fran will be glad to lend a hand, I'm sure.'

Qwilleran squirmed in his chair.

'Yes, of course,' said the women's editor. 'We can work together, Qwill, and I can steer you in the right direction.' Ignoring Qwilleran's bleak reaction, she went on. 'For example, you could start with the Sorbonne Studio; they do society work. Then Lyke and Starkweather; they're the largest decorating firm in town.' She made a swooning gesture. 'David Lyke is absolutely adorable!'

'I'll bet he is,' said Qwilleran in a sullen growl. He had his private opinion of decorators, both male and female.

'There's also Mrs Middy, who does cozy Early American interiors. And there's a new studio called PLUG. It specializes in Planned Ugliness.'

Then Percy made a remark that cast a new light on the proposal. 'This assignment will carry more responsibility,' he said to Qwilleran, 'and naturally your classification will be adjusted. You will be advanced from senior writer to junior editor.'

Qwilleran made a quick computation and came up with a figure that would finance a decent place to live and pay off some old debts. He tugged at his moustache. 'I suppose I could give it a try,' he said. 'How soon would you want me to start?'

'Yesterday! We happen to know that the *Morning Rampage* is breaking with their supplement on October first. We'd like to beat them to the wire.'

That turned the trick. The prospect of scoring a beat on the competition stirred the ink in Qwilleran's veins. His first horrified reaction to *Gracious Abodes* dissolved into a sudden sense of proprietorship. And when Fran Unger gave him a chummy smile and said, 'We'll have fun with this assignment, Qwill,' he felt like saying, Sister, just keep your hands off *my magazine*.

That day, during the lunch hour, Qwilleran went out and celebrated the raise in salary. He bought a can of crabmeat for Koko and a new tie for himself. Another red wool plaid.

Two

Wearing his new tie and the better of his two suits, Qwilleran set forth with some apprehension for his first visit to a decorating studio, bracing himself for an overdose of the precious and the esoteric.

He found the firm of Lyke and Starkweather in an exclusive shopping area, surrounded by specialty shops, art galleries, and tearooms. The entrance was impressive. Huge double doors of exotically grained wood had silver door handles as big as baseball bats.

The interior displayed furniture in room settings, and Qwilleran was pleased to find one room wallpapered in a red plaid that matched his tie. Moose antlers were mounted above a fireplace made of wormeaten driftwood, and there was a sofa covered in distressed pigskin, like the hides of retired footballs.

A slender young man approached him, and the newsman asked to see Mr Lyke or Mr Starkweather. After a delay that seemed inauspicious, a gray-haired man appeared from behind an Oriental screen at the rear of the shop. He had a bland appearance and a bland manner.

'Mr Lyke is the one you should talk to, if it's about publicity,' he told Qwilleran, 'but he's busy with a client Why don't you just look around while you're waiting?'

'Are you Mr Starkweather?' Qwilleran asked.

'Yes, but I think you should talk to Mr Lyke. He's the one . . .'

'I'd appreciate it if you'd tell me about these displays while I'm waiting.' Qwilleran motioned toward the moose antlers.

'There isn't much to tell,' said Starkweather with a helpless gesture.

'What's selling these days?'

'Just about everything.'

'Is there any particular color that's popular?'

'No. They're all good.'

'I see you have some modern stuff over there.'

'We have a little of everything.'

Qwilleran's interviewing technique was not working. 'What do you call that thing?' he asked, pointing to a tall secretary-desk with bulbous base and an inlaid design of exotic birds and flowers.

'It's a desk,' said Starkweather. Then his expressionless face brightened a fraction of a degree. 'Here comes Mr Lyke.'

From behind the Oriental screen came a good-looking man in his early thirties. He had his arm around an elaborately hatted middle-aged woman who was smiling and blushing with pleasure.

Lyke was saying in a deep, chesty voice: 'You go home, dear, and tell the Old Man you've got to have that twelve-foot sofa. It won't cost him a cent more than the last car he bought. And remember, dear, I want you to invite me to dinner the next time you're having that *superb* chocolate cake. Don't let your cook bake it. I want you to bake it yourself – for David.'

While he talked, David Lyke was walking the woman rapidly toward the front door, where he stopped and kissed her temple. Then he said a beautifully timed goodbye, meaningful but not lingering.

When he turned toward Qwilleran, he recomposed his face abruptly from an expression of rapture to one of businesslike aplomb, but he could not change his eyes. He had brooding eyes with heavy lids and long lashes. Even more striking was his hair – snow white and somewhat sensational with his young suntanned face.

'I'm David Lyke,' he growled pleasantly, extending a cordial hand. His eyes flickered downward for only a second, but Qwilleran felt they had appraised his plaid tie and the width of his lapel. 'Come into my office, and we'll talk.'

The newsman followed him into a room that had deep-gray walls. A leopard rug sprawled on the polished ebony floor. Lounge chairs, square and bulky and masculine, were covered in fabric with the texture of popcorn. On the back wall was a painting of a nude figure, her skin tones a luminous blue-gray, like steel.

Qwilleran found himself nodding in approval. 'Nice office.'

'Glad you like it,' the decorator said. 'Don't you think gray is terribly civilized? I call this shade Poppy Seed. The chairs are sort of Dried Fig. I'm sick to death of Pablum Beige and Mother's Milk White.' He reached for a decanter. 'How about a splash of cognac?'

Qwilleran declined. He said he would rather smoke his pipe. Then he stated his mission, and Lyke said in his rumbling voice: 'I wish you hadn't called your magazine *Gracious Abodes*. It gives me visions of lavender gloves and *pêche Melba*.'

'What kind of decorating do you do?' the newsman asked.

'All kinds. If people want to live like conquistadors or English barons or little French kings, we don't fight it.'

'If you can find an important house for us to photograph, we'll put it on the cover of our first issue.'

'We'd like the publicity,' said the decorator, 'but I don't know how our clients will react. You know how it is; whenever the boys in Washington find out a taxpayer has wall-to-wall carpet in his bathroom, they audit his tax returns for the last three years.' He was flipping through a card index. 'I have a magnificent Georgian Colonial job, done in Champagne and Cranberry, but the lamps haven't arrived... And here's an Edwardian town house in Benedictine and Plum, but there's been a delay on the draperies; the fabric manufacturer discontinued the pattern.'

'Could the photographer shoot from an angle that would avoid the missing drapes?'

Lyke looked startled, but he recovered quickly and shook his head. 'No, you'd have to include the windows.' He browsed through the file and suddenly seized an index card. 'Here's a house I'd like to see you publish! Do you know G. Verning Tait? I did his house in French Empire with built-in vitrines for his jade collection.'

'Who is this Tait?' Qwilleran asked. 'I'm new in this city.'

'You don't know the Taits? They're one of the old families living in pseudocastles down in Muggy Swamp. You know Muggy Swamp, of course – very exclusive.' The decorator made a rueful face. 'Unfortunately, the clients with the longest pedigrees are the slowest to pay their bills.'

'Are the Taits very social?'

'They used to be, but they live quietly now. Mrs Tait is unwell, as they say in Muggy Swamp.'

'Do you think they'd let us photograph?'

'People with Old Money always avoid publicity on their real estate,' Lyke said, 'but in this case I might be able to use a little persuasion.'

Other possibilities were discussed, but both the decorator and newsman agreed the Tait house would be perfect: important name, spectacular décor, brilliant color, and a jade collection to add interest.

'Besides that,' said Lyke with a smug smile, 'it's the only job I've succeeded in getting away from the Sorbonne Studio. It would give me a lot of satisfaction to see the Tait house on the cover of *Gracious Abodes*.'

'If you succeed in lining it up, call me immediately,' Qwilleran said. 'We're working against time on the first issue. I'll give you my home phone.'

He wrote his number on a *Daily Fluxion* card and stood up to leave.

David Lyke gave him a parting handshake that was

hearty and sincere. 'Good luck with your magazine. And may I give you some fatherly advice?'

Qwilleran eyed the younger man anxiously.

'Never,' said Lyke with an engaging smile, '*never* call draperies *drapes*.'

Qwilleran returned to his office, pondering the complexities of his new beat and thinking fondly of lunch in the familiar drabness of the Press Club, where the wall color was Sirloin, Medium Rare.

On his desk there was a message to call Fran Unger. He dialed her number reluctantly.

'I've been working on our project,' said the women's editor, 'and I have some leads for you. Have you got a pencil ready? . . . First, there's a Greek Revival farmhouse converted into a Japanese teahouse. And then there's a penthouse apartment with carpet on the walls and ceiling, and an aquarium under the glass floor. And I know where there's an exciting master bedroom done entirely in three shades of black, except for the bed, which is brass . . . That should be enough to fill the first issue!'

Qwilleran felt his moustache bristling. 'Well, thanks, but I've got all the material I need for the first book,' he said, aware that it was a rash lie.

'Really? For a beginner you're a fast worker. What have you lined up?'

'It's a long, involved story,' Qwilleran said vaguely.

'I'd love to hear it. Are you going to the Press Club for lunch?'

'No,' he said with hesitation. 'As a matter of fact, I'm having lunch . . . with a decorator . . . at a private club.'

Fran Unger was a good newspaperwoman, and not easy

to put down. 'In that case, why don't we meet for drinks at the Press Club at five thirty?'

'I'm sorry,' Qwilleran said in his politest voice, 'but I've got an early dinner date uptown.'

At five thirty he fled to the sanctuary of his apartment, carrying a chunk of liver sausage and two onion rolls for his dinner. He would have preferred the Press Club. He liked the dingy atmosphere of the club, and the size of the steaks, and the company of fellow newsmen, but for the last two weeks he had been driven to avoiding his favorite haunt. The trouble had started when he danced with Fran Unger at the Photographers' Ball. Apparently there was some magic in Qwilleran's vintage fox trot that gave her aspirations. She had been pursuing him ever since.

'I can't get rid of that woman!' he told Koko, as he sliced the liver sausage. 'She's not bad-looking, but she isn't my type. I've had all the bossy females I want! Besides, I like zebra fur on zebras.'

He cut some morsels of the sausage as an appetizer for Koko, but the cat was busy snapping his jaws at a thin skein of spider web that stretched between two chair legs.

Only when the telephone rang, a moment later, did Koko pay attention. Lately he had shown signs of jealousy toward the phone. Whenever Qwilleran talked into the instrument, Koko untied his shoelaces or bit the telephone cord. Sometimes he jumped on the desk and tried to nudge the receiver away from Qwilleran's ear.

The telephone rang, and the newsman said to the mouthpiece, 'Hello? . . . Yes! What's the good news?'

Immediately Koko jumped to the desk top and started making himself a pest. Qwilleran pushed him away.

'Great! How soon can we take pictures?'

Koko was pacing back and forth on the desk, looking for further mischief. Somehow he got his leg tangled in the cord, and howled in indignation.

'Sorry, I can't hear you,' said Qwilleran. 'The cat's raising the roof ... No, I'm not beating him. Hold the line.'

He extricated Koko and chased him away, then wrote down the address that David Lyke gave him. 'See you Monday morning in Muggy Swamp,' Qwilleran said. 'And thanks. This is a big help.'

The telephone rang once more that evening, and the friendly voice of Fran Unger came on the wire. 'Well, hello! You're home!'

'Yes,' said Qwilleran. 'I'm home.' He was keeping an eye on Koko, who had leaped up on the desk.

'I thought you had a big date tonight.'

'Got home earlier than I expected.'

'I'm at the Press Club,' said the sugary voice. 'Why don't you come over? We're all here, drinking up a storm.'

'Scram!' said Qwilleran to Koko, who was trying to dial the phone with his nose.

'What did you say?'

'I was talking to the cat.' Qwilleran gave Koko a push, but the cat slanted his eyes and stood his ground, looking determined as he devised his next move.

'By the way,' the wheedling voice was saying, 'when are you going to invite me up to meet Koko?'

'YOW!' said Koko, aiming his deafening howl directly into Qwilleran's right ear.

'Shut up!' said Qwilleran.

'What?'

'Oh, hell!' he said, as Koko pushed an ashtray full of pipe ashes to the floor.

'Well!' Fran Unger's voice became suddenly tart. 'Your hospitality overwhelms me!'

'Listen, Fran,' said Qwilleran. 'I've got a mess on my hands right now.' He was going to explain, but there was a click in his ear. 'Hello?' he said.

A dead silence was his answer, and then a dial tone. The connection had been cut. Koko was standing with one foot planted firmly on the plunger button.

Three

When Qwilleran reported to the Photo Lab on Monday morning to pick up a man for the Muggy Swamp assignment, he found Odd Bunsen slamming gear into a camera case and voicing noisy objections. Bunsen was the *Daily Fluxion*'s specialist in train wrecks and five-alarm fires, and he had just been assigned on a permanent basis to *Gracious Abodes*.

'It's an old man's job,' he complained to Qwilleran. 'I'm not ready to come down off the flagpoles yet.'

Bunsen, who had recently climbed a skyscraper's flagpole to get a close-up of the Fourth of July fireworks, had an exuberance of qualities and defects that amused Qwilleran. He was the most daring of the photographers, had the loudest voice, and smoked the longest and most objectionable cigars. At the Press Club he was the hungriest and the thirstiest. He was raising the largest family, and his wallet was always the flattest.

'If I wasn't broke, I'd quit,' he told Qwilleran as they walked to the parking lot. 'For your private information, I hope this stupid magazine is a fat flop.' With difficulty and mild curses he packed the camera case, tripod, lights and light stands in his small foreign two-seater.

Qwilleran, jackknifing himself into the cramped space that remained, tried to cheer up the photographer. He said, 'When are you going to trade in this sardine can on a real car?'

'This is the only kind that runs on lighter fluid,' said Bunsen. 'I get ten miles to the squirt.'

'You photographers are too cheap to buy gas.'

'When you've got six kids and mortgage payments and orthodontist bills...'

'Why don't you cut out those expensive cigars?' Qwilleran suggested. 'They must cost you at least three cents apiece.'

They turned into Downriver Road, and the photographer said, 'Who lined up this Muggy Swamp assignment for you? Fran Unger?'

Qwilleran's moustache bristled. 'I line up my own assignments.'

'The way Fran's been talking at the Press Club, I thought she was calling the plays.'

Qwilleran grunted.

'She does a lot of talking after a couple of martinis,' said Bunsen. 'Saturday night she was hinting that you don't like girls. You must have done something that really burned her up.'

'It was my cat! Fran called me at home, and Koko disconnected the phone.'

'That cat's going to get you into trouble,' the photographer predicted.

They merged into the expressway traffic and drove in speed and silence until they reached the Muggy Swamp exit.

Bunsen said, 'Funny they never gave the place a decent name.'

'You don't understand upper-class psychology,' said Qwilleran. 'You probably live in one of those cute subdivisions.'

'I live in Happy View Woods. Four bedrooms and a big mortgage.'

'That's what I mean. The G. Verning Taits wouldn't be caught dead in a place called Happy View.'

The winding roads of Muggy Swamp offered glimpses of French châteaux and English manor houses, each secluded in its grove of ancient trees. The Tait house was an ornate Spanish stucco with an iron gate opening into a courtyard and a massive nail-studded door flanked by iron lanterns.

David Lyke greeted the newsmen at the door, ushering them into a foyer paved with black and white marble squares and sparkling with crystal. A bronze sphinx balanced a white marble slab on which stood a seventeen-branch candelabrum.

'Crazy!' said Bunsen.

'I suppose you want some help with your equipment,' Lyke said. He signaled to a houseboy, who gave the young white-haired decorator a worshipful look with soft black eyes. 'Paolo, pitch in and help these splendid people from the newspaper, and maybe they'll take your picture to send home to Mexico.'

Eagerly the houseboy helped Bunsen carry in the heavy camera case and the collection of lights and tripods.

'Are we going to meet the Taits?' Qwilleran asked.

The decorator lowered his voice. 'The old boy's holed up somewhere, clipping coupons and nursing his bad back. He won't come out till we yell *Jade*! He's an odd duck.'

'How about his wife?'

'She seldom makes an appearance, for which we can all be thankful.'

'Did you have much trouble getting their permission?'

'No, he was surprisingly agreeable,' said Lyke. 'Are you ready for the tour?'

He threw open double doors and led the newsmen into a living room done in brilliant green with white silk sofas and chairs. A writing desk was in ebony ornamented with gilt and there was a French telephone on a gilded pedestal. Against the far wall stood a large wardrobe in beautifully grained wood.

'The Biedermeier wardrobe,' said Lyke, raising an eyebrow, 'was in the family, and we were forced to use it. The walls and carpet are Parsley Green. You can call the chairs Mushroom. The house itself is Spanish, circa 1925, and we had to square off the arches, rip up tile floors, and replaster extensively.'

As the decorator moved about the room, straightening lampshades and smoothing the folds of the elaborately swagged draperies, Qwilleran stared at the splendor around him and saw dollar signs.

'If the Taits live quietly,' he whispered, 'why all this?'

Lyke winked. 'I'm a good salesman. What he wanted was a setting that would live up to his fabulous collection of jade. It's worth three quarters of a million. That's not for publication, of course.'

The most unusual feature in the living room was a series of niches in the walls, fronted with plate glass and framed with classic moldings. On their glass shelves were arranged scores of delicately carved objects in black and translucent white, artfully lighted to create an aura of mystery.

Odd Bunsen whispered, 'Is that the jade? Looks like soap, if you ask me.'

Qwilleran said, 'I expected it to be green.'

'The green jade is in the dining room,' said Lyke.

The photographer started to set up his tripod and lights, and the decorator gave Qwilleran notes on the interior design.

'When you write up this place,' he said, 'call the Biedermeier wardrobe an *armoire*, and call the open-arm chairs *fauteuils*.'

'Wait till the guys at the *Fluxion* read this,' said Qwilleran. 'I'll never hear the end of it.'

Meanwhile, Bunsen was working with unusual concentration, taking both color and black-and-white shots. He shifted lights and camera angles, moved furniture an inch one way or another, and spent long periods under the focusing cloth. The houseboy was a willing assistant. Paolo was almost too eager. He got in the way.

Finally Bunsen sank into a white silk chair. 'I've got to park for a minute and have a smoke.' He drew a long cigar from his breast pocket.

David Lyke grimaced and glanced over his shoulder.

'Do you want us all to get shot? Mrs Tait hates tobacco smoke, and she can smell it a mile away.'

'Well, that squelches *that* little idea!' Bunsen said irritably, and he went back to work.

Qwilleran said to him, 'We need some close-ups of the jades.'

'I can't shoot through the glass.'

'The glass can be removed,' said Lyke. 'Paolo, will you tell Mr Tait we need the key to the cases?'

The jade collector, a man of about fifty, came at once, and his face was radiant. 'Do you want to see my jades?' he said. 'Which cases do you want me to open? These pictures will be in color, won't they?' His face had a scrubbed pink gleam, and he kept crimping the corners of his mouth in an abortive smile. He looked, Qwilleran thought, like a powerful man who had gone soft. His silk sports shirt exposed a heavy growth of hair on his arms, and yet there was a complete absence of hair on his head.

The plate-glass panels in the vitrines were ingeniously installed without visible hardware. Tait himself opened them, wearing gloves to prevent smudging.

Meanwhile Lyke recited a speech with affected formality: 'Mr Tait has generously agreed to share his collection with your readers, gentlemen. Mr Tait feels that the private collector – in accumulating works of art that would otherwise appear in museums – has an obligation to the public. He is permitting these pieces to be photographed for the education and esthetic enjoyment of the community.'

Qwilleran said, 'May I quote you to that effect, Mr Tait?'

The collector did not answer. He was too absorbed in

his collection. Reverently he lifted a jade teapot from its place on a glass shelf. The teapot was pure white and paper-thin.

'This is my finest piece,' he said, and his voice almost trembled. 'The pure white is the rarest. I shouldn't show it first, should I? I should hold it back for a grand finale, but I get so excited about this teapot! It's the purest white I've ever seen, and as thin as a rose petal. You can say that in the article: thin as a rose petal.'

He replaced the teapot and began to lift other items from the shelves. 'Here's a Chinese bell, almost three thousand years old ... And here's a Mexican idol that's supposed to cure certain ailments. Not backache, unfortunately.' He crimped the corners of his mouth as if enjoying a private joke that was not very funny.

'There's a lot of detail on those things,' Qwilleran observed.

'Artists used to spend a whole lifetime carving a single object,' Tait said. 'But not all my jades are works of art.' He went to the writing table and opened a drawer. 'These are primitive tools made of jade. Axheads, chisels, harpoons.' He laid them out on the desk top one by one.

'You don't need to take everything out,' said Qwilleran. 'We'll just photograph the carved pieces,' but the collector continued to empty the drawer, handling each item with awe.

'Did you ever see jade in the rough?' he said. 'This is a piece of nephrite.'

'Well, let's get to work,' said Bunsen. 'Let's start shooting this crazy loot.'

Tait handed a carved medallion to Qwilleran. 'Feel it.'

'It's cold,' said the newsman.

'It's sensuous – like flesh. When I handle jade, I feel a prickle in my blood. Do you feel a prickle?'

'Are there many books on jade?' Qwilleran asked. 'I'd like to read up on it.'

'Come into my library,' said the collector. 'I have everything that has ever been written on the subject.'

He pulled volume after volume from the shelves: technical books, memoirs, adventure, fiction – all centered upon the cool, sensuous stone.

'Would you care to borrow a few of these?' he said. 'You can return them at your leisure.' Then he reached into a desk drawer and slipped a button-shaped object into Qwilleran's hand. 'Here! Take this with you for luck.'

'Oh, no! I couldn't accept anything so valuable.' Qwilleran fingered the smooth rounded surface of the stone. It was green, the way he thought jade should be.

Tait insisted. 'Yes, I want you to have it. Its intrinsic value is not great. Probably just a counter used in some Japanese game. Keep it as a pocket piece. It will help you write a good article about my collection.' He puckered the corners of his mouth again. 'And who knows? It may give you ideas. You may become a collector of jade ... and that is the best thing that could happen to a man!'

Tait spoke the words with religious fervor, and Qwilleran, rubbing the cool green button, felt a prickle in his blood.

Bunsen photographed several groups of jade, while the collector hovered over him with nervous excitement. Then the photographer started to fold up his equipment.

'Wait!' said Lyke. 'There's one more room you should see – if it's permissible. Mrs Tait's boudoir is magnificent.' He turned to his client. 'What do you think?'

Qwilleran caught a significant exchange of glances between the two men.

'Mrs Tait is unwell,' the husband explained to the newsmen. 'However, let me see . . .'

He left the room and was gone several minutes. When he returned, his bald head as well as his face was unduly flushed. 'Mrs Tait is agreeable,' he said, 'but please take the picture as quickly as possible.'

With the photographer carrying his camera on a tripod and Paolo carrying the lights, the party followed Tait down a carpeted corridor to a secluded wing of the house.

The boudoir was a combined sitting room and bedroom, lavishly decorated. Everything looked soft and downy. The bed stood under a tentlike canopy of blue silk. The chaise longue, heaped with pillows, was blue velvet. There was only one jarring note, and that was the wheelchair standing in the bay window.

Its occupant was a thin, sharp-featured woman. Her face was pinched with either pain or petulance, and her coloring was an unhealthy blond. She acknowledged the introductions curtly, all the while trying to calm a dainty Siamese cat that sat on a cushion on her lap. The cat had large lavender-blue eyes, slightly crossed.

Bunsen, with an attempt at heartiness, said, 'Well, look what we've got here! A pussycat. A cross-eyed pussycat. Woof, woof!'

'Stop that!' Mrs Tait said sharply. 'You're frightening her.'

In a hushed sickroom voice her husband said: 'The cat's name is Yu. That's the ancient Chinese word for jade.'

'Her name is not Yu,' said the invalid, giving her husband a venomous look. 'Her name is Freya.' She stroked the animal, and the small furry body shrank into the cushion.

Bunsen turned his back to the wheelchair and started to whistle softly while adjusting the lens of his camera.

'It's taken you a long time to snap a few pictures,' the woman observed. She spoke in a peculiarly throaty voice.

In defense Bunsen said, 'A national magazine would take two days to photograph what I've done in one morning.'

'If you're going to photograph my room,' she said, 'I want my cat in the picture.'

A prolonged silence hung quivering in the air as everyone turned to look at the photographer.

'Sorry,' he said. 'Your cat wouldn't hold still long enough for a time exposure.'

Coolly the woman said, 'Other photographers seem to have no difficulty taking pictures of animals.'

Bunsen's eyes snapped. He spoke with strained patience. 'This is a long time exposure, Mrs Tait. I've got to stop the lens down as far as possible to get the whole room in focus.'

'I'm not interested in your technical problems. I want Freya in the picture!'

The photographer drew a deep breath. 'I'm using a wide angle lens. The cat will be nothing but a tiny dot unless you put it right in front of the camera. And then it'll move and ruin the time exposure.'

The invalid's voice became shrill. 'If you can't take the picture the way I want it, don't take it at all.'

Her husband went to her side. 'Signe, calm yourself,' he said, and with one hand waved the others out of the room.

As the newsmen drove away from Muggy Swamp,

Bunsen said: 'Don't forget to give me a credit line on these pictures. This job was a blinger! Do you realize I worked for three hours without a smoke? And that biddy in the wheelchair was the last straw! Besides, I don't like to photograph cats.'

'That animal was unusually nervous,' Qwilleran said.

'Paolo was a big help. I slipped him a couple of bucks.'

'He seemed to be a nice kid.'

'He's homesick. He's saving up to go back to Mexico. I'll bet Tait pays him in peanuts.'

'Lyke told me the jades are worth $750,000.'

'That burns me,' said Bunsen. 'A man like Tait can squander millions on teapots, and I have trouble paying my milk bill.'

'You married guys think you've got all the problems,' Qwilleran told him. 'At least you've got a home! Look at me – I live in a furnished apartment, eat in restaurants, and haven't had a decent date for a month.'

'There's always Fran Unger.'

'Are you kidding?'

'A man your age can't be too fussy.'

'Huh!' Qwilleran contracted his waistline an inch and preened his moustache. 'I still consider myself a desirable prospect, but there seems to be a growing shortage of women.'

'Have you found a new place to live yet?'

'I haven't had time to look.'

'Why don't you put that smart cat of yours to work on it?' Bunsen suggested. 'Give him the classified ads and let him make a few phone calls.'

Qwilleran kept his mouth shut.

Four

The first issue of *Gracious Abodes* went to press too smoothly. Arch Riker said it was a bad omen. There were no ad cancellations, the copy dummied in perfectly, cutlines spaced out evenly, and the proofs were so clean it was eerie.

The magazine reached the public Saturday night, sandwiched between several pounds of Sunday paper. On the cover was an exclusive Muggy Swamp residence in bright Parsley Green and Mushroom White. The editorial pages were liberally layered with advertisements for mattresses and automatic washers. And on page two was a picture of the *Gracious Abodes* editor with drooping moustache and expressionless eyes – the mug shot from his police press card.

On Sunday morning David Lyke telephoned Qwilleran

at his apartment. 'You did a beautiful job of writing,' said the decorator in his chesty voice, 'and thanks for the overstuffed credit line. But where did they get that picture of you? It makes you look like a basset hound.'

For the newsman it was a gratifying day, with friends calling constantly to offer congratulations. Later it rained, but he went out and bought himself a good dinner at a seafood restaurant, and in the evening he beat the cat at the word game, 20 to 4. Koko clawed up easy catchwords like *block* and *blood*, *police* and *politely*.

It was almost as if the cat had a premonition; by Monday morning *Gracious Abodes* was involved with the law.

The telephone jolted Qwilleran awake at an early hour. He groped for his wristwatch on the bedside table. The hands, after he had blinked enough to see them, said six thirty. With sleep in his bones he shuffled stiffly to the desk.

'Hello?' he said dryly.

'Qwill! This is Harold!'

There was a chilling urgency in the managing editor's voice that paralyzed Qwilleran's vocal cords for a moment.

'Is this Qwilleran?' shouted the editor.

The newsman made a squeaking reply. 'Speaking.'

'Have you heard the news? Did they call you?' The editor's words had the sound of calamity.

'No! What's wrong?' Qwilleran was awake now.

'The police just phoned me here at home. Our cover story – the Tait house – it's been burglarized!'

'*What!* ... What did they get?'

'Jade! A half million dollars' worth, at a rough guess. And that's not the worst. Mrs Tait is dead ... Qwill! Are you there? Did you hear me?'

'I heard you,' Qwilleran said in a hollow voice, as he lowered himself slowly into a chair. 'I can't believe it.'

'It's a tragedy per se, and our involvement makes it even worse.'

'Murder?'

'No, thank God! It wasn't quite as bad as *that*. Apparently she had a heart attack.'

'She was a sick woman. I suppose she heard the intruders, and—'

'The police want to talk to you and Odd Bunsen as soon as possible,' said the editor. 'They want to get your fingerprints.'

'They want *our* fingerprints? They want to question *us*?'

'Just routine. They said it will help them sort out the prints they find in the house. When were you there to take pictures?'

'Monday. Just a week ago.' Then Qwilleran said what they were both thinking. 'The publicity isn't going to do the magazine any good.'

'It could ruin it! What have you got lined up for next Sunday?'

'An old stable converted into a home. It belongs to a used-car dealer who likes to see his name in the paper. I've found a lot of good houses, but the owners don't want us to use their names and addresses – for one reason or another.'

'And now they've got another reason,' said the editor. 'And a damn good one!'

Qwilleran slowly hung up and gazed into space, weighing the bad news. There had been no interference from

Koko during this particular telephone conversation. The cat was huddled under the dresser, watching the newsman intently, as if he sensed the gravity of the situation.

Qwilleran alerted Bunsen at his home in Happy View Woods, and within two hours the two newsmen were at Police Headquarters, telling their stories.

One of the detectives said, 'What's your newspaper trying to do? Publish blueprints for burglary?'

The newsmen told how they had gone about photographing the interior of the house in Muggy Swamp and how Tait had produced a key and supervised the opening of the jade cases. They told how he had wanted the rarest items to be photographed.

'Who else was there when you were taking pictures?'

'Tait's decorator, David Lyke ... and the houseboy, Paolo ... and I caught a glimpse of a servant in the kitchen,' said Qwilleran.

'Did you have any contact with the houseboy?'

'Oh, sure,' said Bunsen. 'He worked with me for three hours, helping with the lights and moving furniture. A good kid! I slipped him a couple of bucks.'

After the brief interrogation Qwilleran asked the detectives some prying questions, which they ignored. It was not his beat, and they knew it.

On the way out of Headquarters, Bunsen said: 'Glad that's over! For a while I was afraid they suspected us.'

'Our profession is above suspicion,' said Qwilleran. 'You never hear of a newsman turning to crime. Doctors bludgeon their wives, lawyers shoot their partners, and bankers abscond with the assets. But journalists just go to the Press Club and drown their criminal inclinations.'

When Qwilleran reached his office, his first move was

to telephone the studio of Lyke and Starkweather. The rumbling voice of David Lyke came quickly on the line.

'Heard the news?' Qwilleran asked in tones of gloom.

'Got it on my car radio, on the way downtown,' said Lyke. 'It's a rough deal for you people.'

'But what about Tait? He must be going out of his mind! You know how he feels about those jades!'

'You can bet they're heavily insured, and now he can have the fun of collecting all over again.' The decorator's lack of sympathy surprised Qwilleran.

'Yes, but losing his wife!'

'That was inevitable. Anything could have caused her death at any moment – bad news on the stock market, a gunfight on television! And she was a miserable woman,' said Lyke. 'She'd been in that wheelchair for years, and all that time she made her husband and everyone else walk a tightrope ... No, don't waste any tears over Mrs Tait's demise. You've got enough to worry about. How do you think it will affect *Gracious Abodes*?'

'I'm afraid people will be scared to have their homes published.'

'Don't worry. I'll see that you get material,' Lyke said. 'The profession needs a magazine like yours. Why don't you come to my apartment for cocktails this evening? I'll have a few decorators on tap.'

'Good idea! Where do you live?'

'At the Villa Verandah. That's the new apartment house that looks like a bent waffle.'

Just as Qwilleran hung up, a copyboy threw a newspaper on his desk. It was the Metro edition of the *Morning Rampage*. The *Fluxion*'s competitor had played up the Tait incident on the front page, and there were pointed references to 'a detailed description of the jade collection, which appeared in another newspaper on the eve of the burglary.' Qwilleran smoothed his moustache vigorously with his knuckles and went to the City Room to see the managing editor, but Percy was in conference with the publisher and the business manager.

Moodily, Qwilleran sat at his desk and stared at his typewriter. He should have been working. He should have been shooting for the next deadline, but something was bothering him. It was the *timing* of the burglary.

The magazine had been distributed Saturday evening. It was some time during the following night – late Sunday or early Monday – that the burglary occurred. Within a matter of twenty-four short hours, Qwilleran figured, someone had to (*a*) read the description of the jades and (*b*) dream up the idea of stealing them and (*c*) make elaborate preparations for a rather complex maneuver. They had to devise a plan of entering the house without disturbing family or servants, work out a method of silent access to the ingeniously designed glass-covered niches, arrange for fairly careful packing of the loot, provide a means of transporting it from the house, and schedule all this so as to elude the private police. Undoubtedly Muggy Swamp had private police patrolling the community.

There had been very little time for research, Qwilleran reflected. It would require a remarkably efficient organization to carry out the operation successfully ... unless the thieves were acquainted with the Tait house or had advance knowledge of the jade story. And if that was the case, had they deliberately timed the burglary to make *Gracious Abodes* look bad?

As Qwilleran pondered the possibilities, the first edition of the Monday *Fluxion* came off the presses, and the copyboy whizzed through the Feature Department, tossing a paper on each desk.

The Tait incident was discreetly buried on page four, and it bore an astounding headline. Qwilleran read the six short paragraphs in six gulps. The by-line was Lodge Kendall's; he was the *Fluxion*'s regular man at Police Headquarters. There was no reference to the *Gracious Abodes* story. The estimated value of the stolen jades was omitted. And there was an incredible statement from the Police Department. Qwilleran read it with a frown, then grabbed his coat and headed for the Press Club.

The Press Club occupied a soot-covered limestone fortress that had once been the county jail. The windows were narrow and barred, and mangy pigeons roosted among the blackened turrets. Inside, the old wood-paneled walls had the lingering aroma of a nineteenth-century penal institution, but the worst feature was the noise. Voices swooped across the domed ceiling, collided with other voices, and bounced back, multiplying into a deafening roar. To the newsmen this was heaven.

Today the cocktail bar on the main floor resounded with discussion and speculation on the happening in Muggy Swamp. Jewel thefts were crimes that civilized newsmen could enjoy with relish and good conscience. They appealed to the intellect, and as a rule nobody got hurt.

Qwilleran found Odd Bunsen at that end of the bar traditionally reserved for *Fluxion* staffers. He joined him and ordered a double shot of tomato juice on the rocks.

'Did you read it?' he asked the photographer.

'I read it,' said Bunsen. 'They're nuts.'

They talked in subdued tones. At the opposite end of the mahogany bar the voices of *Morning Rampage* staffers suggested undisguised jubilation. Qwilleran glanced with annoyance at the rival crew.

'Who's that guy down there in the light suit – the one with the loud laugh?' he demanded.

'He works in their Circulation Department,' Bunsen said. 'He played softball against us this summer, and take my word for it – he's a creep.'

'He irritates me. A woman is dead, and he's crowing about it'

'Here comes Kendall,' said the photographer. 'Let's see what he thinks about the police theory.'

The police reporter – young, earnest, and happy in his work – was careful to exhibit a professional air of boredom.

Qwilleran beckoned him to the bar, and said, 'Do you believe that stuff you wrote this morning?'

'As far as the police are concerned,' said Kendall, 'it's an open-and-shut case. It had nothing to do with your publication of the Tait house. It had to be an inside job. Somebody had to know his way around.'

'I know,' said Qwilleran. 'That's what I figured. But I don't like their choice of suspect. I don't believe the houseboy did it.'

'Then how do you explain his disappearance? If Paolo didn't swing with the jades and take off for Mexico, where is he?'

Bunsen said: 'Paolo doesn't fit the picture. He was a nice kid – quiet and shy – very anxious to help. He's not the type.'

'You photographers think you're great judges of character,' Kendall said. 'Well, you're wrong! According to Tait, the boy was lazy, sly, and deceitful. On several occasions Tait threatened to fire him, but Mrs Tait always came to Paolo's defense. And because of her physical condition, her husband was afraid to cross her.'

Bunsen and Qwilleran exchanged incredulous glances, and Kendall wandered away to speak to a group of TV men.

For a while Qwilleran toyed with the jade button that Tait had given him. He kept it in his pocket with his loose change. Finally he said to Bunsen, 'I called David Lyke this morning.'

'How's he taking it?'

'He didn't seem vitally upset. He said the jades were insured and Mrs Tait was a miserable creature who made her husband's life one long hell.'

'I'll buy that. She was a witch-and-a-half. What did he think about Paolo being mixed up in it?'

'At the time I talked to Lyke, that hadn't been announced.'

Bruno, the Press Club bartender, was hovering in the vicinity, waiting for the signal.

'No more,' Qwilleran told him. 'I've got to eat and get back to work.'

'I saw your magazine yesterday,' the bartender said. 'It gave me and my wife a lot of decorating ideas. We're looking forward to the next issue.'

'After what happened in Muggy Swamp, you may never see a next issue,' Qwilleran said. 'Nobody will want to have his house published.'

Bruno gave the newsman a patronizing smile. 'Maybe I

can help you. If you're hard up for material, you can photograph my house. We did it ourselves.'

'What kind of place have you got?' Qwilleran waited warily for the answer. Bruno was known as the poor man's Leonardo da Vinci. His talents were many, but slender.

'I have what they call a monochromatic color scheme,' said the bartender. 'I've got Chartreuse carpet, Chartreuse walls, Chartreuse drapes, and a Chartreuse sofa.'

'Very suitable for a member of your profession,' said Qwilleran, 'but allow me to correct you on one small detail. We *never* call draperies *drapes*.'

Five

Before going to the cocktail party at David Lyke's apartment, Qwilleran went home to change clothes and give the cat a slice of corned beef he had bought at the delicatessen.

Koko greeted him by flying around the room in a catly expression of joy – over chairs, under tables, around lamps, up to the top of bookshelves, down to the floor with a thud and a grunt – making sharp turns in mid-air at sixty miles an hour. Lamps teetered. Ashtrays spun around. The limp curtains rippled in the breeze. Then Koko leaped on the dictionary and scratched for all he was worth – with his rear end up, his front end down, his tail pointed skyward, like a toboggan slide with a flag on top. He scratched industriously, stopped to look at Qwilleran, and scratched again.

'No time for games,' Qwilleran said. 'I'm going out. Cocktail party. Maybe I'll bring you home an olive.'

He put on a pair of pants that had just come from the cleaner, unpinned a newly purchased shirt, and looked for his new tie. He found it draped over the arm of the sofa. There was a hole in it, center front, and Qwilleran groaned. That left only one plaid tie in good condition. He whipped it off the doorknob where it hung and tied it around his neck, grumbling to himself. Meanwhile, Koko sat on the dictionary, hopefully preparing for a game.

'No game tonight,' Qwilleran told him again. 'You eat your corned beef and then have a nice long nap.'

The newsman set out for the party with threefold anticipation. He hoped to make some useful contacts; he was curious about the fashionable and expensive Villa Verandah; and he was looking forward to seeing David Lyke again. He liked the man's irreverent attitude. Lyke was not what Qwilleran had expected a decorator to be. Lyke was neither precious nor a snob, and he wore his spectacular good looks with a casual grace.

The Villa Verandah, a recent addition to the cityscape, was an eighteen-story building curved around a landscaped park, each apartment with a balcony. Qwilleran found his host's apartment alive with the sound of bright chatter, clinking glasses, and music from hidden loudspeakers.

In a pleasant rumbling voice Lyke said: 'Is this your first visit to the Villa Verandah? We call this building the Architects' Revenge. The balconies are designed to be too sunny, too windy, and too dirty. The cinders that hurtle through my living room are capable of putting out an eyeball. But it's a good address. Some of the best people live in this building, several of them blind in one eye.'

He opened a sliding glass door in the glass wall and showed Qwilleran the balcony, where metal furniture stood ankle-deep in water and the wind made ripples on the surface.

'The balconies become wading pools for three days after every rain,' he said. 'When there's a high wind, the railings vibrate and play "Ave Maria" by the hour. And notice our unique view – a panorama of ninety-two other balconies.'

The apartment itself had a warmly livable atmosphere. Everywhere there were lighted candles, books in good leather bindings, plants of the exotic type, paintings in important frames, and heaps of pillows. A small fountain in one corner was busy splashing. And the wallpaper was the most sumptuous Qwilleran had ever seen – like silver straw with a tracery of peacocks.

The predominant note was Oriental. He noticed an Oriental screen, some bowlegged black tables, and a Chinese rug in the dining room. Some large pieces of Far Eastern sculpture stood in a bed of pebbles, lighted by concealed spotlights.

Qwilleran said to Lyke, 'We should photograph this.'

'I was going to suggest something else in this building,' said the decorator. 'I did Harry Noyton's apartment – just a *pied-à-terre* that he uses for business entertaining, but it's tastefully done in wall-to-wall money. And the colors are smart – in a ghastly way. I've used Eggplant, Spinach, and Overripe Melon.'

'Who is Harry Noyton?' Qwilleran asked. 'The name sounds familiar.'

'You must have heard of him. He's the most vocal

"silent partner" in town. Harry owns the ballpark, a couple of hotels, and *probably* the City Hall.'

'I'd like to meet him.'

'You will. He's dropping in tonight. I'd really like to see you publish Harry's country house in Lost Lake Hills – all artsy-craftsy contemporary – but there's an awkward situation in the family at the moment, and it might not be advisable ... Now, come and meet some of the guests. Starkweather is here – with his lovely wife, who is getting to be a middle-aged sot, but I can't say that I blame her.'

Lyke's partner was sitting quietly at one end of the sofa, but Mrs Starkweather was circulating diligently. There was a frantic gaiety in her aging face, and her costume was a desperate shade of pink. She clung to Lyke in an amorous way when he introduced Qwilleran.

'I'm in love with David,' she told the newsman, waving a cocktail glass in a wide arc. 'Isn't he just too overwhelming? Those eyes! And that sexy voice!'

'Easy, sweetheart,' said Lyke. 'Do you want your husband to shoot me?' He turned to Qwilleran. 'This is one of the hazards of the profession. We're so lovable.'

After Lyke disengaged himself from Mrs Starkweather's grip, she clung to Qwilleran's arm and went on prattling. 'Decorators give marvelous parties! There are always lots of *men*! And the food is always so good. David has a marvelous caterer. But the drinks are too potent.' She giggled. 'Do you know many decorators? They're lots of fun. They dress so well and they dance so well. My husband isn't really a decorator. He used to be in the wholesale carpet business. He handles the money at L&S. David is the one with talent. I adore David!'

Most of the guests were decorators, Qwilleran discovered. All the men were handsome, the majority of
them young. The women were less so, but what they
lacked in beauty and youth they made up in vivacity and
impressive clothes. Everyone had an easy charm. They
complimented Qwilleran on his new magazine, the luxuri-
ance of his moustache, and the fragrance of his pipe
tobacco.

Conversation flitted from one subject to another: travel,
fashion, rare wine, ballet, and the dubious abilities
of other decorators. Repeatedly the name of Jacques
Boulanger came up and was dismissed with disapproval.

No one, Qwilleran noticed, was disposed to discuss the
November election or the major-league pennant race or
the situation in Asia. And none of the guests seemed
disturbed by the news of the Tait theft. They were merely
amused that it should have happened to a client of
David's.

One young man of fastidious appearance approached
Qwilleran and introduced himself as Bob Orax. He had an
oval aristocratic face with elevated eyebrows.

'Ordinarily,' he told the newsman, 'I don't follow crime
news, but my family knew the Taits, and I was fascinated
by the item in today's paper. I had no idea Georgie had
amassed so much jade. He and Siggy haven't entertained
for years! Mother went to school with Siggy in Switzerland,
you know.'

'No, I didn't know.'

'Siggy's family had more brains than affluence, Mother
says. They were all scientists and architects. And it was
rather a coup when Siggy married a rich American.
Georgie had *hair* in those days, according to Mother.'

'How did the Taits make their money?' Qwilleran asked.

'In a rather quaint and charming way. Georgie's grandfather made a mint – an absolute *mint* – manufacturing buggy whips. But Mother says Georgie himself has never had a taste for business. Monkey business, perhaps, but nothing that you can put in the bank.'

'Tait was devoted to his jade collection,' said Qwilleran. 'I felt very bad about the theft.'

'That,' said Orax loftily, 'is what happens when you hire cheap help. When Father was alive, he always insisted on English butlers and Irish maids. My family had money at one time. Now we get by on our connections. And I have a little shop on River Street that helps to keep the wolf from the door.'

'I'd like to call on you some day,' said Qwilleran. 'I'm in the market for story material.'

'Frankly, I doubt whether your readers are quite ready for me,' said the decorator. 'I specialize in Planned Ugliness, and the idea is rather advanced for the average taste. But do come! You might find it entertaining.'

'By the way, who is this Jacques Boulanger I keep hearing about?'

'Boulanger?' The Orax eyebrows elevated a trifle higher. 'He does work for the Duxburies, the Pennimans, and all the other old families in Muggy Swamp.'

'He must be good.'

'In our business,' said the decorator, 'success is not always an indication of excellence . . . Bless you! You have no drink! May I get you something from the bar?'

It was not the bar that interested Qwilleran. It was the buffet. It was laden with caviar, shrimp, a rarebit in a chafing dish, marinated mushrooms, stuffed artichoke hearts, and savory meatballs in a dill sauce. As he loaded his plate for the third time, he glanced into the kitchen and saw the large stainless-steel warming oven of a professional caterer. A smiling Oriental caught his eye and nodded encouragement, and Qwilleran signaled a compliment in the man's direction.

Meanwhile a guest with a big, ungainly figure and a craggy face sauntered over to the buffet and started popping tidbits into his mouth, washing them down with gulps from a highball glass.

'I like these kids – these decorators,' he said to the newsman. 'They invite me to a lot of their parties. But how they ever make a living is beyond me! They live in a dream world. I'm a businessman myself – in and out of a dozen enterprises a year – and I make every investment pay off. I'm not in the racket for kicks – like these kids. *You* understand. You're a newspaperman, aren't you?'

'Jim Qwilleran from the *Daily Fluxion*.'

'You newspaper guys are a good breed. You've got your feet on the ground. I know a lot of journalists. I know the managing editors of both papers, and the *Fluxion* sports editor, and your financial writer. They've all been up to my hunting lodge. Do you like hunting and fishing?'

'I haven't done much of it,' Qwilleran admitted.

'To tell the truth, all we do is sit around with a bottle and shoot the breeze. You ought to come up and join us some time . . . By the way, I'm Harry Noyton.'

They shook hands, and Qwilleran said, 'David tells me you have a house that might make good story material for the *Fluxion*'s new decorating magazine.'

Noyton stared at his shoes for a long minute before answering. 'Come in the other room where it's quiet,' he said.

They went into the breakfast room and sat at a marble-topped table – the promoter with his highball glass and Qwilleran with a plate of shrimp and mushrooms.

Noyton said: 'Whatever you've heard about my house in the Hills is no lie. It's terrific! And I give David all the credit – that is, Dave and my wife. She's got talent. I don't have any talent myself. All I did was go to engine college for a couple of years.' He paused and gazed out the window. 'But Natalie is artistic. I'm proud of her.'

'I'd like to see this house.'

'Well ... here's the problem,' said Noyton, taking a long drink from his glass. 'The house is going to be sold. You see, Natalie and I are getting a divorce.'

'Sorry to hear it,' said Qwilleran. 'I've been over that course myself.'

'There's no trouble between us, you understand. She just wants out! She's got this crazy idea that she wants an artistic career. Can you imagine that? She's got everything in the world, but she wants to be creative, wants to starve in an attic studio, wants to make something of her life. That's what she says. And she wants it bad! Bad enough to give up the boys. I don't understand this art bug that gets into women these days.'

'You have children?'

'Two sons. Two fine boys. I don't know how she can have the heart to get up and walk away from them. But those are my terms: I get complete custody of the boys, and the divorce is forever. No willy-wagging. She can't change her mind and decide to come back after a couple of months. I won't play the fool for anyone! Especially not a woman ... Tell me, am I right?'

Qwilleran stared at the man – aggressive, rich, lonely.

Noyton drained his drink, and said, 'I'll send the boys to military school, of course.'

'Is Mrs Noyton a painter?' Qwilleran asked.

'No, nothing like that. She's got these big looms, and she wants to weave rugs and things for decorators to sell. I don't know how she's going to make a living. She won't take any money from me, and she doesn't want the house. Know anybody wants a quarter-million dollars' worth of real estate?'

'It must be quite a place.'

'Say, if you want to write it up for the paper, it might help me to unload the joint. I'm leveling with you, understand.'

'Is anyone living there now?'

'Caretaker, that's all. Natalie's in Reno. I'm living here at the Villa Verandah ... Wait'll I flavor these ice cubes.'

Noyton dashed to the bar, and while he was gone the Japanese caterer quietly removed Qwilleran's plate and replaced it with another, piled high.

'Like I was saying,' Noyton went on, 'I have this apartment that Dave decorated. That boy's got taste! Wish I had that boy's taste. I've got a wood floor imported from Denmark, a built-in bar, a fur rug – the works!'

'I wouldn't mind seeing it.'

'Come on and have a look. It's right here on this floor, in the north wing.'

They left the party, Noyton carrying his highball glass. 'I should warn you,' he said as they walked around the curving corridor, 'the colors are kind of wild.'

He unlocked the door to 15–F and touched a wall switch. Qwilleran gasped.

Pleasant·music burst forth. Rich colors glowed in pools of light. Everything looked soft, comfortable, but rugged.

'Do you go for this modern stuff?' Noyton asked. 'Expensive as hell when it's done right.'

With awe in his voice Qwilleran said: 'This is great! This really gets to me.'

The floor consisted of tiny squares of dark wood with a velvety oiled finish. There was a rug as shaggy as unmown grass and half as big as a squash court.

'Like the rug?' Noyton asked. 'Genuine goat hair from Greece.'

It was surrounded on three sides by a trio of sofas covered in natural tan suede. A chair with inviting body curves was upholstered in something incredibly soft.

'Vicuña,' said Noyton. 'But try that green chair. That's my favorite.'

When Qwilleran relaxed in the green chair and propped his feet on the matching ottoman, an expression of beatitude spread over his face. He stroked the sculptured woolly arms. 'I'd sure like to have an apartment like this,' he murmured.

'And this is the bar,' said Noyton with unconcealed pride as he splashed some liquor in his glass. 'And the stereo is in that old Spanish chest – the only antique in the place. Cost me a fortune.' He sank into the vicuña chair. 'The rent for this apartment is nothing to sneeze at, either, but some good people live in this building – good people to know.' He named two judges, a banker, the retired president of the university, a prominent scientist. 'I know them all. I know a lot of people in this town. Your managing editor is a good friend of mine.'

Qwilleran's eyes were roving over the wall of cantilevered bookshelves, the large desk topped with rust-colored leather, the sensuous rug, and the three – not one, but three – deep-cushioned sofas.

'Yes, Lyke did a great job on the decorating,' he said.

'Say, you look like a regular guy,' Noyton remarked with a crafty look. 'How are you getting along with these decorators?'

'They seem to be a congenial bunch,' said Qwilleran, ignoring the innuendo.

'That's not what I mean. Have you met Bob Orax? He's got a real problem.'

'I'm used to meeting all kinds,' Qwilleran said, more curtly than he had intended. He had a newsman's capacity for identifying with his beat and defending its personnel, and he resented Noyton's aspersions.

Noyton said, 'That's what I admire about you news guys. Nobody throws you. You take everything in your stride.'

Qwilleran swung his feet off the ottoman and hoisted himself out of the green chair. 'Well, what do you say? Shall we go back where the action is?'

They returned to the party, Noyton carrying two bottles of bourbon from his own stock, which he added to Lyke's supply.

Qwilleran complimented the decorator on the Noyton job. 'Wish I could afford an apartment like his. What does a layout like that cost, anyway?'

'Too much,' said the decorator. 'By the way, if you ever need anything, I'll get it for you at cost, plus freight.'

'What I need,' said Qwilleran, 'is a furnished apart-ment. The place where I live is being torn down to make a parking lot, and I've got to be out in ten days.'

'Why don't you use Harry's apartment for a few weeks – if you like it so much?' Lyke suggested. 'He's leaving for Europe, and he'll be gone a month or more.'

Qwilleran blinked. 'Do you think he'd be willing to sublet – at a price I could afford?'

'Let's ask him.'

Noyton said, 'Hell, no, I won't sublet, but if you want to use the joint while I'm gone, just move in.'

'No, I'd insist on paying rent,' Qwilleran said.

'Don't give me that integrity jive! I've had a lot of good treatment from the papers, and this'll give me a chance to say thanks. Besides, it's no skin off my back. Why should I take your money?'

Lyke said to Qwilleran, 'There's a catch, of course. He'll expect you to forward his mail and take telephone messages.'

Qwilleran said, 'There's another catch, too. I've got a cat.'

'Bring him along!' said Noyton. 'He can have his own room and bath. First class.'

'I could guarantee that he wouldn't scratch the furniture.'

'It's a deal. I'm leaving Wednesday. The keys will be at the manager's desk, including the one for the bar. Help yourself to anything. And don't be surprised if I call you twice a day from Europe. I'm a telephone bug.'

Later, Lyke said to the newsman: 'Thanks for getting

me off the hook. Harry was expecting *me* to do his secretary service. I don't know why, but clients think they've hired a wet nurse for life when they call in a decorator.'

It had happened so fast that Qwilleran could hardly believe his good fortune. Rejoicing inwardly, he made two more trips to the buffet before saying good night to his host.

As he left the apartment, he felt a tug at his sleeve. The caterer was standing at his elbow, smiling.

'You got doggie at home?' he asked the newsman.

'No,' said Qwilleran, 'but—'

'Doggie hungry. You take doggie bag,' said the caterer, and he pushed a foil-wrapped package into Qwilleran's hand.

Six

'Koko, old fellow, we're moving!' Qwilleran announced happily on Tuesday morning, as he took the doggie bag from the refrigerator and prepared a breakfast for the cat and himself. Reviewing the events of the previous evening, he had to admit that the decorating beat had its advantages. Never had he received so many compliments or tasted such good food, and the offer of an apartment was a windfall.

Koko was huddling on a cushion on top of the refrigerator – the blue cushion that was his bed, his throne, his Olympus. His haunches were sticking up like fins. He looked uncomfortable, apprehensive.

'You'll like it at the Villa Verandah,' Qwilleran assured him. 'There are soft rugs and high bookshelves, and you can sit in the sun on the balcony. But you'll have to be on your best behavior. No flying around and busting lamps!'

Koko shifted weight. His eyes were large troubled circles of blue.

'Well take your cushion and put it on the new refrigerator, and you'll feel right at home.'

At the *Daily Fluxion* an hour later, Qwilleran reported the good news to Odd Bunsen. They met in the employees' lunchroom for their morning cup of coffee, sitting at the counter with pressmen in square paper hats, typesetters in canvas aprons, rewrite men in white shirts with the cuffs turned up, editors with their cuffs buttoned, and advertising men wearing cufflinks.

Qwilleran told the photographer, 'You should see the bathrooms at the Villa Verandah! Gold faucets!'

'How do you walk into these lucky breaks?' Bunsen wanted to know.

'It was Lyke's idea, and Noyton likes to make generous gestures. He likes to be liked, and he's fascinated by newspaper people. You know the type.'

'Some newspapers wouldn't let you accept a plum like that, but on a *Fluxion* salary you have to take all you can get,' the photographer said. 'Was there any conversation about the robbery?'

'Not much. But I picked up a little background on the Taits. Did it strike you that Mrs Tait had a slight foreign accent?'

'She sounded as if she'd swallowed her tongue.'

'I think she was Swiss. She apparently married Tait for his money, although I imagine he was a good-looking brute before he went bald.'

'Did you notice his arms?' the photographer said.

'Hairiest ape I ever saw! Some women go for that.'

There was a tap on Bunsen's shoulder, and Lodge Kendall sat down on the next stool. 'I knew I'd find you here, goldbricking as usual,' he said to the photographer. 'The detectives on the Tait case would like a set of the photos you took. Enlargements, preferably. Especially any shots that show the jades.'

'How soon do they want them? I've got a lot of printing to do for Sunday.'

'Soon as you can.'

Qwilleran said, 'Any progress on the case?'

'Tait has reported two pieces of luggage missing,' said Kendall. 'He's going away for a rest after the funeral. He's pretty shook up. And last night he went to the storeroom to get some luggage, and his two large overseas bags were gone. Paolo would need something like that to transport the jade.'

'I wonder how he'd get a couple of large pieces of luggage to the airport.'

'He must have had an accomplice with a car. By the time Tait found the stuff missing, Paolo had time to fly to Mexico and disappear forever in the mountains. I doubt whether they'll ever be able to trace the jades down there. Eventually they may turn up on the market, a piece at a time, but nobody will know anything about anything. You know how it is down there.'

'I suppose the police have checked the airlines?'

'The passenger lists for the Sunday-night flights showed several Mexican or Spanish names. Of course, Paolo would use an alias.'

Bunsen said: 'Too bad I didn't take his picture. Lyke suggested it, but I never gave it another thought.'

'You photographers are so stingy with your film,' Kendall said, 'anyone would think you had to buy it yourself.'

'By the way,' said Qwilleran, 'exactly when did Tait discover the jades were missing?'

'About six o'clock in the morning. He's one of those early risers. He likes to go down into his workshop before breakfast and polish stones, or whatever it is he does. He went into his wife's room to see if she needed anything, found her dead, and called the doctor from the bedside phone. Then he rang for Paolo and got no response. Paolo was not in his room, and there were signs of hurried departure. Tait made a quick check of all the rooms, and that's when he discovered the display cases had been rifled.'

'After which,' said Qwilleran, 'he called the police, and the police called Percy, and Percy called me, and it was still only six thirty. It all happened pretty fast. When Tait called the police, did he tell them about the story in *Gracious Abodes*?'

'He didn't have to. The Department had already spotted your story and questioned the advisability of describing valuable objects so explicitly.'

Qwilleran snorted his disdain. 'And where was the cook when all this was happening?'

'The housekeeper gets Sundays off, doesn't come back until eight o'clock Monday morning.'

'And how do they account for Mrs Tait's heart attack?'

'They assume she waked in the night, heard some kind of activity in the living room, and suspected prowlers. Evidently the fright was enough to stop her ticker, which was in bad shape, I understand.'

Qwilleran objected. 'That's a rambling house. The bedroom wing is half a mile from the living room. How come Mrs Tait heard Paolo getting into the display cases – and her husband didn't?'

Kendall shrugged. 'Some people are light sleepers. Chronic invalids always have insomnia.'

'Didn't she try to rouse her husband? There must be some kind of buzzer system or intercom between the two rooms.'

'Look, I wasn't there!' said the police reporter. 'All I know is what I hear at Headquarters.' He tapped his wristwatch. 'I'm due there in five minutes. See you later . . . Bunsen, don't forget those enlargements.'

When he had gone, Qwilleran said to the photographer, 'I wonder where Tait's going for a rest. Mexico, by any chance?'

'You do more wondering than any three guys I know,' said Bunsen, rising from the lunch counter. 'I've got to do some printing. See you upstairs.'

Qwilleran could not say when his suspicions first began to take a definite direction. He finished his coffee and wiped his moustache roughly with a paper napkin. Perhaps that was the moment that the gears meshed and the wheels started to turn and the newsman's deliberation began to focus on G. Verning Tait.

He went upstairs to the Feature Department and found the telephone on his desk ringing urgently. It was a green telephone, matching all the desks and typewriters in the room. Suddenly Qwilleran saw the color scheme of the office with new eyes. It was Pea Soup Green, and the walls were painted Roquefort, and the brown vinyl floor was Pumpernickel.

'Qwilleran speaking,' he said into the green mouthpiece.

'Oh, Mr Qwilleran! Is this Mr Qwilleran himself?' It was a woman's voice, high-pitched and excited. 'I didn't think they'd let me talk to you personally.'

'What can I do for you?'

'You don't know me, Mr Qwilleran, but I read every word you write, and I think your new decorating magazine is simply elegant.'

'Thanks.'

'Now, here's my problem. I have Avocado carpet in my dining room and Caramel *toiles de Jouy* on the walls. Should I paint the dado Caramel Custard or Avocado? And what about the lambrequins?'

When he finally got rid of his caller, Arch Riker signaled to him. 'The boss is looking for you. It's urgent.'

'He probably wants to know what color to paint his dado,' said Qwilleran.

He found the managing editor looking thin-lipped. 'Trouble!' said Percy. 'That used-car dealer just phoned. You have his horsebarn scheduled for next Sunday. Right?'

'It's a remodeled stable,' Qwilleran said. 'Very impressive. It makes a good story. The pages are made up, and the pictures have gone to the engraver.'

'He wants the story killed. I tried to persuade him to let it run, but he insists on withdrawing it.'

'He was hot for it last week.'

'Personally he doesn't object. He doesn't blame us for the mishap in Muggy Swamp, but his wife is worried sick. She's having hysterics. The man threatens to sue if we publish his house.'

'I don't know what I can substitute in a hurry,' said Qwilleran. 'The only spectacular thing I have on hand is a silo painted like a barber pole and converted into a vacation home.'

'Not exactly the image we want to project for *Gracious Abodes*,' said the editor. 'Why don't you ask Fran Unger if she has any ideas?'

'Look, Harold!' said Qwilleran with sudden resolve. 'I think we should take the offensive!'

'What do you mean?'

'I mean – conduct our own investigation! I don't buy the police theory. Pinning the crime on the houseboy is too easy. Paolo may have been an innocent dupe. For all anybody knows, he could be at the bottom of the river!'

He stopped to get the editor's reaction. Percy only stared at him.

'That was no petty theft,' said Qwilleran, raising his voice, 'and it was not pulled off by an unsophisticated, homesick mountain boy from an underdeveloped foreign country! Something more is involved here. I don't know who or what or why, but I've got a hunch—' He pounded his moustache with his knuckles. 'Harold, why don't you assign me to cover this case? I'm sure I could dig up something of importance.'

Percy waved the suggestion away impatiently. 'I'm not opposed to investigative journalism per se, but we need you on the magazine. We don't have the personnel to waste on amateur sleuthing.'

'I can handle both. Just give me the credentials to talk to the police – to ask a few questions here and there.'

'No, you've got enough on your hands, Qwill. Let the police handle crime. We've got to concentrate on putting out a newspaper.'

Qwilleran went on as if he had not heard. He talked

fast. 'There's something suspicious about the timing of that incident! Someone wanted to link us with it. And that's not the only strange circumstance! Too much happened too fast yesterday morning. You called me at six thirty. What time did the police call you? And what time did they get the call from Tait? ... And if Mrs Tait heard sounds of prowlers, why didn't she signal her husband? Can you believe there was no intercom in that house? All that plush decorating, and not even a simple buzzer system between the invalid's bed and the sleeping quarters of her devoted husband?'

Percy looked at Qwilleran coldly. 'If there's evidence of conspiracy, the police will uncover it. They know what they're doing. You keep out of it. We've got troubles enough.'

Qwilleran calmed his moustache. There was no use arguing with a computer. 'Do you think I should make an appearance at the funeral tomorrow?' he asked.

'It won't be necessary. We'll be adequately represented.'

Qwilleran went back to his office muttering into his moustache: 'Play it safe! Don't offend! Support the Advertising Department! Make money!'

'Why not?' said Arch Riker. 'Did you think we were in business to disseminate news?'

At his desk Qwilleran picked up the inoffensive green telephone that was stenciled with the reminder Be Nice to People. He called the Photo Lab.

'When you make those enlargements of the jades,' he said to Bunsen, 'make a set of prints for me, will you? I've got an idea.'

Seven

Qwilleran killed the cover story about the car dealer's remodeled stable and started to worry about finding a substitution. He had an appointment that morning with another decorator, but he doubted that she would be able to produce a cover story on short notice. He had talked with her on the telephone, and she had seemed flustered.

'Oh, dear!' Mrs Middy had said. 'Oh, dear! Oh, dear!'

Qwilleran went to her studio without any buoyant hope.

The sign over the door, lettered in Spencerian script, said *Interiors by Middy*. The shop was located near Happy View Woods, and it had all the ingredients of charm: window boxes filled with yellow mums, bay windows with diamond-shaped panes, a Dutch door flanked by picturesque carriage lanterns, a gleaming brass door knocker. Inside, the cozy charm was suffocating but undeniable.

As Qwilleran entered, he heard Westminster chimes, and then he saw a tall young woman emerge from behind a louvered folding screen at the back of the shop. Her straight brown hair fell like a blanket to her shoulders, hiding her forehead, eyebrows, temples and cheeks. All that was visible was a pair of roguish green eyes, an appealing little nose, an intelligent mouth, a dainty chin.

Qwilleran brightened. He said, 'I have an eleven o'clock appointment with Mrs Middy, and I don't think you're Mrs Middy.'

'I'm her assistant,' said the young woman. 'Mrs Middy is a little late this morning, but then Mrs Middy is always a little late. Would you care to sit it out?' She waved a hand dramatically around the studio. 'I can offer you a Chippendale corner chair, a combback Windsor, or a mammy settle. They're all uncomfortable, but I'll talk to you and take your mind off your anguish.'

'Talk to me, by all means,' said Qwilleran, sitting on the mammy settle and finding that it rocked. The girl sat in the combback Windsor with her skirt well above her knees, and Qwilleran was pleased to see that they were leanly upholstered. 'What's your name?' he asked, as he filled his pipe and lighted it.

'Alacoque Wright, and you must be the editor of the new Sunday supplement. I forget what you call it.'

'*Gracious Abodes*,' said Qwilleran.

'Why do newspapers insist on sounding like warmed-over Horace Greeley?' Her green eyes were kidding him, and Qwilleran liked it.

'There's an element of tradition in newspapering.' He glanced around the studio. 'Same as in your business.'

'Decorating is not really my business,' said the girl

crisply. 'Architecture is my field, but girl architects are not largely in demand. I took this job with Mrs Middy in desperation, and I'm afraid these imitation worm-eaten hutches and folksy-hoaxy mammy settles are warping my personality. I prefer design that reflects the spirit of our times. Down with French Empire, Portuguese Colonial and Swahili Baroque!'

'You mean you like modern design?'

'I don't like to use the word,' said Miss Wright. 'It's so ambiguous. There's Motel Modern, Miami Beach Modern, Borax Danish, and a lot of horrid mutations. I prefer the twentieth-century classics – the work of Saarinen, Mies van der Rohe, Breuer, and all that crowd. Mrs Middy doesn't let me meet clients; she's afraid I'll sabotage her work. . . . And I believe I would,' she added with a feline smile. 'I have a sneaky nature.'

'If you don't meet clients, what do you do?'

'Renderings, floor plans, color schemes. I answer the telephone and sort of sweep up . . . But tell me about you. Do you like contemporary design?'

'I like anything,' said Qwilleran, 'as long as it's comfortable, and I can put my feet on it.'

The girl appraised him frankly. 'You're better looking than your picture in the magazine. You look serious and responsible, but also interesting. Are you married?'

'Not at the moment.'

'You must feel crushed about what happened this weekend.'

'You mean the theft in Muggy Swamp?'

'Do you suppose Mr Tait will sue the *Daily Fluxion*?'

Qwilleran shook his head. 'He wouldn't get to first base. We printed nothing that was untrue or libelous.

And, of course, we had his permission to publish his house in the first place.'

'But the robbery will damage your magazine's image, you must admit,' said Miss Wright.

Just then the Dutch door opened, and a voice said, 'Oh, dear! Oh, dear! Am I late?'

'Here comes Mother Middy,' said the girl with the taunting eyes.

The dumpling of a woman who bustled into the studio was breathless and apologetic. She had been hurrying, and wisps of gray hair were escaping in all directions from the confinement of her shapeless mouse-gray hat.

'Get us some coffee, dear,' she said to her assistant. 'I'm all upset. I just got a ticket for speeding. But the officer was so kind! They have such nice policemen on the force.'

The decorator sat down heavily in a black and gold rocking chair. 'Why don't you write a nice article about our policemen, Mr – Mr—'

'Qwilleran. Jim Qwilleran,' he said. 'I'm afraid that's not my department, but I'd like to write a nice article about you.'

'Oh, dear! Oh, dear!' said Mrs Middy, as she removed her hat and patted her hair.

The coffee came in rosebud-covered cups, and Miss Wright served it with her eyebrows arched in disapproval of the design. Then the decorator and the newsman discussed possibilities for *Gracious Abodes*.

'I've done some lovely interiors lately,' said Mrs Middy. 'Dr Mason's house is charming, but it isn't quite finished. We're waiting for lamps. Professor Dewitt's house is lovely, too, but the draperies aren't hung.'

'The manufacturer discontinued the pattern,' said Qwilleran.

'Yes! How did you know?' She rocked her chair violently. 'Oh, dear! Oh, dear! What to do?'

'The housing?' her assistant whispered.

'Oh, yes, we've just finished some dormitories for the university,' Mrs Middy said, 'and a sorority house for Delta Thelta, or whatever it's called. But those are out of town.'

'Don't forget Mrs Allison's,' said Miss Wright.

'Oh, yes, Mrs Allison's is really lovely. Would you be interested in a residence for career girls, Mr Qwillum? It shows what can be done with a boardinghouse. It's one of those turn-of-the-century mansions on Merchant Street – all very gloomy and grotesque before Mrs Allison called me in.'

'It looked like a Victorian bordello,' said Miss Wright.

'I used crewelwork in the living room and canopied beds in the girls' rooms. And the dining room turned out very well. Instead of one long table, which looks so institutional, I used lots of little skirted tables, like a café.'

Qwilleran had been considering only private residences, but he was willing to publish anything that could be photographed in a hurry.

'What is the color scheme?' he asked.

'The theme is Cherry Red,' said Mrs Middy, 'with variations. Upstairs it's all Cherry Pink. Oh, you'll love it! You'll just love it.'

'Any chance of photographing this afternoon?'

'Oh, dear! That's too soon. People like to tidy up before the photographer comes.'

'Tomorrow morning, then?'

'I'll call Mrs Allison right away.'

The decorator bustled to the telephone, and Alacoque Wright said to Qwilleran: 'Mother Middy has done wonders with the Allison house. It doesn't look like a Victorian bordello any more. It looks like an Early American bordello.'

While the arrangements were being made, Qwilleran made an arrangement of his own with Miss Wright for Wednesday evening, at six o'clock, under the City Hall clock, and he left the Middy studio with a lilting sensation in his moustache. On the way back to the office he stopped at a gourmet shop and bought a can of smoked oysters for Koko.

That evening Qwilleran packed his books in three corrugated cartons from the grocery store and dusted his two pieces of luggage. Koko watched the process with concern. He had not touched the smoked oysters.

Qwilleran said, 'What's the matter? Dieting?'

Koko began to prowl the apartment from one end to the other, occasionally stopping to sniff the cartons and utter a long, mournful howl.

'You're worried!' Qwilleran said. 'You don't want to move.' He picked up the cat and stroked his head reassuringly, then placed him on the open pages of the dictionary. 'Come on, let's have a good rousing game to chase away the blues.'

Koko dug his claws into the pages halfheartedly.

'*Balance* and *bald*,' Qwilleran read. 'Elementary! Two points for me. You'll have to try harder.'

Koko grabbed again.

'*Kohistani* and *koolokamba*.' Qwilleran knew the definition of the first, but he had to look up *koolokamba*. 'A

West African anthropoid ape with the head nearly bald and the face and hands black,' he read. 'That's great! That'll be a handy addition to my everyday vocabulary. Thanks a lot!'

At the end of nine innings Qwilleran had won, 14 to 4. For the most part Koko had turned up easy catchwords like *rook* and *root*, *frame* and *frank*.

'You're losing your knack,' Qwilleran told him, and Koko responded with a long, indignant howl.

Eight

On Wednesday morning Qwilleran and Bunsen drove to the Allison house on Merchant Street. Qwilleran said he hoped some of the girls would be there. Bunsen said he'd like to photograph one of the canopied beds with a girl in it.

The house was a Victorian monster – the lovesong of a nineteenth-century carpenter enamored of his jigsaw – but it was freshly painted, and the windows exhibited perky curtains. Mrs Middy met them at the door, wearing her shapeless hat and a frilly lace collar.

'Where's the girls?' Bunsen shouted. 'Bring on the girls!'

'Oh, they're not here in the daytime,' said Mrs Middy. 'They're working girls. Now, what would you like to see? Where would you like to start?'

'What I want to see,' said the photographer, 'is those bedrooms with canopied beds.'

The decorator bustled around, plumping cushions and moving ashtrays. Then a haggard woman came from the rear of the house. Her face was colorless, and her hair was done up in rollers, covered by a net cap. She wore a housecoat of a depressing floral pattern, but her manner was hearty.

'Hello, boys,' she said. 'Make yourselves at home. I've unlocked the sideboard, if you want to pour a drink.'

'It's too early for hooch,' said Bunsen, 'even for me.'

'You want some coffee?' Mrs Allison turned her face toward the rear of the house, and shouted. '*Elsie, bring some coffee!*' To her guests she said, 'Do you boys like sticky buns? . . . *Elsie, bring some sticky buns!*'

There was a piping, unintelligible reply from the kitchen.

'*Then find something else!*' yelled Mrs Allison.

'It's a nice place you've got here,' Qwilleran said.

'It pays to run a decent establishment,' said the house mother, 'and Mrs Middy knows how to make a place comfortable. She doesn't come cheap, but she's worth every penny.'

'Why did you choose Early American for your house?'

For an answer Mrs Allison turned to the decorator. 'Why did I choose Early American?'

'Because it's homey and inviting,' said Mrs Middy. 'And because it is part of our national heritage.'

'You can quote me,' Mrs Allison said to Qwilleran with a generous gesture. She went to the sideboard. 'Sure you don't want a drink? I'm going to have one myself.'

She poured a straight rye, and as the decorator showed the newsmen about the house, Mrs Allison trailed after them, carrying her glass in one hand and the bottle in the other. Qwilleran made notes on crewelwork, dry sinks, and Queen Anne candlesticks. The photographer formed an attachment for a ship's figurehead over the living-room mantel – an old wood carving of a full-busted mermaid with chipped nose and peeling paint.

He said, 'Reminds me of a girl I used to date.'

'That's one I caught and had stuffed,' said Mrs Allison. 'You should've seen the one that got away.'

Mrs Middy said: 'Look at the skirts on these little café tables, Mr Qwillum. Aren't they sweet? They're slightly Victorian, but Mrs Allison didn't want the interior to be too *pure*.'

'It's all pretty elegant,' Qwilleran said to the house mother. 'I suppose you're fussy about the kind of girls you get in here.'

'You better believe it. They gotta have references and at least two years of college.' She poured another ounce in her glass.

The bedrooms were vividly pink. They had pink walls pink carpet, and even pinker side curtains on the four-poster beds.

'Love this shade of green!' said Bunsen.

'How do the girls react to all this pink?' Qwilleran asked.

Mrs Allison turned to the decorator. 'How do the girls react to all this pink?'

'They find it warm and stimulating,' said the decorator. 'Notice the hand-painted mirror frames, Mr Qwillum.'

Bunsen photographed one bedroom, the living room, a

corner of the dining room, and a close-up of the ship's figurehead. He was finished before noon.

'Come around and meet the girls some evening,' Mrs Allison said, as the newsmen made their goodbyes.

'Got any blondes?' asked the photographer.

'You name it. We got it.'

'Okay, some night when I can get out of washing the dishes and helping the kids with their homework, I'll be around to collect that drink.'

'Don't wait too long. You're not getting any younger,' Mrs Allison said cheerily.

As the newsmen carried the photographic equipment to the car, Mrs Middy came hurrying after them. 'Oh, dear! Oh, dear!' she said. 'I forgot to tell you: Mrs Allison doesn't want you to use her name or address.'

'We always use names,' Qwilleran said.

'Oh, dear! I was afraid so. But she thinks the girls will get crank phone calls if you print the name and address. And she wants to avoid that.'

'It's newspaper policy to tell who and where,' Qwilleran explained. 'A story is incomplete without it.'

'Oh, dear! Then we'll have to cancel the story. What a pity!'

'Cancel it! We can't cancel it! We're right on deadline!'

'Oh, dear! Then you'll have to write it up without the name and address,' said Mrs Middy.

She no longer looked like a dumpling to Qwilleran. She looked like a granite boulder in a fussy lace collar.

Bunsen said to his partner in a low voice: 'You're trapped. Do what the old gal wants.'

'You think I should?'

'We don't have time to pick up another cover story.'

Mrs Middy said: 'Just say that it's a residence for professional girls. That sounds nicer than career girls, don't you think? And don't forget to mention the name of the decorator!' She shook a playful finger at the newsmen.

As they drove away from the house on Merchant Street, Bunsen said, 'You can't win 'em all.'

Qwilleran was not cheered by this philosophy, and they drove in silence until Bunsen said, 'They buried the Tait woman this morning.'

'I know.'

'The chief assigned two photographers. That's pretty good coverage for a funeral. He only sent one to the international boat races last week.'

Bunsen lit a cigar, and Qwilleran opened his window wide.

The photographer said, 'Have you moved into the Villa Verandah with the bigwigs yet?'

'I'm moving in this afternoon. And then I've got a dinner date with Mrs Middy's assistant.'

'I hope she's got references and two years of college.'

'She's quite a dish. Clever, too!'

'Look out for the clever ones,' the photographer warned him. 'The dumb ones are safer.'

Late that afternoon Qwilleran went home, packed his two suitcases, and called a taxi. Then he proceeded to stuff the cat into a canned tuna fish carton with airholes punched in the sides. Suddenly Koko had seventeen legs, all grabbing and struggling at once, and his verbal protests added to the confusion.

'I know! I know!' shouted Qwilleran above the din. 'But it's the best I can do.'

When the seventeen paws, nine ears, and three tails were tucked in, and the cover clapped shut and roped, Koko found himself in a snug, dark, sheltered place, and he settled down. The only sign of life was a glistening eye, seen through one of the airholes.

Once, during the brief ride to the Villa Verandah, the taxi swerved to avoid hitting a bus, and from the back seat came an outraged scream.

'My God!' yelled the driver, slamming on the brakes. 'What'd I do?'

'It's only my cat,' said Qwilleran. 'I've got a cat in one of these boxes.'

'I thought I hit a pedestrian. What is it? A bobcat?'

'He's a Siamese. They're inclined to be outspoken.'

'Oh, yeah. I've seen 'em on television. Ugly buggers.'

Qwilleran's moustache curled. He was never overly generous with gratuities, but he remembered to give the driver a tip lighter than usual.

At the Villa Verandah, Koko produced earsplitting howls in the elevator, but as soon as he was released from his box in the Noyton apartment, he was speechless. For a moment he stood poised with one forepaw lifted, and the place was filled with breathless, listening cat-silence. Then his head swung from side to side as he observed the general features of the room. He walked cautiously across the sleek wood floor. He sniffed the edge of the thick-piled rug and extended one paw experimentally, but withdrew it at once. He nosed the corner of one sofa, examined the hem of the draperies, looked in the waste-basket near the desk.

Qwilleran showed Koko the new location of his sandbox and gave him his old toy mouse. 'Your cushion's on the refrigerator,' he told the cat. 'Make yourself at home.'

An unfamiliar bell rang, and Koko jumped in alarm.

'It's only the phone,' Qwilleran said, picking up the receiver and seating himself importantly behind the fine leather-topped desk.

From the instrument came a voice speaking in careful English. 'I have a transatlantic call for Mr James Qwilleran.'

'Speaking.'

'Copenhagen calling.'

Then came the excited voice of Harry Noyton. 'Would you believe it? I'm in Copenhagen already! How's everything? Did you move in? Did you get settled?'

'Just got here. How was the flight?'

'Some turbulence east of Gander, but it was a good trip on the whole. Don't forward any mail till I give the signal. I'll keep in touch. And one of these days I'll have a scoop for the *Daily Fluxion*.'

'A news story?'

'Something fantastic! Can't talk about it yet ... But here's why I called: Do you like baseball? There's a pair of tickets for the charity game, stuck in my desk calendar. It's a shame to let them go to waste – especially at thirty bucks a throw.'

'I'll probably have to work Saturday.'

'Then give them to your pals at the paper.'

'How do you like Copenhagen?'

'It looks very clean, very tidy. Lots of bicycles.'

'How soon will your news break?'

'Hopefully, within a week,' said Noyton. 'And when it does, the *Fluxion* gets the first crack at it!'

After hanging up, Qwilleran looked for Noyton's calendar. He found it in the desk drawer – a large leatherbound book with a diary on one side and an index for telephone numbers on the other. The baseball tickets were clipped to September 26 – box seats behind the dugout – and Qwilleran wondered whether he should use them or give them away. He could invite Alacoque Wright, break away from the office at noon on Saturday . . .

'Koko!' he snapped. 'Get away from that book!'

The cat had risen noiselessly to the top of the desk and was sinking his claws in the edge of the telephone index. He was trying to play the game. Qwilleran's moustache twitched. He could not resist opening the book to the page Koko had selected.

On it he found the telephone numbers of a Dr Thomas and the well-known law firm of Teahandle, Burris, Hansblow, Maus, and Castle.

'Congratulations!' Qwilleran said to the cat. 'You've cornered a Maus.'

There was also Tappington, the stockbroker, and the phone number of Toledo, the most expensive restaurant in town. And at the bottom of the list there was the name Tait. Not George Tait or Verning Tait, but Signe Tait.

Qwilleran stared at the hastily scrawled name as if it were the ghost of the dead woman. Why had Noyton listed Signe and not her husband? What business did a bigtime promoter have with the invalid wife of a rich, idle collector of jades?

Qwilleran recalled his conversation with Noyton at David's party. The jade theft had been discussed, but the promoter had not mentioned his acquaintance with the late Mrs Tait. And yet he was an unabashed name-dropper, and the Tait name would have been an impressive one to drop.

Qwilleran closed the book slowly and opened it again quickly. He went through the diary, checking Noyton's appointments day by day. He started with September 20 and worked backward to January 1. There was no entry concerning Signe Tait or Muggy Swamp. But the color of ink changed around the first of September. For most of the year it had been blue. Then Noyton switched to black. Signe Tait's phone number was written in black; it had been added within the last three weeks.

Nine

Before leaving the apartment for his date with Alacoque Wright, Qwilleran telephoned David Lyke to inquire about Mrs Tait's funeral.

'You should have been there,' said the decorator. 'There was enough blue blood to float a ship. All the Old Guard who knew Tait's pappy and grandpappy. You never saw so many pince-nez and Queen Mary hats.'

'How was Tait taking it?'

'I wish I could say he looked pale and haggard, but with that healthy flush of his he always looks as if he'd just won at tennis. Why weren't you there?'

'I was working on a cover story. And this afternoon I moved into Harry Noyton's apartment.'

'Good! We're neighbors,' David said. 'Why don't you

come over Saturday night and meet Natalie Noyton? She just got back from Reno, and I'm having a few people in for drinks.'

Qwilleran recalled the excellence of the buffet at the decorator's last party and accepted the invitation with alacrity. After that, he prepared a hasty dinner for Koko – half a can of red salmon garnished with a raw egg yolk – and said: 'Be a good cat. I'll be home late and fix you a snack.'

At six o'clock sharp he met Alacoque Wright under the City Hall clock; her punctuality had an architectural precision. She was wearing a curious medley of green skirt, turquoise top, and blue cape in a weave that reminded Qwilleran of dining-room chair seats somewhere in his forgotten past.

'I made it myself – out of upholstery samples,' she said, peering at him from under a quantity of glossy brown hair that enveloped her head, shoulders, and much of her face.

He took her to the Press Club for dinner, aware that he was being observed by all the regulars at the bar and would have to account, the next day, for his taste in women. Nevertheless, it had to be the Press Club. He had a charge account there, and payday was not until Friday. He ushered his date – she asked Qwilleran to call her Cokey – upstairs to the main dining room, where the atmosphere was quieter and the rolls were sprinkled with poppy seeds.

'Have a cocktail?' Qwilleran invited. 'I'm on the wagon myself, but I'll have a lemon and seltzer to keep you company.'

Cokey looked keenly interested. 'Why aren't you drinking?'

'It's a long story, and the less said about it, the better.' He put a matchbook under one table leg; all the Press Club tables had a built-in wobble.

'I'm on a yoga kick myself,' she said. 'No liquor. No meat. But I'll make us one of nature's own cocktails if you'll order the ingredients and two champagne glasses.'

When the tray arrived, she poured a little cream into each glass, filled it with ginger ale, and then produced a small wooden device from her handbag.

'I carry my own nutmeg and grate it fresh,' she said, dusting the surface of the drinks with brown spice. 'Nutmeg is a stimulant. The Germans put it in everything.'

Qwilleran took a cautious sip. The drink had a bite. It was like Cokey – cool and smooth, with an unexpected pepperiness. 'How did you decide to become an architect?' he asked.

'Maybe you haven't noticed,' said Cokey, 'but there are more architects named Wright than there are judges named Murphy. We seem to gravitate to the drafting board. However, the name is getting me nowhere.' She stroked her long hair lovingly. 'I may have to give up the struggle and find a husband.'

'Shouldn't be difficult.'

'I'm glad you're so confident.' She set her jaw and ground some more nutmeg on her cocktail. 'Tell me what you think of the decorating profession after two weeks in the velvet jungle?'

'They seem to be likable people.'

'They're children! They live in a world of play.' A shadow passed over Cokey's face – the sliver of face that was visible. 'And, just like children, they can be cruel.' She studied the grains of nutmeg clinging to the inside of her empty glass and, catlike, darted out a pink tongue to lick it clean.

A man walked past the table and said, 'Hi, there, Cokey.'

She looked up abruptly. 'Well, hello!' she said with meaning in the inflection.

'You know him?' Qwilleran asked in surprise.

'We've met,' said Cokey. 'I'm getting hungry. May we order?'

She looked at the menu and asked for brook trout with a large garnish of parsley, and a small salad. Qwilleran compared her taut figure with his own well-padded beltline and felt guilty as he ordered bean soup, a hefty steak and a baked potato with sour cream.

'Are you divorced?' Cokey asked suddenly.

Qwilleran nodded.

'That's cool. Where do you live?'

'I moved into the Villa Verandah today.' He waited for her eyes to open wide, and then added in a burst of honesty, 'The apartment belongs to a friend who's gone abroad.'

'Do you like living alone?'

'I don't live alone,' said Qwilleran. 'I have a cat. A Siamese.'

'I adore cats,' Cokey squealed. 'What's your cat's name?'

Qwilleran beamed at her. People who really appreciated animals always asked their names. 'His real name is Kao K'o-Kung, but he's called Koko for everyday purposes. I considered myself a dog man until I met Koko. He's a remarkable animal. Perhaps you remember the murder on Blenheim Place last spring. Koko is the cat who was involved, and if I told you some of his intellectual feats you wouldn't believe me.'

'Oh, I'd believe anything about cats. They're uncanny.'

'Sometimes I'm convinced Koko senses what's going to happen.'

'It's true! Cats tune in with their whiskers.'

'That's what I've been told,' said Qwilleran, preening his moustache absently. 'Koko always gives the impression that he knows more than I do, and he has clever ways of communicating. Not that he does anything uncatlike, you understand. Yet, somehow he gets his ideas across . . . I'm not explaining this very well.'

'I know exactly what you mean.'

Qwilleran looked at Cokey with appreciation. These were matters he could not discuss with his friends at the *Fluxion*. With their beagles and boxers as a frame of reference, how could they understand about cats? In this one area of his life he experienced a kind of loneliness. But Cokey understood. Her mischievous green eyes had mellowed into an expression of rapport.

He reached over and took her hand – the slender, tapering hand that was playing tiddledywinks with stray poppy-seeds on the tablecloth. He said, 'Have you ever heard of a cat eating spider webs – or glue? Koko has started licking gummed envelopes. One day he chewed up a dollar's worth of postage stamps.'

'I used to have a cat who drank soapsuds,' Cokey said. 'They're individualists. Does Koko scratch furniture? It was noble of your friend to let you move into his apartment with a cat.'

'Koko does all his scratching on an old unabridged dictionary,' Qwilleran said with a note of pride.

'How literary of him!'

'It's not really an *old* dictionary,' he explained. 'It's the new edition. The man Koko used to live with bought it for himself and then decided he preferred the old edition, so he gave the new one to the cat for a scratching pad.'

'I admire men who admire cats.'

Qwilleran lowered his voice and spoke confidentially. 'We have a game we play with this dictionary. Koko exercises his claws, and I add a few words to my vocabulary ... This is something I wouldn't want to get around the Press Club, you understand.'

Cokey looked at him mistily. 'I think you're wonderful,' she said. 'I'd love to play the game sometime.'

When Qwilleran arrived home that evening, it was late, and he was exhausted. Girls like Cokey made him realize he was not so young as he used to be.

He unlocked the door of his apartment and was groping for the light switch when he saw two red sparks in the darkened living room. They glowed with a supernatural light He had seen them before, and he knew what they were, but they always gave him a scare.

'Koko!' he said. 'Is that you?'

He flipped the lights on, and the mysterious red lights in Koko's eyes were extinguished.

The cat approached with arched back, question-mark tail, and the backswept whiskers of disapproval. He made vehement one-note complaints.

'I'm sorry,' said Qwilleran. 'Did you think you were abandoned? You'll never believe this, but we went for a walk – a long walk. That's what lady architects like to do on a date – take you for a walk, looking at buildings. I'm bushed!' He sank into a chair and kicked off his shoes without untying the laces. 'For three hours we've been looking at architecture: insensitive massing, inefficient site-planning, trite fenestration . . .'

Koko was howling impatiently at his knee, and Qwilleran picked up the cat, laid him across his shoulder, and patted the sleek fur. He could feel the muscles struggling beneath the pelt, and Koko wriggled away and jumped down.

'Is something wrong?' Qwilleran asked.

'YOW-OW!' said Koko.

He ran to the Spanish chest that housed the stereo set. It was a massive carved piece built close to the floor, resting on four bun-shaped feet. Koko plumped to the floor in front of it, stretched one foreleg, and vainly tried to reach under the chest, his brown tail tensed in a scimitar curve.

Qwilleran uttered a weary moan. He knew the cat had lost his homemade mouse – a bouquet of dried mint leaves tied in the toe of an old sock. He also knew there would be no sleeping that night until the mouse was retrieved. He looked for something to poke under the chest. Broomstick? There was no broom in the kitchen closet; the maids evidently used their own sweeping equipment . . . Fireplace poker? There were no fireplaces at the Villa Verandah. . . . Umbrella? If Noyton owned one, he had taken it to Europe . . . Fishing rod? Golf club? Tennis racquet? The man seemed to have no active hobbies . . . Back-scratcher? Long-handled shoehorn? Clarinet? Discarded crutch?

With Koko at his heels, yowling imperious Siamese commands, Qwilleran searched the premises. He thought wistfully of all the long, slender implements he could use: tree branch, fly swatter – buggy whip.

Eventually he lowered himself to the floor. Lying flat,

he reached under the low chest and gingerly extracted a penny, a gold earring, an olive pit, a crumpled scrap of paper, several dustballs, and finally a familiar gray wad of indefinite shape.

Koko pounced on his mouse, sniffed it once without much interest, and gave it a casual whack with his paw. It went back under the Spanish chest, and Koko sauntered away to get a drink of water before retiring for the night.

But Qwilleran stayed up smoking his pipe and thinking about many things: Cokey and nutmeg cocktails, *Gracious Abodes* and Mrs Middy's lace collar, buggy whips and the situation in Muggy Swamp. Once he went to the wastebasket and fished out the crumpled paper he had found beneath the Spanish chest. There was only a name on it: Arne Thorvaldson. He dropped it in the basket again. The gold earring he tossed in the desk drawer with the paper clips.

Ten

On the day following the funeral, Qwilleran telephoned G. Verning Tait and asked if he might call and deliver the books on jade. He said he always liked to return borrowed books promptly.

Tait acquiesced in a voice that was neither cold nor cordial, and Qwilleran could imagine the crimping of the mouth that accompanied it.

'How did you get this number?' Tait asked.

Qwilleran passed a hand swiftly over his face and hoped he was saying the right thing. 'I believe this is – yes, this must be the number that David Lyke gave me.'

'I was merely curious. It's an unlisted number.'

Qwilleran put Noyton's address book away in the desk, stroked Koko's head for luck, and drove to Muggy Swamp in a company car. It was a wild shot, but he was hoping to see or hear something that would reinforce his hunch – his vague suspicion that all was not exactly as represented on the police record.

He had planned no particular approach – just the Qwilleran Technique. In twenty-five years of newspapering around the country he had enjoyed astounding success in interviewing criminals (described as tight-lipped), old ladies (timid), politicians (cautious), and cowboys (taciturn). He asked no prying questions on these occasions. He just smoked his pipe, murmured encouraging phrases, prodded gently, and wore an expression of sympathetic concern, which was enhanced by the sober aspect of his moustache.

Tait himself, wearing his usual high color and another kind of silk sports shirt, admitted the newsman to the glittering foyer. Qwilleran looked inquiringly toward the living room, but the double doors were closed.

The collector invited him into the library. 'Did you enjoy the books?' he said. 'Are you beginning to feel the lure of jade? Do you think you might like to collect?'

'I'm afraid it's beyond my means at the moment,' said Qwilleran, adding a small falsehood: 'I'm subletting Harry Noyton's apartment at the Villa Verandah, and this little spree is keeping me broke.'

The name brought no sign of recognition. Tait said: 'You can start collecting in a modest way. I can give you the name of a dealer who likes to help beginners. Do you still have your jade button?'

'Carry it all the time!' Qwilleran jingled the contents of his trouser pocket. Then he asked solemnly, 'Did Mrs Tait share your enthusiasm for jade?'

The corners of Tait's mouth quivered. 'Unfortunately,

Mrs Tait never warmed to the fascination of jade, but collecting it and working with it have been a joy and a comfort to me for more than fifteen years. Would you like to see my workshop?' He led the way to the rear of the house and down a flight of basement stairs.

'This is a rambling house,' said Qwilleran. 'I imagine an intercom system comes in handy.'

'Please excuse the appearance of my shop,' the collector said. 'It is not as tidy as it should be. I've dismissed the housekeeper. I'm getting ready to go away.'

'I suppose you'll be traveling to jade country,' said Qwilleran hopefully.

His supposition got no verification.

Tait said: 'Have you ever seen a lapidary shop? It's strange, but when I am down here in this hideaway, cutting and polishing, I forget everything. My back ailment gives me no discomfort, and I am a happy man.' He handed the newsman a small carved dragon. 'This is the piece the police found behind Paolo's bed when they searched his room. It's a fairly simple design. I've been trying to copy it.'

'You must feel very bitter about that boy,' Qwilleran said.

Tait averted his eyes. 'Bitterness accomplishes nothing.'

'Frankly, his implication came as a shock to me. He seemed an open, ingenuous young man.'

'People are not always what they seem.'

'Could it be that Paolo was used as a tool by the real organizers of the crime?'

'That is a possibility, of course, but it doesn't bring back my jades.'

'Mr Tait,' said Qwilleran, 'for what it is worth, I want

you to know I have a strong feeling the stolen objects will be found.'

'I wish I could share your optimism.' Then the collector showed a spark of curiosity. 'What makes you feel that way?'

'There's a rumor at the paper that the police are on the track of something.' It was not the first time Qwilleran had spread the rumor of a rumor, and it often got results.

'Strange they have not communicated with me,' said Tait. He led the way up the stairs and to the front door.

'Perhaps I shouldn't have mentioned it,' Qwilleran said. Then casually he remarked, 'That housekeeper of yours – would she take a temporary job while you're away? A friend of mine will need a housekeeper while his wife is in the hospital, and it's hard to get good help on a short-term basis.'

'I have no doubt that Mrs Hawkins needs work,' said Tait.

'How long before you'll be needing her again?'

'I don't intend to take her back,' said Tait. 'Her work is satisfactory, but she has an unfortunate personality.'

'If you don't mind, then, I'd like to give her phone number to my friend.'

Tait stepped into his library and wrote the information on a slip of paper. 'I'll also give you the name and address of that jade dealer in Chicago,' he said, 'just in case you change your mind.'

As they passed the living room Qwilleran looked hungrily at the closed doors. 'Did Paolo do any damage in opening the cases?'

'No. No damage. It's small comfort,' Tait said sadly, 'but I like to think the jades were taken by someone who loved them.'

As Qwilleran drove away from Muggy Swamp, he felt that he had wasted a morning and two gallons of *Daily Fluxion* gas. Yet, throughout the visit, he had felt a teasing discomfort about the upper lip. He thought he sensed something false in the collector's pose. The man should have been sadder – or madder. And then there was that heart-wringing curtain line: 'I like to think the jades were stolen by someone who loved them.'

'Oh, brother!' Qwilleran said aloud. 'What a ham!'

His morning of snooping had only whetted his curiosity, and now he headed for the place where he might get some answers to his questions. He drove to the shop called PLUG on River Street.

It was an unlikely spot for a decorating studio. PLUG looked self-consciously dapper among the dilapidated storefronts devoted to plumbing supplies and used cash registers.

The merchandise in the window was attractively arranged against a background of kitchen oilcloth in a pink kitten design. There were vases of ostrich plumes, chunks of broken concrete painted in phosphorescent colors, and bowls of eggs trimmed with sequins. The price tags were small and refined, befitting an exclusive shop: $5 each for the eggs, $15 for a chunk of concrete.

Qwilleran walked into the shop (the door handle was a gilded replica of the Statue of Liberty), and a bell announced his presence by tinkling the four notes of 'How Dry I Am.' Immediately, from behind a folding screen composed of old *Reader's Digest* covers, came the genial proprietor, Bob Orax, looking more fastidious than ever among the tawdry merchandise. There were paper flowers pressed under glass, trays decorated with cigar bands, and candelabra made out of steer horns, standing on crocheted doilies. One entire wall was paved with a mosaic of popbottle caps. Others were decorated with supermarket ads and candy-bar wrappers matted in red velvet and framed in gilt.

'So this is your racket!' said Qwilleran. 'Who buys this stuff?'

'Planned Ugliness appeals to those who are bored with Beauty, tired of Taste, and fed up with Function,' said Orax brightly. 'People can't stand too much beauty. It's against the human grain. This new movement is a revolt of the sophisticated intellectual. The conventional middle-class customer rejects it.'

'Do you design interiors around this theme?'

'Definitely! I have just done a morning room for a client, mixing Depression Overstuffed with Mail Order Modern. Very effective. I paneled one wall in corrugated metal siding from an old toolshed, in the original rust. The color scheme is Cinnamon and Parsnip with accents of Dill Weed.'

Qwilleran examined a display of rattraps made into ashtrays.

'Those are little boutique items for the impulse buyer,' said Orax, and he added with an arch smile, 'I hope you understand that I'm not emotionally involved with this trend. True, it requires a degree of connoisseurship, but I'm in it primarily to make a buck, if I may quote Shakespeare.'

Qwilleran browsed for a while and then said: 'That was

a good party at David's place Monday night. I hear he's giving another one on Saturday – for Mrs Noyton.'

'I shall not be there,' said Orax with regret. 'Mother is giving a dinner party, and if I am not on hand to mix good stiff drinks for the guests, Mother's friends will discover how atrocious her cooking really is! Mother was not born to the apron ... But you will enjoy meeting Natalie Noyton. She has all the gagging appeal of a marshmallow sundae.'

Qwilleran toyed with a pink plastic flamingo that lit up. 'Were the Noytons and the Taits particularly friendly?' he asked.

Orax was amused. 'I doubt whether they would move in the same social circles.'

'Oh,' said Qwilleran with an innocent expression. 'I thought I had heard that Harry Noyton knew Mrs Tait.'

'Really?' The Orax eyebrows went up higher. 'An unlikely pair! If it were Georgie Tait and Natalie, that might make sense. Mother says Georgie used to be quite a womanizer.' He saw Qwilleran inspecting some chromium bowls. 'Those are 1959 hubcaps, now very much in demand for salads and flower arrangements.'

'How long had Mrs Tait been confined to a wheelchair?'

'Mother says it happened after the scandal, and that must have been sixteen or eighteen years ago. I was away at Princeton at the time, but I understand it was quite a brouhaha, and Siggy immediately developed her indisposition.'

Qwilleran patted his alerted moustache and cleared his throat before saying, 'Scandal? What scandal?'

The decorator's eyes danced. 'Oh, didn't you *know*? It was a juicy affair! You should look it up in your morgue.

I'm sure the *Fluxion* has an extensive file on the subject.' He picked up a feather duster and whisked it over a tray of tiny objects. 'These are Cracker Jack prizes, circa 1930,' he said. 'Genuine tin, and very collectible. My knowledgeable customers are buying them as investments.'

Qwilleran rushed back to the *Daily Fluxion* and asked the clerk in the library for the file on the Tait family.

Without a word she disappeared among the gray rows of head-high filing cabinets, moving with the speed of a sleepwalker. She returned empty-handed. 'It's not here.'

'Did someone check it out?'

'I don't know.'

'Would you mind consulting whatever records you keep and telling me who signed for it?' Qwilleran said with impatience.

The clerk ambled away and returned with a yawn. 'Nobody signed for it.'

'Then where is it?' he yelled. 'You must have a file on an important family like the Taits!'

Another clerk stood on tiptoe and called across a row of files, 'Are you talking about G. Verning Tait? It's a big file. A man from the Police Department was in here looking at it. He wanted to take it to Headquarters, but we told him he couldn't take it out of the building.'

'He must have sneaked it out,' said Qwilleran. 'Some of those cops are connivers . . . Where's your boss?'

The first clerk said, 'It's his day off.'

'Well, you tell him to get hold of the Police Department and get that file back here. Can you remember that?'

'Remember what?'

'Never mind. I'll write him a memo.'

Eleven

On Saturday afternoon Qwilleran took Alacoque Wright to the ball park, and listened to her views on baseball.

'Of course,' she said, 'the game's basic appeal is erotic. All that symbolism, you know, and those sensual movements!'

She was wearing something she had made from a bedspread. 'Mrs Middy custom-ordered it for a king-size bed,' she explained, 'and it was delivered in queen-size, so I converted it into a costume suit.'

Her converted bedspread was green corduroy with an irregular plush pile like rows of marching caterpillars.

'Very tasteful,' Qwilleran remarked.

Cokey tossed her cascade of hair. 'It wasn't intended to be tasteful. It was intended to be sexy.'

After dinner at a chophouse (Cokey had a crab leg and

some stewed plums; Qwilleran had the works), the newsman said 'We're invited to a party tonight, and I'm going to do something rash. I'm taking you to meet a young man who is apparently irresistible to women of all ages, sizes, and shapes.'

'Don't worry,' said Cokey, giving his hand a blithe squeeze. 'I prefer older men.'

'I'm not *that* much older.'

'But you're so mature. That's important to a person like me.'

They rode to the Villa Verandah in a taxi, holding hands. At the building entrance they were greeted with enthusiasm by the doorman, whom Qwilleran had foresightedly tipped that afternoon. It was not a large tip by Villa Verandah standards, but it commanded a dollar's worth of attention from a man dressed like a nineteenth-century Prussian general.

They walked into the lofty lobby – all white marble, plate glass, and stainless steel – and Cokey nodded approval. She had become suddenly quiet. As they ascended in the automatic elevator, Qwilleran gave her a quick private hug.

The door to David's apartment was opened by a white-coated Oriental, and there was a flash of recognition when he saw Qwilleran. No one ever forgot the newsman's moustache. Then the host surged forward, radiating charm, and Cokey slipped her hand through Qwilleran's arm. He felt her grip tighten when Lyke acknowledged the introduction with his rumbling voice and drooping eyelids.

The apartment was filled with guests – clients of David's chattering about their analysts, and fellow decorators discussing the Spanish exhibition at the museum and the new restaurant in Greektown.

'There's a simply marvelous seventeenth-century Isabellina *vargueno* in the show.'

'The restaurant will remind you of that little place in Athens near the Acropolis. You know the one.'

Qwilleran led Cokey to the buffet. 'When I'm with decorators,' he said, 'I feel I'm in a never-never land. They never discuss anything serious or unpleasant.'

'Decorators have only two worries: discontinued patterns and slow deliveries,' Cokey said. 'They have no real problems.' There was scorn in the curl of her lips.

'Such disapproval can't be purely professional. I suspect you were jilted by a decorator once.'

'Or twice.' She smoothed her long straight hair self-consciously. 'Try these little crabmeat things. They've got lots of pepper in them.'

Although Qwilleran had dined recently and well, he had no difficulty in trying the lobster salad, the crusty brown potato balls flavored with garlic, the strips of ginger-spiced beef skewered on slivers of bamboo, and the hot buttered cornbread filled with ham. He had a feeling of well-being. He looked at Cokey with satisfaction. He liked her spirit, and the provocative face peeking out from that curtain of hair, and the coltish grace of her figure.

Then he glanced over her shoulder toward the living room, and suddenly Cokey looked plain. Natalie Noyton had arrived.

Harry Noyton's ex-wife was plump in all areas except for an incongruously small waist and tiny ankles. Her face was pretty, like a peach, and she had peach-colored hair ballooning about her head.

One of the decorators said, 'How did you like the Wild West, Natalie?'

'I didn't pay any attention to it,' she replied in a small shrill voice. 'I just stayed in a boardinghouse in Reno and worked on my rug. I made one of those shaggy Danish rugs with a needle. Does anybody want to buy a hand-made rug in Cocoa and Celery Green?'

'You've put on weight, Natalie.'

'Ooh, have I ever! All I did was work on my rug and eat peanut butter. I love crunchy peanut butter.'

Natalie was wearing a dress that matched her hair – a sheath of loosely woven wool with golden glints. A matching stole with long crinkly fringe was draped over her shoulders.

Cokey, who was giving Natalie an oblique inspection, said to Qwilleran: 'That fabric must be something she loomed herself, in between peanut-butter sandwiches. It would have been smarter without the metallic threads.'

'What would an architect call that color?' he asked.

'I'd call it a yellow-pink of low saturation and medium brilliance.'

'A decorator would call it Cream of Carrot,' he said, 'or Sweet Potato Soufflé.'

After Natalie had been welcomed and teased and flattered and congratulated by those who knew her, David Lyke brought her to meet Qwilleran and Cokey. He told her, 'The *Daily Fluxion* might want to photograph your house in the Hills. What do you think?'

'Do *you* want it photographed, David?'

'It's your house, darling. You decide.'

Natalie said to Qwilleran: 'I'm moving out as soon as I

find a studio. And then my husband – my ex-husband – is going to sell the house.'

'I hear it's really something,' said the newsman.

'It's super! Simply super! David has oodles of talent.' She looked at the decorator adoringly.

Lyke explained: 'I corrected some of the architect's mistakes and changed the window detail so we could hang draperies. Natalie wove the draperies herself. They're a work of art.'

'Well, look, honey,' said Natalie, 'if it will do you any good; let's put the house in the paper.'

'Suppose we let Mr Qwilleran have a look at it.'

'All right,' she said. 'How about Monday morning? I have a hair appointment in the afternoon.'

Qwilleran said, 'Do you have your looms at the house?'

'Ooh, yes! I have two great big looms and a small one. I'm crazy about weaving. David, honey, show them that sports coat I did for you.'

Lyke hesitated for the flicker of an eyelid. 'Darling, it's at the cleaner,' he said. Later he remarked to Qwilleran: 'I use some of her yardage out of friendship, but her work leaves a lot to be desired. She's just an amateur with no taste and no talent, so don't emphasize the hand-weaving if you publish the house.'

The evening followed the usual Lyke pattern: a splendid buffet, drinks in abundance, music for dancing played a trifle too loud, and ten conversations in progress simultaneously. It had all the elements of a good party, but Qwilleran found himself feeling troubled at David Lyke's last remark. At his first opportunity he asked Natalie to dance, and said, 'I hear you're going into the weaving business on the professional level.'

'Yes, I'm going to do custom work for decorators,' she said in her high-pitched voice that sounded vulnerable and pathetic. 'David loves my weaving. He says he'll get me a lot of commissions.'

She was an ample armful, and the glittering wool dress she wore was delectably soft, except for streaks of scratchiness where the fabric was shot with gold threads.

As they danced, she went on chattering, and Qwilleran's mind wandered. If this woman was banking her career on David's endorsement, she was in for a surprise. Natalie said she was hunting for a studio, and she had a cousin who was a newspaperman, and she loved smoked oysters, and the balconies at the Villa Verandah were too windy. Qwilleran said he had just moved into an apartment there, but refrained from mentioning whose. He speculated on the chances of sneaking a few tidbits from the buffet for his cat.

'Ooh, do you have a cat?' Natalie squealed 'Does he like lobster?'

'He likes anything that's expensive. I think he reads price tags.'

'Why don't you go and get him? We'll give him some lobster.'

Qwilleran doubted whether Koko would like the noisy crowd, but he liked to show off his handsome pet, and he went to get him. The cat was half asleep on his refrigerator cushion, and he was the picture of relaxation, sprawled on his back in a position of utter abandon, with one foreleg flung out in space and the other curled around his ears. He looked at Qwilleran upside down with half an inch of pink tongue protruding and an insane gleam in his slanted, half-closed eyes.

'Get up,' said Qwilleran, 'and quit looking like an idiot. You're going to a soirée.'

By the time Koko arrived at the party, sitting on Qwilleran's shoulder, he had regained his dignity. At his entrance the noise swelled to a crescendo and then stopped altogether. Koko surveyed the scene with regal condescension, like a potentate honoring his subjects with his presence. He blinked not, neither did he move a whisker. His brown points were so artistically contrasted with his light body, his fur was shaded so subtly, and his sapphire eyes had such unadorned elegance that he made David Lyke's guests look gaudily overdressed.

Then the first exclamation broke through the silence, and everyone came forward to stroke the silky fur.

'Why, it feels like ermine!'

'I'm going to throw out my mink.'

Koko tolerated the attention but remained aloof until Natalie spoke to him. He stretched his neck and sniffed her extended finger.

'Ooh, can I hold him?' she asked, and to Qwilleran's surprise Koko went gladly into her arms, snuggling in her woolly stole, sniffing it with serious concentration, and purring audibly.

Cokey pulled Qwilleran away. 'It makes me so mad,' she said, 'when I think of all the trouble I take to stay thin and get my hair straightened and improve my conversation! Then *she* comes in, babbling and looking frizzy and thirty pounds overweight, and everybody goes for her, including the cat!'

Qwilleran experienced a pang of sympathy for Cokey, mixed with something else. 'I shouldn't leave Koko here too long, among all these strangers,' he said. 'It might upset his stomach. Let's take him back to 15-F, and you can have a look at my apartment.'

'I've brought my nutmeg grater,' she said. 'Do you happen to have any cream and ginger ale?'

Qwilleran retrieved Koko from Natalie's stole, and led Cokey around the long curving corridor to the other wing.

When he threw open the door of his apartment, Cokey paused for one breathless moment on the threshold and then ran into the living room with her arms flung wide. 'It's glorious!' she cried.

'Harry Noyton calls it Scandihoovian.'

'The green chair is Danish, and so is the endwood floor,' Cokey told him, 'and the dining chairs are Finnish. But the whole apartment is like a designers' Hall of Fame. Bertoia, Wegner, Aalto, Mies, Nakashima! It's too magnificent! I can't bear it!' She collapsed in the cushions of a suede sofa and put her face in her hands.

Qwilleran brought champagne glasses filled with a creamy liquid, and solemnly Cokey ground the nutmeg on the bubbling surface.

'To Cokey, my favorite girl,' he said, lifting his glass. 'Skinny, straight-haired, and articulate!'

'Now I feel better,' she said, and she kicked off her shoes and wiggled her toes in the shaggy pile of the rug.

Qwilleran lighted his pipe and showed her the new issue of *Gracious Abodes* with the Allison living room on the cover. They discussed its challenging shades of red and pink, the buxom ship's figurehead, and the pros and cons of four-poster beds with side curtains.

Koko was sitting on the coffee table with his back turned, pointedly ignoring the conversation. The curve of his tail, with its uplifted tip, was the essence of disdain, but the angle of his ears indicated that he was secretly listening.

'Hello, Koko,' said the girl. 'Don't you like me?'

The cat made no move. There was not even the tremor of a whisker.

'I used to have a beautiful orange cat named Frankie,' she told Qwilleran sadly. 'I still carry his picture in my handbag.' She extracted a wad of cards and snapshots from her wallet and sorted them on the seat of the sofa, then proudly held up a picture of a fuzzy orange blob.

'It's out of focus, and the color has faded, but it's all I have left of Frankie. He lived to be fifteen years old. His parentage was uncertain, but—'

'Koko!' shouted Qwilleran. 'Get away!'

The cat had silently crept up on the sofa, and he was manipulating his long pink tongue.

Qwilleran said, 'He was licking that picture.'

'Oh!' said Cokey, and she snatched up a small glossy photograph of a man. She slipped it into her wallet but not before Qwilleran had caught a glimpse of it. He frowned his displeasure as she went on talking about cats and grinding nutmeg into their cocktails.

'Now, tell me all about your moustache,' Cokey said. 'I suppose you know it's terribly glamorous.'

'I raised this crop in Britain during the war,' said Qwilleran, 'as camouflage.'

'I like it.'

It pleased him that she had not said 'Which war?' as young women were inclined to do. He said: 'To tell the truth, I'm afraid to shave it off. I have a strange feeling that these lip whiskers put me in touch with certain things – like subsurface truths and imminent happenings.'

'How wonderful!' said Cokey. 'Just like cats' whiskers.'

'I don't usually confide this little fact. I wouldn't want it to get noised around.'

'I can see your point.'

'Lately I've been getting hunches about the theft of the Tait jades.'

'Haven't they found the boy yet?'

'You mean the houseboy who allegedly stole the stuff? That's one of my hunches. I don't think he's the thief.'

Cokey's eyes widened. 'Do you have any evidence?'

Qwilleran frowned. 'That's the trouble; I don't have a thing but these blasted hunches. The houseboy doesn't fit the role, and there's something fishy about the timing, and I have certain reservations about G. Verning Tait Did you ever hear anything about a scandal in the Tait family?'

Cokey shook her head.

'Of course, you were too young when it happened.'

Cokey looked at her watch. 'It's getting late. I should be going home.'

'One more drink?' Qwilleran suggested. He went to the bar with its vast liquor supply and took the cream and ginger ale from the compact refrigerator.

Cokey began walking around the room and admiring it from every angle. 'Everywhere you look there's beautiful line and composition,' she said with rapture in her face. 'And I love the interplay of textures – velvety, sleek woolly, shaggy. And this rug! I worship this rug!'

She threw herself down on the tumbled pile of the luxurious rug. She lay there in ecstasy with arms flung wide, and Qwilleran combed his moustache violently. She lay there, unaware that the cat was stalking her. With his tail curled down like a fishhook and his body slung low,

Koko moved through the shaggy pile of the rug like a wild thing prowling through the underbrush. Then he sprang!

Cokey shrieked and sat up. 'He bit me! He bit my *head*!'

Qwilleran rushed to her side. 'Did he hurt you?'

Cokey ran her fingers through her hair. 'No. He didn't actually bite me. He just tried to take a little nip. But he seemed so . . . *hostile*! Qwill, why would Koko do a thing like that?'

Twelve

Qwilleran would have slept until noon on Sunday, if it had not been for the Siamese Whisker Torture. When Koko decided it was time to get up, he hopped weightlessly and soundlessly onto the sleeping man's bed and lightly touched his whiskers to nose and chin. Qwilleran opened his eyelids abruptly and found himself gazing into two enormous eyes, as innocent as they were blue.

'Go 'way,' he said, and went back to sleep.

Again the whiskers were applied, this time to more sensitive areas – the cheeks and forehead.

Qwilleran winced and clenched his teeth and his eyes, only to feel the cat's whiskers tickling his eyelids. He jumped to a sitting position, and Koko bounded from the bed and from the room, mission accomplished.

When Qwilleran shuffled out of the bedroom, wearing

his red plaid bathrobe and looking aimlessly for his pipe, he surveyed the living room with heavy-lidded eyes. On the coffee table were last night's champagne glasses, the Sunday paper, and Koko, diligently washing himself all over.

'You were a bad cat last night,' Qwilleran said. 'Why did you try to nip that pleasant girl who's so fond of cats? Such bad manners!'

Koko rolled over and attended to the base of his tail with rapt concentration, and Qwilleran's attention went to the rug. There, in the flattened pile, was a full-length impression of Cokey's tall, slender body, where she had sprawled for one dizzy moment. He made a move to erase the imprint by kicking up the pile with his toe, but changed his mind.

Koko, finished with his morning chore, sat up on the coffee table, blinked at the newsman, and looked angelic.

'You devil!' said Qwilleran. 'I wish I could read your mind. That photograph you licked—'

The telephone rang, and he went to answer it with pleased anticipation. He remembered the congratulatory calls of the previous Sunday. Now a new issue of *Gracious Abodes* had reached the public.

'Hello-o?' he said graciously.

'Qwill, it's Harold!' The tone was urgent, and Qwilleran cringed. 'Qwill, have you heard the news?'

'No, I just got out of bed—'

'Your cover story in today's paper – your residence for professional girls – haven't you heard?'

'What's happened?' Qwilleran put a hand over his eyes. He had visions of mass murder – a houseful of innocent girls murdered in their beds, their four-poster beds with pink side curtains.

'The police raided it last night! It's a disorderly house!'

'*What!*'

'They planted one of their men, got a warrant, and knocked the place off.'

Qwilleran sat down unexpectedly as his knees folded. 'But the decorator told me—'

'How did this happen? Where did you get the tip on this – this *house*?'

'From the decorator. From Mrs Middy, a nice little motherly woman. She specializes in – well – residences for girls. Dormitories, that is, and sorority houses. And this was supposed to be a high-class boardinghouse for professional girls.'

'Professional is the word!' said Percy. 'This is going to make us look like a pack of fools. Wait till the *Morning Rampage* plays it up.'

Qwilleran gulped. 'I don't know what to say.'

'There's nothing we can do about it now, but you'd better get hold of that Mrs Biddy—'

'Middy.'

'—whatever she calls herself – and let her know exactly how we feel about this highly embarrassing incident . . . It's an incredible situation per se, and on the heels of the Muggy Swamp mess it's too much!'

Percy hung up, and Qwilleran's stunned mind tried to remember how it had happened. There must be an explanation. Then he grabbed the telephone and dialed a number.

'Yes?' said a sleepy voice.

'Cokey!' said Qwilleran sternly. 'Have you heard the news?'

'What news? I'm not awake yet.'

'Well, wake up and listen to me! Mrs Middy has got me in a jam. Why didn't you tip me off?'

'About what?'

'About Mrs Allison's place.'

Cokey yawned. 'What about Mrs Allison's place?'

'You mean you don't *know*?'

'What are you talking about? You don't make sense.'

Qwilleran found himself with a death grip on the receiver. He took a deep breath. 'I've just been notified that the police raided Mrs Allison's so-called residence for professional girls last night ... It's a brothel! Did you know that?'

Cokey shrieked. 'Oh, Qwill, what a hoot!'

'Did you know the nature of Mrs Allison's house?' His voice was gruff.

'No, but I think the idea's a howl!'

'Well, I don't think it's a howl, and the *Daily Fluxion* doesn't think it's a howl. It makes us look like saps. How can I get hold of Mrs Middy?'

Cokey's voice sobered. 'You want to call her? Yourself? Now? ... Oh, don't do that!'

'Why not?'

'That poor woman! She'll drop dead from mortification.'

'Didn't she know what kind of establishment she was furnishing?' Qwilleran demanded.

'I'm sure she didn't. She's a genius at doing charming interiors, but she's rather ...'

'Rather what?'

'Muddleheaded, you know. Please don't call her,' Cokey

pleaded. 'Let me break the news gently. You don't want to *kill* the woman, do you?'

'I feel like killing somebody!'

Cokey burst into laughter again. 'And in Early American!' she shrieked. 'With all those Tom Jones beds!'

Qwilleran banged the receiver down. 'Now what?' he said to Koko. He paced the floor for a few minutes and then snatched the telephone and dialed another number.

'Hi!' said a childish treble.

'Let me talk to Odd Bunsen,' said Qwilleran.

'Hi!' said the little voice.

'Is Odd Bunsen there?'

'Hi!'

'Who is this? Where's your father? Go and get your father!'

'Hi!'

Qwilleran snorted and was about to slam the receiver down when his partner came on the line.

'That was our youngest,' Bunsen said. 'He's not much for conversation. What's on your mind this morning?'

Qwilleran broke the news and listened to an assortment of croaking noises as the photographer reacted wordlessly.

The newsman said with a sarcastic edge to his voice: 'I just wanted you to know that you may get your wish. You hoped the magazine would fold! And these two incidents in succession may be enough to kill it.'

'Don't blame me,' said Bunsen. 'I just take the pictures. I don't even get a credit line.'

'Two issues of *Gracious Abodes* and two mishaps! It can't be accidental. I'm beginning to smell a rat.'

'You don't mean the competition!'

'Who else?'

'The *Rampage* hasn't got the guts to try any dirty work.'

'I know, but they've got a guy working for them who might try to pull something. You know that loudmouth in their Circulation Department? He played on their softball team, you told me.'

'You mean Mike Bulmer?' Bunsen said. 'He's a creep!'

'The first time I noticed him at the Press Club, I recognized the face, but it took me a long time to place it I finally remembered him. He was mixed up in a circulation war in Chicago a few years back – a bloody affair. And now he's working at the *Rampage*. Ill bet he suggested the raid on the Allison house to the police, and I'll bet the Vice Squad was only too happy to act. You know how it is; every time the *Fluxion* editorial writers run out of ideas, they start sniping at the Vice Squad.' Qwilleran tamped his moustache, and added, 'I hate to say this, but I've got a nasty feeling that Cokey may be involved.'

'Who?'

'This girl I've been dating. Works for Mrs Middy. It was Cokey who suggested publishing Mrs Allison's house, and now I've found out that she knows Bulmer. She said hello to him at the Press Club the other night.'

'No law against that,' Bunsen said.

'It was the way she said it! And the look she gave him! . . . There's something else, too,' Qwilleran began with evident reluctance. 'After the party at David Lyke's last night, I brought Cokey back to my apartment—'

'Ho HO! This is beginning to sound interesting.'

'—and Koko tried to bite her.'

'What was she doing to him?'

'She wasn't doing a thing! She was on the – she was minding her own business when Koko made a pass at her head. He's never done a thing like that before. I'm beginning to think he was trying to tell me something.' There was silence at the other end of the line. 'Are you listening?'

'I'm listening. I'm lighting a cigar.'

'You get remarkably detached when you're home in Happy View Woods on Sunday. I should think you'd be more concerned about this mess.'

'What mess?' Bunsen said. 'I think the Allison thing is a practical joke. It's sort of funny.'

'The half-million-dollar theft wasn't funny!'

'Well,' Bunsen drawled, 'Bulmer wouldn't go *that* far!'

'He might! Don't forget, there's a million dollars' worth of advertising involved. He might see a chance to make himself a nice bonus.'

'And victimize an innocent man just to knife the competition? . . . Naw! You've seen too many old movies.'

'Maybe Tait wasn't victimized,' Qwilleran said slowly. 'Maybe he was in on the deal.'

'Brother, you're really flying high this morning.'

'Goodbye,' said Qwilleran. 'Sorry I bothered you. Go back to your peaceful family scene.'

'Peaceful!' said Bunsen. 'Did you say peaceful? I'm painting the basement, and Tommy just fell in the paint bucket, and Linda threw a rag doll down the john, and Jimmy fell off the porch and blacked his eyes. You call that peaceful?'

When Qwilleran left the telephone, he wandered aimlessly through the apartment. He glanced at the shaggy rug in the living room and angrily scuffed up the pile to erase the imprint. In the kitchen he found Koko sitting on the big ragged dictionary. The cat sat tall, with forefeet pulled in close, tail curled around tightly, head cocked. Qwilleran was in no mood for games, but Koko stared at him, waiting for an affirmative.

'All right, we'll play a few innings,' Qwilleran said with a sigh. He slapped the book – the starting signal – and Koko dug into the edge with the claws of his left paw.

Qwilleran flipped the pages to the spot Koko indicated – page 1102. '*Hummock* and *hungerly*,' he read. 'Those are easy. Find a couple of hard ones.'

The cat grabbed again.

'*Feed* and *feeling*. Two more points for me.'

Koko crouched in great excitement and sank his claws.

'*May queen* and *meadow mouse*,' said Qwilleran, and all at once he remembered that neither he nor Koko had eaten breakfast.

As the man chopped fresh beef for the cat and warmed it in a little canned consommé, he remembered something else: In a recent game Koko had come up with the same page twice. It had happened within the last week. Twice in one game Koko had found *sacroiliac* and *sadism*. Qwilleran felt a curious tingling sensation in his moustache.

Thirteen

On Monday morning, as Qwilleran and Bunsen drove to Lost Lake Hills to inspect the Noyton house, Qwilleran was unusually quiet. He had not slept well. All night he had dreamed and waked and dreamed again – about interiors decorated in Crunchy Peanut Butter and Rice Pudding, with accents of Lobster and Blackstrap Molasses. And in the morning his mind was plagued by unfinished, unfounded, unfavorable thoughts.

He greatly feared that Cokey was involved in the 'practical joke' on the *Fluxion*, and he didn't want it to be that way; he needed a friend like Cokey. He was haunted, moreover, by the possibility of Tait's complicity in the plot, although his evidence was no more concrete than a disturbance on his upper lip and a peculiar experience with the dictionary. He entertained doubts about Paolo's role in the affair; was he an innocent bystander, clever criminal, accomplice, or tool? And was Tait's love affair with his jade collection genuine or a well-rehearsed act? Had the man been as devoted to his wife as people seemed to think? Was there, by any chance, another woman in his life? Even the name of the Taits' cat was veiled in ambiguity. Was it Yu or Freya?

Then Qwilleran's thoughts turned to his own cat. Once before, when the crime was murder, Koko had flushed out more clues with his cold wet nose than the Homicide Bureau had unearthed by official investigation. Koko seemed to sense without the formality of cogitation. Instinct, it appeared, bypassed his brain and directed his claws to scratch and his nose to sniff in the right place at the right time. Or was it happenstance? Was it a coincidence that Koko turned the pages of the dictionary to *hungerly* and *feed* when breakfast was behind schedule?

Several times on Sunday afternoon Qwilleran had suggested playing the word game, hoping for additional revelations, but the catchwords that Koko turned up were insignificant: *oppositional* and *optimism*, *cynegetic* and *cypripedium*. Qwilleran entertained little *optimism*; and *cypripedium*, which turned out to be a type of orchid also called lady's-slipper, only reminded him of Cokey's toes wiggling in the luxuriant pile of the goat-hair rug.

Still, Qwilleran's notion about Koko and the dictionary persisted. A tremor ran through Qwilleran's moustache.

Odd Bunsen, at the wheel of the car, asked: 'Are you sick or something? You're sitting there shivering and not saying a word.'

'It's chilly,' said Qwilleran. 'I should have worn a topcoat.' He groped in his pocket for his pipe.

'I brought a raincoat,' said Bunsen. 'The way the wind's blowing from the northeast, we're going to get a storm.'

The trip to Lost Lake Hills took them through the suburbs and into farm country, where the maple trees were beginning to turn yellow. From time to time the photographer gave a friendly toot of the horn and wave of his cigar to people on the side of the road. He saluted a woman cutting grass, two boys on bicycles, an old man at a rural mailbox.

'You have a wide acquaintance in this neck of the woods,' Qwilleran observed.

'Me? I don't know them from Adam,' said Bunsen, 'but these farmers can use a little excitement. Now they'll spend the whole day figuring who they know that drives a foreign car and smokes cigars.'

They turned into a country road that showed the artful hand of a landscape designer, and Qwilleran read the directions from a slip of paper. ' "Follow the lakeshore, first fork to the left, turn in at the top of the hill." '

'When did you make the arrangements for this boon-doggle?' the photographer wanted to know.

'At Lyke's party Saturday night.'

'I hope they were sober. I don't put any stock in cocktail promises, and this is a long way to drive on a wild-goose chase.'

'Don't worry. Everything's okay. Natalie wants David to get some credit for decorating the house, and Harry Noyton is hoping our story will help him sell the place. The property's worth a quarter million.'

'I hope his wife doesn't get a penny of it,' Bunsen said. 'Any woman who'll give up her kids, the way she did, is a tramp.'

Qwilleran said: 'I got another phone call from Denmark this morning. Noyton wants his mail forwarded to Aarhus. That's a university town. I wonder what he's doing there.'

'He sounds like a decent guy. Wouldn't you know he'd get mixed up with a dame like that?'

'I don't think you should judge Natalie until you've met her,' Qwilleran said. 'She's sincere. Not overly bright, but sincere. And I have an idea people take advantage of her gullibility.'

The house at the end of the winding drive was of complex shape, its pink-brick walls standing at odd angles and its huge roof timbers shooting off in all directions.

'It's a gasser!' said Bunsen. 'How do you find the front door?'

'Lyke says the house is organic contemporary. It's integrated with the terrain, and the furnishings are integrated with the structure.'

They rang the doorbell, and while they waited they studied the mosaic murals that flanked the entrance – swirling abstract designs composed of pebbles, colored glass, and copper nails.

'Crazy!' said Bunsen.

They waited a considerable time before ringing the bell again.

'See? What did I tell you?' the photographer said. 'No one home.'

'It's a big house,' said Qwilleran. 'Natalie probably needs roller skates to get from her weaving studio to the front door.'

A moment later there was a click in the lock, and the door swung inward a few inches, opened with caution. A woman in a maid's uniform stood there, guarding the entrance inhospitably.

'We're from the *Daily Fluxion*,' Qwilleran said.

'Yes?' said the maid, standing her ground.

'Is Mrs Noyton home?'

'She can't see anybody today.' The door began to close.

'But we have an appointment.'

'She can't see anybody today.'

Qwilleran frowned. 'We've come a long way. She told us we could see the house. Would she mind if we took a quick look around? We expect to photograph it for the paper.'

'She doesn't want anybody to take pictures of the house,' the maid said. 'She changed her mind.'

The newsmen turned to look at each other, and the door snapped shut in their faces.

As they drove back to town, Qwilleran brooded about the rude rejection. 'It doesn't sound like Natalie. What do you suppose is wrong? She was very friendly and agreeable Saturday night.'

'People are different when they're drinking.'

'Natalie was as sober as I was. Maybe she's ill, and the maid took it on herself to brush us off.'

'If you want my opinion,' said Bunsen, 'I think your Natalie is off her rocker.'

'Stop at the first phone booth,' said Qwilleran. 'I want to make a call.'

From a booth at a country crossroad the newsman dialed the studio of Lyke and Starkweather and talked to David 'What's going on?' he demanded. 'We drove all the way to Lost Lake Hills, and Natalie refused to see us. The maid wouldn't even let us in to look at the layout.'

'Natalie's a kook,' David said. 'I apologize for her. I'll take you out there myself one of these days.'

'Meanwhile, we're in a jam – with a Wednesday deadline and no really strong story for the cover.'

'If it will help you, you can photograph my apartment,' said David. 'You don't have to give me a credit line. Just write about how people live at the Villa Verandah.'

'All night. How about this afternoon? How about two o'clock?'

'Just give me time to buy some flowers and remove some art objects,' the decorator said. 'There are a few things I wouldn't want people to know I have. Just between you and me, I shouldn't even have them.'

The newsmen had a leisurely lunch. When they eventually headed for the Villa Verandah, Qwilleran said, 'Let's stop at the pet shop on State Street. I want to buy something.'

They were battling the afternoon traffic in the downtown area. At every red light Bunsen saluted certain attractive pedestrians with the motorist's wolf whistle, touching his foot tenderly to the accelerator as they passed in front of his car. For every traffic officer he had a loud quip. They all knew the *Fluxion* photographer, and one of them halted traffic at a major intersection while the car with a press card in the windshield made an illegal left turn into State Street.

'What do you want at the pet shop?' Bunsen asked.

'A harness and a leash for Koko, so I can tie him up on the balcony.'

'Just buy a harness,' said the photographer. 'I've got twelve feet of nylon cord you can have for a leash.'

'What are you doing with twelve feet of nylon cord?'

'Last fall,' Bunsen said, 'when I was covering football games, I lowered my film from the press box on a rope, and a boy rushed it to the Lab. Those were the good old days! Now it's nothing but crazy decorators, ornery women, and nervous cats. I work like a dog, and I don't even get a credit line.'

The newsmen spent three hours at David Lyke's apartment, photographing the silvery living room, the dining room with the Chinese rug, and the master bedroom. The bed was a low platform, a few inches high, completely covered with a tiger fur throw, and the adjoining dressing room was curtained off with strings of amber beads.

Bunsen said, 'Those beads would last about five minutes at my house – with six kids playing Tarzan!'

In the living room the decorator had removed several Oriental objects, and now he was filling the gaps with bowls of flowers and large vases of glossy green leaves. He arranged them with a contemptuous flourish.

'Sorry about Natalie,' he said, jabbing the stem of a chrysanthemum into a porcelain vase. 'Now you know the kind of situation a decorator has to deal with all the time. One of my clients gave his wife the choice of being analyzed or having the house done over. She picked the decorating job, of course, and took out her neuroses on me ... There!' He surveyed the bouquet he had arranged, and disarranged it a little. He straightened some lampshades. He pressed a hidden switch and started the fountain bubbling and splashing in its bowl of pebbles. Then he stood back and squinted at the scene with a critical eye. 'Do you know what this room needs?' he said. 'It needs a Siamese cat on the sofa.'

'Are you serious?' Qwilleran asked. 'Want me to get Koko?'

Bunsen protested. 'Oh, no! No nervous cats! Not in a wide-angle time exposure.'

'Koko isn't nervous,' Qwilleran told him. 'He's a lot calmer than you are.'

'And better looking,' said David.

'And smarter,' said Qwilleran.

Bunsen threw up his hands and looked grim, and within a few minutes Koko arrived to have his picture taken, his fur still striated from a fresh brushing.

Qwilleran placed the cat on the seat of the sofa, shifted him around at the direction of the photographer, folded one of the velvety brown forepaws under in an attitude of lordly ease, and arranged the silky brown tail in a photogenic curve. Throughout the proceeding Koko purred loudly.

'Will he stay like that without moving?' Bunsen asked.

'Sure. He'll stay if I say so.'

Qwilleran gave Koko's fur a final smoothing and stepped back, saying, 'Stay! Stay there!'

And Koko calmly stood up, jumped to the floor, and walked out of the room with vertical tail expressing his indifference.

'He's calm, all right,' said Bunsen. 'He's the calmest cat I ever met.'

While the photographer finished taking pictures, Koko played with the dangling beads in David's dressing room and sniffed the tiger bedthrow with fraternal interest. Meanwhile David was preparing something for him to eat.

'Just some leftover chicken curry,' the decorator

explained to Qwilleran. 'Yushi came over last night and whipped up an eight-boy *rijstafel*.'

'Is he the one who cooks for your parties? He's a great chef!'

'He's an artist,' David said softly.

David poured ginger ale for Qwilleran and Scotch for Bunsen.

The photographer said: 'Does anyone want to eat at the Press Club tonight? My wife's giving a party for a gaggle of girls, and I've been kicked out of the house until midnight.'

'I'd like to join you, but I've got a date,' said David. 'I'll take a raincheck, though. I'd like to see the inside of that club. I hear it's got all the amenities of a medieval bastille.'

The two newsmen went to the Press Club bar, and Bunsen switched to double martinis while Qwilleran switched to tomato juice.

'Not such a bad day after all,' said Qwilleran, 'although it started out bad.'

'It isn't over yet,' the photographer reminded him.

'That David Lyke is quite a character, isn't he?'

'I don't know what to think about that *bedroom* of his!' said Bunsen, rolling his eyes.

Qwilleran frowned. 'You know, he's an agreeable joe, but there's one thing that bugs me: he makes nasty cracks about his friends. You'd think they'd get wise, but no. Everyone thinks he's the greatest.'

'When you've got looks and money, you can get away with murder.'

During the next round of drinks Qwilleran said, 'Do

you remember hearing about a scandal in the Tait family fifteen or twenty years ago?'

'Fifteen years ago I was still playing marbles.'

Qwilleran huffed into his moustache. 'You must have been the only marble-player with five o'clock shadow.' Then he signaled the bartender. 'Bruno, do you recall a scandal involving the G. Verning Tait family in Muggy Swamp?'

The bartender shook his head with authority 'No, I don't remember anything like that. If there'd been anything like that, I'd know about it. I have a memory like a giraffe.'

Eventually the newsmen went to a table and ordered T-bone steaks.

'Don't eat the tail,' Qwilleran said. 'I'll take it home to Koko.'

'Give him your own tail,' said the photographer. 'I'm not sharing my steak with any overfed cat. He lives better than I do.'

'The leash is going to work fine. I tied him up on the balcony before I left But I have to buckle the harness good and tight or he'll wiggle free. One fast flip and a tricky stretch – and he's out! That cat's a Houdini.' There were other things Qwilleran wanted to confide about Koko's capabilities, but he knew better than to tell Bunsen.

After the steaks came apple pie à la mode, following which Qwilleran started on coffee and Bunsen started on brandy.

Qwilleran said, as he lighted his pipe, 'I worry about Natalie – and why she wouldn't let us in today. That whole Noyton affair is mystifying. See what you can make out of these assorted facts: Natalie gets a divorce for reasons that are weak, to say the least, although we have only her husband's side of the story. I find an earring in the apartment that Harry Noyton is supposed to use for business entertaining. I also find out that he knows Mrs Tait. Then she dies, and he leaves the country hurriedly. At the same time, Tait's jades are stolen, after which he also prepares to leave town . . . What do you think?'

'I think the Yankees'll win the pennant.'

'You're crocked!' Qwilleran said. 'Let's go to my place for black coffee. Then maybe you'll be sober enough to drive home at midnight.'

Bunsen showed no inclination to move.

'I should bring the cat in off the balcony, in case it rains,' Qwilleran said. 'Come on! We'll take your car, and I'll do the driving!'

'I can drive,' said Bunsen. 'Perfectly sober.'

'Then take that salt shaker out of your breast pocket, and let's go.'

Qwilleran drove, and Bunsen sang. When they reached the Villa Verandah, the photographer discovered that the elevator improved the resonance of his voice.

' "Oh, how I hate to get up in the morrr-nin'—" '

'Shut up! You'll scare the cat.'

'He doesn't scare easy. He's a cool cat,' said Bunsen. 'A real cool cat.'

Qwilleran unlocked the door of 15-F and touched a switch, flooding the living room with light.

'Where's that cool cat? I wanna see that cool cat.'

'I'll let him in,' Qwilleran said. 'Why don't you sit down before you fall down? Try that green wing chair. It's the most comfortable thing you ever saw.'

The photographer flopped into the green chair, and

Qwilleran opened the balcony door. He stepped out into the night. In less than a second he was back.

'He's gone! Koko's gone!'

Fourteen

A twelve-foot nylon cord was tied to the handle of the balcony door. At the end of it was a blue leather harness buckled in the last notch, with the belt and the collar making a figure eight on the concrete floor.

'Somebody stole that cool cat,' said the photographer from his position of authority in the green wing chair.

'Don't kid around,' Qwilleran snapped at him. 'This worries me. I'm going to call the manager.'

'Wait a minute,' said Bunsen, hauling himself out of the chair. 'Let's have a good look outside.'

The two men went to the balcony. They were met by a burst of high wind, and Bunsen had to steady himself.

Qwilleran peered at the adjoining balconies. 'It's only about five feet between railings. Koko could jump across, I guess.'

Bunsen had other ideas. He looked down at the land-scaped court, fifteen stories below.

Qwilleran shuddered. 'Cats don't fall from railed balconies,' he said, without conviction.

'Maybe the wind blew him over.'

'Don't be silly.'

They gazed blankly around the curve of the building. The wind, whistling through the balcony railings, produced vibrating chords like organ music in a weird key.

Bunsen said, 'Anybody around here hate cats?'

'I don't think so. I don't know. That is, I haven't—' Qwilleran was staring across the court, squinting through the darkness. The façade of the south wing was a checkerboard of light and shadow, with many of the apartments in darkness and others with a dull glow filtering through drawn draperies. But one apartment was partially exposed to view.

Qwilleran pointed. 'Do you see what I see? Look at that window over there – the one where the curtains are open.'

'That's David Lyke's place!'

'I know it is. And his TV is turned on. And look who's sitting on top of it, keeping warm.'

The doors of a Chinese lacquer cabinet were open, and the TV screen could be seen, shimmering with abstract images. On top, in a neat bundle, sat Koko, his light breast distinct against the dark lacquer and his brown mask and ears silhouetted against the silvery wall.

'I'm going to phone Dave and see what this is all about,' said Qwilleran.

He dialed the switchboard, asked for Lyke's apartment, and waited a long time before he was convinced no one was home.

'No answer,' he told Bunsen.

'What now?'

'I don't know. Do you suppose Koko got lonesome and decided to go visiting?'

'He wanted some more of that curried chicken.'

'He must have hopped from balcony to balcony – all the way around. Crazy cat! Lyke must have let him in and then gone out himself. He said he had a date.'

'What are you going to do?' Bunsen said.

'Leave him there till morning, that's all.'

'I can get him back.'

'What? How could you get him back? He couldn't hear you with the door closed over there, and even if he could, how would he open the sliding door?'

'Want to bet I can't get him back?' The photographer leaped up on the side railing of the balcony and teetered there, clutching the corner post.

'No!' yelled Qwilleran. 'Get down from there!' He was afraid to make a sudden move toward the man balancing on the narrow toprail. He approached Bunsen slowly, holding his breath.

'No sweat!' the photographer called out, as he leaped across the five-foot gap and grabbed the post of the next balcony. 'Anything a cat can do, Odd Bunsen can do better!'

'Come back! You're out of your mind! . . . No, stay there! Don't try it again!'

'Odd Bunsen to the rescue!' yelled the photographer, as he ran the length of the balcony and negotiated the leap to the next one. But first he plucked a yellow mum from the neighbor's window box and clenched it in his teeth.

Qwilleran sat down and covered his face with his hands.

'Ya hoo!' Bunsen crowed. 'Ya hoo!'

His war cries grew fainter, drowned by the whistling wind as he progressed from railing to railing around the inside curve of the Villa Verandah. Here and there a resident opened a door and looked out, without seeing the acrobatic feat being performed in the darkness.

'Ya hoo!' came a distant cry.

Qwilleran thought of the three double martinis and the two – no, three – brandies that Bunsen had consumed. He thought of the photographer's wife and six children, and his blood chilled.

There was a triumphant shout across the court, and Bunsen was waving from Lyke's balcony. He tried the sliding door; it opened. He signaled his success and then stepped into the silvery-gray living room. At his entrance Koko jumped down from his perch and scampered away.

I hope, Qwilleran told himself, that nincompoop has sense enough to bring Koko back by land and not by air.

From where the newsman stood, he could no longer see Bunsen or the cat, so he went indoors and waited for the errant pair to return. While waiting, he made two cups of instant coffee and put some cheese and crackers on a plate.

The wait was much too long, he soon decided. He went to the corridor and listened and looked down its carpeted curve. There was no sign of life – only mechanical noises from the elevator shaft and the frantic sounds of a distant TV. He returned to the balcony and scanned the south wing. There was no activity to be seen in Lyke's apartment, except for the busy images on the TV screen.

Qwilleran gulped a cup of coffee and paced the floor. Finally he went to the telephone and asked the operator to try Lyke's apartment again. The line was busy.

'What's that drunken fool doing?'

'Pardon?' said the operator.

Returning once more to the balcony, Qwilleran stared across the court in exasperation. When his telephone rang, he jumped and sprinted for it.

'Qwill,' said Bunsen's voice, several tones lower than it had been all evening. 'We've got trouble over here.'

'Koko? What's happened?'

'The cat's okay, but your decorator friend has *had* it.'

'What do you mean?'

'Looks as if Lyke's dead.'

'No! . . . No!'

'He's cold, and he's white, and there's an ugly spot on the rug. I've called the police, and I've called the paper. Would you go down to the car and get my camera?'

'I gave you the car keys.'

'I put them in my raincoat pocket, and I dropped my raincoat in your front hall. I think I'd better stay here with the body.'

'You sound sober all of a sudden,' Qwilleran said.

'I sobered up in a hurry when I saw this.'

By the time Qwilleran arrived at Lyke's apartment with Bunsen's camera, the officers from the police cruiser were there. Qwilleran scanned the living room. It was just as they had photographed it in the afternoon, except that the TV in the Chinese cabinet was yakking senselessly and there was a yellow mum on the carpet, where Bunsen had dropped it.

'As soon as I came through the door,' Bunsen said to Qwilleran, 'Koko led me into the bedroom.'

The body was on the bedroom floor, wrapped in a gray silk dressing gown. One finger wore a large star sapphire that Qwilleran had not seen before. The face was no longer handsome. It had lost the wit and animation that made it attractive. All that was left was a supercilious mask.

Qwilleran glanced about the room. The tiger skin had been removed from the bed, neatly folded, and laid on a bench. Everything else was in perfect order. The bed showed no indication of having been occupied.

Bunsen was hopping around the room looking for camera angles. 'I just want to get one picture,' he told the officers. 'I won't disturb anything.' To Qwilleran he said, 'It's hard to get an interesting shot. The Picture Desk won't run gory stuff any more. They get complaints from the PTA, little old ladies, the American Legion, the DAR, vegetarians—'

'What did you do with Koko?' Qwilleran said.

'He's around here somewhere. Probably destroying the evidence.'

Qwilleran found Koko in the dining room, sitting under the table as if nothing had happened. He had assumed his noncommittal pose, gathered in a comfortable bundle on the gold-and-blue Chinese rug looking neither curious nor concerned nor guilty nor grieved.

When the detectives from the Homicide Bureau arrived, Qwilleran recognized a pair he had met before. He liked the heavy-set one called Hames, a smart detective with an off-duty personality, but he didn't care for Wojcik, whose nasal voice was well suited to sarcasm.

Wojcik gave one look at Qwilleran and said, 'How'd the press get here so fast?'

The patrolman said: 'The photographer was here when we arrived. He let us into the apartment. He's the one who found the body and reported it.'

Wojcik turned to Bunsen. 'How did you happen to be here?'

'I came in through the window.'

'I see. This is the fifteenth floor. And you came in through the window.'

'Sure, there are balconies out there.'

Hames was ogling the sumptuous living room. 'Look at this wallpaper,' he said. 'If my wife ever saw this—'

Wojcik went into the bedroom and after that onto the balcony. He looked at the ground fifteen stories below, and he gauged the distance between balconies. Then he cornered Bunsen. 'Okay, how did you get in?'

'I told you—'

'I suppose you know you smell like a distillery.'

Qwilleran said: 'Bunsen's telling the truth. He jumped from balcony to balcony, all the way from my place on the other side.'

'This may be a silly question,' said the detective, 'but do you mind if I inquire *why*?'

'Well, it's like this,' said the photographer. 'We were across the court—'

'He came to get my cat,' Qwilleran interrupted. 'My cat was over here.'

Hames said: 'That must be the famous Siamese that's bucking for my job on the force. I'd like to meet him.'

'He's in the dining room under the table.'

'My wife's crazy about Siamese. Some day I've got to break down and buy her one.'

Qwilleran followed the amiable detective into the dining room and said quietly: 'There's something I ought to tell you, Hames. We were here this afternoon to photograph the apartment for *Gracious Abodes*, and David Lyke removed some valuable art objects before we took the pictures. I don't know what he did with them, but they were valuable, and I don't see them anywhere.'

There was no reaction from the detective, who was now down on his knees under the table.

'As I recall,' Qwilleran went on, 'there was a Japanese screen in five panels, all done in gold. And a long vertical scroll with pictures of ducks and geese. And a wood sculpture of a deer, almost life-size, and very old, judging from its condition. And a big china bowl. And a gold Buddha about three feet high.'

From under the table Hames said, 'This guy's fur feels like mink. Are these cats very expensive?'

It was Wojcik who roused the neighbors. The apartment across the hall was occupied by an elderly woman who was hard of hearing; she said she had retired early, had heard nothing, had seen no one. The adjoining apartment to the east was vacant; the one on the other side produced a fragment of information.

'We're not acquainted with Mr Lyke,' said a man's voice, 'but we see him on the elevator occasionally – him and his friends.'

'And we hear his wild parties,' a woman's shrill voice added.

'We didn't hear anything tonight,' said the man, 'except his television. That struck us as being unusual. Ordinarily he plays stereo . . . Music, you know.'

'He doesn't play it. He *blasts* it,' the woman said. 'Last week we complained to the manager.'

'When we heard his TV,' the man went on, 'we decided there must be a good show, so we turned our set on. After that I didn't hear anything more from his apartment.'

'No voices? No altercation of any kind?' the detective asked.

'To tell the truth, I fell asleep,' said the man. 'It wasn't a very good show after all.'

Wojcik nodded to the woman. 'And you?'

'With the TV going and my husband snoring, who could hear a bomb go off?'

When Wojcik returned, he said to Qwilleran, 'How well did you know the decedent?'

'I met him for the first time a couple of weeks ago – on assignment for the *Fluxion*. Don't know much about him except that he gave big parties, and he seemed to be well liked – by both men and women.'

The detective said, 'He was a decorator, hmmm?'

'Yes,' said Qwilleran crisply, 'and a damn good one.'

'When was the last time you saw him?'

'This afternoon, when we photographed the apartment. Bunsen and I invited him to dinner at the Press Club, but he said he had a date.'

'Any idea who it was?'

'No, he just said he had a date.'

'Did he live alone?'

'Yes. That is, I presume he lived alone.'

'What do you mean by that?'

'There's only one name on his mailbox.'

'Any help working here?'

'At parties he had two people working in the kitchen

and serving. The building management supplies cleaning service.'

'Know any of his relatives or close friends?'

'Just his partner at the decorating studio. Better try Starkweather.'

By that time the coroner's man and the police photographer had arrived, and Wojcik said to the newsmen, 'Why don't you two pack up and clear out?'

'I'd like to get the doctor's statement,' said Qwilleran, so I can file a complete story.'

Wojcik gave him a close look. 'Aren't you the *Fluxion* man who was involved in the Tait burglary?'

'I wasn't *involved* in it,' said Qwilleran. 'I just happened to write a story about Mr and Mrs Tait's house – a few days before their houseboy made off with their jades if one can believe the statement made by the Police Department.'

From the dining room Hames called out: 'Have you noticed? This cat's eyes turn red in the dark.'

After a while Wojcik said to the newsmen: 'Death caused by a bullet wound in the chest. Fired at close range. About ten o'clock. Weapon missing. Robbery apparently no motive ... That's all. Now, do us a favor and go home. You probably know more than we do. I think your paper goes around setting these things up.'

To retrieve Koko, Qwilleran had to crawl under the dining table and forcibly remove the cat, who seemed to have taken root.

Hames walked the newsmen to the door. 'Your Sunday supplement looks good,' he said. 'All those elegant homes! My wife says I should scare up a little graft so we can live like that.'

'I think the magazine's a good idea,' Qwilleran said, 'but it's been rough going. First the Tait setback, and then—'

'Come on, clear out!' snapped Wojcik. 'We've got work to do.'

'Say!' said Hames. 'My wife sure liked those four-poster beds you photographed on Merchant Street. Do you know where I could buy something like that?'

Qwilleran looked distressed. 'That was another unfortunate coincidence! I wish I knew why the Vice Squad picked that particular weekend to raid the place.'

'Well,' said Hames, 'I don't know how it happened but I know the Police Widows' Fund just received a sizable donation from the Penniman Foundation ... Now, what did you say was missing? Five-panel gold-leaf screen? Three-foot gold Buddha? Kakemono with ducks and geese? Antique wood carving of deer? Porcelain bowl? Are you sure it was a five-panel screen? Japanese screens usually have an even number of panels.'

Slowly and thoughtfully the newsmen returned to 15-F Bunsen carrying his camera, Qwilleran carrying the cat on his shoulder.

'The Penniman Foundation!' he repeated.

'You know who the Pennimans are, don't you?' said Bunsen.

'Yes, I know who they are. They live in Muggy Swamp. And they own the *Morning Rampage*.'

Fifteen

Qwilleran phoned in the details of David Lyke's murder to a *Fluxion* rewrite man, and Bunsen called his wife. 'Is the party over, honey? ... Tell the girls I'll be right there to kiss 'em all good night ... Nothing. Not a thing. Just sat around and talked all evening ... Honey, you know I wouldn't do anything like that!'

The photographer left the Villa Verandah to return to Happy View Woods, and Qwilleran began to worry about Koko's prolonged tranquillity. Was the cat demonstrating feline sangfroid or had he gone into shock? Upon returning to the apartment, he should have prowled the premises, inspected the kitchen for accidental leftovers, curled up on his blue cushion on top of the refrigerator. Instead, he huddled on the bare wood floor beneath the desk, with eyes wide, looking at nothing. His attitude suggested that he was cold. Qwilleran covered him with his old corduroy sports coat, arranging it like a tent over the cat, and received no acknowledgment – not even the tremor of an ear.

Qwilleran himself was exhausted after the scare of Koko's disappearance, Bunsen's hair-raising performance, and the discovery of Lyke's body. But when he went to bed, he could not sleep. The questions followed him from side to side as he tossed.

Question: Who would want to eliminate the easygoing openhanded David Lyke? He was equally gracious to men and women, young and old, clients and competitors, the help in the kitchen and the guests in the living room. True, he spoke out of the other side of his mouth when their backs were turned, but still he charmed them all.

Question: Could the motive be jealousy? Lyke had everything – looks, talent, personality, success, friends. He had had a date that night. Perhaps the woman had been followed by a jealous friend or a jealous husband. Or – there was another possibility – perhaps the date had not been with a woman.

Question: Why was Lyke wearing an important ring and no other apparel, except a dressing gown? And why had the bedcover been removed and neatly folded in the middle of the evening? Qwilleran frowned and blew into his moustache.

Question: Why had the neighbors heard no commotion and no shot? Perhaps the audio on Lyke's television had been turned up to full volume purposely, before the shot was fired. And the neighbors had attributed everything they heard to a television program. Wonderful invention, television.

Question: Where had Koko been during the whole episode? What had he seen? What had he done? Why did he now appear to be stunned?

Qwilleran tossed from his left side to his right for the hundredth time. It was dawn before he finally fell asleep, and then he dreamed of telephone bells. Readers were phoning him with unanswerable questions. *Brrrring!* 'What colors do you mix to get sky-blue-pink?' *Brrrring!* 'Where can I buy a Danish chair made in Japan?' And the managing editor, too. *Brrrring!* 'Qwill, this is Harold. We're going to carpet the Press Room. What do you think about Bourbon Brown?'

When the ringing telephone finally dragged Qwilleran from his confused sleep, he said a mindless 'Hello' into the mouthpiece.

The voice at the other end said, simply, 'Starkweather,' and then waited.

'Yes?' said Qwilleran, groping for words. 'How are you?'

'Isn't it – isn't it terrible?' said Lyke's partner. 'I haven't slept all night.'

Yesterday's events came tumbling back into Qwilleran's mind. 'It was a shock,' he agreed. 'I don't understand it.'

'Is there anything – I mean – could you . . .' There was a prolonged pause.

'Can I do anything for you, Mr Starkweather?'

'Well, I thought – if you could find out what – what they're going to say in the paper . . .'

'I reported the item myself,' said Qwilleran. 'I phoned it in last night – just the bare facts based on the coroner's report and the detective's statement. It'll be in the first edition this morning. If there's to be any follow-up story, the editor will probably call me in ... Why are you concerned?'

'Well, I wouldn't want – I wouldn't like anything to reflect – you know what I mean.'

'Reflect on the studio, you mean?'

'Some of our customers, you know – they're very—'

'You're afraid the papers will make it too sensational? Is that what you're trying to say? I don't know about the *Morning Rampage*, Mr Starkweather. But you don't need to worry about the *Fluxion*. Besides, I don't know what anyone could say that would be damaging to the studio.'

'Well, you know – David and his parties – his friends. He had a lot of – you know how these young bachelors are.'

Qwilleran was now fully awake. 'Do you have any idea of a possible motive?'

'I can't imagine.'

'Jealousy, maybe?'

'I don't know.'

'Do you think it had anything to do with David's Oriental art collection?'

'I just don't know,' said Starkweather in his helpless tone of voice.

Qwilleran persisted. 'Do you know his collection well enough to determine if anything is missing?'

'That's what the police wanted to know last night.'

'Were you able to help them?'

'I went over there right away – over to David's apartment'

'What did you find?'

'Some of his best things were locked up in a closet. I don't know why.'

'I can tell you why,' said Qwilleran. 'Dave removed them before we took pictures yesterday.'

'Oh,' said Starkweather.

'Did you know we were going to take pictures of Dave's apartment?'

'Yes, he mentioned it. It slipped my mind.'

'Did he tell you he was going to remove some of the art?'

'I don't think so.'

'Dave told me there were certain things he didn't want the public to know he had. Were they extremely valuable?'

Starkweather hesitated. 'Some of the things were – well—'

'They weren't hot, were they?'

'What?'

'Were they stolen goods?'

'Oh, no, no! He paid plenty.'

'I'm sure he did,' said Qwilleran, 'but I'm talking about the source of the stuff. He said, 'There are some things I shouldn't even have.' What did he mean by that?'

'Well, they were – I guess you'd say – museum pieces.'

'A lot of well-heeled collectors own items of museum caliber, don't they?'

'But some of David's things were – well – I guess they should never have left the country. Japan, that is.'

'I see,' said Qwilleran. He thought a moment. 'You mean they were ostensibly protected by the government?'

'Something like that.'

'National treasures?'

'I guess that's what they call them.'

'Hmm . . . Did you tell the police that, Mr Starkweather?'

'No.'

'Why not?'

'They didn't ask anything like that.'

Qwilleran enjoyed a moment's glee. He could picture the brusque Wojcik interrogating the laconic Starkweather. Then he thought of one more question. 'Can you think of anyone who has shown particular interest in these "protected" items?'

'No, but I wonder . . .'

'What? What do you wonder, Mr Starkweather?'

Lyke's partner coughed. 'Is the studio liable – I mean, if there's anything illegal – could they . . .'

'I doubt it. Why don't you get some sleep, Mr Starkweather? Why don't you take a pill and try to get some sleep?'

'Oh, no! I must go to the studio. I don't know what will happen today. This is a terrible thing, you know.'

When Starkweather hung up, Qwilleran felt as if he'd had all his teeth pulled. He went into the kitchen to make some coffee, and found Koko stretched out on the refrigerator cushion. The cat was lying on his side with his head thrown back and his eyes closed. Qwilleran spoke to him, and not a whisker moved. He stroked the cat, and Koko heaved a great sigh in his sleep. His hind foot trembled.

'Dreaming?' said Qwilleran. 'What do you dream about? Chicken curry? People with guns that make a loud noise? I'd sure like to know what you witnessed last night.'

Koko's whiskers twitched, and he threw one paw across his eyes.

The next time the telephone rang, it interrupted Qwilleran's shaving, and he answered in a mild huff. He considered shaving a spiritual rite – part ancestor worship, part reaffirmation of gender, part declaration of respectability – and it required the utmost artistry.

'This is Cokey,' said a breathless voice. 'I just heard the radio announcement about David Lyke. I can't believe it.'

'He was murdered, all right.'

'Do you have any idea who did it?'

'How would I know?'

'Are you mad at me?' Cokey said. 'You're mad at me because I suggested publishing the Allison house.'

'I'm not mad,' said Qwilleran, letting his voice soften a little. It occurred to him that he might want to question Cokey about a few things. 'I'm shaving. I've got lather all over my face.'

'Sorry I called so early.'

'I'll give you a ring soon, and we'll have dinner.'

'How's Koko?'

'He's fine.'

After saying goodbye, Qwilleran had an idea. He wiped the lather from his face, waked Koko, and placed him on the dictionary. Koko arched his back in a tense, vibrating stretch. He turned his whiskers up, rolled his eyes down, and yawned widely, showing thirty teeth, a corrugated palate, five inches of tongue, and half his gullet.

'Okay, let's play the game,' Qwilleran said, after a prolonged yawn of his own.

Koko turned around three times, then rolled over and assumed a languid pose on the open pages of the dictionary.

'Game! Game! Play the game!' Qwilleran dug his fingernails into the pages to demonstrate.

Coyly Koko rolled over on his back and squirmed in a happy way.

'You loafer! What's the matter with you?'

The cat just narrowed his eyes and looked dreamy.

It was not until Qwilleran waved a sardine under Koko's nose that he agreed to cooperate. The game was uneventful, however: *maxillary* and *maypop*, *travel* and *trawlnet*, *scallion* and *Scandinavian*. Qwilleran had hoped for more pertinent catchwords. He had to admit, though, that a couple of them made sense. The sardine can said PRODUCT OF NORWAY.

Qwilleran hurried to the office and tackled the next issue of *Gracious Abodes*, but his mind was not on the magazine. He waited until he thought Starkweather would be at the studio, and then he telephoned Mrs Starkweather at home.

She burst into tears. 'Isn't it awful?' she cried. 'My David! My dear David! Why would anyone want to do it?'

'It's hard to understand,' said Qwilleran.

'He was so young. Only thirty-two, you know. And so full of life and talent. I don't know what Stark will do without him.'

'Did David have enemies, Mrs Starkweather?'

'I don't know. I just can't think. I'm so upset.'

'Perhaps someone was jealous of David's success. Would anyone gain by his death?'

The tears tapered off into noisy sniffing. 'Nobody would gain very much. David lived high, and he gave everything away. He didn't save a penny. Stark was always warning him.'

'What will happen to David's half of the business?' Qwilleran asked in a tone as casual as he could manage.

'Oh, it will go to Stark, of course. That was the agreement. Stark put up all the money for the business. David contributed his talent. He had so much of that,' she added with a whimper.

'Didn't Dave have any family?'

'Nobody. Not a living soul. I think that's why he gave so many parties. He wanted people around him, and he thought he had to buy their affection.' Mrs Starkweather heaved a breathy sigh. 'But it wasn't true. People just naturally adored David.'

Qwilleran bit his lip. He wanted to say: Yes, but wasn't he a cad? Didn't he say cutting things about the people who flocked around him? Don't you realize, Mrs Starkweather, that David called you a middle-aged sot?

Instead he said, 'I wonder what will happen to his Oriental art collection.'

'I don't know. I really don't know.' Her tone hardened. 'I can think of three or four spongers who'd like to get their hands on it, though!'

'You don't know if the art is mentioned in David's will?'

'No, I don't.' She thought for a moment. 'I wouldn't be surprised if he left it to that young Japanese who cooks for him. It's just an idea.'

'What makes you think that?'

'They were very close. David was the one who set Yushi up in the catering business. And Yushi was devoted to David. We were all devoted to David.' The tears started again. 'I'm glad you can't see me, Mr Qwilleran. I look awful. I've been crying for hours! David made me feel young, and suddenly I feel so old.'

Qwilleran's next call was to the studio called PLUG. He recognized the suave voice that answered.

'Bob, this is Qwilleran at the *Fluxion*,' he said.

'Yes, indeed!' said Orax. 'How the wires are buzzing this morning! The telephone company may declare an extra dividend.'

'What have you heard about Dave's murder?'

'Nothing worth repeating, alas.'

'I really called,' said Qwilleran, 'to ask about Yushi. Do you know if he's available for catering jobs? I'm giving a party for a guy who's getting married.'

Orax said: 'I'm sure Yushi will have plenty of time now that David has departed. He's listed in the phone book under Cuisine Internationale ... Are we going to see you at the Posthumous Pour?'

'What's that?'

'Oh, didn't you know?' said Orax. 'When David wrote his will, he provided for one final cocktail bash for all his friends – at the Toledo! No weeping! Just laughter, dancing and booze until the money runs out. At the Toledo it runs out very fast.'

'David was a real character,' Qwilleran said. 'I'd like to write a profile of him for the paper. Who were his best friends? Who could fill me in?'

Orax hummed on the line for a few seconds. 'The Starkweathers, of course, and the Noytons, and *dear* Yushi, and quite a few unabashed freeloaders like myself.'

'Any enemies?'

'Perhaps Jacques Boulanger, but these days it's hard to tell an enemy from a friend.'

'How about the girls in his life?'

'Ah, yes, girls,' said Orax. 'There was Lois Avery, but

she married and left town. And there was a creature with long straight hair who works for Mrs Middy; I've forgotten her name.'

'I think,' said Qwilleran, 'I know the one you mean.'

Sixteen

Qwilleran took a taxi to the Sorbonne Studio. He had telephoned for an appointment, and a woman with an engaging French accent had invited him to arrive *tout de suite* if he desired a *rendez-vous* with Monsieur Boulanger at the atelier.

In the taxi he thought again about Cokey. Now he knew! Koko had sensed her deception. Koko had been trying to convey that information when he nipped Cokey's head and licked the photograph from her wallet.

Qwilleran had caught only a glimpse of the picture, but he was fairly sure whose likeness the cat had licked: that arty pose, that light hair. Now he knew! Cokey – so candid, so disarming – was capable of a convincing kind of duplicity. She had allowed Qwilleran to introduce David, and the decorator had played the game with only a meager wavering of his sultry gaze. Was he playing the gentleman on a spur-of-the-moment cue? Or was there some pre-arranged agreement?

If Cokey had deceived Qwilleran once, she had probably deceived him twice. Had she engineered the embarrassment about the Allison house? Did she have connections at the *Morning Rampage*?

'Is this the place you want?' asked the cabdriver, rousing Qwilleran from his distasteful reverie. The taxi had stopped in front of a pretentious little building, a miniature version of the pavilions that French monarchs built for their mistresses.

The interior of the Sorbonne Studio was an awesome assemblage of creamy white marble, white carpet, white furniture, and crystal chandeliers. The carpet, thick and carved, looked like meringue. Qwilleran stepped on it cautiously.

There was an upholstered hush in the place until a dark-skinned young woman of rare beauty appeared from behind a folding screen and said, '*Bon jour, m'sieu*. May I 'elp you?'

'I have an appointment with Mr Boulanger,' said Qwilleran. 'I'm from the *Daily Fluxion*.'

'*Ah, oui*. Monsieur Boulanger is on the tele*phone* with a cli*ent*, but I will announce your pre*sence*.'

With a sinuous walk she disappeared behind the folding screen, which was mirrored, and Qwilleran caught a reflection of himself looking smugly appreciative at her retreating figure.

In a moment a handsome Negro, wearing a goatee, came striding out from the inner regions. 'Hello, there,' he said with a smile and an easy manner. 'I'm Jack Baker.'

'I have an appointment with Mr Boulanger,' said Qwilleran.

'I'm your man,' said the decorator. 'Jacques Boulanger to clients, Jack Baker to my relatives and the press. Come into my office, *s'il vous plaît.*'

Qwilleran followed him into a pale-blue room that was plush of carpet, velvety of wall, and dainty of chair. He glanced uneasily at the ceiling, entirely covered with pleated blue silk, gathered in a rosette in the center.

'Man, I know what you're thinking.' Baker laughed. 'This is a real gone pad. *Mais malheureusement*, it's what the clients expect. Makes me feel like a jackass, but it's a living.' His eyes were filled with merriment that began to put Qwilleran at ease. 'How do you like the reception salon? We've just done it over.'

'I guess it's all right if you like lots of white,' said Qwilleran.

'Not white!' Baker gave an exaggerated shudder. 'It's called Vichyssoise. It has an undertone of Leek Green.'

The newsman asked: 'Is this the kind of work you do for your customers? We'd like to photograph one of your interiors for *Gracious Abodes*. I understand you do a lot of interiors in Muggy Swamp.'

The decorator hesitated. 'I don't want to seem uncooperative, *vous savez*, but my clients don't go for that kind of publicity. And, to be perfectly frank, the designing I do in Muggy Swamp is not, *qu'est-ce qu'on dit*, newsworthy. I mean it! My clients are all squares. They like tired clichés. Preferably French clichés, and those are the worst! Now, if I worked for the *nouveaux riches* in Lost Lake Hills, I could show you design with imagination and daring. Not so much taste, but more spirit.'

'Too bad,' said Qwilleran. 'I was hoping we could get an important society name like Duxbury or Penniman.'

'I wish I could oblige,' said the decorator. 'I really do. I dig the newspaper scene. It was an American newsman in Paris who introduced me to my first client – Mrs Duxbury, as a matter of fact.' He laughed joyously. 'Would you like to hear the whole mad tale? *C'est formidable!*'

'Go ahead. Mind if I light my pipe?'

Baker began his story with obvious relish. 'I was born right here in this town, on the wrong side of the wrong side of the tracks, if you know what I mean. Somehow I made college on a scholarship and came out with a Fine Arts degree, which entitled me – *ma foi!* – to work for a decorating studio, installing drapery hardware. So I saved my pennies and went to Paris, to the Sorbonne. *C'est bien ça.*' The decorator's face grew fond. 'And that's where I was discovered by Mr and Mrs Duxbury, a couple of beautiful cats.'

'Did they know you were from their own city?'

'*Mais non!* For kicks I was speaking English with a French accent, and I had grown this picturesque beard. The Duxburys bought the whole exotic bit – bless them! – and commissioned me to come here and do their thirty-room house in Muggy Swamp. I did it in tones of Oyster, Pistachio, and Apricot. After that, all the other important families wanted the Duxburys' Negro decorator from Paris. I had to continue the French accent, *vous savez.*'

'How long have you kept the secret?'

'It's no secret any longer, but it would embarrass too many people if we admitted the truth. So we all enjoy the harmless little *divertissement*. I pretend to be French, and they pretend they don't know I'm not. *C'est parfait!'* Baker grinned with pleasure as he related it.

The young lady with the ravishing face and figure walked into the office carrying a golden tray. On it were delicate teacups, slices of lemon, a golden teapot.

'This is my niece, Verna,' said the decorator.

'Hi!' she said to Qwilleran. 'Ready for your fix? Lemon or sugar?' There was no trace of a French accent. She was very American and very young, but she poured from the vermeil teapot with aristocratic grace.

Qwilleran said to Baker, 'Who did the decorating in Muggy Swamp before you arrived on the scene?'

The decorator gave a twisted smile. '*Eh bien*, it was Lyke and Starkweather.' He waited for Qwilleran's reaction, but the newsman was a veteran at hiding reactions behind his ample moustache.

'You mean you walked away with all their customers?'

'*C'est la vie*. Decorating clients are fickle. They are also sheep, especially in Muggy Swamp.'

Baker was frank, so Qwilleran decided to be blunt. 'How come you didn't get the G. Verning Tait account?'

The decorator looked at his niece, and she looked at him. Then Jack Baker smiled an ingratiating smile. 'There was some strong feeling in the Tait family,' he said, speaking carefully. '*Pourtant*, David Lyke did a good job. I would never have used that striped wallpaper in the foyer, and the lamps were out of scale, but David tried hard.' His expression changed to sorrow, real or feigned. 'And now I've lost my best competition. Without competition, where are the kicks in this game?'

'I'm thinking of writing a profile on David Lyke,' said

Qwilleran. 'As a competitor of his, could you make a statement?'

'Quotable?' asked Baker with a sly look.

'How long had you known Lyke?'

'From 'way back. When we were both on the other side of the tracks. Before his name was Lyke.'

'He changed his name?'

'It was unpronounceable and unspellable. Dave decided that Lyke would be more likable.'

'Did you two get along?'

'*Tiens!* We were buddies in high school – a couple of esthetes in a jungle of seven-foot basketball players and teen-age goons. Secretly I felt superior to Dave because I had parents, and he was an orphan. Then I came out of college and found myself working for him – measuring windows and drilling screwholes in the woodwork so David Lyke could sell $5,000 drapery jobs and get invited to society debuts in Muggy Swamp. While I'd been grinding my brain at school and washing dishes for my keep, he'd been making it on personality and bleached hair and – who knows what else. It rankled, man; it rankled!'

Qwilleran puffed on his pipe and looked sympathetic.

'*Dites donc*, I got my revenge.' Baker smiled broadly. 'I came back from Paris and walked away with his Muggy Swamp clientele. And to rub it in, I moved into the same building where he lived, but in a more expensive apartment on a higher floor.'

'You live at the Villa Verandah? So do I.'

'Sixteenth floor, south.'

'Fifteenth floor, north.'

'*Alors*, we're a couple of status-seekers,' said Baker.

Qwilleran had one more question. 'As a competitor of David's, and a former friend, and a neighbor, do you have any educated guesses as to the motive for his murder?'

The decorator shrugged. '*Qui sait*? He was a ruthless man – in his private life as well as in business.'

'I thought he was the most,' said Verna.

'*Vraiment, chérie*, he had a beautiful façade, but he'd cut your throat behind your back, as the saying goes.'

Qwilleran said, 'I've never met anyone with more personal magnetism.'

'*Eh bien!*' Baker set his jaw, and looked grim.

'Well, I'll probably see you around the mausoleum,' said the newsman, as he rose to leave.

'Come up to the sixteenth floor and refuel some evening,' the decorator said. 'My wife's a real swinger in the kitchen.'

Qwilleran went back to the office to check proofs, and he found a message to see the managing editor at once.

Percy was in less than genial mood. 'Qwill,' he said abruptly, 'I know you were not enthusiastic about taking the *Gracious Abodes* assignment, and I think I was wrong in pressing it on you.'

'What do you mean?'

'I'm not blaming you for the succession of mishaps per se, but it does seem that the magazine has been accident-prone.'

'I didn't like the idea at the beginning,' said Qwilleran, 'but I'm strong for it now. It's an interesting beat.'

'That thing last night,' said Percy, shaking his head. 'That murder! Why does everything happen on your beat? Sometimes there are psychological reasons for what we call a jinx. Perhaps we should relieve you of the assignment. Anderson is retiring October first . . .'

'Anderson!' Qwilleran said with undisguised horror. 'The church editor?'

'Perhaps you could handle church news, and *Gracious Abodes* could be turned over to the Women's Department, where it belonged in the first place.'

Qwilleran's moustache reared up. 'If you'd let me dig into these crimes, Harold, the way I suggested, I think I could unearth some clues. There are forces working against us! I happen to know, for example, that the Police Widows' Fund got a sizable donation from the owners of the *Morning Rampage* around the same time the Vice Squad raided the Allison house.'

Percy looked weary. 'They're getting one from us, too. Every September both papers make a donation.'

'All right, then. Maybe it wasn't a payoff, but I'll bet the timing wasn't accidental. And I suspect a plot in the Muggy Swamp incident, too.'

'On what do you base your suspicions?'

Qwilleran smoothed his moustache. 'I can't reveal my source at this time, but with further investigation—'

The editor slapped his hand on the desk with finality. 'Let's leave it the way I've suggested, Qwill. You put next Sunday's magazine to bed, and then let Fran Unger take over.'

'Wait! Give me one more week before you make a decision. I promise there'll be a surprising development.'

'We've had nothing but surprising developments for the last fifteen days.'

Qwilleran did not reply, and he did not move away from Percy's desk. He just stared the editor in the eye and waited for an affirmative – a trick he had learned from Koko.

'All right. One more week,' said the editor. 'And let's hope no one plants a bomb in the Press Room.'

Qwilleran went back to the Feature Department with hope and doubt battling for position. He dialed the *Fluxion*'s extension at Police Headquarters and talked to Lodge Kendall. 'Any news on the murder?'

'Not a thing,' said the police reporter. 'They're going through Lyke's address book. It's an extensive list.'

'Did they get any interesting fingerprints?'

'Not only fingerprints, but pawprints!'

'Let me know if anything breaks,' Qwilleran said. 'Just between you and me, my job may depend on it.'

At six o'clock, as Qwilleran was leaving for dinner, he ran into Odd Bunsen at the elevator.

'Hey, do you want those photographs of the Tait house?' Bunsen said. 'They've been cluttering up my locker for a week.' He went back to the Photo Lab and returned with a large envelope. 'I made blowups for you, same as I made for the police. What do you want them for?'

'Thought I'd give them to Tait.'

'That's what I figured. I did a careful job of printing.'

Qwilleran went to the Press Club, loaded a plate at the all-you-can-eat buffet, and took it to the far end of the bar, where he could eat in solitude and contemplate the day's findings: Lyke's relationship with Cokey, his unfashionable beginnings, the boyhood friendship that went sour, the national treasures that should have stayed in Japan, and the vague status of Yushi. Once during the day Qwilleran had tried to telephone Cuisine Internationale, but Yushi's answering service had said the caterer was out of town.

While the newsman was drinking his coffee, he opened the envelope. The photographs were impressive. Bunsen had enlarged them to eleven-by-fourteen and let the edges bleed. The bartender was hovering near, wiping a spot on the bar that needed no wiping, showing curiosity.

'The Tait house,' Qwilleran said. 'I'm going to give them to the owner.'

'He'll appreciate it. People like to have pictures of their homes, their kids, their pets – anything like that.' Bruno accompanied this profound observation with a sage nod.

Qwilleran said: 'Did you ever hear of a cat licking glossy photos? That's what my cat does. He also eats rubber bands.'

'That's not good,' said the bartender. 'You better do something about it.'

'You think it's bad for him?'

'It isn't normal. I think your cat is, like they say, disturbed.'

'He seems perfectly happy and healthy.'

Bruno shook his head wisely. 'That cat needs help. You should take him to a psycatatrist.'

'A psyCATatrist?' said Qwilleran. 'I didn't know there was such a thing.'

'I can tell you where to find a good one.'

'Well, thanks,' said the newsman. 'If I decide to take Koko to a headshrinker, I'll check back with you.'

He went to the buffet for a second helping, wrapped a slice of turkey in a paper napkin, and took a taxi home to the Villa Verandah.

As soon as he stepped off the elevator on the fifteenth floor, he started jingling his keys. It was his signal to Koko. The cat always ran to the door and raised his shrill Siamese yowl of greeting. As part of the ritual, Qwilleran would pretend to fumble with the lock, and the longer he delayed opening the door, the more vociferous the welcome.

But tonight there was no welcoming clamor. Qwilleran opened the door and quickly glanced in Koko's three favorite haunts: the northeast corner of the middle sofa; the glass-topped coffee table, a cool surface for warm days; and the third bookshelf, between a marble bust of Sappho and a copy of *Fanny Hill*, where Koko retired if the apartment was chilly. None of the three offered any evidence of cat.

Qwilleran went to the kitchen and looked on top of the refrigerator, expecting to see a round mound of light fur curled on the blue cushion – headless, tailless, legless, and asleep. There was no Koko there. He called, and there was no answer. Systematically he searched under the bed, behind the draperies, in closets and drawers, even inside the stereo cabinet. He opened the kitchen cupboards. In a moment of panic he snatched at the refrigerator door. No Koko. He looked in the oven.

All this time Koko was watching the frantic search from the seat of the green wing chair – in plain view but invisible, as a cat can be when he is silent and motionless. Qwilleran gave a grunt of surprise and relief when he finally caught sight of the hump of fur. Then he became concerned. Koko was sitting in a hunched position with his shoulder blades up and a troubled look in his eyes.

'Are you all right?' the man said.

The cat gave a mouselike squeak without opening his mouth.

'Do you feel sick?'

Koko wriggled uncomfortably and looked in the corner of the chair seat. A few inches from his nose was a ball of fluff. Green fluff.

'What's that? Where did you get that?' Qwilleran demanded. Then his eyes traveled to the wing of the chair. Across its top a patch of upholstery fabric was missing, and the padding was bursting through.

'Koko!' yelled Qwilleran. 'Have you been chewing this chair? This expensive Danish chair?'

Koko gave a little cough, and produced another wad of green wool, well chewed.

Qwilleran gasped. 'What will Harry Noyton say? He'll have a fit!' Then he raised his voice to a shout, 'Are you the one who's been eating my ties?'

The cat looked up at the man and purred mightily.

'Don't you dare purr! You must be crazy – to eat cloth! You're out of your mind! Lord! That's all I need – one more problem!'

Koko gave another wheezing cough, and up came a bit of green wool, very damp.

Qwilleran dashed to the telephone and dialed a number.

'Connect me with the bartender,' he said, and in a moment he heard the hubbub of the Press Club bar like the roar of a hurricane. 'Bruno!' he shouted. 'This is Qwilleran. How do I reach that doctor? That psycatatrist?'

Seventeen

The morning after Koko ate a piece of the Danish chair Qwilleran telephoned his office and told Arch Riker he had a doctor's appointment and would be late.

'Trouble?' Riker asked.

'Nothing serious,' said Qwilleran. 'Sort of a digestive problem.'

'That's a twist! I thought you had a stomach like a billy goat.'

'I have, but last night I got a big surprise.'

'Better take care of it,' Riker advised. 'Those things can lead to something worse.'

Bruno had supplied Dr Highspight's telephone number, and when Qwilleran called, the voice of the woman who answered had to compete with the mewing and wailing of countless cats. Speaking with a folksy English accent, she told Qwilleran he could have an appointment at eleven o'clock that morning. To his surprise she said it would not be necessary to bring the patient. She gave an address on Merchant Street, and Qwilleran winced.

He prepared a tempting breakfast for Koko – jellied consommé and breast of Press Club turkey – hoping to discourage the cat's appetite for Danish furniture. He said goodbye anxiously, and took a bus to Merchant Street.

Dr Highspight's number was two blocks from the Allison house, and it was the same type of outdated mansion. Unlike the Allison house, which was freshly painted and well landscaped, the clinic was distinctly seedy. The lawn was full of weeds. There were loose floorboards on the porch.

Qwilleran rang the doorbell with misgivings. He had never heard of a psycatatrist, and he hated the thought of being rooked by a quack. Nor did he relish being made the victim of another practical joke.

The woman who came to the door was surrounded by cats. Qwilleran counted five of them: a tiger, an orange nondescript, one chocolate brown, and two sleek black panthers. From there his glance went to the woman's run-over bedroom slippers, her wrinkled stockings, the sagging hem of her housedress, and finally to her pudgy middle-aged face with its sweet smile.

'Come in, love,' she said, 'before the pussies run out in the road.'

'My name's Qwilleran,' he said. 'I have an appointment with Dr Highspight.'

His nose recorded faint odors of fish and antiseptic, and his eye perused the spacious entrance hall, counting cats.

They sat on the hall table, perched on several levels of the stairway, and peered inquisitively through all the doorways. A Siamese kitten with an appealing little smudged face struck a businesslike pose in a flat box of sand that occupied one corner of the foyer.

'Eee! I'm no doctor, love,' said the woman. 'Just a cat fancier with a bit of common sense. Would you like a cuppa? Go in the front room and make yourself comfy, and I'll light the kettle.'

The living room was high-ceilinged and architecturally distinguished, but the furniture had seen better days. Qwilleran selected the overstuffed chair that seemed least likely to puncture him with a broken spring. The cats had followed him and were now inspecting his shoelaces or studying him from a safe distance. He marveled at a cat's idea of a safe distance – roughly seven feet, the length of an average adult's lunge.

'Now, love, what seems to be the bother?' asked Mrs Highspight, seating herself in a platform rocker and picking up a wild-looking apricot cat to hold on her lap. 'I was expecting a young lad. You were in such a dither when you called.'

'I was concerned about my Siamese,' said Qwilleran. 'He's a remarkable animal, with some unusual talents – and very friendly. But lately his behavior has been strange. He's crazy about gummed envelopes, masking tape, stamps – anything like that. He licks them!'

'Eee, I like to lick envelopes myself,' said Mrs Highspight, rocking her chair vigorously and stroking the apricot cat. 'It's a caution how many flavors they can think up.'

'But you haven't heard the worst. He's started eating

cloth! Not just chewing it – swallowing it! I thought the moths were getting into my clothes, but I've found out it's the cat. He's nibbled three good wool ties, and last night he ate a chunk out of a chair.'

'Now we're onto something!' said the woman. 'Is it always wool that he eats?'

'I guess so. The chair is covered with some kind of woolly material.'

'It won't hurt him. If he can't digest it, he'll chuck it up.'

'That's comforting to know,' said Qwilleran, 'but it's getting to be a problem. It was a costly chair that he ate, and it doesn't even belong to me.'

'Does he do it when you're at home?'

'No, always behind my back.'

'The poor puss is lonesome. Siamese cats need company, they do, or they get a bit daft. Is he by himself all day?'

Qwilleran nodded.

'How long has he lived with you?'

'About six months. He belonged to my landlord, who was killed last March. Perhaps you remember the murder on Blenheim Place.'

'Eee, that I do! I always read about murders, and that was a gory one, that was. They done him in with a carving knife. And this poor puss – was he very fond of the murdered man?'

'They were kindred spirits. Never separated.'

'That's your answer, love. The poor puss has had a shock, like. And now he's lonesome.'

Qwilleran found himself rising to his own defense. 'The cat's very fond of me. We get along fine. He's affectionate, and I play with him once in a while.'

Just then a large smoky-blue cat walked into the room and made a loud pronouncement.

'The kettle's boiling,' said Mrs Highspight. 'Tommy always notifies me when the kettle's boiling. I'll fetch the tea things and be back in a jiff.'

The company of cats kept their eyes on Qwilleran until the woman returned with cups and a fat brown teapot.

'And does he talk much, this puss of yours?' she asked.

'He's always yowling about one thing or another.'

'His mother pushed him away when he was a kit. That kind always talks a blue streak and needs more affection, they do. Is he neutered?'

Qwilleran nodded. 'He's what my grandmother used to call a retired gentleman cat.'

'There's only one thing for it. You must get him another puss for a companion.'

'Keep two cats?' Qwilleran protested.

'Two's easier than one. They keep each other entertained and help wash the places that's hard to reach. If your puss has a companion, you won't have to swab his ears with cotton and boric acid.'

'I didn't know I was supposed to.'

'And don't bother your head about the feed bill. Two happy cats don't eat much more than one cat that's lonesome.'

Qwilleran felt a tiny breath on his neck and turned to find the pretty little Siamese he had seen in the entrance hall, now perched on the back of his chair, smelling his ear.

'Tea's ready to pour,' Mrs Highspight announced. 'I like a good strong cup. There's a bit of milk in the pitcher, if you've a mind.'

Qwilleran accepted a thin china cup filled with a mahogany-colored brew, and noted a cat hair floating on its surface. 'Do you sell cats?' he asked.

'I breed exotics and find homes for strays,' said Mrs Highspight. 'What your puss needs is a nice little Siamese ladylove – spayed, of course. Not that it makes much difference. They still know which is which, and they can be very sweet together. What's the name of your puss?'

'Koko.'

'Eee! Just like Gilbert and Sullivan!' Then she sang in a remarkably good voice, ' "For he's going to marry Yum *Yum*, te dum. Your anger pray bury, for all will be merry. I think you had better succumb, te dum." '

Tommy, the big blue point, raised his head, and howled. Meanwhile, the Siamese kitten was burrowing into Qwilleran's pocket.

'Shove her off, love, if she's a bother. She's a regular hoyden. The females always take a liking to men.'

Qwilleran stroked the pale fur, almost white, and the kitten purred delicately and tried to nibble his finger with four little teeth. 'If I'm going to get another cat,' he said, 'maybe this one—'

'Eee, I couldn't let you have that one. She's special, like. But I know where there's an orphan needs a good home. Did you hear about that Mrs Tait that died last week? There was a burglary, and it was in all the papers.'

'I know a little about it,' said Qwilleran.

'A sad thing, that was. Mrs Tait had a Siamese female, and I don't fancy her husband will be keeping the poor puss.'

'What makes you think so?'

'Eee, he doesn't like cats.'

'How do you know all this?'

'The puss came from one of my litters, and the missus – rest her soul! – had to call on me for help. The poor puss was so nervous, wouldn't eat, wouldn't sleep. And now the poor woman's gone, and no telling what will become of the puss . . . Let me fill your teacup, love.'

She poured more of the red-black brew with its swirling garnish of tea leaves.

'And that husband of hers,' she went on. 'Such a one for putting on airs, but – mind this! – I had to wait a good bit for my fee. And me with all these hungry mouths to feed!'

Qwilleran's moustache was signaling to him. He said that, under the circumstances, he would consider adopting the cat. Then he tied the shoelace the cats had untied, and stood up to leave. 'How much do I owe you for the consultation?'

'Would three dollars be too much for you, love?'

'I think I can swing it,' he said.

'And if you want to contribute a few pennies for the cup of tea, it goes to buy a bit of a treat for the pussies. Just drop it in the marmalade crock on the hall table.'

Mrs Highspight and an entourage of waving tails accompanied Qwilleran to the door, the Siamese kitten rubbing against his ankles and touching his heart. He dropped two quarters in the marmalade jar.

'Call on me any time you need help, love,' said Mrs Highspight.

'There's one thing I forgot to mention,' Qwilleran said. 'A friend visited me the other evening, and Koko tried to bite her. Not a vicious attack – just a token bite. But on the head, of all places!'

'What was the lady doing?'

'Cokey wasn't doing a thing! She was minding her own business, when all of a sudden Koko sprang at her head.'

'The lady's name is Cokey, is it?'

'That's what everybody calls her.'

'You'll have to call her something else, love. Koko thought you were using his name. A puss is jealous of his name, he is. Very jealous.'

When Qwilleran left the cattery on Merchant Street, he told himself that Mrs Highspight's diagnosis sounded logical; the token attack on Cokey was motivated by jealousy. At the first phone booth he stopped and called the Middy studio.

On the telephone he found Cokey strangely gentle and amenable. When he suggested a dinner date, she invited him to dinner at her apartment. She said it would be only a casserole and a salad, but she promised him a surprise.

Qwilleran went back to his office and did some writing. It went well. The words flowed easily, and his two typing fingers hit all the right keys. He also answered a few letters from readers who were requesting decorating advice:

'May I use a quilted *matelassé* on a small *bergère*?'

'Is it all right to place a low credenza under a high clerestory?'

In his agreeable mood Qwilleran told them all, 'Yes. Sure. Why not?'

Just before he left the office at five thirty, the Library chief called to say that the Tait clipping file had been returned, and Qwilleran picked it up on his way out of the building.

He wanted to go home and shave before going to Cokey's, and he had to feed the cat. As soon as he stepped off the elevator on the fifteenth floor, he could hear paeans of greeting, and when he entered the apartment Koko began a drunken race through the rooms. He went up over the backs of chairs and down again with a thud. He zoomed up on the stereo cabinet and skated its entire length, rounded the dining table in a blur of light fur, cleared the desk top, knocked over the wastebasket – all the while alternating a falsetto howl with a baritone growl.

'That's the spirit!' said Qwilleran. 'That's what I like to see,' and he wondered if the cat sensed he was getting a playmate.

Qwilleran chopped some chicken livers for Koko and sautéed them in butter, and he crumbled a small side order of Roquefort cheese. Hurriedly he cleaned up and put on his other suit and his good plaid tie. Then it was six thirty, and time to leave. For a few seconds he hesitated over the Tait file from the Library – a bulky envelope of old society notes, obsolete business news, and obituaries. His moustache pricked up, but his stomach decided the Tait file could wait until later.

Eighteen

Cokey lived on the top floor of an old town house, and Qwilleran, after climbing three flights of stairs, was breathing hard when he arrived at her apartment. She opened the door, and he lost what little breath he had left.

The girl who greeted him was a stranger. She had cheekbones, temples, a jawline, and ears. Her hair, that had formerly encased her head and most of her visage like a helmet of chain mail, was now a swirling frame for her face. Qwilleran was fascinated by Cokey's long neck and graceful chinline.

'It's great!' he said. His eyes followed her as she moved about the apartment doing domestic and unnecessary little tasks.

The furnishings were spare, with an understated Bohemian smartness; black canvas chairs, burlap curtains in the honest color of potato sacks, and painted boards supported by clay plant pots to make a bookcase. Cokey had created a festive atmosphere with lighted candles and music. There were even two white carnations leaning out of a former vinegar bottle.

Her economies registered favorably with Qwilleran. There was something about the room that looked sad and brave to a resident of the Villa Verandah. It touched him in a vulnerable spot, and for one brief moment he had a delirious urge to support this girl for life, but it passed quickly. He pressed a handkerchief to his brow and remarked about the music coming from a portable record player.

'Schubert,' she said sweetly. 'I've given up Hindemith. He doesn't go with my new hairdo.'

For dinner she served a mixture of fish and brown rice in a sauce flecked with green. The salad was crunchy and required a great deal of chewing, retarding conversation. Later came ice cream made of yogurt and figs, sprinkled with sunflower seeds.

After dinner Cokey poured cups of herb tea (she said it was her own blend of alfalfa and bladder wrack) and urged her guest to take the most comfortable chair and prop his feet on a hassock that she had made from a beer crate, upholstering it with shaggy carpet samples. While he lighted his pipe, she curled up on the couch – an awning-striped mattress on legs – and started knitting something pink.

'What's that?' Qwilleran gasped, and almost inhaled the match he intended to blow out.

'A sweater,' she said. 'I knit all my own sweaters. Do you like the color? Pink is going to be part of my new image, since I had no luck with the old image.'

Qwilleran smoked his pipe and marveled at the omnipotence of hairdressers. Billions are spent for neurophysiological research to control human behavior, he reflected. Beauty shops would be cheaper.

For a while he watched the angular grace of Cokey's hands as she manipulated the knitting needles, and suddenly he said: 'Tell me honestly, Cokey. Did you know the nature of the Allison house when you suggested publishing it?'

'Honestly, I didn't,' she said.

'Did you happen to mention it to that fellow from the *Morning Rampage*?'

'What fellow?'

'Mike Bulmer in their Circulation Department. You seem to know him. You spoke to him at the Press Club.'

'Oh, *that* one! I don't really know him. He bought some lamps from Mrs Middy last spring and gave her a bad check; that's why I remembered him.'

Qwilleran felt relieved. 'I thought you were keeping secrets from me.'

Cokey stopped knitting. She sighed. 'There's one secret I'd better confess, because you'll find out sooner or later. You're so snoopy!'

'Occupational disease,' said Qwilleran. He lighted his pipe again, and Cokey watched intently as he knocked it on the ashtray, drew on it, peered into it, filled it, tamped it, and applied a match.

'Well,' said Cokey, when that was done, 'it's about David Lyke. When you took me to his party and introduced him, I pretended we had never met.'

'But you had,' said Qwilleran. 'In fact, you carry his picture in your handbag.'

'How did you know?'

'You spilled everything on my sofa Saturday night, and Koko selected Lyke's picture and started licking it.'

'You and your psychic cat are a good team!'

'Then it's true?'

She shrugged helplessly. 'I was one of the hordes of women who fell for that man. Those bedroom eyes! And that voice like a roll of drums! ... Of course, it never amounted to anything. David charmed everyone and loved no one.'

'But you still carry his picture.'

Cokey pressed her lips together, and her eyelashes fluttered. 'I tore it up – a few days ago.' Then all at once it became necessary for her to repair her lipstick, change the records, snuff the candles on the dinner table, put the butter in the refrigerator. When she had finished her frantic activity, she sat down again with her knitting. 'Let's talk about you,' she said to Qwilleran. 'Why do you always wear red plaid ties?'

He fingered his neckwear tenderly. 'I like them. This one is a Mackintosh tartan. I had a Bruce and a MacGregor, too, but Koko ate them.'

'*Ate* them!'

'I was blaming the moths, but Koko was the culprit. I'm glad he didn't get this one. It's my favorite. My mother was a Mackintosh.'

'I never heard of a cat eating ties.'

'Wool-eating is a neurotic symptom,' Qwilleran said with authority. 'The question is: Why didn't he touch the

Mackintosh? He had plenty of opportunity. He ruined all the others. Why did he spare my favorite tie?'

'He must be a very considerate cat. Has he eaten anything else?'

Qwilleran nodded gloomily. 'You know that Danish Modern chair in my apartment? He ate a piece of that, too.'

'It's wool,' Cokey said. 'Animal matter. Maybe it tastes good to neurotic cats.'

'The whole apartment is full of animal matter: vicuña chairs, suede sofas, goat-hair rug! But Koko had to pick Harry Noyton's favorite chair. How much will I have to pay to get it reupholstered?'

'Mrs Middy will do it at cost,' said Cokey, 'but we'll have to order the fabric from Denmark. And how can you be sure Koko won't nibble it again?'

Qwilleran told her about Mrs Highspight and the plan to adopt the Tait cat. 'She told me Tait is unfond of cats. She also said he's slow to pay his bills.'

'The richer they are, the harder it is to collect,' said Cokey.

'But is Tait as rich as people think? David hinted that the decorating bill was unpaid. And when we discussed the possibility of publishing the Tait house, David said he thought he could use persuasion; it sounded as if he had some kind of leverage he could employ. Actually, Tait agreed quite readily. Why? Because he was really broke and inclined to cooperate with his creditor? Or for some other obscure reason?' Qwilleran touched his moustache. 'Sometimes I think the Muggy Swamp episode is a frame-up. And I still think the police theory about the houseboy is all wet.'

'Then what's happened to him?'

'Either he's in Mexico,' said Qwilleran, 'or he's been murdered. And if he's in Mexico, either he went of his own accord or he was sent there by the conspirators. And if he was sent, either he has the jades with him or he's clean. And if he has the jades, I'll bet you ten to one that Tait is planning a trip to Mexico in the near future. He's going away for a rest. If he heads west, he'll probably wind up in Mexico.'

'You can also go west by heading east,' said Cokey.

Qwilleran reached over and patted her hand. 'Smart girl.'

'Do you think he'd trust the houseboy with the jades?'

'You've got a point. Maybe Paolo didn't take the loot. Maybe he was dispatched to Mexico as a decoy. If that's the case, where are the jades hidden?'

The answer was a large silence filling the room. Qwilleran clicked his pipe on his teeth. Cokey clicked her knitting needles. The record player clicked as another disc dropped on the turntable. Now it was Brahms.

Finally Qwilleran said, 'You know that game Koko and I play with the dictionary?' He proceeded with circumspection. 'Lately Koko's been turning up some words that have significance . . . I shouldn't talk about it. It's too incredible.'

'You know how I feel about cats,' said Cokey. 'I'll believe anything.'

'The first time I noticed it was last Sunday morning. I had forgotten to fix his breakfast, and when we played the dictionary game he turned up *hungerly*.'

Cokey clapped her hands. 'How clever!'

'On the next try he turned up *feed*, but I didn't catch on

until he produced *meadow mouse*. Apparently he was
getting desperate. I don't think he really cares for mice.'

'Why, that's like a Ouija board!'

'It gives me the creeps,' said Qwilleran 'Ever since the
mystery in Muggy Swamp, he's been flushing out words
that point to G. Verning Tait, like *bald* and *sacroiliac*. He
picked *sacroiliac* twice in one game, and that's quite a
coincidence in a dictionary with three thousand pages.'

'Is Mr Tait bald?'

'Not a hair on his head. He also suffers from a back
ailment . . . Do you know what a koolokamba is?'

Cokey shook her head.

'It's an ape with a bald head and black hands. Koko
dredged that one up, too.'

'Black hands! That's poetic symbolism,' Cokey said.
'Can you think of any more?'

'Not every word pertains to the situation. Sometimes
it's *visceripericardial* or *calorifacient*. But one day he
found two significant words on one page: *rubeola* and
ruddiness. Tait has a florid complexion, I might add.'

'Oh, Qwill, that cat's really tuned in!' Cokey said. 'I'm
sure he's on the right track. Can you do anything about
it?'

'Hardly.' Qwilleran looked dejected. 'I can't go to the
police and tell them my cat suspects the scion of a fine old
family . . . Still, there's another possibility . . .'

'What's that?'

'It may be,' said Qwilleran, 'that the police suspect Tait,
too, and they're publishing the houseboy theory as a
cover-up.'

Nineteen

Qwilleran arrived home from Cokey's apartment earlier than he had expected. Cokey had chased him out. She said they both had to work the next day, and she had to fix her hair and iron a blouse.

When he arrived at the Villa Verandah, Koko greeted him with a table-hopping routine that ended on the desk. The red light on the telephone was glowing. The phone had been ringing, Koko seemed to be saying, and no one had been there to answer.

Qwilleran dialed the switchboard.

'Mr Bunsen called you at nine o'clock,' the operator told him. 'He said to call him at home if you came in before one a.m.'

Qwilleran consulted his watch. It was not yet midnight and he started to dial Bunsen's number. Then he changed

his mind. He decided Cokey was right about the importance of image. He decided it would not hurt to enhance
his own image – the enviable one of a bachelor carousing
until the small hours of the morning.

Qwilleran emptied his coat pockets, draped his coat on
a chairback, and sat down at the desk to browse through
the Tait file of newspaper clippings. Koko watched,
lounging on the desk top in a classic pose known to lions
and tigers, curving his tail around a Swedish crystal
paperweight.

The newsprint was in varying shades of yellow and
brown, depending on the age of the news item. Each was
rubber-stamped with the date of publication. It was hardly
necessary to read the stamp; outmoded typefaces, as well
as mellowed paper, gave a clue to the date.

First Qwilleran shuffled through the clippings hastily,
hoping to spot a lurid headline. Finding none in a cursory
search, he started to read systematically: three genera-
tions of Tait history in chronological disorder.

Five years ago Tait had given a talk at a meeting
of the Lapidary Society. Eleven years ago his father
had died. There was a lengthy feature on the Tait
Manufacturing Company, apparently one of a series on
family-owned firms of long standing; organized in 1883
for the manufacture of buggy whips, the company was
now producing car radio antennas. Old society clippings
showed the elder Taits at the opera or charity func-
tions. Three years ago G. Verning Tait announced his
intention of manufacturing antennas that looked like
buggy whips. A year later a news item stated that the Tait
plant had closed and bankruptcy proceedings were being
instituted.

Then there was the wedding announcement of twenty-four years ago. Mr George Verning Tait, the son of Mr and Mrs Verning H. Tait of Muggy Swamp, was taking a bride. The entire Tait family had gone to Europe for the ceremony. The nuptials had been celebrated at the home of the bride's parents, the Victor Thorvaldsons of—

Qwilleran's eyes popped when he read it. 'The Victor Thorvaldsons of Aarhus, Denmark.'

He leaned back in his chair and exhaled into his moustache.

'Koko,' he said, 'what do you suppose Harry Noyton is pulling off in Aarhus?'

The cat opened his mouth to reply, but there was not enough breath behind his comment to make it audible.

Qwilleran's watch said one o'clock, and he hurried through the rest of the clippings until he found what he was looking for. Then he dialed Odd Bunsen's number excitedly.

'Hope I didn't get you out of bed,' he said to the photographer.

'How was your date, you old tomcat?' Bunsen demanded.

'Not bad. Not bad.'

'What were you doing on Merchant Street this morning?'

'How do you know I was on Merchant Street?'

'Aha! I saw you waiting for a bus on the southwest corner of Merchant and State at eleven fifty-five.'

'You don't miss a thing, do you?' Qwilleran said. 'Why didn't you stop and give me a lift?'

'I was going in the other direction. Brother! You were getting an early start. It wasn't even lunchtime.'

'I had a doctor's appointment.'

'On Merchant Street? Ho ho HO! Ho ho HO!'

'Is that all you called about? You're a nosy old woman.'

'Nope. I've got some information for you.'

'I've got some news for you, too,' said Qwilleran. 'I've found the skeleton in the Tait closet.'

'What is it?'

'A court trial. G. Verning Tait was involved in a paternity suit!'

'Ho ho HO! That old goat! Who was the gal?'

'One of the Taits' servants. She got a settlement, too. According to these old clippings it must have been a sensational trial.'

'A thing like that can be a rough experience.'

'You'd think a family with the Taits' money and position would settle out of court – at any cost,' Qwilleran said. 'I covered a paternity trial in Chicago several years ago, and the testimony got plenty raw ... Now, what's on *your* mind? What's this information you've got for me?'

'Nothing much,' said Bunsen, 'but if you're going to send those photographs to Tait, you'd better make it snappy. He's leaving the country in a couple of days.'

'How do you know?'

'I ran into Lodge Kendall at the Press Club. Tait's leaving Saturday morning.'

'For Mexico?' asked Qwilleran as his moustache sprang to attention.

'Nope. Nothing as obvious as that! You'd like it if he was heading for Mexico, wouldn't you?' the photographer teased.

'Well, where is he going?'

'Denmark!'

* * *

Qwilleran waked easily the next morning after a night of silly dreams that he was glad to terminate. In one episode he dreamed he was flying to Aarhus to be best man at the high-society wedding of two neutered cats.

Before leaving for the office, he telephoned Tait and offered to deliver the photographs of the jade the next day. He also inquired about the female cat and was appalled to hear that Tait had put her out of the house to fend for herself.

'Can you get her back?' Qwilleran asked, controlling his temper. He had a particular loathing for people who mistreated animals.

'She's still on the grounds,' Tait said. 'She howled all night. I'll let her come back in the house ... How many photos do you have for me?'

Qwilleran worked hard and fast at the office that day, while the clerk in the Feature Department intercepted all phone calls and uninvited visitors with the simple explanation that permits no appeal, no argument, no exceptions. 'Sorry, he's on deadline.'

Only once did he take time out, and that was to telephone the Taits' former housekeeper.

'Mrs Hawkins,' he said, taming his voice to an aloof drawl, 'this is an acquaintance of Mr Tait in Muggy Swamp. I am being married shortly, and my wife and I will need a housekeeper. Mr Tait recommends you highly—'

'Oh, he does, does he?' said a musical voice with impudence in the inflection.

'Could you come for an interview this evening at the Villa Verandah?'

'Who'll be there? Just you? Or will the lady be there?'

'My fiancée is unfortunately in Tokyo at the moment, and it will be up to me to make the arrangements.'

'Okey doke. I'll come. What time?'

Qwilleran set the appointment for eight o'clock. He was glad he was not in need of a housekeeper. He wondered if Mrs Hawkins was an example of Tait's ill-advised economies.

By the time Mrs Hawkins presented herself for the interview, the rain had started, and she arrived with dripping umbrella and a dripping raincoat over a gaudy pink and green dress. Qwilleran noted that the dress had the kind of neckline that slips off the shoulder at the slightest encouragement, and there was a slit in the side seam. The woman had sassy eyes, and she flirted her shoulders when she walked. He liked sassy, flirtatious females if they were young and attractive, but Mrs Hawkins was neither.

With exaggerated decorum he offered her a glass of sherry 'against the weather,' and poured a deep amber potion from Harry Noyton's well-stocked bar. He poured an exceptionally large glass, and by the time the routine matters had been covered – experience, references, salary – Mrs Hawkins had relaxed in the cushions of a suede sofa and was ready for a chatty evening.

'You're one of the newspaper fellows that came to the house to take pictures,' she announced at this point, with her eyes dancing at him. 'I remember your moustache.' She waved an arm at the appointments of the room. 'I didn't know reporters made so much money.'

'Let me fill your glass,' said Qwilleran.

'Aren't you drinking?'

'Ulcers,' he said with a look of self-pity.

'Lordy, I know all about *them*!' said Mrs Hawkins. 'I cooked for two people with ulcers in Muggy Swamp. Sometimes, when Mr Tait wasn't around, *she* would have me fix her a big plate of French fried onion rings, and if there's anything that doesn't go with ulcers, it's French fried onion rings, but I never argued. Nobody dared argue with her. Everybody went around on tippytoe, and when she rang that bell, everybody dropped everything and rushed to see what she wanted. But I didn't mind, because – if I have my druthers – I druther cook for a couple of invalids than a houseful of hungry brats. And I had help out there. Paulie was a big help. He was a sweet boy, and it's too bad he turned out to be no good, but that's the way it is with foreigners. I don't understand foreigners. *She* was a foreigner, too, although it was a long time ago that she came over here, and it wasn't until near the end that she started screaming at all of us in a foreign language. Screaming at her husband, too. Lordy, that man had the patience of a saint! Of course, he had his workshop to keep him happy. He was crazy about those rocks! He bought a whole mountain once – some place in South America. It was supposed to be chock-full of jade, but I guess it didn't pan out. Once he offered me a big jade brooch, but I wouldn't take it. I wasn't having any of *that*!' Mrs Hawkins rolled her eyes suggestively. 'He was all excited when you came to take pictures of his knick knacks, which surprised me because of the way he felt about the *Daily Fluxion*.' She paused to drain her glass. 'This is good! One more little slug? And then I'll be staggering home.'

'How did Mr Tait feel about the *Fluxion*?' Qwilleran asked casually, as he refilled Mrs Hawkins's glass.

'Oh, he was dead set against it! Wouldn't have it in the house. And that was a crying shame, because everybody knows the *Fluxion* has the best comics, but ... that's the way he was! I guess we all have our pecu-peculiarities. ... Whee! I guess I'm feeling these drinks.'

Eventually she lapsed into a discourse on her former husband and her recent surgery for varicose veins. At that point Qwilleran said he would let her know about the housekeeping position, and he marched her to a taxi and gave her a five-dollar bill to cover the fare.

He returned to the apartment just as Koko emerged from some secret hiding place. The cat was stepping carefully and looking around with cautious eyes and incredulous ears.

'I feel the same way,' Qwilleran said. 'Let's play the game and see if you can come up with something useful.'

They went to the dictionary, and Koko played brilliantly. Inning after inning he had Qwilleran stumped with *ebionitism* and *echidna*, *cytodiagnosis* and *czestochowa*, *onychophore* and *opalinid*.

Just as Qwilleran was about to throw in the sponge, his luck changed. Koko sank his claws into the front of the book, and the page opened to *arene* and *argue*. On the very next try it was *quality* and *quarreled*. Qwilleran felt a significant vibration in his moustache.

Twenty

The morning after Mrs Hawkins's visit and Koko's stellar performance with the dictionary, Qwilleran waked before the alarm clock rang, and bounded out of bed. The pieces of the puzzle were starting to fall into place.

Tait must have had a grudge against the *Fluxion* ever since the coverage of the paternity trial. The family had probably tried to hush it up, but the *Fluxion* would naturally insist that the public has a right to know. None of the agonizing details had been spared. Perhaps the *Rampage* had dealt more kindly with the Taits; it was owned by the Pennimans, who were part of the Muggy Swamp clique.

For eighteen years Tait had lived with his grudge, letting it grow into an obsession. Despite his subdued exterior, he was a man of strong passions. He probably hated the *Fluxion* as fervently as he loved jade. His ulcers were evidence of inner turmoil. And when the *Fluxion* offered to publish his house, he saw an opportunity for revenge; he could fake a theft, hide the jades, and let them be recovered after the newspaper had simmered in its embarrassment.

What would be a safe hiding place for a teapot as thin as a rose petal? Qwilleran asked himself as he prepared Koko's breakfast.

But would Tait go to such lengths for the meager satisfaction of revenge? He would need a stronger motive. Perhaps he was not so rich as his position indicated. He had lost the manufacturing plant; he had gambled on a jade expedition that failed to produce; he owed a large decorating bill. Had he devised a scheme to collect insurance? Had he and his wife argued about it? Had they quarreled on the night of the alleged theft? Had the quarrel been violent enough to cause a fatal heart attack?

Qwilleran placed Koko's breakfast on the kitchen floor, slipped into his suit coat, and started filling his pockets. Here and there around the apartment he collected his pipe, tobacco pouch, matches, card case, a comb, some loose silver, his bill clip, and a clean handkerchief, but he could not find the green jade button that usually rattled around in his change pocket. He remembered leaving it on the desk top.

'Koko, did you steal my lucky piece?' Qwilleran said.

'YARGLE!' came the reply from the kitchen, a yowl gargled with a throatful of veal kidneys in cream.

Once more Qwilleran opened the envelope of photographs he was going to deliver to Tait. He spread them on the desk: wide-angle pictures of beautiful rooms, medium shots of expensive furniture groupings, and close-ups of the jades. There was a perfect shot of the rare white teapot as well as one of the bird perched on the back of a lion. There were the black writing desk, ebony and black marble heavily ornamented with gilded bronze; the table supported by a sphinx; the white silk chairs that did not look comfortable.

Koko rubbed against Qwilleran's ankles.

'What's on your mind?' the man said. 'I made your breakfast. Go and finish it. You've hardly touched that food!'

The cat arched his back, curved his tail into a question mark, and walked back and forth over the newsman's shoes.

'You're getting your playmate today,' Qwilleran said. 'A little cross-eyed lady cat. Maybe I should take you along. Would you like to put on your harness and go for a ride?'

Koko pranced in figure eights with long-legged grace.

'First I've got to punch another hole in your harness.'

The kitchen offered no tools for punching holes in leather straps: no awl, no icepick, no sixpenny nails, not even an old-fashioned can opener. Qwilleran managed the operation with the point of a nail file.

'There!' he said, as he went to look for Koko. 'I defy you to slip out of it again! ... Now, where the devil did you go?'

There was a wet, slurping, scratching sound, and Qwilleran wheeled around. Koko was on the desk. He was licking a photograph.

'Hey!' yelled Qwilleran, and Koko jumped to the floor and bounded away like a rabbit.

The newsman examined the prints. Only one of them was damaged. 'Bad cat!' he said. 'You've blistered this beautiful photo.'

Koko sat under the coffee table, hunched in a small bundle.

It was the Biedermeier armoire he had licked with his sandpaper tongue. The surface of the photograph was still sticky. From one angle the damage was hardly noticeable. Only when the light hit the picture in a certain way could the dull and faintly blistered patch be noticed.

Qwilleran examined it closely and marveled at the detail in Bunsen's photo. The grain of the wood stood out clearly, and whatever lighting the photographer had used gave the furniture a three-dimensional quality. The chased metal around the tiny keyhole was in bold relief. A fine line of shadow accentuated the edge of the drawer across the bottom.

There was another thin dark line down the side panel of the armoire that Qwilleran had not noticed before. It sliced through the grain of the wood. It hardly made sense in the design or construction of the cabinet.

Qwilleran felt a prickling in his moustache, and stroked it hurriedly. Then he grabbed Koko and trussed him in his harness.

'Let's go,' he said. 'You've licked something that gives me ideas!'

It was a long and expensive taxi ride to Muggy Swamp. Qwilleran listened to the click of the meter and wondered if he could put this trip on his expense account. The cat sat on the seat close to the man's thigh, but as soon as the taxi turned into the Tait driveway, Koko was alerted. He rose on his hind legs, placed his front paws on the window and scolded the landscape.

Qwilleran told the driver, 'I want you to wait and take me back to town. I'll probably be a half hour.'

'Okay if I go to the railway station and get some breakfast?' the man asked. 'I'll stop the meter.'

Qwilleran tucked the cat under his left arm, coiled the leash in his left hand, and rang the doorbell of the Spanish mansion. As he stood waiting, he detected a note of neglect about the premises. The grass was badly in need of cutting. Curled yellow leaves, the first of the season to fall, were swirling around the courtyard. The windows were muddied.

When the door opened, it was a changed man who stood there. Tait, despite his high color, looked strained and tired. The old clothes and tennis shoes he wore were in absurd contrast to the black-and-white marble elegance of the foyer. Muddied footprints had dried on the white marble squares.

'Come in,' said Tait. 'I was just packing some things away.' He made an apologetic gesture toward his garb.

'I brought Koko along,' said Qwilleran coolly. 'I thought he might help in finding the other cat.' And he thought, Something's gone wrong, or he's scared or the police have been questioning him. Have they linked the murder of his decorator with the theft of his jades?

Tait said, 'The other cat's here. It's locked up in the laundry room.'

Koko squirmed, and was transferred to Qwilleran's shoulder, where he could survey the scene. The cat's body was taut, and Qwilleran could feel a vibration like a low-voltage electric current.

He handed the envelope of photographs to Tait and accepted an offhand invitation into the living room. It had changed considerably. The white silk chairs were shrouded with dust covers. The draperies were drawn across the windows. And the jade cases were dark and empty.

One lamp was lighted in the shadowy room – a lamp on the writing desk, where Tait had apparently been working. A ledger lay open there, and his collection of utilitarian jades was scattered over the desk – the primitive scrapers, chisels, and ax heads.

Tait yanked a dust cover off a deskside chair and motioned Qwilleran to sit down, while he himself stood behind the desk and opened the envelope. The newsman glanced at the ledger upside down; it was a catalog of the jade collection, written in a precise, slanted hand.

While the jade collector studied the photographs, Qwilleran studied the man's face. This is not the look of grief, he thought; this is exhaustion. The man has not been sleeping well. His plan is not working out.

Tait shuffled through the photographs, crimping the corners of his mouth and breathing heavily.

'Pretty good photography, isn't it?' said Qwilleran.

'Yes,' Tait murmured.

'Surprising detail.'

'I didn't realize he had taken so many pictures.'

'We always take more than we know we can use.'

Qwilleran cast a side-glance at the armoire. There was no fine dark line down the side of the cabinet – at least, none that could be discerned from where he sat.

Tait said, 'This desk photographed well.'

'It has a lot of contrast. Too bad there's no picture of the Biedermeier wardrobe.' He watched Tait closely. 'I don't know what happened. I was sure Bunsen had photographed the wardrobe.'

Tait maneuvered the corners of his mouth. 'It's a fine piece. It belonged to my grandfather.'

Koko squirmed again and voiced a small protest, and the newsman stood up, strolled back and forth and patted the silky back. He said: 'This is the first time this cat has gone visiting. I'm surprised he's so well behaved.' He walked close to the armoire, and still he could see no fine dark line.

'Thank you for the pictures,' Tait said. 'I'll go and get the other cat.'

When the collector left the room, Qwilleran's curiosity came to a boil. He walked to the armoire and examined the side panel. There was indeed a crack running vertically from top to bottom, but it was virtually invisible. Qwilleran ran his finger along the line. It was easier to feel than to see. Only the camera with its uncanny vision had observed clearly the hairline joining.

Koko was struggling now, and Qwilleran placed him on the floor, keeping the leash in his hand. Experimentally he ran his free hand up and down the crevice. He thought, it *must* be a concealed compartment. It's got to be! But how does it open?' There was no visible hardware of any kind.

He glanced toward the foyer, listened for approaching footsteps, then applied himself to the puzzle. Was it a touch latch? Did they have touch latches in the old days? The cabinet was over a hundred years old.

He pressed the side panel and thought that it had a slight amount of give, as if it were less than solid. He pressed again, and it responded with a tiny cracking noise like the sound of old, dry wood. He pressed the panel hard along the edge of the crack – first at shoulder level, then higher, then lower. He reached up and pressed it at the top, and the side of the armoire slowly opened with a labored groan.

It opened only an inch or two. Cautiously Qwilleran increased the opening enough to see what was inside. His lips formed a silent exclamation. For a moment he was transfixed. He felt a prickle in his blood, and he forgot to listen for footsteps. Koko's ears were pivoting in alarm. Tennis shoes were coming noiselessly down the corridor, but Qwilleran didn't hear. He didn't see Tait enter the room ... stop abruptly ... move swiftly. He heard only the piercing soprano scream, and then it was too late.

The scene blurred in front of his eyes. But he saw the spike. He heard the snarls and blood-chilling shrieks. There was a shock of white lightning. The lamp crashed. In the darkness he saw the uplifted spike ... saw the spiraling white blur ... felt the tug at his hand ... heard the great wrenching thud ... felt the sharp pain ... felt the trickle of blood ... and heard a sound like escaping steam. Then all else was still.

Qwilleran leaned against the armoire and looked down. Blood was dripping from his fingertips. The leash was cutting into his other palm, and twelve feet of nylon cord were wound tightly around the legs of G. Verning Tait, who lay gasping on the floor. Koko, anchored at the other end of the leash, was squirming to slip out of his harness. The room was silent except for the hard breathing of the prisoner and the hissing of a female cat on top of the Biedermeier armoire.

Twenty-One

The nurse in the First Aid room at the *Fluxion* bandaged the slash on Qwilleran's hand.

'I'm afraid you'll live,' she said cheerfully. 'It's only a scratch.'

'It bled a lot,' he said. 'That spike was razor-sharp and a foot long! It was actually a jade harpoon used for spearing walrus in the Arctic.'

'How appropriate – under the circumstances,' said the nurse with an affectionate side-glance at Qwilleran's moustache.

'Lucky I didn't get it in the stomach!'

'The wound looks clean,' said the nurse, 'but if it gives you any trouble, see a doctor.'

'You can skip the commercial,' Qwilleran said. 'I know it by heart.'

She patted the final strip of adhesive tape, and admired her handiwork.

The nurse had made a good show of the bandage. It did nothing for Qwilleran's typing efficiency, but it enhanced his story when he faced his audience at the Press Club that evening. An unusually large number of *Fluxion* staffers developed a thirst at five thirty, and the crowd formed around Qwilleran at the bar. His published account had appeared in the afternoon edition, but his fellow staffers knew that the best details of any story never get into print.

Qwilleran said, with barely suppressed pride: 'It was Koko who alerted me to the hoax. He licked one of Bunsen's photos and drew attention to the secret compartment.'

'I used sidelighting,' Bunsen explained. 'I put a light to the left of the camera at a ninety-degree angle, and it showed up the tiny crack. The camera caught it, but the eye would never know it was there.'

'When I discovered the swing-out compartment packed full of jade,' said Qwilleran, 'I was so fascinated that I didn't hear Tait coming. First thing I knew, a cat shrieked, and there was that guy coming at me with an Eskimo harpoon, a spike *this long*!' He measured an exaggerated twelve inches with his hands. 'Koko was snarling. The other cat was flying around, screaming. And there was that maniac, coming at me with a spike! Everything went out of focus. Then – crash! Tait fell flat on his face.' Qwilleran displayed his bandaged hand. 'He must have hurled the spike as he fell.'

Arch Riker said, 'Tell them how your cat tripped him up.'

Qwilleran took time to light his pipe, while his audience waited for the inside story: 'Koko was on a long leash, and he flew around in circles so fast – all I could see was a smoke ring in midair. And when Tait crashed to the floor, his legs were neatly trussed up in twelve feet of cord.'

'Crazy!' said the photographer. 'Wish I'd been there with a movie camera.'

'I picked up the jade spike and kept Tait down on the floor while I called the police on that gold-plated French phone.'

'When you go, you go first class,' Bunsen said.

Then Lodge Kendall arrived from Headquarters. 'Qwill was right all along,' he told everyone. 'The houseboy was innocent. Tait has told the police that he staked Paolo to a one-way fare to Mexico, then transferred the jade to the wardrobe cabinet and threw one piece behind Paolo's bed. And you remember the missing luggage? He'd given it to the boy himself.'

'Was it the insurance money he was after?'

'Chiefly. Tait wasn't an astute businessman. He'd lost the family fortune, and he needed a large sum of cash to invest in another harebrained scheme ... But there was something else, too. He hates the *Fluxion*. Ever since they played up his role in a paternity case.'

'I'd like to know why he didn't settle that claim out of court,' Qwilleran said.

'He tried, but he was up against dirty politics, he claims. It seems there was another Tait, a cousin of George Verning, who was running for Congress that year, and the paternity claim was timed accordingly. Somebody figured the voters wouldn't know one Tait from another, and apparently it was true. The guy lost the election.'

Qwilleran said, 'Did Tait tell the police anything about his proposed trip to Denmark?'

'Nobody mentioned it at Headquarters.'

'Well,' said Riker, 'I'll tune in tomorrow for the next installment. I'm going home to dinner.'

'I'm going home to feed Koko a filet mignon,' said Qwilleran. 'After all, he saved my neck.'

'Don't kid yourself,' Bunsen said. 'He was chasing that female cat.'

'I dropped her off at the pet hospital,' Qwilleran said. 'She had an infected wound in her side. That guy probably gave her a kick when he threw her out.'

Qwilleran had floated high on excitement all afternoon, but when he arrived home he succumbed to exhaustion. Koko reacted the same way. The cat lay on his side, legs stiffly extended, one ear bent under his head – to all appearances a dead cat except for a thoughtful look in half-open eyes. He ignored his dinner.

Qwilleran went to bed early, and his dreams were pertinent and convincing. He dreamed that Percy was saying, 'Qwill, you and Koko have done such a good job on the Tait case, we want you to find David Lyke's murderer,' and Qwilleran said, 'The investigation may take us to Japan, Chief,' and Percy said, 'Go right ahead! You can have an unlimited expense account.' Qwilleran's moustache twitched in his sleep. So did the cat's whiskers. Koko was dreaming, too.

Early Saturday morning, while Qwilleran was snoring gently and his subconscious was wrestling with the Lyke mystery, the telephone began ringing insistently. When it succeeded in shaking him awake, he reached groggily toward the bedside table, found the receiver, and heard the operator say: 'This is Aarhus, Denmark. I have a call for Mr James Qwilleran.'

'Speaking,' Qwilleran croaked in his early-morning voice.

'Qwill, this is Harry,' came a transatlantic shout. 'We just heard the news!'

'You did? In Denmark?'

'It came over the radio.'

'It's a big shame. He was a nice guy.'

'I don't know about *him*,' said Noyton. 'I only knew her. He must have cracked up.'

'Who cracked up?'

'What's the matter? Aren't you awake yet?'

'I'm awake,' said Qwilleran. 'What are you talking about?'

'Is this Qwill? This is Qwilleran, isn't it?'

'I think so. I'm a little groggy. Are you talking about the murder?'

'Murder!' shouted Noyton. 'What murder?'

Qwilleran paused. 'Aren't you talking about David Lyke?'

'I'm talking about G. Verning Tait! What's happened to David?'

'He's dead. He was shot last Monday night.'

'David dead! My God! Who did it?'

'They don't know. It happened in his apartment. In the middle of the evening.'

'Somebody break in?'

'It doesn't appear so.'

'Why would anyone want to kill David? He was a fantastic guy!'

'What was it you heard on the radio over there?' Qwilleran asked.

'About Tait's arrest. Mrs Tait's family couldn't believe it when they heard the news.'

Qwilleran sat up straight. 'You know her family?'

'Just met them. Fine people. Her brother's working with me on the hush-hush deal I told you about. Don't forget: I promised you the *Fluxion* will get the scoop!'

'What's the nature of it?'

'I'm financing a fantastic manufacturing process. Qwill, I'm going to be the richest man in the world!'

'Is it a new invention?'

'A scientific discovery,' Noyton said. 'While the rest of the world is fooling around with outer space, the Danes are doing something for mankind here and now.'

'Sounds great!'

'Until I got over here, I didn't know what it was all about. I just took her word that it was something world-shaking.'

'Whose word?'

'Mrs Tait's.'

'She tipped you off to her brother's discovery?'

'Well, you see, Dr Thorvaldson needed financing, and she knew her husband couldn't swing it. She'd heard about me and thought I could handle it. Of course, she wanted a kickback – under the table, so to speak.' Noyton paused. 'This is all off-the-record, of course.'

Qwilleran said: 'Tait was heading for Denmark. He probably expected to invest the insurance money.'

There was some interference on the line.

'Are you still there?' Qwilleran said.

Noyton's voice had faded. 'Listen, I'll call you tomorrow – can you hear me? – as soon as everything's sewed up legally ... This is a lousy connection ... Hope they nab David's killer. So long! Call you within twenty-four hours.'

It was Saturday, but Qwilleran went into the office to work ahead on the next issue of *Gracious Abodes*. He was determined, now, that Fran Unger should not get the magazine away from him. He hoped also to see Percy and say 'I told you so,' but the managing editor was attending a publishers' conference in New York. During the day Qwilleran made two important phone calls – one to the hospital to inquire about the cat, and one to the Middy Studio to make a dinner date with Cokey.

When he went home in the late afternoon to feed Koko, he found a scene of frantic activity. Koko was careening drunkenly around the apartment. He was playing with his homemade mouse – a game related to hockey, basketball, and tennis, with elements of wrestling. The cat skidded the small gray thing over the polished floor, pounced on it, tossed it in the air, batted it across the room, pursued it, made a flying tackle, clutched it in his forepaws, and rolled back and forth in ecstasy until the mouse slipped from his grasp, and the chase began again. With an audience Koko was inclined to vaunt his prowess. As Qwilleran watched, the cat dribbled the mouse the length of the living room, gave it a well-aimed whack, and scored a goal – directly under the old Spanish chest. Then he trotted after it, peered under the low chest, and raised his head in a long, demanding howl.

'No problem,' said Qwilleran. 'This time I'm equipped.'

From the hall closet he brought the umbrella that Mrs Hawkins had so conveniently forgotten. The first sweep under the chest produced nothing but dust, and Koko increased the volume of his demands. Qwilleran got down on the floor and poked the finial into far dark corners, fishing out the jade button that had disappeared a few days before. Koko's clamor was loud and unceasing.

The next sweep of the umbrella brought forth something pink!

Not exactly pink, Qwilleran told himself, but almost pink ... and it looked vaguely familiar. He had an idea what it was. And he knew very well how it had managed to get there.

'Koko!' he said sternly. 'What do you know about this?'

Before the cat could answer with a gutteral sound and a wrestling match with an invisible enemy, Qwilleran went to the telephone and rapidly dialed a number.

'Cokey,' he said, 'I'm going to be late picking you up. Why don't you take a cab to the Press Club and meet me there? ... No, just a little business emergency I've got to handle ... All right. See you shortly. And I may have some news for you!'

Qwilleran turned back to the cat. 'Koko, when did you eat this pink stuff? Where did you find it?'

When Qwilleran arrived at the Press Club, Cokey was waiting in the lobby, sitting in one of the worn leather sofas.

'There's trouble,' she said. 'I can read it in your face.'

'Wait till we get a table, and I'll explain,' he said. 'Let's sit in the cocktail lounge. I'm expecting a phone call.'

They went to a table with a red-checked tablecloth, well patched and darned.

'There's been an unexpected development in connection with David's murder,' Qwilleran began, 'and Koko's involved. He was in David's apartment when the fatal shot was fired, and he apparently ate some wool. When I brought him home that night, he looked odd. I thought he'd had a fright. Now I'm inclined to think it was a stomachache. I suppose cats get stomachaches.'

'He couldn't digest the wool?' Cokey said.

'He might have managed the wool, but there was something else in the cloth. After he came home, he must have upchucked the whole thing and hidden it under the Spanish chest I found it an hour ago.'

Cokey clapped her hands to her face. 'And you recognized it? Don't tell me you actually *recognized* it!'

'Yes, and I think it would have looked familiar to you, too. It was a yellowish-pink wool with gold metallic threads.'

'Natalie Noyton! That handwoven dress she wore to the party!'

Qwilleran nodded. 'It appears that Natalie was in Dave's apartment Monday night, and she may have been there when he was shot. At any rate, it was something that had to be reported to the police, so I took the peach-colored wool over to Headquarters. That's why I was late.'

'What did they say?'

'When I left, they were hustling out to Lost Lake Hills. Our police reporter promised to call me here if anything develops.'

'I wonder why Natalie didn't come forward and volunteer some information to the police?'

'That's what worries me,' said Qwilleran. 'If she had information to give, and the killer knew it, he might try to silence her.

The domed ceiling of the club multiplied the voices of the Saturday-night crowd into a roar, but above it came an amplified announcement on the public-address system: 'Telephone for Mr Qwilleran.'

'That's our night man at Police Headquarters. I'll be right back.' He hurried to the phone booth.

When he returned, his eyes had acquired a darkness.

'What's wrong, Qwill? Is it something terrible?'

'The police were too late.'

'Too late?'

'Too late to find Natalie alive.'

'Murdered!'

'No. She took her own life,' said Qwilleran. 'Evidently a heavy dose of alcohol and then sleeping pills.'

A sad wail came from Cokey. 'But why? Why?'

'Apparently it was explained in her diary. She was hopelessly in love with her decorator, and he wasn't one to discourage an affair.'

'That I know!'

'Natalie thought Dave was ready to marry her the moment she got a divorce, and she wanted him so desperately that she agreed to her husband's terms: no financial settlement and no request for child custody. Then last weekend it dawned on her that Dave would never marry her – or anyone else. When Odd Bunsen and I turned up at her house Monday morning and she refused to see us, she must have been out of her mind with disappointment and remorse and a kind of hopeless panic.'

'I'd be blind with fury!' said Cokey.

'She was blind enough to think she could set things right by killing David.'

'Then it was Natalie—'

'It was Natalie ... Afterward, she went home, dismissed the maid, and lived through twenty-four hours of hell before ending it. She's been dead since Tuesday night.'

There was a long silence at the table.

After a while Qwilleran said, 'The police found the peach-colored dress in her closet. The shawl had quite a lot of fringe missing.'

Then the menus came, and Cokey said: 'I'm not hungry. Let's go for a walk – and talk about other things.'

They walked, and talked about Koko and the new cat whose name was Yu or Freya.

'I hope they'll be happy together,' said Cokey.

'I think we're all going to be happy together,' said Qwilleran. 'I'm going to change her name to Yum Yum. I've got to change your name, too.'

The girl looked at him dreamily.

'You see,' said Qwilleran, 'Koko doesn't like it when I call you Cokey. It's too close to his own name.'

'Just call me Al,' said Alacoque Wright with a wistful droop in her voice and a resigned lift to her eyebrows.

It was Monday when the news of Harry Noyton's Danish enterprise appeared on the front page of the *Daily Fluxion* under Qwilleran's by-line. In the first edition a typographical error had substituted 'devious' for 'diverse,' but it was a mistake so customary that the item would have been disappointing without it:

'Harry Noyton, financier and promoter of devious business interests,' said the bulletin, 'has acquired the worldwide franchise for a Danish scientist's unique contribution to human welfare – calorie-free beer with Vitamin C added.'

On the same day, in a small ceremony at the Press Club, Qwilleran was presented with an honorary press card for his cat. On it was pasted Koko's identification photo, with eyes wide, ears alert, whiskers bristling.

'I took his picture,' said Odd Bunsen, 'that night in David Lyke's apartment.'

And Lodge Kendall said, 'Don't think I had an easy time getting the police chief and fire commissioner to sign it!'

When Qwilleran returned to the Villa Verandah that evening, he entered the apartment with his fingers crossed. He had brought Yum Yum home from the hospital at noon, and the two cats had had several hours in which to sniff each other, circle warily, and make their peace.

All was silent in the living room. On the green Danish chair sat Yum Yum, looking dainty and sweet. Her face was a poignant triangle of brown, and her eyes were enormous circles of violet-blue, slightly crossed. Her brown ears were cocked at a flirtatious angle. And where the silky hairs of her pelt grew in conflicting directions on her white breast, there was a cowlick of fur softer than down.

Koko sat on the coffee table, tall and masterful, with a ruff of fur bushed around his neck.

'You devil!' said Qwilleran. 'There's nothing neurotic

about you, and there never was! You knew what you were doing all the time!'

With a grunt Koko jumped down from the table and ambled over to join Yum Yum. They sat side by side in identical positions, like bookends, with both tails curled to the right, both pairs of ears worn like coronets, both pairs of eyes ignoring Qwilleran with pointed unconcern. Then Koko gave Yum Yum's face two affectionate licks and lowered his head, arching his neck gracefully. He narrowed his eyes, and they became slits of catly ecstasy as the little female recognized her cue and washed inside his ears with her long pink tongue.

the
wrap-up
list

STEVEN ARNTSON

Houghton Mifflin
HOUGHTON MIFFLIN HARCOURT
Boston   New York   2013

Houghton Mifflin is an imprint of Houghton Mifflin Harcourt Publishing Company.

www.hmhbooks.com

The text of this book is set in Fournier MT Std.

Library of Congress Cataloging-in-Publication Data

Arntson, Steven, 1973–
The wrap-up list / by Steven Arntson.
p. cm.
Summary: "When sixteen-year-old Gabriela's death is foretold by a letter, she must
complete her 'wrap-up list' before she's forced to say goodbye."—Provided by publisher.
ISBN 978-0-547-82410-9
[1. Death—Fiction. 2. Hispanic Americans—Fiction.] I. Title.
PZ7.A7415Wr 2013
[Fic]—dc23
2012014035

Manufactured in United States of America
DOC 10 9 8 7 6 5 4 3 2 1
4500390451

seven days before
departure day

death letter

Some people die from heart attacks, and some from falling off ladders. Some are killed in car accidents. Some drown. Some, like my grandfather Gonzalo, die in war.

But some people don't die—they depart. Whether this is a good or a bad thing is debatable, but departures are always interesting, so when the bell rings at the end of seventh period I'm not surprised that Iris springs up and places one pale hand firmly on my forearm. She digs her red nails in. "Hurry, Gabriela!" she says.

I allow myself to be pulled from the classroom as Mr. Harpting, our history instructor, hopelessly calls out a reading assignment to his former audience. Iris and I are already in the hall, and Harpting's voice is lost amid the afterschool rush.

Outside, cars and buses clog the sunny hilltop turnaround. Iris drags me down the front steps, her long, straight blond hair glowing like a beacon. At the entrance to the student parking lot, a voice behind us calls, "Where are you guys going?" I turn to see Sarena running to catch up, her trumpet case bouncing against one thigh. I explain as she reaches us: "Iris thinks the Singing Man's departing today—" I hold out my free hand to her, and she grabs on. Her braided black hair, lustrous in the afternoon sun, shines. She sings: *"Ca-a-a-ro mio be-e-e-n!"* reprising the song we heard the Singing Man perform yesterday. "Hey, Gabriela," she says, reminded, "did you think about those lyrics?"

I wince. "I'm sorry," I say. "I will."

"That's okay," she replies. She's disappointed, and I feel bad. Sarena plays trumpet and sometimes sings in her dad's band—a jazz orchestra called the Washington Fifteen, which is the house act at the Caballero Hotel downtown. Her dad told her she could compose a song for the group, and she asked me to write the lyrics, because she thinks I have a way with words. I was thrilled at first, but now I regret it. I can't seem to get started.

Iris pulls us both through the parking lot, where mostly juniors and seniors loiter, playing car radios and socializing. I see Sylvester Hale leaned against the hood of his new pepper red sports car—he's in his letterman's jacket, surrounded by friends who also wear letterman's jackets. His pretty, wide-set eyes glance my direction for a moment, and my legs wobble, but Iris keeps pulling, and soon we're past.

"Hey—" another voice calls.

"Grab him!" I say to Sarena. It's Raahi standing outside his beat-up hatchback with some friends. Raahi's older than the three of us, eighteen, a thin kid with a head of thick, wavy black hair. He's one of those rare seniors who don't mind being friends with underclassmen. I met him last year in Mr. Wilkson's American Geography class.

Sarena extends her hand, holding out her trumpet case. Raahi takes her wrist, turning us into a chain of four as we head down the hill, leaving Raahi's car. He doesn't even bother to lock it up.

The four of us are a known group at school. Once, when we were sitting in a row in art class (left to right: Iris, me, Raahi, and Sarena), Mr. Jensen spontaneously used our skin tones as an example of a color gradient. I feel strange about that, but I guess it's true — cream color, light brown, brown, dark brown. Our school isn't very diverse in this regard, so I guess it struck Jensen as a noteworthy moment of life mimicking art.

"Iris thinks the Singing Man is departing today," Sarena explains to Raahi.

He nods, mock serious, and says, "Iris thinks someone's departing *every* day."

"I heard that!" Iris yells over at us.

"One time she thought Ms. Lime was going to depart," I recall.

"Remember when she thought *I* was going to?" says Sarena.

"And last week it was Sylvester," I say, "because of his new car."

"But *how* did he get that car?" says Iris, trying laughingly to defend herself. "It appeared out of nowhere."

We arrive at the bottom of the hill, where Cougar Way intersects Eighth. I hear the Singing Man before I see him — a big, operatic voice that suggests the exact sort of person who comes into view across the street: an elderly, portly Italian gentleman. He's wearing a blue suit and a thin red tie. The first time we saw him, a few weeks ago, Iris was immediately sure he was going through his wrap-up, and when he kept performing each day, the rest of us were inclined to agree — the Singing Man was scheduled to depart.

Here's how departures work. First, you're contacted by one of the Deaths, the creatures who oversee the process, usually with a letter saying "Dear So-and-So, your days are numbered." Then you correspond, deciding how much time you need and what you want to wrap up before you're taken. In the Singing Man's case, he wanted to sing, obviously.

No one knows why Deaths select particular people. There are plenty of theories, but it's basically random beyond the fact of one statistic: departures account for one percent of all fatalities.

Sarena says all of the Singing Man's songs are famous Italian arias, with lyrics along the lines of "Don't leave — it's bad when you go." Today, he belts his a cappella melodies with particular gusto. "Have we heard this one?" I ask Sarena. The Singing Man's repertoire is pretty limited, but this melody is unfamiliar.

"No, we haven't," says Sarena.

"This is the day. *For sure!*" says Iris as a delivery truck rumbles past, interrupting our view. "He saved this song for today. It's his swan song."

As the truck exits the intersection and the Singing Man returns to view, my eyes widen.

No matter how many times you encounter them, the Deaths are startling creatures. The one who appears today is Gretchen, whom I've seen a few times before. Like all the Deaths, she's about eight feet tall, extremely skinny, and grayish silver, as if you're seeing her through a screen that filters the colors out. The Deaths live in a place called the Silver Side (where everything is presumably colored silver?) and only come visiting here when they're drawn for a departure. Today, Gretchen is wearing a dark gray jacket over a silvery, flowing, ankle-length dress, and slate-colored heels. She approaches slowly, walking like they all do, as if through water — for some reason the Deaths experience our atmosphere as if it's thick, and a little buoyant. They always look like they're crossing the bottom of a swimming pool. Gretchen's salt and pepper hair floats hugely around her, and her dress pushes and pulls against her frame, moved by unseen currents. She looks about fifty years old, but the Deaths are much older than they look (centuries, millennia in some cases). Her face, long and skinny, is expressionless, and my eyes are drawn to the dark slits, like gills, to either side of her nose.

"We're going to see it!" Iris whispers frantically. She clutches one of my hands in excitement.

Gretchen stands to one side while the Singing Man finishes his last song. A number of people see what's going on and stop to watch. When the Singing Man falls silent, no one applauds, but he bows. Then he turns to Gretchen. She extends one hand toward him, as if they're being introduced. He reaches out hesitantly, and their fingers close. The Singing Man straightens up—the way you might if an ice cube were dropped down the back of your shirt. He takes a deep, surprised breath.

Then, beginning at his hand where he's touching Gretchen and spreading through his body, everything about him from his pink skin to his blue coat to his red tie turns silvery gray. His eyes close, and he exhales. His thinning hair lifts slightly around him, weightless, submerged. He stands still for a few moments, and then his lids flutter, confused, until his gaze settles on Gretchen.

"Thank you," he says politely, his voice barely audible to me across the street. Then he and Gretchen turn together, and begin to walk away—toward the Fields.

"Let's go!" says Iris, excited.

I roll my eyes. *"Why* do you always have to follow them? I can't. I've got homework."

"Sarena?" says Iris, but Sarena holds up her trumpet case,

indicating her need to practice. "Raahi?" Iris sees his answer in his eyes, and without even a goodbye she rushes off, leaving us staring after her for the few moments it takes her to disappear up the street after her quarry.

"Want a lift home?" Raahi asks me. He gestures back up the hill to the parking lot, where his car is presumably still sitting with all the doors unlocked.

"No thanks, it's nice out," I say.

"Raahi," says Sarena, "have you gotten any more news?" Sarena always asks about this. I feel awkward broaching the subject, but for some reason she and Raahi seem able to talk about it.

"No," he replies. "I doubt there'll be any at this point."

"Have you started . . . packing?" I ask.

"A little," he says. "I'm not supposed to bring much. You get on the bus with just a duffel bag. But I'm putting away other stuff, for Mom — so she doesn't have to do it."

There's a lot in these words. Raahi doesn't say, for instance, *in case I don't come back*, though he's surely thinking it. He's said as much during the past few weeks.

Raahi has been drafted. He got his card last month, and he'll be leaving for basic training next Tuesday. In all honesty, I'm a little excited for him — jealous, even. I don't say it, because he's obviously scared, but it kind of sounds like an adventure. It has crossed my mind to volunteer when I'm old enough (I'm barely sixteen right now).

"Heading back up the hill?" Raahi asks Sarena.

"Yeah," she says.

"Can I carry your trumpet?"

"Sure, okay," says Sarena, handing it over.

The two of them say goodbye to me and head back up. I watch them go — short Sarena and lanky Raahi. Since he got his card, his demeanor has totally changed from what I've always known. I don't think I'd ever seen him in a bad mood before the last few weeks. He isn't the first senior at school to have his name come up, but he's the first who's a friend of mine.

I continue ruminating on the matter as I walk toward home. The U.S. isn't technically at war yet. A month and a half ago we closed our borders to people from countries with "questionable sympathies," but few shots have been fired. It's about looking tough for now. The most popular quote from the television pundits so far has been "Speak softly and carry a big stick," which President Roosevelt said over a century ago. Several commentators have pointed out the possibility that this African proverb originated in the very country we're about to attack. It's strange to think that the stick mentioned in that proverb is partly composed of seniors from Central High.

The other term that's discussed frequently is *victory*. When you go to war, it's important to have a clear sense of what you mean by *victory*, so you know when to stop fighting. Something about that strikes me funny. I imagine a football team arguing over the nature of victory. It seems kind of obvious. For instance, World War II: the free world fought against fascism. That's pretty clear. At school I learned that World War II is called the Good War.

World War II is the war my grandfather Gonzalo fought in. He disappeared somewhere in Africa, maybe Tunisia. He died serving his country, according to his conscience. I think he's a hero, and so do my dad and my aunt Ana. If I had the chance to make the same choice as Gonzalo, I'd follow his footsteps. I would fight.

Aunt Ana and Dad love to talk about Gonzalo. He was the son of a peasant farmer in Mexico, and spoke imperfect English. It's because of him that my grandmother Fidelia, whom I called Abuela, moved here; because of him that my dad was born here; because of him that I'm growing up here, barely sixteen years old and poised at the start of the next war.

I'm still thinking about Raahi when I reach my block. As I turn onto my street, I encounter a sudden and strong smell of flowers—hyacinths or hydrangeas (which is the one that blooms in early spring?). I breathe deep. It's one of my most favorite scents—not a nice, neat smell, but a kind of wild one. You have to wrestle with it. Sometimes it makes me sneeze, and it always sends my mind in romantic directions. I recall something Raahi told me the other day: that he has not been kissed. He's eighteen, about to ship off to war. For a moment, I imagine a fantasy for him in which a beautiful girl kisses him just as he's about to step onto a boat/plane/train.

Iris, who's my best friend, hasn't been kissed either. This is especially perplexing to me, because not only is she nice, funny, and unquestionably a knockout, but she was asked to freshman prom by nine different guys. She said no to all of them. I can't fault her for being picky—she deserves someone special—but even I went to freshman prom. Iris stayed home and played Scrabble with her parents.

My date to freshman prom was Norbert Ganz. We didn't kiss—we were just friends. I smile now thinking of Norbert, who doesn't even attend Central High anymore. I may not ever see him again, but I have the feeling that as I get older it will become pretty funny that the name of my date to freshman prom was Norbert Ganz. Norb, we called him.

My apartment building is an old five-story brick rectangle nestled between two other five-story brick rectangles. (They are all very nice rectangles, well-maintained and with pretty flourishes at each cornice.) I enter the lobby and walk the red carpet to the numbered mailboxes on the wall, by the long mirror. I watch my reflection pass across and observe myself. I'm kind of a frumpy girl, but not uncute, with a frame that's both scrawny and chubby (which could perhaps be my miracle if the Church ever beatifies me: "St. Gabriela, it is Said, was Blessede by the Lorde to be both Scrawnye and Chubbye").

My curly brown hair is a mix of my dad's dark, wiry curls and my mom's wavy, blond locks. I've got light brown skin and a handful of freckles across my nose.

The mailboxes are set into a massive iron rectangle, as old as the building itself. I retrieve apartment 305's mail from its keyed cubby and proceed to the elevator, which is also as old as the building. It's the kind that has an iron accordion gate you pull back. When the car arrives, I enter and select floor three. I leaf idly through the stack of mail as the room glides up. There's a bank statement and an ad for a sporting goods store. The gas bill. A dumb magazine Dad reads called *Fiscal Frontrunners*. Then there is one more letter.

The elevator dings. The doors open.

They wait.

They close.

I'm still inside, staring at the final envelope. It's light red. There's no stamp on it, no return address, and no address for the recipient. There's only a first name. My name.

It's a Death Letter.

The elevator begins to descend — someone has called it back to the lobby. Quickly, I cover the letter in the other mail, so when the doors open on the ground floor I appear to Mr. Sanders to be absorbed in a deep (though unlikely) meditation on closeout golf cleats. I step out and he steps in.

I return outside and start walking. Dad's magazine and the other mail falls through my fingers, and I grip the letter tight, crumpling it a little, thinking that it cannot be there. Not for me. I'm in a daze. I take a left turn and a right turn, moving absently, my mind possessed with a static turbulence, like boiling water.

I find myself standing outside of St. Mary's, my church. It's a long building with a humble steeple, stretching for half the block. I enter through the double doors. I dip my fingers in the baptismal font and cross myself, then proceed along the dark nave, structured in even rows of pews. The church is hung with somber banners, quotes about remembrance, mortality, repentance — the sober mist of Lent has begun already to descend here, though it doesn't start until next week. There are a few people inside, widely dispersed, all deep in prayer, heads bowed. No one notices me.

I slide into an empty pew, lay down my book bag, and hold the red letter before me. Hands shaking, I quietly tear it open and remove a single sheet of rose-colored paper and a rose-colored return envelope with the name HERCULE typed on it. The letter is only a few lines long, but for a moment I can't read it. My brain rejects the alphabet. I see shapes, but they are hieroglyphs — not even hieroglyphs: bugs. I focus my eyes with a great act of will, and run them over the words.

Dear Gabriela,
You've been chosen for departure. How about next Wednesday? That gives you a week. Save a dance for me.
— *Hercule*

There are tears on my cheeks, which leaked out without me noticing. I dry my eyes on my sleeve, then stand and pull my book bag over my shoulder. I exit the church and head home.

breaking the news

The Rivera living room, by my mom's decree, is spare and well-kept, representative of what she does for a living (interior design consultation for Lockton's Department Store). There's a blue vinyl couch, a long, narrow coffee table, and two bentwood chairs. A small stand holds the telephone and telephone directory.

The rest of the place is cluttered with Dad's stuff, which, though various, is invariable in its oldness. The dining room table, visible from the entryway as I open the front door, is piled with (among other things) a yellowed folio of newspapers, the PQR volume of an out-of-print genealogical encyclopedia, and a brick of cellophane-sealed greeting cards tied with a faded vellum bow. On the floor adjacent there's a group of office boxes labeled DEACC JAN, DEACC FEB, and DEACC MAR. Dad works for the Municipal Archives, and he loves his work, often rescuing things that the archives is getting rid of.

Mom and Dad are in the living room as I enter. Dad is standing, holding the telephone receiver to his ear. He's wearing his work clothes: brown pants and a brown suit jacket on top of a blue shirt and a wide black tie, which curves over his ample belly. His long, curly hair is held in a gray-streaked ponytail. He looks angry, and this set of his features only increases when he sees me. He says roughly into the phone, "Never mind, she just walked in." He hangs up, glaring.

Mom is sitting on the couch, legs crossed, one pale arm slung casually over the back. She's less prone to worry than Dad, though they keep a united front when it comes to my whereabouts. She looks coolly at me and pushes a long strand of blond hair behind one ear, as if readying that ear to receive the explanation for my lateness.

For a second, I'm not sure what I'm going to do. I open my mouth hesitantly, and then, with the force of a ruptured water main, I cry out. I fall to the floor, my book bag opens, and books and papers fan out across the rug.

Dad rushes to me. He kneels and places his hands on my shuddering back, his anger vanished in an instant. Mom is right behind him.

"Gabriela . . . ?" she says.

I try to collect my wits, but I can't. Still sobbing, I hold out the letter.

Dad sits heavily next to me on the floor when he sees it. He opens the rose-colored page. After a long pause, he says, *"Oh."* His tone is the one he uses for when someone points out something he's overlooked, like *"Oh,* I didn't know we had an unopened jar of red pepper flakes in the pantry." After another pause he says, "This is some kind of . . ." The last word here would be *joke,* but he knows it's not a joke. He begins again: "There must be a . . ." He stops before saying *mistake.*

Slowly, silently, we move from the floor to the couch. My mom's shoulders start to shake. She says, "Hm, hm, hm," crying and shrugging.

"I want to keep going to school," I say. When kids like myself are chosen for departure, they can decide if they want to continue their education or leave off. I'm surprised I have the presence of mind to discuss this right now.

"We'll get you a Pardon," says Mom, reading my thoughts. "Write and ask!" Her tone is a little angry, and I can't tell if it's anger at Hercule, my Death, for sending the letter or at me for receiving it.

"Demand one!" says Dad, wiping his nose on his sleeve.

"You can't *demand* a Pardon," says Mom.

"Well, you can't *ask* for one either," says Dad. They're both right: you can't demand, and you can't ask. There's only one way to get a Pardon. You've got to be tricky.

After a quiet dinner of canned soup, we end up watching TV in the living room. It's easier than talking about the only thing we have to talk about right now, but just barely. The news is bad. War is coming—the fact of the draft is enough to convince just about anyone, and speculation focuses not on *if*, but on *when*. Some think we could begin within months, such is the speed of mobilization. It seems awfully fast (and yet, I may be long gone by then).

Eventually I go to my room, assuring Mom and Dad that I'll come out if I need anything. I leave them sitting on opposite sides of the couch, still suffering the insubstantial anger with each other that they initiated with their sharp words over my Pardon. But I see Dad starting to move toward Mom as I exit. They need comfort right now more than they need to be correct.

I close my bedroom door and sit quietly at my desk. I kick off my sneakers. Normally on a night like this I'd be stressed about school. But I don't have to do homework anymore. I drag my gaze up to my wall calendar. I put a finger on today's date: Wednesday, March third. I examine the squares following, counting down silently to myself. *Six, five, four* . . . I land finally on next Wednesday. That box is labeled ASH WEDNESDAY, the beginning of Lent. My hand trembles.

I pry my eyes away, and they move on to the only other pieces of décor on my desk: two grainy, black-and-white portraits. I've had these for as long as I can remember. The photo on the left is of a young Latino man wearing a U.S. Army uniform. This is my grandfather Gonzalo. Sometimes when I'm under a lot of stress, looking at this photo calms me. Gonzalo has a sensitive, open expression, and I think he was probably a kind man. He has my father's slightly pocked dark skin, and there's a hint of a smile around his lips. The photo was taken shortly before he left for Africa. It's a very noble image. Gonzalo's eyes are looking ahead. He knows he's doing the right thing. I feel patriotic when I look at this picture. In fact, for years patriotism was the only feeling it evoked in me. I remember as a kid making up different stories about Gonzalo. Some of them, to think back on it, were kind of gruesome. One I remember, probably based on a movie, was Gonzalo saving his buddies by jumping on a hand grenade. I used to tell these stories to my grandmother, much to my parents' chagrin. But Abuela liked them. She would say, "Yes, that's Gonzalo," verifying that my tales caught the spirit of the man: risking life and limb to carry an injured soldier back from enemy lines, giving away his last meal to a refugee, fighting bravely on while others panicked and fled.

As I got older, and I kept looking at his picture on my desk, I started to notice something that I'd missed before — Gonzalo's eyes in this photo are aglow with a deep and subtle amusement. I see a similar twinkle in my dad's eyes sometimes, and in my own. It runs through all of us Riveras. Gonzalo thought it was a little funny to get this portrait taken, so reeking with nobility. Of course he had no idea that he'd disappear within two weeks of leaving for Tunisia, never to be heard from again. If he'd received a letter to that effect in advance, I wonder if his eyes would sparkle so.

The other photo on my desk is of an elegant white couple. They're dressed expensively, the woman with a jeweled necklace and the man with glinting diamond cuff links. They're in their thirties, both smiling, but their eyes don't sparkle like Gonzalo's. The man, who could be called dashing except for the cruel bent of his eyebrows, looks imperiously at the camera. The woman glances disinterestedly to one side. These are my mother's parents, the Mason-Hunts. I'm fascinated by this picture because I'm repelled by it. These two are still alive somewhere, as far as I know. I've never met them. They objected to Mom's marriage to Dad and disowned her. I guess they said all kinds of things about Dad's "values" and the "kind of people" he came from—the regular euphemisms for being brown.

It's weird to think that I'm the physical embodiment of an idea these two found so distasteful. The very person I am—my hair, my skin, my eyes. Somewhere, wherever they are, the Mason-Hunts wish they could have prevented my birth. I guess they'll probably never know about my Death Letter. If they did, though, I wonder—would they be pleased? Would they feel somehow vindicated?

The clear difference between these photos often helps me orient myself, and with a last look at the nobility and humor of

Gonzalo's eyes, I pull a blank sheet from my desk drawer. At the top I write "Wrap-Up List."

Every kid learns about Wrap-Up Lists in school: a person's attempt to organize what they want to finish before their time runs out. The list is sent to the attending Death, who renders Influence — which is sometimes supernatural and other times merely advisory.

The image suggested by the term *Wrap-Up List* implies that you have things to wrap — your lifetime of pursuits and accomplishments. But I'm barely sixteen. I'm still more or less in my original container. Nonetheless, I start writing out some ideas. I throw them onto the page quickly, without much thought. "Millionaire," I scrawl. "Famous. First kiss." As these appear, they produce an effect I hadn't anticipated. I feel . . . even worse. The list is stupid. Writing "First kiss" imparts a swift and awful sense of hopelessness, and when I follow it with "Make the cheer squad," I drop the pen to the desktop.

At the very moment I'm confronted with this painful missive from my own interior, I'm rescued by a knock on my bedroom door.

"Come in!" I say, relieved.

Dad enters, his big shoulders bulking through. "Sorry to disturb you, Gabby," he says, frowning as he remembers that I've forbidden him to call me that (since I started high school last year).

"It's okay, Dad."

"I just phoned St. Mary's." (He says the name of our church like you'd say *S'Mores:* S'Mary's.) "I talked to Father Ernesto. He's there if you'd like to see him."

"Now?" I say.

"Yes."

I stand, folding my poor list and sliding it into my pocket. "Let's go," I say.

It's typical to consult with a priest when something important happens — just to get some perspective. Maybe a non-Catholic would go to a counselor, or a psychotherapist. My family goes to Father Ernesto. I don't know how much I believe in the doctrines of my religion — I'm neither here nor there on a lot of it, and if my mood was a little different at present I'd probably be angry at Dad for his presumption. But because I'm scared, I'm glad.

Dad's car is a big old station wagon with wood paneling. It's dusty and worn, and the back seats and hatchback trunk are filled to the ceiling with boxes — stuff Dad has rescued from the Municipal Archives. He can't bring himself to get rid of any of it, but Mom won't allow it in the apartment either.

We don't really need to drive to St. Mary's — it's only a few blocks away — but I don't mind. I crack my window as the car picks up speed and the cool springtime air rushes in. I'm hoping for the scent of the flowers I smelled earlier, but no luck.

Shortly, we pull into the parking lot between the church

and the rectory. The church is long, low, and obscure at night, its steeple grazed by two bluish lights shining from the roof. The rectory is an inviting building next door, an old two-story farmhouse with a lit gravel walk to the front porch. Dad rings the bell, which plays the opening bars of "Let All Mortal Flesh Keep Silence." An instant later, the door opens.

"Welcome, Riveras! Please come in," says Father Ernesto, his accent thick, his voice friendly. He's a large man who moves with a slow dignity that always has impressed me (even after I learned that it's the result of knee problems). He's clean-shaven, with an aged, rectangular face capable of expressing everything from gleeful solicitousness to mortal strictness. He's wearing his priest's collar and a dark suit, obviously expecting our visit. We follow him slowly past the stairwell that ascends to his and Father Salerno's apartments, and we enter a sitting room where the fireplace burns low, with three chairs gathered before it.

We sit. The fire crackles.

"Gabriela," says Father, "I'm glad you've come on this difficult night. I would like to know what I can do, personally, for you. You know that your family is very special to me."

I do know this. Father Ernesto is the priest who married Gonzalo and Abuela. He also married my parents, and oversaw Mom's conversion to the church. He baptized and confirmed me. His face is a monument, and his words a benevolent force.

"I was working on my Wrap-Up List," I say.

"I'm glad," says Father Ernesto. "It's a blessing."

"I don't know if I think so," I say. (When I was in Confirmation classes I was the one kid who ever challenged Father Ernesto, and he liked me for it. It's because of that, in fact, that I have any faith at all—Father was a good example to me that religion didn't have to replace thoughtfulness.)

"All things made by God can be blessings," he says now, an easy parry. "Of course it isn't always so simple," he adds.

"Yeah, it's just . . ." I say. I fall silent, embarrassed.

Father turns to my dad. "Señor Rivera," he says, "could Gabriela and I have a moment alone?" Without a word, Dad stands and exits smoothly, closing the front door behind him as he steps out onto the porch.

I unfold in my chair enough to pull my Wrap-Up List out of my jeans pocket. I grit my teeth, and through that reluctant gate recite: "Millionaire. Famous. First kiss." The words squeak through. Fortunately, Father Ernesto stops me before I have to say "Make the cheer squad."

"Gabriela," he says, "I see you making an unhappy expression."

"Yeah," I sigh.

"Do you remember when in Confirmation class we discussed the guiding statement St. Mary's had chosen?"

"'Spirit of Service,'" I say. It was a big deal two years ago when the church chose that motto. And kids had made fun of it because it's also the slogan of a nearby gas station. It seemed emblematic of how out of touch the church was. But right now it doesn't seem funny.

"And the verse we chose, to remind us?"

"'Each of you should use whatever gift you have received to serve others,'" I quote.

"Perhaps it's worth considering, as you create your list," says Father Ernesto.

"You're right, Father," I say.

"I'll add one thing more, also, Gabriela. I know your family holds your grandfather in high esteem, and rightly so. Think of his sacrifice, too — that he gave his own life to ensure the safety of his family, his descendants." It's funny that I was just looking at Gonzalo's picture but somehow needed this pointed out to me.

Dad and I have a quiet drive back home. He doesn't ask me what Father Ernesto said to me, and I don't volunteer. It's always been so. Dad has a respect for the Church that borders on fear. Tonight, the silence between us isn't awkward — I'm too occupied with my own thoughts. I'm imagining better items for my list. I'm thinking about *Heal the Sick* and also *Money for Church Expansion* (because I know St. Mary's wants to remodel the sanctuary). I consider *Win the War*.

Back home, Mom has made some dessert — strawberries and cream — but I don't want any. I've got work to do. I return to my room, leaving my parents figuring out if they're still mad at each other, I expect — if they can even remember what they were arguing about before. (I've learned that this isn't a necessary component of their disagreements. They have great faith in their annoyance even when they can't recall its origin.)

I close my bedroom door, sit at my desk, and open my list before me. I cross out every item I'd previously written. I'm feeling better. Before I begin again, though, I take another look at Gonzalo's portrait, thinking about what Father Ernesto said. It's true, my grandfather made a heroic decision. I look into his noble, distant gaze . . .

But there is that gleam in his eyes. That tricky amusement, which has nothing to do with nobility. I don't know what it is, but it makes me want to smile. "Spirit of Service," I say to Gonzalo, and then: "Free Wash and Wax with Every Oil Change!"

At that moment, a waft of spring air blows through my window, carrying with it that scent — the bracing and rich smell of flowers that sends my heart fluttering hopefully.

Now, I think, glancing over the crossed-out items of my original list. One item sticks out: First kiss, I had written. I write it again now, at the top of my new list, but a little different:

1. First Kiss — for Iris

The words appear as by divine inspiration. I glance at Gonzalo. His eyes sparkle. He's laughing. *Spirit of Service!*

I imagine my Death, Hercule, getting my Wrap-Up List and seeing this item. I smile wider. I move my pen to the next line down and write: "2. First Kiss — for Raahi." This is followed quickly by "3. First Kiss — for Sarena." (She could probably use one, too, since I'm handing them out.)

I let out an unexpected snort, which I do sometimes by accident when something's funnier than I thought it'd be. I clap a hand over my mouth. I wonder if Father Ernesto would approve . . .

Then I write, "4. First kiss — for me, from Sylvester." I feel I've earned it, after generously supplying these other kisses. Who would begrudge me?

I round out the list with a final item. This appears on almost every Wrap-Up List that has ever been created. I pen it quickly, although it's the most important thing on the whole piece of paper:

5. *Pardon*

A Pardon means, "You can go back home, Gabriela, and live the rest of your life as if none of this ever happened." Deaths never give these out willingly, though. Granting a Pardon is some kind of misfortune for them. If a Death gives a Pardon, that Death disappears — for fifty years at least, sometimes forever.

But you can manage it if you're smart. Every Death has

what's called a Noble Weakness. This is a good deed that, if you accomplish it, forces them to let you go. They conceal this Noble Weakness with great care, and guessing it is difficult because it could be almost anything. If you ask for a Pardon on your Wrap-Up List, your Death will give you a Hint. Solve the Hint and accomplish the correct Deed, and you'll be Pardoned.

It almost never happens.

I look over my list. I've heard of people with hundreds of items, but it's said that Deaths don't like long lists. This is enough, anyway, and I'm still amused about Hercule reading it. Having to exert his precious Influence for the sake of a bunch of kisses!

1. First Kiss — for Iris
2. First Kiss — for Raahi
3. First Kiss — for Sarena
4. First Kiss — for me, from Sylvester
5. Pardon

I spare another glance at Gonzalo, whose eyes glint approvingly. The Mason-Hunts, for their part, seem to neither approve nor disapprove. As usual, I can't convince myself that they'd care what I do. They look right through me.

I jot a copy of the list for myself and seal the original into Hercule's rose return envelope. I leave the apartment quietly, walk the hall, and step into the elevator. As I descend, I experience an unexpected memory from last year. I don't know why it hits me at this moment, but my brain is very insistent.

It's the memory of me entering Central High for the first time, freshman year. I was looking for my homeroom, thinking I'd never find my way—not because I was lost but because it seemed like there was nowhere to get to. The place was full of people, but to me it felt lonesome, alien—purposeless. I was caught totally off-guard by this.

My junior high had been a small school full of kids from St. Mary's, but Central High wasn't where my onetime Sunday school cohorts ended up. Due to district dividing lines, I became a Central High Cougar instead of a South High Jaguar. Every face I saw that morning was unknown to me.

My debut report card that year was almost straight Fs. I was put on academic probation and sent to Ms. Lime, the school's most pear-shaped English instructor (since hers was the only class I was passing). At our first meeting, Ms. Lime asked me, "What are your goals, Gabriela?"

I said I didn't have any. It was true—with no place to be, and no place to go, how could I have goals? "I feel like I'm in limbo," I said. Ms. Lime took the term in the popular sense, not being Catholic, but I intended its ecclesiastical meaning—the place, neither heaven nor hell, where unbaptized babies go. Limbo is not like purgatory. In purgatory, you have a purpose—to cleanse your soul so you can get to heaven.

Limbo is a permanent state, with neither the risk of damnation nor the possibility of salvation. A tractionless finale.

Ms. Lime, despite her limited acquaintance with the doctrine, offered me some good advice. "You need goals," she said. We laid out a sheet, and she wrote "Gabriela's Goals" at the top. I remember staring at the name: Gabriela. I'd always been Gabby before, but now I found myself transformed. I saw the first possibility of my situation — that I was on the verge of becoming someone new.

It wasn't easy at first. "Gabriela's Goals" seemed empty, fake, like a paper house that would never keep out the weather. But I applied myself, and the goals Ms. Lime and I placed on that sheet solidified. My new name became my real name. Over the course of the next several months, I made some friends and improved my grades (two of my goals). I worked my way off of academic probation. At my last meeting with Ms. Lime, she told me she was proud of me. "You had a shock this year," she said. "Life was bigger and colder than you thought. But you've made your direction. You're on your way."

Now, as the reminiscence ends, I feel the cold blow back in as strongly as I've ever felt it. I see my little life amid a void — weightless, directionless, infinite. All victories in such a kingdom are won in vain. All castles are paper.

I drop my letter into the rigid mouth of the outgoing mail slot, and the awful chill passes through me as if I were nothing.

six days before
departure day

the announcement

The following morning, I arrive in Ms. Lime's English class as the opening bell sounds. Behind me is Wendy Overton, who leans toward me anxiously as I sit and hisses, *"Pop quiz!"*

Wendy is one of those kids who seem able to do almost anything. She's a short, slightly stocky girl, who some days looks almost like a guy — but when she comes to school dressed in her cheer uniform (like today), she's the picture of cuteness. She enjoys the distinction of being the only member of the cheer squad both small enough to get thrown into the air *and* strong enough to throw other cheerleaders into the air (both a *flyer* and a *base*, in parlance). Additionally, she's the only cheerleader who's also in the marching band — she plays flute. But every superhuman creature has a weakness, and Wendy's is English. I often let her cheat off of my quizzes, because I like her—even though I'm also a little jealous of her (I tried out for cheer squad last year and didn't make it). This morning, though, I don't respond to her at all. I just stare straight ahead.

Iris enters. "Hi, Wendy, how's it going?" she says, pausing behind me.

"Pop quiz," says Wendy, very focused.

Iris sits next to me and lays a hand on my desk to get my attention. She wants to tell me what happened yesterday with the Singing Man. When I don't look over at her, she says, "Gabriela? You okay?"

The intercom at the front of the room crackles to life, and Principal Kreisler's nasal voice sounds through the old speaker. "Hello, Cougars. It's Thursday, March fourth. Hamburgers and tater tots. Put Sunday night's game on your calendar, playoff against the South High Jaguars, seven p.m. (Go Cougs), and please attend the varsity fundraiser in the parking lot after school today—dunk tank with starting receiver Sylvester Hale. Lastly, on a sad note, Gabriela Rivera has been selected for departure. Please offer your condolences." The intercom clicks off.

The whole class turns to look at me with a collective gasp of disbelief. I knew this was coming—I had Mom call it in, thinking I'd get it over all at once.

"Gabriela!" Ms. Lime exclaims, shocked.

Iris is standing next to me—she has jumped out of her chair.

Ms. Lime delays the pop quiz and initiates a peer discussion session on the reading, during which some kids approach me as Principal Kreisler recommended, and offer condolences.

I turn to Iris. "Want to skip?" I ask.

Everyone's eyes are on me as we go.

We walk toward the Marking Street Café, which is Iris's favorite coffee shop. I've never liked it. It's where the Deaths usually go to get coffee, and Iris has always been fascinated with them. She never passes up a chance to see one or two.

When we arrive there's a line of middle-aged business-people waiting to place orders, and one Death among them, a good three feet taller than everyone else. His head nearly brushes the ceiling. His straight gray hair floats in broad curves around his shoulders, and his silvery sharkskin suit glimmers. Iris leans toward me and whispers, "Greeley." I'm sure she doesn't know them all, but she knows a lot of them. Greeley orders coffee and disappears out the door, aquatic and slow, while we're still in line.

Iris and I get a pot of black tea to share and find a table by the window. Once we're seated, she says, "Gabriela, what the *hell?*" She slaps the tabletop with one hand. "Is this for *real?*"

I produce Hercule's letter and pass it to her.

"Oh, I can't *believe* it," she says.

As she reads, I pour us each a cup of tea. "Have you ever heard of Hercule?" I ask.

"No. This letter is awful, by the way — what an ass! 'Save a dance for me.'" I know what her next question will be. Before she asks, I produce the copy I made of my Wrap-Up List. I hesitate for a moment out of embarrassment, but finally hand it over. She's my best friend, after all.

She looks it over soberly, and her expression changes from deep concern to what I might call scandalized admiration.

"*This?*" she says, shaking the list. "*This?*"

"Yeah," I say.

"You *mailed* this? To your *Death?*" She continues rattling the page.

"That's right," I say.

"Gabriela, I can't *believe* you!" Her eyes sparkle, and I can tell she's thrilled with it. She laughs. "I shouldn't be surprised!"

"What do you mean?" I say.

"Well, it's just . . . you're just . . ." She tries to find the words, but there is apparently no term for the thing I am. She lays the list the table and puts one red nail on the first item. "So, you think I need a first kiss?"

"Um, maybe?"

"All right, I probably do," she says, obviously touched to find herself on the page.

Then we're interrupted by voices: "Gabriela! *Gabriela!*" Sarena and Raahi rush through the café door, past the line, to our table.

"The announcement — " says Sarena.

"We heard — " says Raahi, close behind.

"*Is it true?*" they say in unison.

My expression tells the tale.

Sarena says, "I can't believe it! Did you get a date?"

"Next Wednesday," I say.

"*A week?*" says Raahi.

"This . . . this is just *stupid!*" says Sarena. She brushes her braids back with an annoyed flick of her wrist. They both seem angry, like my parents did last night. "You've got to get a *Pardon!*" she says.

"That's right," says Iris. "We have no time to lose."

Sarena and Raahi grab chairs and sit on either side of me, and we all look to Iris. She's been interested in this stuff since forever. She knows more about the Deaths, more about departure, more about getting Pardons, than just about anyone. "The first step is already complete," she says. "Gabriela sent her Wrap-Up List to Hercule. When we get his reply, we can start doing research."

"We have to find his Noble Weakness, right?" says Raahi.

"Right," says Iris. "And Gabriela has to accomplish it."

"And his weakness can be *anything?*" says Sarena.

Iris rolls her eyes. "Our schools are failing us," she laments. It's true we don't learn much about all of this at school, but it's understandable. Departures are only one percent of all fatalities, after all. "Hercule's Noble Weakness will be a significant act relating to *generosity*. It won't be small, like baking someone a birthday cake. It will require a lot of you, Gabriela."

"Like jumping on a hand grenade," I say.

"Sort of," says Iris. "It could have to do with putting yourself in danger to save someone's life. But don't get yourself killed — you can't use a Pardon if you're dead."

"What if you never have an opportunity to save someone's life?" says Raahi.

"Well, you can promise to do it," says Iris.

"That counts?" says Sarena.

"Promises count if you really mean them," says Iris. "Deaths can tell the attitude of your heart, though — if you don't mean it, it won't work."

"I'd jump on a hand grenade to save your life, Iris," I say.

"But would you *really*, Gabriela? Think it over."

"I really would," I say. "You're my best friend! Nothing's going to come along to change that."

Iris narrows her eyes, and there's something in her gaze — an intensity that's so focused it makes me a little uncomfortable, and I look away. Iris continues. "The Noble Weakness could relate to almost anything. Maybe giving your time — nursing a sick person, for instance. Or giving up your space — inviting someone to live with you. It could even be giving up possessions. Some are very specific, and some are more general. There's no telling. We'll have to wait for the Hint."

After spending a few hours in further speculation and several cups of coffee, we return to school in the afternoon to watch a little of the dunk tank fundraiser for the football team. The spectacle is in full swing when we arrive. Students swarm around the tank, chatting in groups, watching, some lined up to take a shot. I notice Sylvester Hale's dad standing near the edge of the crowd, talking with one of the assistant coaches. Mr. Hale is a big booster for the football team, and he's easy to spot not only because of his gleaming, bald head, but because he has only one arm. The other he lost, I gather, in the military, though I don't know the story of it. I've always steered clear of the man. He gets really angry sometimes, and I even saw him forcibly removed from a football game once after he stormed onto the field in a rage. At the moment, he's not really doing anything. Just chatting with people.

Finally my eyes land on Sylvester, the star of the event, poised over the water on his collapsible seat. He's slouched, casual, hands on his knees. No one has dunked him yet. His hair is rakish, and his skin curves generously over his fit frame. Every bend of him transfixes my eye. I wonder how many girls here are dreaming of him right now.

The transparent sides of the dunk tank are adorned with amusing imagery, intended, I suppose, to make the dunking process more fun. At the top of the tank, painted clouds and birds, and a smiling sun wearing sunglasses. Below the water line, a school of grinning fish, a diminutive underwater castle, and some underwater houses that resemble a regular neighborhood. I'd think they would have put a bunch of merpeople down there, or King Triton and his servants, but there's no one. The castle and houses look kind of lonely. It's as if Sylvester's about to be dumped into a ghost town.

"Wendy's next," Sarena observes. "She'll dunk him for sure." Raahi is standing next to Sarena, and I notice how much taller he is than her—maybe a foot taller. I noticed that yesterday, too, I recall, when they were walking up the hill together after school, Raahi carrying Sarena's trumpet. That seems like a thousand years ago.

"Go-o!" shouts Iris. She's not generally interested in football, but she appears enthusiastic for Wendy to hit that bull's-eye.

Coach Frank hands Wendy three blue and green beanbags stenciled with the Cougars logo. Wendy looks around at her audience. Everyone knows and respects her potential for doing just about anything (except pass English). Sylvester, a little nervous, lets fly a sudden insult: "You throw like a girl!" he says, though she has not yet thrown anything. His voice, brassy and confident, causes some good-natured laughter in the crowd.

Wendy turns to Coach Frank. She hands two of the three beanbags back to him, leaving her with only one. A hush falls over us all as she steps to the chalk line on the ground. She eyes the target. Then she carefully pitches her single beanbag underhand—throwing like a girl! It arcs gracefully straight to the target and strikes it dead-on. Sylvester's seat flops, and he plunges into the water with a manly bellow. The crowd goes wild.

"She's so cool!" says Sarena.

"Yeah," says Iris, as I attentively watch Sylvester climb, dripping, from the plunge.

After fielding more heartfelt condolences from classmates and friends both dear and distant, I lead Iris, Sarena, and Raahi back to the apartment to see if the mail has arrived. We enter the lobby and approach the wall of mailboxes. I nervously open 305's cubby, which sings on its old hinges, and pull forth the mail. Among the junk and bills there's a red envelope, blank but for my name.

We all stare at it. I say, "Um, is anyone hungry?" I slip the envelope into my jacket pocket. "Do you guys want to come up?"

Mom and Dad are both home. "Hello, honey," says Mom casually, with a tone in her voice that makes it obvious she and Dad have been waiting for me. Furthermore, I think that neither of them went to work today. They've both been home, worrying, and they're still radiating the anger and grief they expressed last night.

Dad says to my friends, "Iris, Sarena, Raahi, it's nice to see you." My parents have hosted these three plenty of times during living room study sessions, field trips, et cetera. We've all watched scary movies together and eaten birthday cake. They've all attended the weekly Rivera Family Tuesday Night Dinner.

"Did you pick up the mail, Gabriela?" Mom asks.

I place the stack on the coffee table. "Hercule wrote back, but I haven't opened it yet," I say. Fortunately, everyone is understanding about my reluctance.

While my parents assemble chicken tacos, my friends and I clear the dining room table, which is covered with some of Dad's recent acquisitions from the archives. There's a blue box labeled BUREAU OF TOURISM (which Raahi takes to the hall closet and places atop three other boxes similarly labeled), a stack of old record sleeves tied into a block with twine (which Sarena stashes in the corner next to a historic set of regional memoirs), and a metal tin that opens to reveal some unused Yosemite-themed postcards (which I put on the desk in Dad's study). We finish just as my parents enter with tacos and bowls of reheated pozole. Our plates are massive antique disks painted with peacocks, which belonged to Mom's parents, the Mason-Hunts.

"Let's pray," says Dad. We all fold our hands obediently. Dad is the leader of a prayer group at church and often says the closing prayer there. Unlike most people I've known who pray publicly, Dad is always brief. ("If Jesus was truly a man," he told me once, "then He can be bored.") "Dear Lord Jesus," he prays, "thank you for this food, and the knowledge to prepare it. Thank you for bringing Raahi, Sarena, and Iris here this evening as we try to understand your will and live in accordance with your wishes. Amen."

"Amen," I echo.

. . .

After dinner, Raahi and Sarena both have to go. Sarena has sound check with the Washington Fifteen at the Caballero, and Raahi told his mom he'd be home—she's anxious after him, since he's leaving for basic training early next Tuesday. (Raahi's mom, Charvi, is an amazing woman. She's a senior officer for an American corporation with business interests in India. She's extremely tough, independent, intelligent, and according to Raahi, worried about him and wanting him home for dinner.)

Iris and I clear the table. I see Dad about to give me a reprieve from my chores, but he stops himself. I imagine him thinking, "Maybe Gabriela should do her chores, to enjoy the normality of them." I feel bad. It's hard for me, sure, to have found out I have only a handful of days left, but it may be harder in some ways for my parents. They've known me longer than I have.

While I wash the dishes and enjoy the normality, Iris calls her parents to tell them she's going to spend the night here. She hands me the phone so I can talk to her dad, which is awkward, but Mr. Van Voorhees just wants me to know how sorry he is to hear the news. He passes the phone to Mrs. Van Voorhees, and she says the same.

Then, finally, Iris and I go to my room. To look at the letter my Death has sent me.

hints

Deaths are tricksters. They never give a straight answer about anything. Instead of sending answers, Deaths send Hints.

I sit at my desk, and Iris settles onto the edge of my bed, feet dangling. She kicks off her shoes as I tear open the letter, and shoes and envelope fall to the carpet. I unfold the page. There's no "Dear Gabriela" this time—it's just my original handwritten list, with Hercule's annotations scribbled below.

1. First Kiss—for Iris
—A cavalier request, Gabriela.
2. First Kiss—for Raahi
—See #1.
3. First Kiss—for Sarena
—See #1.

4. First Kiss — for me, from Sylvester
— A bedroom for books.
— The Fields.
5. Pardon
— Always about to disappear.

"Are these *Hints?*" I say. They don't look like Hints.

"They are," says Iris.

Numbers 1, 2, and 3 seem like a chastisement. Maybe I *was* being cavalier. I don't know. It's not every day you find out you've got a week to live. "'A bedroom for books,'" I muse. "Shelf? Bookcase?" I feel Iris's eyes boring into me, and I meet her gaze. "What?" I say.

"Do you feel it?" she asks.

"Feel what?"

"The *Influence,*" she says. "As soon as you opened this, Hercule started helping you."

"I don't feel anything," I say. I focus on the Hints, and suddenly the solution to the first line of Number 4 jumps out, like a fish leaping into a boat. "Got it!" I say, surprised.

"What? Which one?"

"'A bedroom for books'! Where are all of our books right now?" I say.

"In our bags?"

"Not a bag — a *room*. *Lockers*. Our lockers at school."

"Maybe there's something in your locker," says Iris.

"A love note?" I laugh. It's improbable, but now that I have the magical aid of my Death, who knows? "Funny to think," I say. "Normally I go to my locker every day, but if this Hint hadn't appeared . . ."

"You might never have gone back there, after getting your Death Letter," says Iris.

After this, we divvy my desk into halves so Iris can do homework while I keep figuring. The minutes pass, and my early success fades. The other Hints prove impenetrable. Next to me, Iris scrawls formulas for her chemistry class, but she keeps peeking at my list, obviously more interested in helping me than in calculating molecular weights.

Eventually, our energies flag. It's gotten late. I lend Iris a pair of flannel pajamas, and while she puts them on, I go say good night to Mom and Dad in the living room. I bring my Wrap-Up List with me, thinking I'll show them Hercule's Hints, but by the time I've reached the couch where they're sitting together watching TV, I've changed my mind. I'm not sure why. I've folded the list in half and am holding it by my side, nearly out of sight. Maybe I'm embarrassed that I'm going to depart in the first place. I'm not sure.

"Good night," I say, even as their twin gazes flick back and forth between my face and the folded list.

"The Hints," says Dad, gesturing at the paper. "Could we see them, Gabby?"

"Gabriela," says Mom, "maybe we can help."

"Er, not right now, okay?" I say. I crumple the folded sheet, trying to wish it into a pocket I don't have.

"Then *when?*" says Dad.

"Maybe tomorrow . . ." I say.

"Maybe?" Dad echoes. "Gabriela, your mother and I want to help you."

I really wish I had a pocket. Why don't pajamas have pockets? The list seems to be getting bigger, and maybe glowing, and beeping.

Then, out of nowhere, Dad's hand flicks out — he grabs it from me.

My eyes grow large with surprise. Dad is not that kind of guy. He's someone who discusses; who talks it out with you; who, maybe, issues ultimatums. He would never —

But he has. Before he can even glance at the sheet, my own hand leaps. I grab the list back from him, and an angry stalemate of stern glares follows.

"Gabriela!" says Mom, loudly, and her tone speaks volumes. It says, *I am going to severely chastise your father after you leave the room because that was uncalled for. However, the fault is partly yours, and you should apologize now so we don't all go to bed angry.*

I'm flushed and outraged, but she's right. "I'm sorry, Dad," I say. "But — you have to respect me."

Dad glowers.

"We both want to help, Gabriela," says Mom. "But we'll wait until you decide it's time."

"Good night," I say.

"Good night," says Mom.

"Good night, Gabriela," says Dad. "I'm sorry."

"Let's forget it," I say. I pause, and then smile. "That's *final*," I add. Saying "That's final" to Dad is kind of a joke. He says it sometimes when he doesn't want to entertain further discussion.

He blanches when I say it now, but then sees the humor in it. He snorts suddenly, just like I do when something strikes me funny. "Okay," he says. "Don't forget your rosary," he adds.

"I won't."

"What would you like for breakfast tomorrow?"

"Maybe . . . chicken fajitas?"

"No maybes," says Dad. "Chicken fajitas is *final*."

As I retreat down the hall, I hear Mom's intense and quiet voice as she begins to tell Dad off. I wish she wouldn't, even though he deserves it. I just don't want anyone arguing right now.

Back in my room, I find Iris changed into her borrowed PJs.

"I have to say my rosary really quick," I tell her, going to my desk.

She's seen me do it plenty of times. As she gets under the covers, I take out my set of plastic beads. I place the cross between thumb and forefinger and begin, silently — the Apostles' Creed, the Our Father, a handful of Hail Marys and the Doxology get me past the introductory block to the first Mystery. On Thursdays I usually pray the Luminous Mysteries. The first is the baptism of Christ, when the heavens open and the Spirit of God descends like a dove. It's normally a comforting image — up there in heaven, something like a dove — but tonight I imagine old pigeons waddling in gutters, bobbing heads, rigid pinkish toes, twitchy red-rimmed eyes. I look down at the plastic loop in my lap. The cross looks like a bird foot.

I return the rosary to my desk, flip off the lights, and climb into bed next to Iris. You know how you can tell, in the darkness, if someone's eyes are open? I've always found that strange.

"That was fast," says Iris.

"I couldn't finish," I say.

There's a rustling under the covers, and Iris's hand finds mine. "We'll figure this out, Gabriela," she says. "We'll start research tomorrow. We can go to the archives after school."

"Once we find out Hercule's Noble Weakness, then what?"

"Then you'll perform it, or sincerely promise to. Finally, in the Fields, right before you cross under the Oaks, you tell Hercule that you did it. He'll Pardon you, and you'll walk back home."

"Naked," I say.

"Right," says Iris. (That's a well-known thing about people who get Pardons—it's as if they came so close to their end that they lost even their clothes.) "Don't worry, though," she adds. "I'll bring an extra dress and meet you on the way back. I don't want you to be cold."

The covers rustle again. Iris turns toward me and puts her arms around me. We're both shivering.

five days before
departure day

bedroom for books

The next morning is Friday. Mom, Dad, Iris, and I eat a brief, early breakfast of chicken fajitas. It looks like Mom and Dad are both planning to go to work today. Dad's in his brown suit, and Mom is wearing her slacks. We eat quietly, and neither they nor I bring up Hercule's Hints. I mention to Dad that Iris and I will stop by the archives after school, and I can tell he's glad.

Iris and I are both curious what I'll find in my locker today, but she heads to Ms. Lime's room once we arrive at school, to give me a little privacy. I walk the busy hall, lined with uniform gray doors. I reach mine, twirl in the combination, and find my books within, looking well-rested.

A scrap of paper washes out and slips to the ground. Such is the rush before first period that three passersby step on it before I can pick it up. When I finally get it in hand, I see that it's a note.

meet me at the 45th street canal. noon saturday — sylvester

My eyes widen. It's the height of unlikelihood, and I begin to understand what Iris was talking about last night when she spoke of the Influence. My mind fills with scenarios of Sylvester confessing the most improbable of crushes on me. Even the Hint that led me here, "A bedroom for books," brims with romance.

Minutes later, I take my regular seat in Ms. Lime's class between Iris and the window. Normally Wendy is behind me, but she's been unexpectedly displaced this morning by Raahi and Sarena. Raahi reaches forward and puts his hand on my shoulder.

"Hi," he says.

"Good morning!" I reply, startled to find them skipping their own classes for the sole purpose of hanging out with me here.

The bell rings, and I look to the front of the room to find that Ms. Lime is not up there. Instead, there's a soldier. He's dressed in fatigues, standing at parade rest, soberly surveying the room.

"Everyone," says Ms. Lime from her desk by the far wall, "the military is on campus today to inform us about the draft. It shouldn't take long." She turns to the soldier. "Go ahead,

Sergeant Mistletoe." The sergeant's name catches the class, and me, by surprise. I glance around. Everyone's trying to figure out if it's some kind of joke. Milo Stathopoulos, a huge linebacker on the football team, mouths the word to himself slowly (*Mis-el-tow?*), a confounded expression on his face.

But the sergeant's name tag corroborates Ms. Lime's assertion. I think, *Mistletoe! First kiss!* I turn in my seat and spot Sylvester at the back of the room, sitting with some of his buddies. He doesn't seem to notice me, though, and my excitement fades — it's silly to assume that everything that happens to me now will be the result of Hercule's Influence. The sergeant has no doubt been named Mistletoe since he was born.

"*Selective Service* is the preferred term, ma'am," says the sergeant to Ms. Lime. Then he addresses the class. "I'll make this brief, everyone," he says. His voice shakes a bit, and there's a tiny gleam of sweat at his temple. The sergeant is nervous. I wonder how old he is. His uniform is a little misleading. I think he might be in his twenties — not much older than all of us, really.

"If you have received a letter from the government conscripting you for compulsory service," he says, "compliance is mandatory. You will be assigned a doctor and receive a physical examination. You will have two weeks to put your affairs in order before reporting for active duty. I expect some of you have . . ." He trails off and turns to Ms. Lime. "Are these sophomores?" he asks. "Mostly," she replies. He continues: "I expect some of you have friends who have received draft letters.

It is very important for you to encourage them to remember that the draft was ratified by your government and signed into law by the president."

Then a voice I didn't expect to hear is raised from the back of the room. It's Sylvester. "Is there any way to volunteer *before* you get drafted?" he asks. That's a strange question.

"U.S. citizens eighteen years or older can volunteer at the downtown recruiting office," says Mistletoe.

"My birthday's next week," says Sylvester. "Can I volunteer now, just so it's on record?"

"Hey, Sylvester," says Raahi, turning in his seat, "I'll give you my draft card if you give me your birthday." Some kids laugh at this.

"No, draft cards are not transferable," says Mistletoe.

"I *want* to volunteer," says Sylvester. These words could sound challenging — a blow aimed at Raahi's patriotism — but Sylvester's tone is too earnest. "If we look strong, maybe there won't be a war."

"No, there will be," says a new voice: Iris. "It's already begun," she says. "Gabriela is proof of it."

My face grows suddenly hot, and I'm thankful my complexion isn't prone to blushing. I'm mystified about what kind of point she's trying to make, as is the rest of the class. She continues:

"Departures are always one percent of all fatalities," she says. "So when they increase, it means deaths from other causes will also increase. And departures are up *five percent* in the last six months. Five percent! That's thousands — tens of thousands — above normal."

This gives the class pause, me included. It hadn't occurred to me that my situation was attributable to anything other than bad luck. The notion that I'm part of the measurable cost of an approaching war strikes me as profoundly as a slap in the face.

Mistletoe is looking right at me. "I'm sorry to hear this, young lady," he says. And his eyes seem sad, which surprises me. Just like with Gonzalo, I'm able only with special effort to see that there's a whole person beneath the uniform. But my surprise at realizing this pales in comparison to the surprise I see in Mistletoe's own face. Because, I realize with sudden clarity, he didn't expect to feel sad either. Uniforms aren't an illusion worked only on the audience — the soldier believes it, too. As Mistletoe and I share this moment, we're both instructed. He thought, perhaps for years and certainly when he got up this morning, that when he puts on the uniform, he takes off his feelings. When he puts on the soldier, he takes off the man.

They forget themselves, I think, amazed.

"Thank you for your time today, Sergeant," says Ms. Lime, breaking the spell. "I'm sure you have other classes to visit."

"Yes, ma'am," says Mistletoe. He salutes us, the expression on his face a mixture of relief and dismay. He strides quickly out.

the archives

It's sunny after school, with a slight chilly breeze. Iris and I catch the bus out to the Municipal Archives, about a thirty-minute ride south of downtown.

The archives building was once stately, I imagine: a stone façade with granite pillars and a grand staircase leading to a pair of twenty-foot-tall double doors trimmed in brass. In later years, it turned out this wasn't such a good design, so the city started remodeling it. A wood and metal wheelchair ramp was added, partly covering the stairs. They sealed the big doors and installed an energy-efficient set of revolving ones. The windows across the front received bright white vinyl frames. The original grand idea looked good, but it didn't work. Now it's a mess, but smarter.

Iris and I, inexperienced revolving door operators, make the mistake of both entering the same compartment, and we emerge into the lobby in a laughing tangle, to find my dad observing us from behind the front counter. "Welcome to the Municipal Archives!" he says, brushing his shoulders in mock officiousness.

"Hi, Dad," I say.

"Hello, Mr. Rivera," says Iris.

"I hope you two have an appointment . . . ?"

"Dad," I chide (there's a rule in the teenager handbook that one must never be amused by parental clowning). He steps from behind the counter, and we hug. "I laid a little groundwork for you," he says. "These are the cards we have for Hercule." He hands me a clipboard with a list of records locations attached. "Most are military," he says. "Hercule hasn't generated a new record for over fifty years." As he speaks, his levity drains.

"Thanks, Dad," I say.

"Iris knows the way down." He gestures across the room. Iris comes here frequently to do exactly this sort of research on various Deaths, so she leads us to the stairwell, which descends past three small landings. The natural light of the lobby diminishes as we enter the yellow murk of the basement's filament bulbs.

"When were you last down here?" I ask.

"Couple weeks ago," says Iris. "You?"

"Sixth-grade field trip," I say.

"Really? Even though your dad works here?"

"Yeah . . ." I say, thinking, *I'm a bad daughter!* I could have stopped by, just to say hi. Maybe I could have brought him cookies. Would it have been so hard?

We reach the bottom of the stairs and enter a low-ceilinged vestibule with dark veneered walls. I glance at the clipboard and at the labels on the doorways. Straight ahead is MH 2435–4658, a typed sign with a handwritten addendum on the side reading 6707, MB7–ML07. Below that, in blue, in a different handwriting, G2.

Iris sees my confusion and holds out a hand for the clipboard. I pass it to her. She sizes it up quickly and steps toward our first objective, M6819, passing through a doorway the sign above which does not include the range containing that record. "This one would have been moved," she explains.

We travel the downward-slanting hall, the air dusty and dry. A few of the hallway bulbs have burned out, leaving dark sections that obscure some of the black-and-white photographs decorating both walls. The subjects of the photos are young soldiers in posed portraits, their uniforms perfect, their eyes confident. Not long ago, I would have been filled with patriotism to see them there, looking so handsome and brave. Now I think immediately of Sergeant Mistletoe. They forget themselves. Or they were trying to, anyway. To be the image. I've imagined myself a soldier plenty of times. And in my more recent history, I donned the short blue skirt and white gloves for cheerleader tryouts. I remember looking at myself in the locker room mirror, straightening my collar, trying to embody the spirit and image of cheerleaderishness. Trying to suppress whatever in me didn't conform to that.

I see past the uniforms in these old photos without too much difficulty. In this one, of a pale, skinny teen with curly hair as thick as wool, it's easy. He's looking down. He's remembering his life at home, everything he's about to lose. Maybe he's replaying an argument with his parents, trying to win it. The next one is easy, too — a girl dressed in a nurse's uniform. She gazes directly at the camera with a sharp wit. She's trying to see a way out. None of these kids are soldiers. There's no such thing as a soldier.

My dad and aunt always talk in reverent tones about Grandfather Gonzalo. They respect him so deeply — but they hardly knew him. I wonder what all of our lives would be like now if Gonzalo had not gone to war. What if he'd stayed home with Abuela, and raised my aunt and dad? What if he was my living grandfather now, joining us for Tuesday Night Dinner every week?

When I reach the end of the hall, I look back along the line of photos, the overhead lights flaring off the glass covers and glazing the images. Frail, confused, struggling, funny, smart, beautiful young people. They put on their uniforms and imagined they'd return in triumph, heroes.

I rush to catch up to Iris in the next room.

I find her leaning over a drawer she's pulled from a large square card catalog. It seems like she's leafing through it, but as I near her I notice she's not really doing anything. She's just standing there, staring down. I get closer and see that her eyes are closed. Her fingers are gripping the drawer tightly. I take a sudden breath, startled — it's one of those moments when you see someone's in pain but you can't tell what's causing it. I've never seen her like this before.

"Are you okay, Iris?" I say, stopping my approach a few paces off.

"Sorry," she mutters, her eyes flicking open. My words seem to have broken her trance, and she begins flipping through the cards in the drawer. She brushes an imaginary speck from her cheek.

"What's wrong?" I say.

"Nothing."

"But it *is* something." I reach out and take her wrist, pulling her from the cards. Her mouth closes tightly, and then, suddenly, she's in tears. She lunges forward and throws her arms around me. For a second I think this is about my looming departure — she's sad that she might lose her best friend. And maybe that's part of it . . . but there's more, I can tell. I put my arms around her, and she sobs quietly, her body shaking. I rub her back, not sure what to do.

Eventually, the storm passes. Iris straightens. "Well," she says. She puts one hand on the table next to the card catalog and leans on it. Obviously, I expect her to explain. She looks ruefully down at her red nails, then off into the retreating lanes of shelved records that surround us. "Gabriela," she says, more tears hovering at the edge of each word as she continues: "it was sweet of you to put my first kiss on your Wrap-Up List."

"Oh, I wanted to," I say.

"But." Iris's mouth snaps shut. She takes her hand from the table and laces her fingers roughly, twisting them.

"Iris, *what is it?*" I say, feeling afraid with the sense of unknowing.

"Maybe you don't want this," she says.

"Tell me," I say.

She looks at me with an awful, desolate expression. And, though I don't know what's coming, I suddenly understand that Iris herself has been wearing some kind of uniform all the while I've known her. Perhaps she even forgot herself, if that's what she wanted — discarded herself in favor of something simpler. But somehow my Wrap-Up List has torn the veil. She's seen herself anew, and what's worse, she thinks this is the last moment of our friendship, because of what she's about to tell me. I suddenly flash back to that moment when I told her that I'd jump on a hand grenade for her. When she'd looked at me so seriously, and I'd looked away.

"That kiss," she says, her voice quivering. "It would have to be with a girl."

I open my mouth to respond before I've fully understood what she's just said. But when I do understand, no words emerge. Part of what leaves me speechless is that I never suspected it. In fact, I think I have never suspected this of anyone I've ever personally met. But as her words drop into me, I see the truth in a thousand recollections—her getting asked to freshman prom by so many guys and saying no to them all. Always finding fault with everyone who has a crush on her. I remember also the way she's always contriving small talk with Wendy. *Wendy.*

The other part of what leaves me speechless, though, is more shameful. I feel uncomfortable. I haven't ever known anyone like this. I think I didn't really believe in it. And *Iris,* of all people. She's so . . . so well-disguised.

"I . . . er . . ." says my jaw, abandoned by my brain.

"It's okay," says Iris. She returns to the card catalog and pulls a card out of it. "It doesn't matter." She says this with a heavy blankness, and I sense her retreating back inside herself.

Gabriela, I think, *you have got to do better than this.* I rally against the confounding invasion of surprise and shock. I reach out and again take Iris by the arm.

"It does matter," I say. I'm not thinking about what *it* is right now—I'm thinking only about my friend, her eyes red, standing miserably before me.

We stand frozen together, me with one hand on her arm, she looking down at my brown fingers on her pale skin. The room is silent. She's waiting to see if I reject her. And who knows if I could have? For a moment, I think I nearly did.

Now it's my turn to lunge clumsily forward. I throw my arms around her. *"I'm sorry!"* I blubber, apologizing for I'm not sure what—for something that almost happened.

We're both crying. And Iris likes girls. That fact has not yet begun to unfold. I feel it there, lodged deep, like a hard seed that doesn't yet know it's been planted.

"Why didn't you tell me before?" I say over her shoulder.

"I just . . ." says Iris, sniffling. "The stakes were high."

"Was it because I'm Catholic?" As I say the words, I think of my dad. He would not be pleased if he ever learned of this.

"Maybe," says Iris.

There's much more, but we've said enough for now. We fall silent, and step apart from each other, momentarily shy. Then Iris holds up the card she previously removed from the catalog. "I'm going to go get this," she says. She disappears into the shelves and a few moments later emerges holding an old manila file. *"Here,"* she says cheerfully. She lays it on the table and opens it.

It contains a single sheet of paper. "Hercule's last documented departure," she says. "This is a copy, not the original." She runs a red fingernail along the small lines of type.

Stops. Stares.

"Oh," she says.

"What?" I ask. She turns the page so I can see.

TRANSCRIPTION FROM OFFICIAL
DOCUMENTS
PROVIDED BY: TUNISIAN DEPARTURE
AUTHORITY
Attending Death: Hercule

Site: Tunisian Fields (Formerly Berber Fields of
Carthage), Olive Grove
Departing Person: Gonzalo Rivera. Citizenship:
    Mexico, residing USA
Departure Status: Pardoned. Trns. to —————

"Gonzalo Rivera?" I say. "But . . . ?" I look at Iris. "But . . . ?"

"I've never seen anything like this," she says, nervousness in her voice.

"Hercule couldn't have been . . ."

"He was your grandfather's attending Death," she says quietly.

"But Gonzalo didn't depart," I say. "He was killed in action."

"You never knew that for sure."

"Isn't there a thing about Deaths never visiting the same family twice?"

"Yes, there is a thing," said Iris. "Deaths usually steer clear of friends and relatives because they're worried people will find out their Noble Weakness and share the information." Then she points silently to the line that reads "Departure Status."

"*Pardoned,*" I say. "But that doesn't make sense either. If he was Pardoned, why didn't he come home?"

"The Pardon was transferred—that's what this means." She points to the words "Trns. to."

"Transferred?"

"Your grandfather gave it away."

"You can do that?" I say. "But . . . who got it? It's blank."

"The Tunisian authority never found out. It was during the war, so it's lucky this record exists at all. Even luckier that a copy got sent here."

"I can't believe my dad never found this," I say.

"He wouldn't have known unless he was looking for something about Hercule," says Iris. "None of these are cross-referenced. But Gabriela, the main thing is that there was a Pardon issued. And that means——"

"My grandfather discovered Hercule's Noble Weakness."

I hear footsteps in the hall, and my dad rounds the corner. "I had a minute free, so . . ." He squints at us in the low yellow light. He can tell something's up.

I take the folder from Iris and hold it out to him.

four days before
departure day

meet me at the canal

The discovery that Gonzalo departed with Hercule is hugely important for my family. Dad makes a photocopy of the record. He shows Mom as soon as she gets home, and then he goes to Aunt Ana's to tell her and her family. When he returns from that, his eyes are red from crying. Grandfather Gonzalo's disappearance has been a loose thread in our lives for as long as I can remember. Now that thread has been pulled, and the mystery is more convoluted than ever. Pardoned — how? Pardon transferred — to whom? What happened to Gonzalo out there in the Tunisian Fields when he took his final walk with Hercule?

Needless to say, I have trouble getting to sleep. In my room in the wee hours, I spend some time staring at Hercule's Hints, and some time staring at my picture of Gonzalo. I put my head down on my desk and close my eyes. I think about Iris.

Her confession has me ruminating over our friendship, wondering about things that have happened between us. Times we've slept in the same bed together. Times Iris has called me cute. A weird, panicked feeling grows. I do not want to be . . . but if I am . . . (but I don't think so) . . . ? And the Church, it goes without saying. Years of Bible study. Dad. I remember one time when he and I were out walking — we saw two men holding hands. He muttered, under his breath, a word I hadn't heard before: *maricas*. I didn't know it, but his tone was one I never forgot: disgust.

Iris said, "Maybe you don't want this." And at the moment, tossing in bed and worried — not just about her but about myself, about my own nature — I understand something that she knew better than I. In telling me, she gave me something. I don't know what it is yet. It's only just starting to grow.

I'm not sure when I doze off, but I awaken with a start, jerking my head from my desk and blurting, *"Whazat?"*

Morning sun streams through the windows. Its warmth on my back is what awakened me. I glance at my watch. Ten o'clock. I have a feeling there's . . . somewhere I'm supposed to be?

Then I remember: "meet me at the 45th street canal."

I don't have much time. I rush to the bathroom and look at the tired girl in the mirror, slumping under a mop of mussed hair. I attack my curls with a brush for a few minutes, reducing but not eliminating the thicket. I apply eyeliner and mascara, then pull on my favorite jeans and a long-sleeved shirt with fleur-de-lis designs stitched into it. I hope it's cute.

As I prepare, I wonder if maybe I needn't worry—with Hercule's Influence, I could probably show up wearing a barrel and a chicken mask and still look good. But my vanity won't allow this.

Mom and Dad are on the couch watching the weekend news report. "Morning," I say, a little awkwardly.

"Good morning, sweetie," says Mom. She and Dad both stand and hug me, which isn't what usually happens when I enter a room. "How are you feeling?" Mom asks.

"I don't know," I say. "Late, I guess."

"Late?"

"I'm meeting . . . Sarena. For coffee."

"Oh," says Mom, and I get the sense from her tone that she and Dad have been waiting around in hopes of having a talk with me.

"I'll be back," I say. "Back for dinner." Then I remember that I still haven't shown them Hercule's Hints. Maybe this is a good moment—just get it over with. But before I can enact this idea, Dad says, "I want to talk to you about Confession, Gabby. I'd like you to go before Mass tomorrow."

This startles me. Then it makes sense. Then it makes me mad, the presumptuousness of it. "I'll think about it," I say.

"This could be your last Confession, Gabriela," he says firmly. "You have to go. That's *final*." He's not joking. His eyes glow with frustration and fear.

"It won't be my last," I say, equally firm. "I'm going to confess plenty of things, for the rest of my life!" When I say *life*, my voice cracks. Seeing Dad's emotion has started me down the same path. I turn and stride quickly to the front door.

"Gabriela—" says Mom.

I'm gone.

The Snake River winds down wooded hillsides from Snake Lake, which lies near the mountain pass. When the river reaches town, it flows into a straight cement canal, which chaperones it through three neighborhoods and releases it to the southeast. The mile or so of its urban passage, known as "the canal," features gravel paths and a few overpasses. It's a popular place to go for a stroll, or for a talk.

Sylvester's right where he said he'd be. He's sitting on a metal bench wearing a green hooded sweatshirt and jeans. A burned-out cigarette dangles forgotten from his fingers. He's watching the stream of passing joggers, moms, and retirees that daily occupy the walking path. When I see him, I can scarcely believe he's here to meet *me*. He's the kind of person I always encounter by accident, whose orbit is unknowable. I stand at a distance for a while, watching him, convincing myself that I'm really supposed to walk up to him and say "Hi." I give my hair a quick fluff and smooth my eyebrows. I walk up to him.

"Hi," I say.

He absentmindedly ashes his extinguished cigarette. "Hi," he replies. He scoots over, inviting me to sit, which I do, my skin prickling as I approach closer to him than I've ever been. He smells of smoke, sweat, and soap, having come here straight from football practice.

"So," he says, "which Death contacted you?"

"He's named Hercule," I reply. I sit patiently, hoping perhaps for some condolences, but Sylvester offers none. He puts his cigarette to his lips and finally discovers that it's out. He tosses it on the gravel and produces a pack from his shirt pocket. "Want one?" he asks.

"Sure." I've never smoked, but why not? Sylvester lights one and passes it to me. I puff on it.

"Don't puff," he says. "Inhale."

Taking this advice starts me into a coughing fit. Sylvester laughs as I hand the cigarette back. He holds it to his lips. Air tumbles past the ember. When he exhales, he tells me why he's asked me here. The explanation emerges with the smoke.

"I'm going to depart, too," he says. He sighs out the rest of the breath. "I haven't told anyone."

I'm dumbfounded. Like my parents a few days back, I first think that there's a mistake. My second thought is that Iris was right—*finally right!*—about one of her suspicions.

"Which Death?" I say, not because it's an important question; it's just the first to jump into my head.

"Hercule," Sylvester replies.

"That . . . can't be," I say. Some totally obscure Death contacts both of us at once? But Sylvester does not appear to be putting me on. "That's my Death," I insist. "Not even Iris has heard of him."

"Yeah," says Sylvester, strangely unsurprised. "I tried to do some research, but forget it. It doesn't matter."

There are a million things I could say here, all foolish. As the catalog flits past my mind's eye, I select the most foolish of all and speak it before I have time to think twice. "Sylvester . . . I have . . . a . . . crush? On . . . um . . . *you*."

His eyes widen. For a moment, he seems to be weighing whether or not this is a joke. Then, he smiles. "Well!" he proclaims. He sits up straight, and smoothes the front of his sweatshirt comically. He starts puffing his cigarette, clowning on the way I did it before (*puffpuffpuff*). "Why didn't you say anything?" he asks. (*Puffpuffpuff.*)

"I don't know," I say. "Shy, I guess."

He nods. "No time for that now," he says. He takes a long draw on the cigarette, and emits the smoke in a gray stream. "I have a question for you, Gabriela." He reaches into his pocket and produces a folded piece of paper. I recognize it instantly as he opens it. It's his Wrap-Up List, with Hercule's Hints scrawled on it. Sylvester's list contains many more items than mine. His first, at the very top, says, "Enlist in the Army." Hercule's Hint below that:

— *Volunteer.*

I recall Sylvester's question of Sergeant Mistletoe yesterday — whether there was any way to volunteer before turning eighteen. This is not the item to which Sylvester directs my attention now, though. He points at the bottom of the page, to the last line, which reads, as mine does, "Pardon." Below it, Hercule has scrawled the following Hint:

— *Wait for Gabriela.*

We observe this together.

"So I waited," says Sylvester, "and here you are."

"I . . . I . . ." I stutter. "Maybe some other Gabriela?" This seems highly unlikely. "I'm . . . I'm . . ." I'm not getting anywhere, but Sylvester helps me out:

" . . . hoping to get kissed?" he says. He squints at me, some of the humor returning to his eyes. "Is that on your Wrap-Up List, maybe?" He says this with a droll tone that I have difficulty interpreting — is he making fun? Showing off his deductive skills?

He stands, tosses his cigarette to the gravel, and stamps it out. "Have you been to the Fields?" he asks. He's not wondering if I've *ever* been there. He's wondering if I've been since I learned I was going to depart. I recall instantly the second half of Hercule's Hint about my first kiss: — *The Fields.*

"I'll drive," he says.

the fields

Sylvester opens the passenger door to his shiny red sports car for me, and I step in. The interior smells of new leather — an intoxicating, slightly nauseating scent.

I pull the seat belt across my lap as Sylvester starts the engine. He grins. "Safety first," he says as I click the strap into place. "You're marked for departure, you know."

"Better that than dying in a car crash today," I reply. Then, something occurs to me. "This car!" I exclaim. "Hercule got you this?"

"The dealership was raffling it," says Sylvester. "Hercule told me to buy a ticket, and I won." He backs the car from the parking stall, then guns the engine and races to the end of the lot. I place both hands on the dashboard and Sylvester chuckles, obviously getting some satisfaction from scaring me. We pull into the street, and he darts around two slower cars and runs a yellow light.

In moments, we're out of downtown, racing along the winding road toward the Fields. My initial fears fade as Sylvester's competence as a driver impresses itself upon me and I give in to the thrill of the trip. We speed through a neighborhood of warehouses and finally curve into the pinewoods and onto a bumpy, single-lane road.

The sun diminishes in a high mist, and its sharp light fades. It's almost always foggy out here. As we go deeper into the woods, colors fade to gray. Fog curls onto the road. Sylvester hits his headlights but doesn't slow. Branches scrape the sides of the car. The fuzzy lights of an oncoming sedan appear, and it blips by, driven by a woman about my mom's age. Her red taillights shrink away behind us.

Soon, we reach the parking lot. Sylvester decelerates across the gravel and parks, and we step out into the cold. It's drizzling here, and the drops of rain pop against the roof and the ground. Sylvester stands next to me. "Come on," he says. He offers me his arm, and I take it.

Immediately beyond the parking lot is a gazebo set in a small rose garden, where class field trips usually start. We look at the map there, which shows the public Fields stretching out to a dotted line labeled DEPARTURE. Only Deaths and departing people can go beyond that, and no one returns from there. That is, no one beyond the very few who earned Pardons at the last moment and walked back. There's rumored to be a grove of oaks out there.

Sylvester and I wander among the roses, where a few bushes

try to bloom in the fog. "I hope it doesn't rain," I say. Sylvester is quiet, but I can tell he understands that I'm not referring to right now. "I just don't see *why*," I add. "Why *us*."

"I tried to ask Hercule when I wrote to him," says Sylvester, "but . . ." He trails off, indicating that Hercule's response was unsatisfactory. "It's not worth worrying about."

"Yeah." Everything I've ever read on this subject reaches a similarly inconclusive conclusion. Some people just get chosen. Young. Old. Rich. Poor. White. Brown. Americans. Russians. Mexicans serving in the U.S. Army deployed in Tunisia.

My hair is wet from the drizzle, and a damp chill penetrates my clothes. I shiver, and Sylvester puts an arm around me as we proceed onto the lawn. Anyone can come here, so the city maintains it, mowing and watering the turf. The grass is loaded with moisture, and after a few steps my feet are wet.

The rose garden disappears behind, and we're surrounded by the small circle of grass we can see through the fog. The ground grows rougher as we walk, and the even, green turf turns to a scrubby, shorn field. I don't see the sign until it's right in front of us: DEPARTURE. Beyond, the unshorn grass grows waist high, brown and dead from winter, out of range of the city's lawn mowers.

Stacked by the edge are countless piles of rocks — cairns built up by the relatives of departing souls.

I release Sylvester's arm and step to the dividing line. I push forward, and feel the invisible resistance of the boundary — it pushes back at you, like you're lying on the surface of a pool, too buoyant to sink. The deeper you press, the more firmly it presses back. No one knows how these forces work, though plenty of people study them.

I lean in and float there in the air. *Not yet, Gabriela,* the boundary seems to say, holding me off.

Sylvester joins me. He stretches out his arms as he leans in, too, letting the boundary support him. "My dad went to the Fields a few times in Vietnam," he says. "I guess they bring lotus flowers for the person, instead of stacking rocks."

"Was he in the war?" I ask.

"Yeah."

"You want to go, too," I say. "You asked about enlisting in class."

Sylvester shakes his head, and a lock of hair falls along the firm line of his nose. I resist a strong inclination to reach out and brush it aside, to touch his cheek. "He doesn't want me to, but I'm going to do it. I'll trick him into being proud of me."

"Trick him?"

"The old man," says Sylvester. He smiles humorlessly. "I doubt anyone else could understand. It's between us."

"Try me," I say.

Sylvester glances over, and I return his gaze. After my role as confidante to Iris yesterday, I'm feeling like I can handle almost anything.

"Well, it doesn't make sense," he says, "but just try to believe it makes sense to *me.*"

"Okay."

"My dad's angry—about his arm. He always has been. His missing arm, you know? *The Arm.* When I was a kid, he told me it was the military's fault he lost it. That they could have saved it if there'd been a decent medic in the field. He blames his arm for all kinds of stuff—Mom leaving him, losing his job. So, there's that." Sylvester pauses, then continues. "The other thing is, he blames *me* for stuff, too. Sometimes the same stuff. I know it sounds crazy, but I think I *am* that arm. Like his own fingers. But I never do things right." Sylvester's voice descends as he says this, and his eyes narrow. "But I'll show him. I'm going to enlist. And I'm going to be a *medic*." He looks over at me, to check my response to this. "*The Arm* is going back out there. It's going to do what he wishes it had done."

I think my face is blank. Sylvester's right—it doesn't make sense . . . but it does, in a way. It reminds me of something I learned in catechetics class, and I quote it aloud now from memory: "If thine enemy hunger, feed him . . . : in so doing thou shalt heap coals of fire on his head."

Sylvester looks surprised. "What's that?" he says.

"St. Mary's," I say. "We memorized verses about service. I like that one, because you're being nice to be mean."

"Yeah, that's it," says Sylvester. "Not that it matters any-way—turns out I'm departing the day before I turn eighteen."

"When?"

"Tomorrow," he says, with pronounced casualness. "Tomorrow at midnight. During the fight."

"During the fight?" I repeat, emphasizing each word. I don't know why it surprises me, but it does. *The fight!* It's a forbidden event, after the last game of the season. I didn't go last year, but I heard it whispered about. It happens at midnight, on the football field, between the Cougars football team and whoever they just played (this year, the South High Jaguars).

"Hercule's going to take me right off the field!"

"Have you told *anyone?*" I ask. "Your dad?"

"Yeah, I told him. I didn't want to, but I kind of had to." He pauses. "What about you? Have you talked to Hercule about *your* date?"

"Next Wednesday," I say.

"Ah," he says, closing his eyes to imagine how great it must be to have so much time.

We fall silent, neither sure what to say, bodies pressing into the boundary, floating in midair.

Then, I smell it. The blooms — the hyacinths, or hydrangeas, or whatever they are. The scent is really strong, and I wonder if they grow out *there,* out past the boundary, but my wonderment is overwhelmed by the effect of the scent upon me. I feel like I'm waking up after a long nap. My body fills with sensation.

I turn to face Sylvester, looking at him for the first time without reserve, drinking him up. He is achingly, unbelievably beautiful. I reach out and touch his shoulder as he, also, breathes deep. When I have his attention, I take a step back from the boundary and sit on the wet, brown grass. The cold damp immediately soaks through my jeans, but I scarcely notice.

He joins me, kneeling next to me.

"Do you smell the blooms?" I ask.

His clear eyes are locked onto me. I'm close enough to see small beads of water poised at the ends of his eyelashes.

He leans toward me. His breath smells of cigarettes — not a stale smell but a rich one, mixing with the sweat and soap of football practice, and now with the stinging profusion of the unseen blossoms. As he draws near, I close my eyes . . .

Suddenly he grabs my shoulders. My eyes snap open to see him grinning before me, prankish. I pull back. "Hey!" I say.

"Is this going to be your *very first kiss?*" he says, leering comically.

I twist in his grasp, confused. "Quit it," I say.

Before he can respond, we're interrupted.

A foot bumps into my shoulder, and from above there's a surprised exclamation. Someone is falling over us, wheeling around and landing hard. Sylvester and I quickly uncompromise ourselves, wide-eyed, to see a tall, slim figure on the ground.

It is a Death.

"*Of all the* — " he curses, wallowing in the wet grass.

"I'm *sorry!*" I say, as the creature collects himself. He stands, smoothing his gray suit, glaring. He extends a scornful silver finger toward us, frowning, eyes smoldering, before stalking off into the fog in the direction of the parking lot, still straightening his pants.

Sylvester and I sit as silent as stones, startled nearly out of our skins. Then he makes a sudden hissing sound, like air coming out of a bicycle tire. He's . . . laughing! His eyes bug. He wheezes.

It hadn't occurred to me that this was funny, but when it does, I let out a sudden snort. We quickly become hysterical. Our voices boom into the fog. It feels good. I'm sure the Death hears us as he makes his morbid way toward town.

"His *expression!*" I croak.

"He was *pissed!*" Sylvester gasps.

It's a long time before we've recovered. I think it must be the funniest thing that's ever happened.

could have beens

I'm home for dinner, as promised. It's a quiet affair at first, Mom, Dad, and I focused on our plates, which contain fettuccine with Alfredo sauce. Mom doesn't usually cook, but sometimes, if Dad comes home late from work, she'll rise to the occasion and make fettuccine with Alfredo sauce. I twirl my fork among the milky strands.

"I'll go to Confession tomorrow," I say.

Confession has never been my favorite sacrament (or even my seventh favorite). But it will ease Dad's mind, I know. And although I'm expecting to get a Pardon, as the days pass I . . . I want to wrap things up right, just in case.

"Thank you, Gabriela," says Dad, to his pasta. "That means a lot to me. It's the right thing."

"Dad," I say, "have you thought any more about Gonzalo? What Iris and I found?"

"Ana called today to talk more," he says. "We can't believe it. After all these years."

"You never suspected his death was a departure."

"No, never."

"Or that he was Pardoned."

"By *Hercule*," Mom jumps in.

There's a pause. Mom and Dad are both looking at me. Again, I realize I haven't shown them my Wrap-Up List, or Hercule's Hints. But I'm going to now. It's time.

Without saying anything, I stand and fetch the list and Hints from my room. I hand it to Mom, and Dad leans over her shoulder. They read it. And they think . . . Oh, I don't know what they think. I can't stand it. "So, there you go!" I say.

"Have you and Iris gotten any ideas about your Pardon?" says Dad.

"Not yet," I say.

We fall silent. Mom passes the page back to me. This is awful. I can't believe I thought my list was such a great idea before.

"Gabriela, are you still planning to go to the football game tomorrow night?" Mom asks.

"I think so," I say.

"Your father and I have decided *not* to go," she says. "We talked it over. We want you to enjoy it with your friends."

"Oh, that's not—" I say. I can tell that "We talked it over" really means "We argued about it."

"That's final," says Dad. He smiles sadly.

I want to protest further, but I don't. It will make things easier if they aren't there. "I might spend the night at Iris's house afterwards," I say, crafting a quick alibi against attending the midnight fight. Then I revise, "Actually, at *Sarena's* house." I don't know at first what prompts this revision, but as soon as I realize, I feel awful. I'm so at loose ends about Iris that I'm avoiding even an imaginary overnight with her. I am a rotten person. "Actually," I re-revise, "it *is* at Iris's house, I just remembered, but, um, we're starting at Sarena's house? Then going to Iris's house after that?"

My parents watch as I flounder before them for no apparent reason.

Just before bed, the phone rings. Dad answers, and holds it out to me. "It's Iris," he says.

I put the receiver to my ear. "Hi," I say.

"Hi."

"Um, how are you?" I ask, feeling awkward.

"I've been thinking about your grandfather," says Iris, jumping right in with high enthusiasm. "It's like nothing I've ever heard of! And get this—I did some more research into Hercule's other departures."

"You did?" I say. It hadn't even occurred to me to do more research.

"In the last three hundred years, he's given two Pardons aside from your grandfather's. And *both were also transferred*."

"You mean, both were given away?" I say.

"Right. It might not mean anything, but it's quite a coincidence, don't you think?"

"Ugh," I say, reeling from what seems an endless parade of unknowables. "I wish we could somehow . . . I don't know, *kidnap* him. Tie him up and . . . and force him to tell us!"

Iris laughs musically. "That would be great," she says. Then there's a long pause. "Wait just a *second.*"

I wait. "Iris? Are you still there?"

"Gabriela," she says, her voice a whisper. "What if we really could?"

"Could what?" I say.

"Kidnap him."

"What are you talking about?" I'm whispering now, too.

"I need to think about this more . . . but just tell me — *would* you?"

"I . . . Yes, I would," I say.

"Meet me tomorrow. At Marking Street, after you're done with church."

Click — the line goes dead without even a goodbye.

"Gabriela?" says Dad from the kitchen. "Everything all right?"

Funny question.

Mom, Dad and I end up in the living room later, watching TV. The news reports are distressing, and it's unavoidable that we start talking about the war. But Mom and Dad don't agree — they never do.

"Yes, dear," says Dad to Mom, "but what you don't understand is that war can save lives."

"Maybe it can, but it never does," says Mom.

"No one can know the future," says Dad.

"So there you are," says Mom.

"I'm going to bed," I say, standing.

I brush my teeth and change into my pajamas, feeling the emotional coldness blowing in from the otherwise silent living room, where the TV blithely continues. Mom and Dad are making a show of reading magazines, but they aren't really reading. They're thinking about what they could have said to win the argument.

I think my parents have an okay relationship overall, but sometimes I wonder — they went through so much to be together, with Dad enduring the racism of Mom's parents, and Mom converting to Catholicism. Seeing them bicker over the evening news is sad. As the years pass, the marriage they fought for is settling into acid.

It makes me think again about uniforms. When Mom and Dad fell in love, was it with the person or with some disguise put on to impress? On the other hand, maybe they really did love each other, and now they've forgotten — each presumptively dressing the other in the uniform of their own annoyance. When do you see the person, and when the façade? I'm not sure if I know what those terms mean anymore.

I return to my room and sit on the edge of my bed. I take

out my rosary, but I don't pray. Instead, I remember something from last year — another time when Ms. Lime and I were meeting to talk about my difficult transition into high school. My parents were arguing more than ever, and I think my own troubles were the cause of some of it. They were both worried about me. I really don't think Mom and Dad would ever get divorced, but things were bad back then, and that subject was on my mind. It just seemed like they'd get tired of arguing and call it quits. I was seething about this when I met with Ms. Lime. I could barely speak, just stared vengefully out the window. Ms. Lime said, "Gabriela, sometimes regular words aren't enough. Sometimes when I'm really upset, I write poetry. Do you ever write poetry?"

This struck me as a stupid idea, and in a snit I snatched up a pencil from Ms. Lime's desk and scribbled a little haiku on a pink sticky note (five syllables, seven, five). I still remember it:

> *Divorce divorce div*
> *orce divorce divorce divorce*
> *Divorce divorce div*

I shoved it across the table. Ms. Lime read it. After a moment, she said, "You're right, Gabriela. Divorce doesn't fit."

I've been interested in writing ever since.

· · ·

When the memory finishes, I return my rosary to my desk, close my bedroom door, turn out the light, and slip under the covers.

I'm wide awake. There's too much swirling in my head, and each thought sends me onto a different tangent, but the strongest is this: I thought I was going to get kissed today. Everything added up — both of Hercule's Hints seemed ful-filled — and then Sylvester was a jerk. Why did he grab me like that? Why make a joke about it? It doesn't make sense. It's cruel.

I remember the way he held out his arm so chivalrously in the parking lot. There was something awkward about that, as if he were imitating a movie . . .

Finally, I get it. Maybe I didn't see it before because it didn't seem possible, since Sylvester is a senior. But as Sherlock Holmes said, when you've eliminated the impossible, what-ever remains, however improbable, must be the truth. And the truth is: Sylvester was *nervous*, because he likes me.

I envision us again walking into the fog of the Fields, to the boundary. The smell of flowers blows from the unknown glade. We sit together in the cold. Jewels of water cling to his pretty eyelashes.

I imagine what I wish had happened. That it had been ten-der. That Sylvester was confident and gentle. That he leaned in slowly. That his soft lips touched mine.

three days before
departure day

confession

Mom, Dad, and I are up early. They dress in their nice church clothes, whereas I wear a warm outfit appropriate for the football game later on (jeans, long-sleeved shirt, sweater, parka). We ride the old elevator to the lobby, step onto the staircase at the front of the building, and stop. We stare down into the street.

Usually the neighborhood is empty when we leave for early Mass, but today things prove a far cry from the usual. Instead of the peaceful, quiet lull of a day yet to begin, there are hundreds, maybe thousands, of people walking by, filling both traffic lanes and both sidewalks. They're all dressed in black. It's a human river, confusing and beautiful for a moment until I see the signs and banners, and the surreality dissipates. I glance at Dad in time to see him draw the same conclusion as I: this is a protest march, against the war.

"We'll have to walk with them for a couple blocks," says

Dad. The *we* and *them* of his statement clearly express not only his sympathies but mine and Mom's by extension. Not even a week ago I'd have felt perfect solidarity with him on this point. Dad sees what I used to see — the nobility. Maybe he has to believe in that, for the sake of his own father. But more and more I'm seeing something different.

We descend the front steps and join the march. We do not match the uniform of the occasion, as Dad is dressed in brown, Mom in green, and I in blue.

Immediately ahead of us, carried over the crowd by a group of pallbearers, is a long black coffin. We skirt around it. Stenciled across the side are the words SONS AND DAUGHTERS.

As we go by, I notice something about one of the pallbearers. He's marching precisely on the left side of the coffin. One sleeve of his black jacket is pinned up, empty. It's Mr. Hale, Sylvester's dad. His face is tired, his chin dusted with stubble. I wonder if Sylvester knows his father is out here protesting the war he wants to volunteer for.

Soon Mom, Dad, and I turn off the route of the march, toward St. Mary's. There's another group standing at the intersection, with signs that indicate their opposition to the marchers, and their support of the war. They seem less organized, not all dressed any particular color or trying to create a spectacle beyond their hasty-looking placards. As we pass, my dad nods to one of them, a man wearing a fly-fishing vest with a sign that says SOME THINGS ARE WORTH FIGHTING FOR.

· · ·

The humble bulk of St. Mary's looms before us minutes later, and we enter.

Our parish is a mix of middle- and low-income people, including a significant population of Mexicans and Koreans. I've noticed that ethnicity influences people's seating choices. Our church, like lots of Catholic churches, is called cruciform, which means it's cross shaped, with the altar in the middle (at the intersection of the metaphorical crossbeams). The short arms of the cross, areas called transepts, each contain rows of seats. I was still a kid when I noticed that we always sat with Aunt Ana and her husband, Hector, in the west transept, with other Latino families. The east transept, across the way, is where the Koreans sit, and the long middle, the seating down what's called the nave, is everybody else — mostly white people of Irish and English descent.

These divisions are partly linguistic. If you look at the missals everyone follows the service with, there are Spanish translations in the west transept, Korean ones in the east transept, and English in the nave. One thing I kind of like about the early service at St. Mary's is that the Mass is performed in Latin. It doesn't matter what language you speak — God is from Rome.

Plenty of parishioners are turned out for early Mass today, and as is usually the case, it's an older crowd. I don't see many kids here. Most families seem to prefer the nine thirty or eleven o'clock service, both of which are in English. The early service is a little more like how things used to be, in the Church of antiquity: Latin, candles, and incense as compared to English, electricity, and incense. Incense is the common denominator. The strong, weighty frankincense burns into the air even now. It's interesting: to smell frankincense, and to experience the churchly state of mind it imparts, you have to come here. You choose it. You send yourself through these doors, where the wheezy organ blows. But the other smell I've been encountering lately — the flowers — that smell is ready to hijack you anywhere. It's blowing around in the wind, the organs of hydrangeas piping universally.

We dip our fingers in the font of holy water and genuflect before the altar. We find seats next to Ana, Hector, and their kids, Juan (eight years old) and Pia (thirteen months old). Ana and Hector are both friendly, plump people, and they both give me hugs — it's the first they've seen me since I got my Death Letter. My aunt's eyes look teary as she contemplates me.

Mom and Dad stand apart. I wonder what it's like to wake up in bed next to someone and know they're mad at you. Even as they regain consciousness after a solid night of slumber, their anger is waiting for them, like the morning paper full of what happened yesterday.

Dad glances at me and gestures significantly behind us to a door at the rear of the transept — the confessional.

Confession at St. Mary's is not like Confession in the movies. When I attended confirmation classes, we learned about the Second Vatican Council, which happened in the 1960s. It was a meeting where the Church decided to liberalize itself. Catholic rituals in movies are usually pre–Vatican II, when

Confession involved a closet with an opaque grating between you and the priest. At St. Mary's, Confession takes place in an office, where you meet with Father Ernesto or Father Salerno and talk things over.

Our family's priest has always been Father Ernesto. He pretty much *is* the Church for us Riveras, since forever. Sometimes though, I'll admit, Father Salerno is easier to deal with in Confession, partly because I don't know him very well, and partly because he doesn't speak Spanish.

I'm embarrassed that I don't have any Spanish beyond one semester of it last year in school. Neither Dad nor Aunt Ana ever encouraged me, though they're both fluent. It bothers me more and more. Six months ago, at the tail end of my largely miserable freshman year, my fifteenth birthday was coming up. Mom, Dad, and I were in the community hall after Mass, and this kid, Herman, about two years younger than me, asked me, "Gabriela, will you have your quinceañera here in the community hall?"

"Quinceañera?" I replied. "What's that?"

Herman looked at me like I was from Mars—but I didn't know what he was talking about. No one ever asked if I wanted a quinceañera any more than they'd asked if I wanted to be confirmed the year before that. I was simply not consulted about such things.

There's one person lined up in advance of me for Confession—a middle-aged white lady who's wearing knee-length boots and a purple dress. She enters the office and closes the door. Her confession lasts about ten minutes, and when she emerges our eyes meet briefly. We both think, *I'm curious about your sins.*

I take a deep breath of sanctifying frankincense and enter. The sounds of pre-Mass socializing are blocked as I close the door to find Father Ernesto sitting, waiting, an empty chair next to him.

Father Ernesto is like a force of nature. He knew Gonzalo. He was with Abuela when she passed away. He is, in his realm of authority, unquestionable. Today, he's wearing the robes of his office (white, with a colorful stole) over his black suit and priest's collar. He stands and hugs me. "Hola, Gabriela," he says. "It's good to see you." He gestures to the empty chair. He probably arranges this carefully — facing him, but not facing him too much. Given the gravity of all he hears, I'm sure he's had plenty of practice selecting an angle that allows for hesitation but encourages disclosure. I sit in the chair to find it warm — the body heat of the woman who confessed before me is still radiating from it.

"How are you doing?" he asks, his voice friendly and concerned.

"All right," I say. "I'm still trying to figure out my Pardon."

"I hope it's God's will," says Father Ernesto. "Have you thought about receiving Extreme Unction, Gabriela?"

"Oh, I don't know about that . . ." I say.

"It's not just for old people, you know," Father replies, then pauses. "But this is not why you're here today," he says. He holds out one old hand, passing the conversation to me.

"I've missed Mass a few times," I confess. It's true that missing services is a sin, and I've used nonattendance as a smoke screen before, but it won't work today. Father Ernesto sits, waiting. It is time for me to decide what this is going to be about. I consider for a moment and finally say, "Father, I have a question. About what the Church believes. I have a friend —"

Father interrupts me, saying, "Is it really a friend, Gabriela, or is it you? Remember, the sanctity and privacy of Confession protects you."

"Oh, no," I say, polishing the air before me with both hands, "it really is a friend. *Not* me." Did I rush too quickly to say that? Would it be so bad for him to think it was me? I don't know. "I was wondering about the Church's stance. About people who . . . who prefer their same gender."

"I assume you mean this in an intimate sense," says Father Ernesto. "Is your friend a boy or a girl?"

The question surprises me. "Um, girl," I say. "That doesn't matter, though, does it?"

"No," says Father Ernesto, "but it is different for women sometimes. For a man, it absolutely cannot be — obviously it's a mortal sin. But for a woman, perhaps it's not always so serious."

I stare at him. I'd expected him to tell me that Iris's soul was in jeopardy, but instead he seems to be saying . . . actually, I don't know what he's saying. Is he saying women's sins count for less? And that's a good thing? Questions vie with one another in my mind until I finally say, "I don't understand."

"Understanding is not always ours to enjoy," says Father Ernesto. His tone gives me pause. It's a little harsh, clipped. He sounds like Dad does with his "That's final"—getting mad because he doesn't really know the answer.

When Iris told me about herself, it was like she'd planted a seed of thought in me. And that seed has been resting ever since. Now, in an instant, it opens.

Suddenly I *see* Father Ernesto. Maybe for the first time in my life, I really see him. And he is not Father Ernesto. He is Jaime Ernesto, wearing a priest's collar. He is a man, an old man. He's giving me advice, and I am deciding . . . that he's wrong.

"Thank you, Father," I say. "That's all I wanted to know."

Father Ernesto relaxes, thinking his battle won. "Thank you for your confession, Gabriela," he says, though I've scarcely confessed anything. He raises a hand and makes the sign of the cross before me. "As God's instrument, and with the power of the Holy Spirit, I pronounce your sins forgiven." He pauses. "Let me say, Gabriela," he adds, "that we're each given different struggles in life. One man struggles with one thing, and another with another. As we live, we ask the Lord's help."

I stand to leave, but pause. This may be the last conversation the two of us ever have, and there's something I need him to know. "Thank you for your advice all these years, Father. And for being so kind to my family."

"Of course, Gabriela."

"I'm growing up now," I continue. "I think, in the future, we might disagree about some things."

Father Ernesto smiles. "I suppose so," he says. I can see in his eyes that he understands what has just happened here.

the planning meeting

After church, I walk to the Marking Street Café, where I find Iris sitting by the window drinking tea. The sudden perspective that descended upon me in the confessional is still with me. I feel like I'm seeing her for the first time. My best friend.

As I sit, Iris reaches into her shoulder bag and produces a few magazines, with plain covers but for their title: *The Journal of the Association of Departure Science*. Iris is the only person I know who quarterly wades through this publication, reading articles such as "Interchange Superalterability: An Exclusion-Based Analysis" and "The Infinite Field Hypothesis, viz. Atemporality."

"Iris," I say, "before we get into that, there's something I need to ask you. Something . . . sort of personal."

Iris lifts her cup and blows on the tea. "Go ahead," she says.

"When you said, um . . . when you said it would have to be a girl. I was wondering, well . . . I was wondering what you think of *Wendy*."

Iris's cup becomes very heavy, and it pulls her arm to the table. She smiles, and really doesn't need to say anything more. She gestures toward the magazines she's brought. "Let's talk about what I mentioned on the phone," she says.

"Kidnapping . . . ?" I say.

"I think we can do it," she says. "I'm putting some ideas together, from different places. I don't know if anyone's ever tried it, but I think if we give Hercule the right . . . *encouragement,* we could drag him into our world a little early."

"Encouragement?" I say.

"First, I'll get together a list of all of Hercule's known departures. And we should perform the summoning in your venue — the place you're going to depart from."

"But I don't know where that is," I say.

"Where do you *want* to depart from? Usually people get to choose."

This gives me a shiver, as I recall Sylvester's upcoming departure from the football field, scheduled to transpire in just a handful of hours. I almost tell Iris about it, but I stop myself, feeling bound to respect his desire for secrecy. "Hey," I say, as I realize something.

"What is it?" says Iris.

"The first letter I got from Hercule. Do you remember?

The last sentence — we thought he was joking. *Save a dance for me*. I think he was being serious. I think . . . I think I'm going to depart from the Caballero."

Iris's face lights up. "It must be!" she says. She claps her hands together. "And we need to bring something Hercule has touched — your Death Letter, I think. Do you still have it? Oh my god, Gabriela — we are going to do this!"

"But how will we get into the Caballero? We can't just perform a summoning out on the dance floor — " I cut myself off, as, at that instant, the answer to my question enters the café.

Sarena is carrying her trumpet case, and has her band uniform slung over one arm. She waves to us as she lines up to get coffee. Iris and I watch her place her order. She brings her steaming cup to our table, where she consumes it in one businesslike gulp. Then she finally notices how intensely we're observing her.

"Hi, Sarena," says Iris.

"Hi, Sarena," I say.

She looks back and forth between us. "What is it?"

"Can I ask you for a favor?" I say.

the game

Iris, Sarena, and I walk to campus, brimming with excitement over our plan to sneak into the Caballero tomorrow night and kidnap my Death. It's almost enough to make me forget that within a few hours we're going to witness Sylvester's departure.

The parking lot is starting to fill with cars already: kids in the band, or on the team, who have to show up early, and a few people who like to tailgate. I see a familiar hatchback. There's Raahi with some friends, seniors I don't know very well, leaning against his back bumper. In his trunk are fixings for hamburgers and a jug of punch. Raahi holds up his glass toward us.

"Punch?" he says.

"We're headed to the music building," I say.

Raahi turns to his friends. "Watch my car," he says. He quickly pours each of us a glass of punch, hands them around, and walks with us.

"Raahi," I say, once we're out of earshot of the parking lot, "we're going to kidnap my Death tomorrow night, and I was wondering if—"

"What?" he says, punch sloshing from his cup.

"Oh, right," I say. I've gotten so used to the idea already, I forgot it might be unexpected. "Yeah—Iris and I figured out how. So, anyway, I was wondering if—"

"Kidnap your *Death?"* says Raahi. We've stepped under a breezeway that connects the main campus to the music building, and Raahi lays a steadying hand on one of the metal supports. He looks from one of us to the next, searching for a clue that we're joking.

"Right," I say firmly.

"So, can you give us a lift to the Caballero?" says Sarena. "Around two or three in the morning?"

"And then stick around to help out?" says Iris.

"Help . . . out?" says Raahi.

"Help tie him up, for instance, once we've got him," says Iris.

"You guys . . ." says Raahi. He shakes his head in disbelief. He drinks the remainder of his punch. "All right," he says. "Count me in."

We arrive at the music building shortly after, to see many members of the marching band congregating by the front doors. Sarena greets them.

"See you after halftime," I say.

She hugs me. "See you then."

Raahi accompanies Sarena to the doors of the music building. As I watch them go, something occurs to me.

"What are you looking at?" Iris asks.

"Them," I whisper, gesturing.

"What about . . ." says Iris, and then: "Oh . . . *really?*"

"I think so," I say. And it *is* so. I'm surprised I hadn't put it together before. Raahi has a crush on Sarena.

Our school is nuts for football. I know there are other sports, but does anyone play them? We like football so much that it was we Cougars who years ago spearheaded an extended season in our division, which starts in September and doesn't wind up until March. More kids get to play, more kids get to cheer, and more kids start to care about football. We've sent lots of students to college on football scholarships, and some Cougars have even played in the NFL.

Our athletics field was the most expensive project Central High ever undertook. It cost more than the school itself, actually. The field is built into the hill, with the home team seating dug in on the uphill side and the away team seating on bleachers on the downhill side. The field between is presently lit with blaring halogen lights a hundred feet overhead. It's perfectly even, perfectly mowed, and perfectly green. The lines of play are precisely limed.

Iris and I visit the concession stand, which has just opened.

There's already a line of dressed-up kids standing next to their dates (or hoping their dates are on the way, or hoping someone will ask them out).

We buy sodas, and while Iris stops by the bathroom, I climb about halfway up the home seats, to our regular spot next to the railing. Beyond the bleachers to my left stretches the scrubby, undeveloped hillside, already darkening as the sun drops. Straight ahead, across the perfect green rectangle of the football yardage, the visiting side is starting to fill with a colorful patchwork of parkas. I recognize some of the people over there from church—Latino faces hailing from the South End—and I hear snippets of Spanish.

I take my Wrap-Up List from my pocket and spend a few moments contemplating it. The most frustrating Hint at the moment is the one that seems to hold the most promise—Hercule's identical responses to all of my "first kiss" entries.

—A cavalier request, Gabriela.

As Spanish phrases continue to float my way from across the field, my long-slumbering language skills very unexpectedly begin to stir (*Yawn! Did someone say something? Wow, I've been asleep for a while—look how long my hair is!*).

Cavalier. I stare at the word on my Wrap-Up List. "*Caballero,*" I whisper.

"What'd you say?" Iris asks as she slides into the seat next to me.

I'm thrilled, and suddenly a little playful. I fold the list quickly and return it to my pocket with an ironic glance. "That's classified, miss," I say.

"Did you just figure something out?" says Iris. "Tell me!"

I smile silently.

Within twenty minutes the concession stand has a line thirty people deep, and the only vacancy in the home bleachers is a reserved block at the front, which the marching band now enters to occupy. The crowd cheers, and Iris and I stand and yell, "Sarena! Sarena!" when she appears. I see Wendy, too. Since she's both a musician and a cheerleader, she has special permission to wear her cheer outfit in the marching band. Her short sleeves and miniskirt are tough to miss.

Raahi joins us as Ms. Garibaldi, the band director, raises her baton.

"Were you hanging out with Sarena this whole time?" I ask.

"Yeah," he says casually.

The band members raise their instruments, and a voice booms over the field from the announcer's booth. "Ladies and gentlemen, please stand for the playing of the national anthem." Everyone, on both sides of the field, rises. I've been through this many times, and it has never occurred to me to wonder about it, but looking down on the field now, with its demarcations, and across at families I know from St. Mary's, as we all ritualistically cover our hearts . . . it's just like church.

When the first notes are played, everyone, and everything, comes to a halt. People walking toward their seats stop walking. The football players gathered by the sidelines stand still. The concession stand stops vending. Every hand covers every heart, and everyone in the whole place is thinking, *We are about to go to war.*

I don't know what to feel. There are young people here, like Raahi, who have received draft letters. There are probably people here who were in this morning's protest march, too. I glance at Raahi. His expression is unreadable.

Sarena nails the high note, and everyone, I'm sure, mentally places the word that belongs there: *free.* This field, divided into yards. All of us here to root for our teams. The new insight I was granted this morning is still with me, and as I look around now, I clearly see the nature of this strange spectacle. I remember, not even a week ago, thinking it was silly to argue over something as self-evident as *victory.* But now I see. The players, the cheerleaders, the band, even the crowd — this entire stadium and everything that takes place in it is a uniform we have all decided to put on together. To forget ourselves.

As the ritual of Mass prepares the congregation to receive the Body of Christ, so the cheer squad prepares the fans to receive the varsity team. The cheerleaders spring onto the empty field, vigorous in their blue uniforms, skirts, and white gloves, gathering at the fifty-yard line and leading the specta-tors on both sides in a round of "We've Got Spirit, How About You?"

Then the starting teams—our defense and the Jaguars' offense—take the field. Normally I feel great excitement at this point, an impatience for things to get started. But not to-night. As Sylvester jogs on, fans in the home bleachers stand and hoot, and my blood runs cold. It's awful to imagine what he must be feeling as he begins the last hours of his life.

The whistle blows, and the game begins.

The first quarter is a little boring. Sylvester doesn't do much. Each team scores a field goal, and Iris and I drink our sodas. Things remain tied up through the second quarter. During this stretch, I begin to hear sounds from the hillside to the left of the bleachers: voices, shouts, and laughter. I peer into the semidark and see a bunch of kids playing their own football game out there in the patchy overflow light. These are the little brothers and sisters of the players on the field. Many of them I recognize—some are siblings of kids from school, and some are from St. Mary's. They're all mixed to-gether, boys and girls. I nudge Iris and direct her attention to this alternative spectacle.

"Hey!" she calls over to the kids. "What are your teams called?" This question, shouted from out of nowhere, proves confusing. The kids look at one another first, and then toward us, shielding their eyes against the field lights. I repeat Iris's question, louder: "What are your teams called?"

"No names," a little boy yells back, his brown face nearly obscured by the hood of his sweatshirt.

"These aren't real teams," explains the girl next to him, maybe his older sister.

The kids go into a huddle. The girl who shouted appears to be the quarterback of the team with the ball. She holds one hand flat like a football field and diagrams a strategy on her palm with her index finger. They make their play, tossing a blue plastic football along the hillside, retreating into the shadows. I watch until they disappear. I wonder how that girl will endure her transformation from player into cheerleader as she gets older—all of these kids gradually mapping themselves onto the spectacle that's being demonstrated for them on the real field.

The second quarter ends. Once the teams exit, the announcer says: "Now, under the direction of Nadine Garibaldi, your Cougars Marching Band!" Ms. Garibaldi stands at the front of the bleachers, and the band takes the field in rows. Sarena is right after the drum major, and we all stand and shout: "Sarena! Sarena!" Neighboring fans look over, amused by our enthusiasm.

The band moves through its formations, spelling Go! and Win! with their bodies (in both cases, Wendy, in her cheer uniform, is the dot on the exclamation point). They zip expertly through "Baby Elephant Walk" and other marching treacle. When they finish and make their exit, the cheerleaders replace them, initiating a spirited call and response on "Fight! Fight! Fight!" (fight, fight, fight).

Iris and I go for more soda and find Sarena in line at the concession stand. She's taken off her tall marching hat, but is otherwise still dressed in full regalia—brass buttons, epaulets, creases.

"Go!" I say, as we reach her.

"Win!" says Iris.

Being in the band must be weird. You're simultaneously respected and mocked for it. And Sarena is like that, too—a cool dork.

The three of us return to the stands, where Raahi congratulates Sarena on her performance and invites her to sit next to him, which she does.

The game resumes. Sylvester is subbed out, and I watch him on the sidelines, talking with teammates and joking around. He seems perfectly normal. At the end of the quarter, he approaches Coach Frank and asks to be sent back in.

The coach assents, and the final quarter commences with the Cougars in possession on the Jaguars' eighteen-yard line. The whistle blows. The ball is hiked. Sylvester runs long, sprinting straight to the end zone. The quarterback, Jeff Dounais, scrambles as a hole appears in the defensive line. Jaguars pour through. Jeff panics and launches the ball in an overpowered pass, above the heads of the players. The moment the pass is released and its poor trajectory becomes clear, the fans start thinking about the next play; this one is as good as over.

So it's a surprise when Sylvester jumps for it. And it gets even more surprising. His body sails into the air. His fingers stretch. They intersect with the ball, and pull it down. He lands hard, falls, rolls, and stands.

Touchdown!

The crowd, after a moment of startled disbelief, goes bonkers. I cheer, too, but my excitement is tempered by something no one else knows: Sylvester can't jump that high. I expect that catching an impossible game-winning touchdown pass was on his Wrap-Up List.

The game is more or less in the bag. After Sylvester's catch, the quality of play diminishes. The teams aren't thinking about this match anymore. They're thinking about what comes next: the fight, at midnight.

the fight

After a few last-minute time-outs, the final whistle blows. The crowd slips the bonds of spectatorship. Parents walk onto the field to say hi to the players. Children chase one another up and down the yards. The game from the hillside briefly and gloriously reinvents itself on the now-vacant field. The cash register rings for the last time, and the lights in the concession stand go out. Engines turn over in the distant parking lot.

Iris, Raahi, Sarena, and I climb off the bleachers and walk around behind, in the shadows, where some other kids are loitering. I see Wendy nearby, with a few cheerleaders. We don't really know one another very well, and she looks surprised when I approach.

"Gabriela," she says, "I was so sorry to hear about your departure."

"Oh, that," I say dismissively. "I'm going to get a Pardon. Listen, I wanted to invite you—I'm going to be at the Caballero on Wednesday. The Washington Fifteen are playing. If you want to come, and anyone else . . ."

"Definitely!" says Wendy. I can tell she's touched that I invited her. "I'll bring a bunch of people."

I turn my gaze toward the bright green field. It's continuing to empty quickly. There's barely anyone left. Parents are gone. School officials and the groundskeepers are disappearing fast. It's so strange—everyone knows what's going to happen, but no one does anything to stop it.

"Are you staying for the fight?" I ask.

"All the cheerleaders are," she says, a note in her voice that suggests she isn't thrilled about it.

When I return to my friends, they're curious—especially Iris. "What was that about?" she asks.

"I invited Wendy to my departure," I say. "And you guys, too, if you want to bring any guests or anything, I hope you will—to the Caballero."

"Really?" says Sarena, struck.

"I think it's a good place to do it," I say.

"Well, I'll bring a fifteen-piece jazz orchestra with me!" she says.

"Gabriela," says Raahi, "I want to be there, but . . ." He doesn't finish. He doesn't have to.

"Oh, Raahi!" I say. "God, I can't believe—I didn't think—"

"It's okay."

"You're leaving . . ."

"Tuesday morning," he says.

Then: *wham!* The field lights turn off. It's easy to forget that none of the game here could have happened except for these lights. A hazy crescent moon and the dots of a few stars now glow above, but all that remains of the world down here is black and purple shadows.

"Whoa," I say but am drowned out by the *whoa*s of everyone around me.

"Right on cue," says Sarena. "There's only us kids here, now. We can head out front."

"If we can find the front," says Iris.

"Never fear!" says Sarena, and she flicks on a flashlight. It must be fun to be in the band and know about these things in advance.

Everyone who was standing in the nearby shadows, maybe twenty kids, walks to the field, while other flashlights descend from campus. It's ghostly and beautiful to see them accumulate at the base of the home bleachers, at the fifty-yard line. It's so dark that I can barely see across the field.

"What happens now?" Iris asks.

"We wait," Sarena replies. "The teams are already in the end zones."

"I'm kind of dreading this," I say.

"Everyone is," says Sarena.

I imagine Jaguars and Cougars gathering nervously out there in the black.

The audience grows to about a hundred kids. Sarena stands, looking for her fellow musicians. There are about fifteen members of the marching band here, and they walk onto the field now with members of the cheer squad.

Everyone's uniforms are deliberately disheveled. Some cheerers have only one glove on, or one shoe. One girl has replaced her miniskirt with blue jeans, and has put the skirt around her neck like a collar. Band members have their coats on backwards, or half-draped off their shoulders. The sousaphone player has his pants around his ankles, boxer shorts extending from the bottom of his blue coat, bare legs pale.

The band begins the national anthem. It sounds terrible. The instruments are out of tune, and everyone is purposefully playing wrong notes. The cheer squad make clumsy jumps, falling down, laughing. Some spectators squeal the obscenities they never shout during football games. When Sarena hits the high note, where "free" belongs, it's not the right note — it's one note below. I'm laughing by the time the performance finishes, but it's also kind of profound. Football is so ritualistic — there's something false about it. But this awful performance and the fight to follow . . . it's like the difference between a war story and a real war. The difference between a staged photo and a scared soldier.

The ragtag anthem ends, the dropped-pants sousaphonist waddling off last. Sarena returns to us.

"That was beautiful," says Iris.

The music achieved its intended effect—everyone's attentions are directed into the empty field. It's silent, flashlights flickering along the green.

"I hear them," says someone, and then I do, too.

In movies, armies always scream at each other as they approach the clash, psyching themselves up, but that doesn't happen here—maybe because the event is unsanctioned, or maybe for some other reason. The field is quiet as the two groups appear. Some players are still dressed in football jerseys, with the padding removed; others are in street clothes. Neither side is running fast—just jogging—but as they close in, I can see the adrenaline in their movements. It's true, I think, what Sarena said: none of them want this.

Then, quite unexpectedly, a voice booms out across the field. *"STOP!"*

I turn toward it, as does everyone. The teams halt their approach, confused, possibly relieved. They don't need to be told twice.

A figure steps from the shadows—it's Sylvester. He walks onto the field between the two groups. He isn't looking at either team, though they're all watching him attentively. Rather, he's focused on the visiting bleachers, the darkness. He holds up a hand and points. Flashlights follow his instruction, reaching across to the other sideline to illuminate the two shadowy figures there.

One of them I recognize immediately — Sylvester's father. I can see his pinned up coat sleeve. He's still dressed in his black suit from this morning, when I saw him in the protest. His hand holds a bouquet of red flowers — lotus blossoms.

The figure standing next to him I don't recognize. He is very, very tall.

The players on the field are as still as stones as the two forms make their slow way toward us, Sylvester's dad taking two paces for every one taken by the Death next to him, who moves through the thick currents of our air as a plow through heavy ground.

"Hercule," I whisper. I hope Iris hears me — I want her to know, but I find I can't raise my voice.

He's very thin, like all the Deaths, and silvery gray from his shiny dress shoes to his somewhat rumpled suit. His face is long, his expression tired, distant. Around his head float the thin wisps of his medium-length gray hair.

I scarcely know what I'm doing, but I find myself on my feet. I take Iris's hand, and then I'm rushing forward, past the transfixed audience, onto the field as Hercule and Mr. Hale reach Sylvester. I hear Sylvester's voice. He's crying. Iris clutches my shoulder, and I clutch hers. We've come as near as we dare, standing now among the statuary of the two terrified varsity teams.

Hercule extends one large gray hand.

Sylvester sobs more loudly, hopeless, then quiets himself. Finally, he reaches out.

He grasps Hercule's hand, and as his fingers close, he takes a deep, startled breath, and his eyes close. The color vanishes up the sleeve of his jersey, then from his neck and face. Within moments he is as gray as smoke. His hair lifts gently, moving in the newly buoyant air, and he exhales.

His lids flutter. He looks around, confused.

"It's over," says his father, his raspy voice cracking.

Sylvester releases Hercule's hand and looks down at his body. He turns to his father, who holds out the bouquet to him. Sylvester takes it, and the blooms turn gray instantly. Both father and son are crying, tears leaving brilliant tracks on their cheeks in the flashlight beams. They turn and begin to walk, approaching to within a few feet of Iris and me.

"Sylvester," I croak as he passes. He doesn't seem to hear me, but Hercule and Mr. Hale both turn. Mr. Hale, his voice measured and profoundly calm, says, "There's a wake tomorrow, at my home. You're welcome to attend." He says the address — maybe Iris will remember it.

Then, my eyes meet Hercule's. I see a glimmer of recognition. He knows me.

The group moves past us, continuing their slow walk toward the exit. Every eye is glued to them. Mr. Hale puts his hand on Sylvester's shoulder as they step into the shadows and disappear — toward the Fields.

The fight is over.

two days before
departure day

the wake

I'm not sure what time it is when I get home, maybe one or two a.m., and I arrive to find Mom and Dad waiting for me in the living room. They were called by both Iris's and Sarena's parents. They know what happened. They're angry and scared. I sit with them on the couch and tell them what I saw — that Sylvester's Death was Hercule.

Dad wants to pray for Sylvester, and it seems like a good idea. We close our eyes and fold our hands. Dad's words are beautiful and heartfelt. He ends by saying, "May our will be the same as yours, Lord," which is a common ending. Then he adds, "May your will be the same as ours." He is thinking about me — thinking about his desire for me to live.

After, Dad suggests that I should be grounded for attending the fight, but this suggestion is quickly taken off the table. It's clear that such punishments are meaningless to me now, so we decide, sort of by consensus, that although I'm not grounded hopefully I'll feel a bit contrite about how much I made my parents worry. This seems reasonable, and the three of us, exhausted both physically and emotionally, hug one another and go to bed.

The next morning, an early phone call from the school informs me that all classes are canceled today—because of Sylvester's unexpected departure. Shortly after this, Iris calls, and about twenty minutes later I arrive at the Marking Street Café to find her seated by the window. We hug.

"Sylvester told me before," I blurt. "I wanted you to know, but he was keeping it a secret."

"Yes, well, did you ever kiss him?" she asks.

"Er," I say, "no. We . . . it almost happened. Out in the Fields, like Hercule said, but then it didn't. I'm glad, though." I say this with confidence, but I don't really know what I'm feeling on the subject.

Just then, Raahi and Sarena walk in, and we get down to business—the plan for the kidnapping tonight. Raahi will drive, and he'll pick everyone up around two thirty. I'll bring my Death Letter. Iris will bring the list of Hercule's former known departures. Sarena will bring the key to the back entrance of the Caballero. It is all arranged.

Then Iris says, "Do you guys want to go to Sylvester's wake? Mr. Hale invited us last night."

"I can drive us," says Raahi.

We pile into his car, outside the café. Iris and Sarena sit in back, and I take the passenger seat. Iris tells Raahi the address. We drive north.

Raahi is introspective, and I know what he's thinking about. "Tomorrow," I say, turning to him.

"Yeah," he agrees.

"Listen, Raahi, I have to tell you something . . . about my Wrap-Up List," I say.

Iris and Sarena both lean forward, pushing between Raahi's and my seats. This does not make things less awkward.

"What about it?" says Raahi.

"Um, you're on it," I say.

"Me?" He turns to me, taking his eyes off the road.

"Red light!" Iris observes. Raahi applies the brakes, and we come to a quick stop.

"Hercule's Hint wasn't very clear," I say, "but I think — for your item, that is — I think you need to be at the Caballero Wednesday night. I don't suppose there's any way for you to, um, get a deferment?" I ask. "Just for a day?"

"What did you put on your list?" Raahi asks.

"Green light," says Iris.

"I feel a little private about it," I mumble. Raahi isn't insistent. It probably doesn't matter anyway — so far my Wrap-Up List is a bust. Sylvester's departed. Raahi will be on a bus to Fort Jackson tomorrow morning. Iris . . . is complicated. It's all complicated.

· · ·

We enter Valley View Estates—a neighborhood of single-wide trailer homes. Some of the homes are rundown, with siding peeling off and rusting hulks of old cars in the yards. Others are meticulously kept, featuring fussed-over beds of petunias and gingerbread around the windows. There's a man unloading an old refrigerator from a hand truck, and an elderly woman drinking a glass of orange juice on a stoop.

"I wonder why Sylvester went to Central High and not North End," says Raahi. "This is really far from school."

Mr. Hale's house is obvious, because there are cars parked up and down the block from it, and the front door is open behind the screen door. His is neither the best- nor the worst-kept trailer in the neighborhood. The yard is a simple square of grass, brown and a little weedy. Raahi parks at the curb, and we walk the narrow cement path to the porch. I hear voices through the screen door, and the sound of a TV—a broadcast football game.

I knock, and a shadow disengages from inside. Mr. Hale approaches through the hall and opens the screen.

"Mr. Hale," I say, "we're all friends of Sylvester's."

"Hello, Gabriela," he says. He's still wearing his black suit from yesterday, with its pinned-up sleeve. His breath smells of whiskey. He steps across the threshold onto the porch with us, and I see that he isn't wearing any shoes—just black socks. He closes the door behind him and sits on the stoop. We sit, too. "Thank you for stopping by," he says. "Gabriela, I heard your news. When will you depart?"

"Midnight Wednesday," I say. "At the Caballero."

"I'd like to attend," he says. He looks at me intensely. "I know Sylvester told you. You and I were the only ones." He pauses, sighs. "Years ago, when I lost my arm, I thought I'd get used to it. But you never do. In fact, it gets worse with time." He rubs the stump through his coat, and a waft of acidic sweat floats past us. "I had to fight for him," he says, "all his life. Fighting to keep him during the divorce. Fighting to send him to the right school. Fight, fight, fight," he chants, bitterly recalling the football cheer. "Fighting to keep him from war."

"He wanted to volunteer," I say but don't offer anything else.

"Yes. I wouldn't allow it. When I think of myself as a kid . . . ah, just a damn *kid*." He shakes his head.

"I'm leaving tomorrow for basic training," says Raahi, suddenly.

Mr. Hale turns to him. "You volunteered, son?" he asks.

"No, drafted."

"What's your name?"

"I'm Raahi."

"They make it seem a fate worse than death, don't they, to refuse," says Mr. Hale.

"Refuse?" says Raahi. The word comes off his tongue as if it's from a foreign language.

"But consider this, son — at least it *is* a fate, and not death." Mr. Hale turns to me. "Perhaps you'll see him, Gabriela, out there in the Fields. If you do, tell him his dad loves him."

"I'm sure he knows that," I say.

"Remind him," says Mr. Hale. "You kids always need reminding." He looks out across his patchy lawn and pulls a pack of cigarettes from his shirt pocket. He lights one with that economy of motion earned through years of practice. Inside the house, the announcer on the TV yells excitedly. Mr. Hale turns to Raahi. "To refuse," he says, punctuating his words with the lit cigarette: "To be a *coward*. And to have the opportunity to live with that." He throws the cigarette into the yard without taking a single draw on it. "Thank you all for coming," he says, standing. "I have to get back to my family now." Without another word, he returns inside. The screen door closes behind him with a clap.

I think about what Sylvester said — that he wanted to become a medic to finally impress his dad. To heap coals on his head. I could have told Mr. Hale just now, and I think it would have worked. But I'm glad I didn't.

My gaze drifts into the yard, where Mr. Hale's virgin cigarette sputters a final ribbon of smoke and goes out.

fidelia

As Raahi guides the car back toward our neighborhood, we're all quiet. I can tell from Raahi's expression that the conversation with Mr. Hale hit him hard.

"Turn left, Raahi," I say as we pause at an intersection. He obeys, going the opposite direction from our neighborhood. "I want to visit Abuela," I explain. "My grandmother's grave."

Raahi guides the car to Broadsprings cemetery, and we park in the lot. Iris and I lead the way. (She knows where we're going because we came out here together last year when we were doing an assignment on family histories, for Ms. Gulich. I took a rubbing from Abuela's gravestone to use as my visual aid. Maybe that was a little morbid, but it turned out to be one of the few assignments my freshman year that I did well on.)

We walk the well-maintained grounds, past the place where all the headstones read SMITH and HUXLEY, and past where they all read SONG and KIM, before reaching the neighborhood of our town's deceased Riveras. It's not surprising that things get grouped like that, I suppose. At one time, it may even have been required. These days I think it's more like what Dad says about our seating choices at Mass every week — "We sit with your aunt and uncle." Glancing at my friends now, though, I think I'd prefer to be buried in a mixed-up graveyard. Washingtons, Mehtas, and Van Voorheeses.

We find Abuela's grave looking well cared for. Dad comes here every Wednesday, and Aunt Ana every Saturday. There are fresh flowers in a vase, white daisies, which I'm sure Ana bought.

We stand silently around the headstone, which reads FIDELIA RIVERA.

"She never knew that her husband departed," I say. "She thought he was killed in action."

"I remember you saying you used to tell her stories about that," says Iris.

"Yeah — all kinds of crazy things," I say. "I remember one where Gonzalo jumped on a hand grenade. All the stories were about him being a hero." I kneel and gently place my hand on Abuela's stone, next to her name. I feel a little self-conscious, my friends watching me, but I continue anyway. I close my eyes and visualize her face, as well as I can remember it. She was a strict-looking woman who never smiled, but she was very kind. She taught me how to play lotería, which is kind of like bingo. I remember her being almost infinitely patient. "Hi, Abuela," I say. "It's Gabriela. I wanted to come tell you something. Maybe Dad or Aunt Ana already told you. We found out that Gonzalo didn't get killed in action. He departed!" I pause. "Maybe he told you that himself, if you guys are together now. I hope you're together. Oh, and if you think of it, could you ask Gonzalo what my Death's Noble Weakness is? I think he might know. Maybe you or he could tell me in a dream. It's okay if not. I hope everything is good for you, Abuela. I hope you and Gonzalo are happy. I pray for you every week at Mass. I miss you." I look up at my friends, who all seem respectful and a little awkward. I smile. "Anyone have anything they want to tell my grandma?" I ask.

"Hi, Abuela," said Iris.

"Hi," says Sarena, waving.

"Gabriela, are your mom's parents buried here, too?" asks Raahi.

"No, they're still alive somewhere," I say. "I don't know where. They disowned Mom when she married Dad."

"Oh, right," says Raahi. "I think you told me that. The . . . Martins, or something?"

"The Mason-Hunts. It's funny, all the ways people can go out of your life, huh? Abuela died from cancer. Gonzalo departed. And Mom's parents — they just opted out."

"I'm glad none of us are going to go out of one another's lives," says Iris.

"Me, too," I say.

the day before
departure day

the summoning

The apartment is dark at two thirty in the morning, when I wander into the perfectly still living room. It's as if no one has ever set foot in it before. I wonder if the whole world was like that, early on — an environment in which nothing had happened. Before God started making creatures. "On the third day, the LORD created two-bedroom apartments, and He saw that it was good. Next day, He created apartment dwellers."

I'm caught in a thicket of emotions as I make my way out — nervousness, guilt, hesitation, uncertainty. I ride the elevator, leave the building, and sit on the front steps waiting for Raahi.

Sneaking out is harder for Raahi than for me. He has to get past his mom, who is a very involved parent (and her only son is leaving for basic training in the morning). I imagine him pushing his car quietly down the block without starting it, so he's well out of earshot when he turns the engine over.

He's right on time to pick me up. We stop by Sarena's house next. She had it harder than either of us — she had to steal her dad's key to the back entrance of the Caballero.

We go to Iris's house last. She has it the hardest of all, because we're looking to her to get us through this.

Raahi parks in an alley behind the hotel. Sarena fumbles forever with the key at the back door, but finally we find ourselves standing, shivering (more from nerves than from cold) in a nondescript hallway dinged from countless collisions with countless musicians and staff people over countless decades. At a dim intersection, we turn right and step abruptly out onto the stage of the Caballero Restaurant.

I've seen Sarena play plenty of times with the Washington Fifteen, but I've never stood up here. Nor have I ever been in the Caballero at three a.m. It's a dark, silent cavern. There's no lighting at all beyond little dots of strung lights and a few spots shining on the walls, apparently always left on. The dance floor is a plot of empty boards. It seems impossible that a place this big would be completely, utterly empty. "Hello?" Iris says, her tiny voice ringing.

"*Hello?*" says Sarena, louder. "*Anybody here?*"

We climb down to the dance floor. The boards creak. I suppose they creak when people dance on them, too, but there's always so much other noise you can't hear it. The four of us stand, grinning stupidly at one another. Then Sarena says, "Hey, hold on a sec. Raahi, follow me."

She walks off the dance floor to the large circular dinner tables beyond, Raahi following. They reach the far wall and cross to the bar. Sarena places four shot glasses on the polished wood, selects a bottle from the shelf, and splashes liquor into each glass. She hands two to Raahi, takes two herself, and they return to us.

We clink the glasses together and drink. I've never tasted hard alcohol, and I think Iris hasn't either. While Sarena and Raahi swallow easily, we both sputter.

"What is it?" I say.

"Vodka," says Sarena.

Iris, still coughing, says, "I have no idea how this is going to go, you guys." She holds out a hand to me, and I give her my Death Letter. She places it in the middle of the floor. "Gabriela, you stand here, and the rest of us off to the side."

We follow her directions. Iris holds up the page she's working from, and explains: "This is the list of Hercule's known departures, from about seventeen fifty to, well—to yesterday," she says, showing everyone the sheet, which ends with "Sylvester Hale." "I'll read it, starting with the oldest."

"How long will it take, once we summon him?" says Sarena.

"Seconds . . . minutes? I don't know. I don't think anyone's ever done this," says Iris. Then she begins. "Anne Hawthorne," she says. She pauses to see if anything preliminary might occur. Nothing does. The room is silent. The dance floor gleams dully. "Fidel Guerrez," she continues. "Rita Heifitz. Henry Mallahan." She pauses again. I feel growing relief—maybe this won't work. Maybe we'll end up just a bunch of scared idiots.

"Itta Bernard," says Iris. "Chung Hee Sung."

"How many more?" whispers Raahi. It's funny that he whispers—none of the rest of us are whispering.

"Five, and then Gabriela," says Iris, and continues: "Amy Fuller. Regina McIntyre. Quincey Ibrahim. Gonzalo Rivera." She pauses. "Sylvester Hale," she says. We stand motionless. Finally, she says, "Gabriela Rivera."

Well, I'm ready to go home now, I think. *It's past my bedtime.* But then I must have blinked.

There's a chair in the middle of the dance floor, where no chair was before. It's upholstered in sparkly gray, with a low back. Carved claw-foot legs.

And seated on it is a very tall man. He's wearing a gray smoking jacket over an untucked dress shirt and dark, silvery slacks. His clothing floats aquatically around him. His legs are crossed, right ankle on left knee. In one hand he holds a gray glass of wine aloft, as if making a toast. He's smiling, his face raised, his eyes closed. His thin, gray hair floats over his head. I recognize him instantly—Hercule.

And the air is full of the merry tinkle of his laugh. He's right in the middle of something, which he probably began wherever he was when we summoned him. "—and so *I* said,

'Well, my dear, if that's what you want, I'm afraid I can't help you!' Haaaa-hahahaa!" His voice booms through the restaurant.

His smile fades quickly as he hears the silence around him. He freezes. His eyes flick open. He drops his glass, which bounces and then rolls across the dance floor. He stands, looking around in panic, and screams — a high shriek that pierces the air: "KIDNAP! KIDNAAAP!"

Before any of us can do anything, he runs. Like all Deaths, his movements look as though they're happening underwater. His loose jacket and slacks billow around him as he takes two large, slow strides, which deliver him straight to the wall at the left of the stage. He collides, rebounds, and falls onto his back, where he lies motionless. He begins to snore.

Raahi, terrified, whispers, "Is he dead?"

It would normally be pretty funny for someone to ask if a snoring person was dead, but no one laughs. Iris rushes forward. Of all of us, she's spent the most time around Deaths and is a little less starstruck. She rolls Hercule onto his side, and his snoring quiets. She looks up at us. "Help me tie him." She extricates a long coil of rope from her bulging purse.

Sarena comes to her aid as Raahi and I watch, fascinated.

"You brought *rope?*" I say.

Hercule is quickly secured from shoulders to feet. I finally get a good look at his face, which is long and pinched-looking, with a prominent silvery nose between the quotation marks of his little gill slits. As her denouement, Iris produces a black sleeping mask, which she places over Hercule's eyes. His thin hair floats, ghostly and weightless.

"Why a sleeping mask?" says Sarena.

"I don't know," says Iris. "It just seems like a good idea, right?"

Then Hercule speaks. We all jump as his voice booms out, not having realized that he'd regained consciousness. *"I wish to know,"* he says loudly, *"the identities of my abductors!"* His tone contains none of the panic that characterized it before. It's authoritative and angry.

"G-Gabriela Rivera," I say, voice quaking.

"Ah, *Gabriela,*" Hercule says. "A pleasure, I'm sure."

"We all did it," says Iris. "All . . . ten of us."

"That's right," says Raahi.

"You're surrounded," says Sarena.

"All *four* of you," says Hercule. He licks his lips.

I glance nervously at Iris, and see that her face is lit with triumph. She turns to me and whispers, "Time and venue."

"Hercule," I say, "I want to discuss my departure. When and where."

"What would you *like?*" he says, acidly.

"Midnight on Wednesday," I say. "Here, at the Caballero."

"Fine," he replies.

"Hercule," says Iris, "we want you to give Gabriela a Pardon."

"Of course you do," says Hercule.

"So," says Iris, "tell us your Noble Weakness."

Hercule doesn't respond right away. His broad mouth frowns. His shoulders straighten in their restraints. "Listen to me, *children*," he says distastefully. He takes a breath, and then intones, his deep voice inhumanly loud, resounding through the empty restaurant: "I am *Death!*"

Raahi begins stuttering, pushed by this into a kind of panic: "Right, certainly, okay, *yes sir* . . ."

Sarena puts both hands over her heart.

I look at Iris. Her triumphant expression is unchanged. She says, "There are some irregularities we'd like to discuss, Hercule."

"Like *what?*" he responds, a little frustrated that he didn't scare her, I think.

"Like, why was I on Sylvester's Wrap-Up List?" I ask suddenly.

Iris shoots me a surprised look.

"He showed me, the day I met him," I explain to her. "Hercule told him to wait for me."

"Wait for *you?*" says Iris. "You in particular?"

"For his Pardon."

"I hate to interrupt," says Hercule, "but that list is none of your affair."

"*Fine,*" says Iris, momentarily piqued at both Hercule and me. "Hercule, we also know you attended Gabriela's grandfather."

Hercule wiggles in his ropes. "These chafe," he says.

"Why have you chosen Gabriela?" she says. "Deaths never attend relatives of those they've already attended."

"Untie me, please," says Hercule.

"No. You might try to harm us."

"The longer you leave me trussed like an Easter ham, my dear, the more attractive such a proposition becomes," Hercule growls.

"My grandfather's Pardon was transferred," I say.

Hercule sighs. He stops wriggling. "It wasn't any use to him," he says.

"I don't understand," I say.

"I have no investment in that, young lady," says Hercule.

"Why are you being such a *prick?*" says Raahi suddenly. This comment completely derails the conversation. I see Hercule's surprise behind the sleeping mask. Then he smiles.

"Well, young man, I *apologize*," he says. "I shall reform myself and strive to be a more upstanding *prisoner*." He turns his masked face toward me. "The story of your grandfather, Gabriela, was not unusual in wartime. I arrived to find him seated alone at the base of an olive tree, suffering a bullet wound to the gut, delivered some time previous by an Italian rifle. He was dying when I took him, so you can understand when I say his Pardon was no use to him. He would return to life only to finish dying. So he decided to give it away."

"Oh," I say. This was a story I never thought to tell to

Abuela: Gonzalo giving up his own Pardon in his last moments of life.

"But he guessed your Noble Weakness," says Iris.

"Did you receive my response to your Wrap-Up List?" Hercule asks.

"Yes," I reply.

"Then you know everything I'm prepared to disclose on that subject." He snaps his mouth shut.

"Well, then, I . . ." I say. I glance at my friends to find them all looking at me expectantly. It seems silly to give up now—but I find myself feeling, suddenly, tired. Ready to go home. "You know what, Hercule," I say, "I guess I don't need anything from you. I'm sorry for the inconvenience. You can go back to whatever you were doing."

"You're sure, Gabriela?" says Iris.

"Yeah," I say.

"Very well, Hercule," says Iris, "*we dismiss you!*"

There's a moment of silence, and then Hercule seems to find something amusing. He giggles. Snorts. His mouth opens wide, showing his sharp, gray teeth, and he belts out a robust laugh. He rolls onto his chest and begins to guffaw into the floor. He hiccups and sniffles.

"What's so funny?" I say.

"Nothing," he replies.

"Hercule," says Iris, "how do we send you back?"

The question launches him into another torrent of hilarity.

This fit ends with a long, pleasurable sigh, and he says, "This is so much better than the party you took me from. I should thank you."

"Answer the question please," says Iris.

"My dear," says Hercule, "when a Death comes to collect someone, he does not leave until that someone is *collected*."

oatmeal

I open my eyes. I'm in my bed. My room is full of early morning light. Through the window, I see a pale blue sky with a few burnished clouds over the roof of the building across the street.

"Gabriela," says a voice. I don't recognize it. I squint into the shadows at the corner. There, sitting by my desk, is a tall old man. Very, very tall. His gangly legs, clothed in slate-colored slacks, are bent sharply at the knees. His head droops near the ceiling, and his face is long and thin. His little gills are tender gray at the sides of his prominent silvery nose.

The shreds of last night return—sneaking out of the Caballero with Hercule in tow. He wouldn't fit into Raahi's car, and I decided to walk back with him. Before we parted ways, Iris, Sarena, and I said our goodbyes to Raahi. We all hugged him. Sarena cried, and I thought Raahi was about to confess his feelings for her. But he didn't.

The bus to take him to Fort Jackson left at five this morning; he probably got home just in time to grab his bag. I imagine him on that bus now, duffel on his lap.

"Do Deaths sleep?" I ask, a little dizzy as I sit up.

"No, we do not," says Hercule, "so you can imagine how this situation has tried my patience. It is now morning, however, and I wish to go to Marking Street."

"To the café?" I say. "You don't need my permission."

"Nor do I desire it," says Hercule. A wisp of hair floats before his eyes, and he brushes it aside with his long, silvery fingers. "However, I require your *presence*. You and I are, for the moment, inextricable from one another."

"Inextricable?"

"Do you know that word, young lady?" says Hercule.

"Yes, I know that word."

"Well, it should fade with time. Deaths are compelled to be their most attentive on first arrival — typically the moment of departure. In this case, however, I've been summoned a bit early, *as you know*. Therefore, I must cajole your company."

I pull my hands across my tired face.

"Also," Hercule continues, "I've heard *noises*. I believe your father has left for work, and your mother is preparing breakfast. Is it her habit to awaken you? If so, you may wish to forewarn her of my presence."

That's a good point. I stand, and Hercule stands also.

"Exactly how close to me do you have to be?" I ask.

"Not sure yet."

We step into the hall and walk to the living room. The radio is on, playing music, and I smell cinnamon: Mom is making oatmeal. I motion to Hercule and whisper, "Stay back."

I enter the room alone, smiling to my mom, who's behind the kitchen counter.

"Good morning, honey," she says. "I'm making some — "

Then, with a lunge, Hercule springs forward from his concealment as if shot from a cannon, stumbling, clothes and hair swimming around him, his face frozen in an embarrassed half smile.

Mom screams — something I've never heard her do before. Then she plucks the pot of oatmeal from the stovetop and flings it at Hercule. It strikes him right on the forehead with an audible *bap*, and he careers to the side, into the sofa, and crashes down. Oatmeal everywhere.

I intervene as Mom rounds the kitchen counter with a meat cleaver in one hand. "Mom, this is *Hercule!*" I shout. "My Death!"

Hercule struggles to a sitting position, whitish clumps of steaming oatmeal rolling down his gray jacket and slacks. Mom slows her advance. Her fury dissipates as my words sink in.

"We summoned him so we could question him — Iris and I, and Raahi and Sarena," I explain. "Now he has to stay here until it's time."

Mom places the cleaver on the coffee table. She sits opposite Hercule on the disheveled couch. "Here?" she says.

"Um, yes," I say, looking around the apartment. "Here."

Mom nods, accepting this extraordinary circumstance with perfect calm. "Do you eat?" she asks Hercule.

"As a rule, yes," says Hercule, "though not generally oatmeal." He seems a little amused even as he rubs his forehead, where a bruise has begun. "However," he continues, "I have at the moment a pressing need to visit the Marking Street Café."

"Let's clean you up," says Mom. "I apologize, please understand . . ." Mom is a hands-on kind of person. She fetches a sponge from the kitchen and begins removing oatmeal from Hercule's clothes.

"Oh, totally unnecessary," says Hercule, holding out his arms so she doesn't miss anything.

When she's finished, Mom pulls on her coat.

"You're coming with us?" I say.

"I could use some coffee."

Hercule is a slow companion, pushing as he must with each step through our thick world. Mom offers him her arm, which he takes, laying his large gray hand on the sleeve of her coat. We stop at a few intersections to wait for the light, though there's no cross traffic — as if we're walking with a police officer.

We reach the Marking Street Café to find Iris sitting at an outside table, with tea and scone, her blond hair tied in a hasty bun. She looks worried when she sees us. She's hoping I'm not mad.

I hug her. "I'm not mad," I say.

"I had a feeling you'd come here," she says. "Hercule will want to gossip."

"The word is *discuss*," says Hercule.

"Alexandre and Dido are inside," says Iris.

"Can you go in without me?" I ask.

"I shall try," says Hercule, and he steps into the café, ducking his head under the lintel.

"He has to stay close to you?" says Iris, fascinated.

I nod.

"It's nice to see you, Mrs. Rivera," says Iris.

"You, too, Iris," says Mom. "And thank you . . . for wanting to help." Her tone suggests that although she's doubtful of the value of this help, she's touched by the intentions behind it.

Inside, Hercule stands before Alexandre and Dido. Alexandre wears a gray trench coat, and Dido a gray V-neck vest over her gray shirt. Hercule gesticulates, his smoking jacket wafting spectrally around him as he tells the tale of his abduction. I find myself embarrassed by him. What does it say about me that Hercule is appropriate to oversee my departure? All I have to go on is an obscure link between him and my grandfather. It's distressing that such an annoying, judgmental, presumptuous Death is drawn to my family.

He returns after a few minutes, holding a steaming cup of black coffee, which he places on our table. "Did you have a nice chat with your friends?" Iris asks.

"Those two," he says, "will inform my friends." He sits next to me, towering.

"Everyone who didn't hear your punch line?" I ask.

"Excuse me?" Hercule lifts one hawkish, silver brow inquisitively.

"Your punch line. When we summoned you, you said something about 'If that's what you want, I can't help you.'"

Hercule's face brightens. His large hands grip the edge of the table, and it shakes with his mirth. *"Priceless! Priceless!"* he cackles. "I vanished before their very eyes!"

When the volume of his joy diminishes, Mom says, quietly, "So — tomorrow."

"Your daughter has asked that I await the stroke of midnight," says Hercule, "which is a reasonable (and, I might add, *extremely common*) stipulation."

"Mom," I say, "are we going to have Tuesday Night Dinner tonight? I'd like to."

"Oh, yes — we can," she says. "I'll call Ana — " She cuts herself off. Then, without warning, she leaps to her feet. Iris's tea and Hercule's coffee go flying as she lunges at Hercule and grabs his jacket collar, shaking him. *"Grant her a Pardon!"* she yells.

"My! Good! Woman!" sputters Hercule, head bobbling, fingers pawing uselessly in Mom's iron grip.

She releases him with a defeated cry. No one is sure what to say, and we sit sullenly, our drinks drizzling to the ground.

"Iris and I can go get the groceries?" I say awkwardly. "Do you want, um, a roast?"

"Oh, you two don't have to—"

"I'd love to help, Mrs. Rivera," says Iris.

I glance at Hercule. He's straightening his smoking jacket. "Hercule?" I say.

"Hm?" He's brushing imaginary crumbs from his gray shoulders.

"Do you mind a little grocery shopping?" I ask.

He sighs.

"We'll walk to McPherson's, Mom, and meet you back home."

Then, from her purse, Iris unexpectedly produces a small point-and-shoot camera. "Mrs. Rivera," she says, "before we go . . . could I get a picture of the three of you? I thought, well—I don't know if you'd mind. But I was thinking, since this is all so unusual . . ."

"You're going to write an article?" I ask. "For the *Journal of Departure Science*?"

"I thought I'd try," she says.

"That's a *great idea!*" I say. In the midst of all of my own dilemmas, this seems even better than great. I immediately take an intense interest in staging the photo. I put my Death between Mom and me. "Hercule," I say, "you should smile, and Mom and I will look sad."

"No, I will not participate in this," says Hercule.

"Come on," I say.

family dinner

Hercule, Iris, and I walk the few blocks to McPherson's. The appearance of Iris's camera has improved my mood—it feels good to help with something.

We roll our black shopping cart into the brightly lit produce aisle, where we're greeted by a seemingly limitless number of photographic opportunities. Such as that big crate mounded full of Red Delicious apples.

"Hercule, would you push the cart, and we could take a picture of you waiting while I choose apples."

"No," says Hercule, but he lays his hands on the handle of the cart. Immediately the whole black thing turns silver, like it's been dipped in paint.

"Does everything you touch do that?" says Iris.

"Everything I *grasp*," says Hercule.

"If you let go, does it come back?"

Hercule lets go, and the cart returns to black. "But not people, when it's their time," he adds. "If you two really want to see something, you should take a picture of me juggling. I can juggle four balls."

I almost laugh, but Hercule looks serious.

"Four *apples*, if you like," he says. He picks up four bright red apples, all of which immediately turn silver in his hands.

He begins to juggle them.

And it is amazing.

Not only does he effortlessly manage the apples, a feat in itself, but as soon as he catches one, it turns silver, and as soon as he tosses it, it turns red again. They wink red, silver, red, silver as they weave through the cascade of throws. Stranger still is that Hercule's movements, as always, are executed as if underwater, the wide sleeves of his gray smoking jacket billowing, his hands pushing against the thick air, but the apples fly normally in quick arcs. Back and forth. Red, silver. A crowd gathers. Two cashiers desert their stations to come and watch, and four or five people produce cameras before Iris remembers hers and finally snaps the photo.

When Hercule returns the apples to the crate, I say, "That was incredible!"

He is obviously pleased. "What's next on your shopping list?" he asks.

"The roast," I say. We head to the meat counter, where we take a great picture of Hercule browsing the various cuts.

· · ·

Iris parts ways with us after shopping so she can go home and get her parents, and Hercule and I return to the apartment. Mom begins preparing the roast, and I decide to dress up. I head to my bedroom, Hercule trailing.

"Please stand outside the door," I say.

"I shall try," he says.

We manage this, and I commence examining the contents of my closet. I pull down a blue dress.

"So, do you have any questions for me?" Hercule asks idly from the hall, sounding bored.

"Well," I say, holding the dress before me in the mirror, "your Hints haven't been very easy."

"They aren't intended to be."

I place the blue dress on my bed and take out a red strapless, which I throw on quickly. My curly hair falls over my bare shoulders. It looks okay, but a little too much like I'm headed back to freshman prom. "I figured out the thing about *cavalier*," I say. "It's the Caballero. So I've invited everyone on my list. But Raahi won't be there—he left this morning, for basic training."

"Sorry to hear it," says Hercule.

"Also," I say, "Iris likes girls."

"She does?"

"I thought you should know, before you start Influencing things too much."

"Noted," says Hercule. Then, "Once you're at the restaurant, Gabriela, what do you intend to do to accomplish the items on your list?"

"Um, isn't that your department?" I say.

"You expect *me* to do everything."

"Well . . . yes?" I put the red strapless dress back on the hanger and replace it in the closet. I hold up the blue dress again.

"Certainly no one could request anything of *you*."

"Request anything?" I say.

"A cavalier request."

I drop the dress just as I pull it over my knees. "The song!" I say. I haven't given it a thought since all of this began — the lyrics I promised to write for Sarena, for her to sing at the Caballero.

When I enter the living room wearing the blue dress, Mom sees me from the kitchen. "You look *beautiful!*" she says.

"Thank you," says Hercule from behind me.

"Can I help with anything?" I ask.

Just then, there's a knock at the door. It's Sarena and Iris, with Iris's parents and Sarena's mother. Iris's parents look sort of like twins, both slim and well-dressed, with short blond hair. Sarena's mother is a large, tall woman with dark skin, hair braided similarly to her daughter's. She's smiling as she steps through the doorway with a platter of potato salad in her hands.

Then, the potato salad has been dumped on the floor. In the moment after, the caesar salad Iris's dad has brought also lands with a clang, lettuce erupting from the metal bowl. There's a scream, a shout, and everything is confusion. Croutons and square chunks of boiled potato scatter as Iris's parents and Sarena's mother panic at the sight of Hercule looming behind me.

I leap in to offer explanations, which doesn't help, because Hercule leaps after (as he must), and the next thing I know we're chasing our own guests down the hall toward the elevator.

Eventually, it gets sorted out. Everyone returns inside, and we all participate in the effort to clean up the mess and separate the scrambled salads. Iris's parents go into the kitchen while Iris and Sarena and her mom put the extra leaves in the dining room table under my supervision.

As the apartment fills with the scent of the roast, Dad enters, straight from work. He's dressed in a brown suit jacket and corduroy pants, and holds a platter stacked with frozen tamales, which he just bought at Central Carnicería. He smiles as he sees me, but when he sees Hercule he shouts, jumps, and drops the tamales, which clatter frostily across the parquet floor.

I leap forward, causing Hercule to leap forward . . . I could be doing a better job. In the hallway, I shout, "Dad, Dad! Didn't Mom tell you?"

Eventually, we retrieve him. Hercule says, "Pleasure to

meet you, Mr. Rivera." Dad crouches down silently to retrieve his tamales, a few long strands of his gray hair waving loose where they came undone during his panic.

He delivers the bruised tamales to the kitchen, and I hear him speaking sharply to Mom. "You could have *mentioned*," he says.

"Because I had nothing else to do today, you mean?" Mom replies.

I feel my ears growing hot. You know what—I've had enough of their bickering. I storm into the kitchen, dragging Hercule gracelessly behind me, and find them facing off before the stove.

"Quit it!" I say, sternly. Iris's mom and dad, who were arranging the tamales on a cooking sheet, turn demurely away as I scold my parents. "Why do you two always argue about *nothing?*" I say.

"I'm sorry, Gabriela," says Mom. "You're right."

"If you're going to act like children," I say, "I'm going to treat you like children. Now—apologize." I put my hands on my hips, and wait. Hercule, cramped against the kitchen ceiling behind me, also waits.

"Sorry, Grace," says Dad.

"I'm sorry, too," says Mom.

"Kiss and make up," I demand.

They kiss, a reluctant peck.

"Now *behave*. Dad, can I get you a beer?"

I fetch one from the refrigerator, and Dad, Hercule, and

I return to the living room and sit on the couch with Iris and Sarena and her mom.

Dad takes the band out of his hair. I've always liked it when his hair falls around his shoulders. It looks dignified. "Will you go to Mass tomorrow, Gabriela?" he asks.

"Yes," I say. I appreciate that he doesn't assume I'll go. He's really asking.

There's another knock at the door. It opens to reveal Aunt Ana; her husband, Hector; and Juan and Pia. They've made an enormous platter of sopapillas, covered with drizzled honey and powdered sugar.

In moments, it's on the floor, broken into pieces, globs of honey and puffs of sugar flying as Ana and Hector panic at the sight of Hercule. Ana recoils back through the doorway, carrying Pia and dragging Juan, and Hector bravely puts up his dukes.

I jump up and resolve things enough that everyone comes inside, and we begin the process of rescuing the pastries. Dad and Juan duck-walk good-humoredly around the entryway, collecting and stacking them in a tired-looking pile on the platter. I'm about to take it to the kitchen when there's another knock on the door. I look around the room—odd, I think everyone is already here.

Dad opens it, and as the unexpected visitors are revealed . . . I drop the platter. The sopapillas take a messy bounce, flying again.

In the doorway stand Raahi and his mother, Charvi.

Iris and Sarena leap from the living room couch. *"How?"* says Iris. *"Raahi!"* says Sarena.

They enter. Charvi's wearing a navy blue sweater and gray slacks, and her shining black hair is piled copiously atop her head, fixed with two long green pins. It is her turn to be surprised when she spots Hercule. *"Great Scott!"* she says with her precise British accent. She's holding a pot of kheer, a dessert Raahi introduced me to, and fortunately manages to keep hold of it.

Juan takes charge of the recovery of the twice-dropped sopapillas, and the rest of us go to the living room, anxious to hear the story.

"What happened?" I ask Raahi.

"I decided not to go," he replies.

"And the Army was . . . *okay* with that?" says Iris.

"No, I don't think they'll be okay with it," he says.

"But what's going to happen?" I say.

"I'll be arrested, probably."

"Will you . . . um, go on the *run?*" says Sarena, clenching her hands in her lap.

Raahi smiles. "No," he says. He looks at his mom, and she puts one arm around her tall, skinny son. "Mom and I talked it over. We're just going to take what comes. Tomorrow, maybe, they'll find me. I want to thank you, Gabriela — it was talking to Mr. Hale that helped me make up my mind. I was already thinking about it, but after seeing him I knew what I had to do."

Juan has industriously recovered the sopapillas from the entryway, and he takes them to the kitchen. He returns now and, full of curiosity, sidles up next to Hercule and gives him an experimental poke with one finger.

"Juan, *no!*" says Aunt Ana, racing in. She grabs him away from Hercule, who smiles vaguely. So far, I'm thankful for Hercule's presence. I'd worried that he'd be a grim reminder of what awaits me at midnight tomorrow, but the opposite is proving true: the novelty of him distracts from it.

When the roast is ready, we gather around the table. We fold our hands, and Dad gives a blessing: "Dearest Lord, thank you for our family and friends, and for this opportunity to gather with them in your name. And thank you for our . . . special guests tonight. Everyone is welcome at the table of God."

The dishes are passed hand to hand. There's hardly any diminution of talk. It's almost like a regular Tuesday dinner. Hercule eats politely, and talks politely, answering questions and explaining common misapprehensions about Deaths — what they can and can't do. One major issue is the afterlife. Hercule explains that Deaths don't know if there is one or not.

"So, what do you do with people?" says Mom. "I thought you took them into the afterlife."

"We take them to the end of the Fields," says Hercule. "You call them the Oaks here, I believe."

"Fascinating," whispers Iris under her breath.

"Taking notes?" I ask. She nods.

"I've heard that departures are on the rise right now," says Aunt Ana, who has proven as curious about Hercule as her son, Juan.

"I wouldn't know," says Hercule. "I keep my own garden."

"Speaking of your garden," says Iris, "it's certainly strange to have you here while we're struggling with all of your Hints. Because you could just tell us."

"No, I can't," he says.

"Can't or won't?" she presses.

"Trust me when I say," he replies, "that these things are done as they *must* be done. There is no caprice in it."

"Hercule," says Ana, leaning forward. "I understand that you attended my father, Gonzalo."

Of course I knew this would come up, and yet it still surprises me.

"Sir," says Dad, "please tell us. I never knew him. My sister" —he gestures to Ana— "barely met him . . ."

"I'm honored to relate the story," says Hercule. He begins the tale he told me before, but as he proceeds this time, different details emerge. After explaining his arrival in the olive grove, and Gonzalo's mortal wound, he says, "My presence seemed to amuse him, in fact. There was a twinkle in his eye, you might say, that I haven't often encountered with souls on the verge of death. He struggled to his feet, despite his condition, and said . . ." Hercule pauses, and turns to me. "Do you speak Spanish, Gabriela?" he asks.

"No," I say.

"Well, he stood there, in his bloody uniform," Hercule says, "and said, 'Hello, sir. Welcome to my demise.' Isn't that wonderful? Shortly thereafter, he and I walked together to the Fields. As you all know, we Deaths become more active during war. It is not our pleasure, I assure you, but simply our nature. The day I departed with Gonzalo, there were others in the Fields, taking soldiers from all sides of the conflict: Italians, Frenchmen, Tunisians, Germans, Americans, Egyptians . . . It was astounding, so many former enemies walking together in the gray. Some were accompanied by loved ones, but most were alone. Gonzalo linked arms with a Tunisian soldier, a stranger to him. They did not even speak a common language."

"My daughter showed me a document the other day," says Dad, "which indicated that Gonzalo earned a Pardon."

"He did," says Hercule, "but it was useless to him. If he returned to life, he would have died within minutes from his injury. So he decided to give it away."

"This is real, then—the true story?" says Dad.

"Thank you," says Ana, who has raised her napkin to dab away tears.

Next, perhaps a bit bored with topics historical, little Juan asks Hercule if he has any funny stories. Hercule waves a hand to indicate a mountain of such stories behind him and proceeds to tell one about a particularly demanding departing woman. The tale ends with Hercule saying, "Well, my dear, if that's what you want, I'm afraid I can't help you!" Everyone laughs.

After the meal, we gather in the living room for broken sopapillas and coffee. As we eat, Dad stands and taps an empty wineglass with his fork. He's going to make a toast. Immediately, tears spring to my eyes.

"Everyone, everyone," he says. "Thank you for coming to this very special dinner tonight. You know, those things in life that matter most—"

I wonder what the rest would have been, if he could have finished. I imagine him working on the speech, writing it out carefully. But he delivers only these first words before his voice cracks. He stands perfectly still, his glass raised, lips trembling.

I go to him and wrap my arms around him. *"I refuse!"* he barks, at no one. *"I refuse!"* His fingers tangle in my hair. It is awful to be grieved.

writing

After the guests have all left and my parents have turned in for the night—after it is very late—I find myself alone with Hercule in my room. I'm at my desk, shoes off. He's next to the window, clothes and hair wafting gently.

"Your parents' makeup kiss was not very convincing," he observes.

"I agree," I say, thinking back on it.

"Do you think they could both use a good *first kiss?*"

I eye Hercule. "Are you making fun of me?" I say.

"Not at all," he says, in a way that makes me think he is making fun of me.

"You sound like you're making fun."

He shakes his head.

"Well," I say, "they've been harping on one another for a long time."

Hercule gazes through the window into the darkness outside. "I wonder if you have the energy to comply with your friend's request of you. There's not much time left."

"What's your Noble Weakness, Hercule?" I ask. "I'm not going to figure it out, you know."

"'Always about to disappear,'" says Hercule, and he snorts approvingly at the ingenuity of his riddling. "Pardons are such selfish things anyway, don't you think, Gabriela? And isn't your list an attempt to provide for others?"

"I guess so," I say.

"Don't sit on your hands now. You have a role to play. Start writing. You like to write, don't you?"

"I . . . I don't really know," I say. I pull a blank sheet of paper and a pencil from my top desk drawer while Hercule looks on disapprovingly.

"Don't give me a disapproving look right now, please," I say.

"I am not giving you a disapproving look."

"Yes, you are — you still are."

"Am not. This is my sad look."

"Sad?"

"That you're so young. You don't even know yet if you like to write." He pauses. "As to your difficulty getting started, let me say this: there's no answer but to try. Have you read Samuel Beckett? He once said, 'Try again. Fail again. Fail better.'" Hercule closes his eyes. When he opens them, he says, "Let me tell you a little more about your grandfather's death. Something I didn't reveal during dinner, which is simply this:

When I first met Gonzalo in the olive grove, he stood and greeted me as I said, but he did one other thing as well. He recited a poem, which was dedicated to his family."

"He wrote poetry?" I say. "Do you remember it?"

"It was like a prayer, and there was a general principle to it that might be of use to you. He wrote about the people he cared about." Hercule pauses and looks out my window again, down on the lamplit street. "Your father does the same, doesn't he? He writes prayers for people in your church." Hercule reaches out and cracks open my bedroom window. "Think of someone you care about," he says.

A waft of cool air enters through the crack. And riding upon it is the strong smell of flowers—the very smell that's been my intermittent companion all week. I breathe deeply. Hercule does, too.

"They're hydrangeas," I say.

"They're *hyacinths*," he replies.

"Hercule," I say, "your Hint, about my first kiss. You wrote 'The Fields.' But Sylvester and I went there and it didn't happen."

"You have a complaint?" says Hercule.

"No, just . . . an observation, that it didn't work out."

"Wrap-up items do not always work out," says Hercule. "I'm not a magician, you know."

"But I thought you were," I say. "I thought you could make things happen."

"I can only encourage things that *might* happen. For instance, some events with relevance to your Wrap-Up List *might* transpire tomorrow night at the Caballero, given the correct circumstances."

The smell of the flowers reminds me intensely of that day — Sylvester and I. I find myself wishing for him . . . wishing for another try at that kiss. He messed it up, but maybe he'd do better with a second chance.

I pick up my pen.

I write.

departure day

ash wednesday

A dream: I'm in the living room of the apartment, watching TV with Mom. It's a report about the war, and we can see the troops marching while the announcer describes it. Then fighting begins, and it's impossible to say what's happening — war is too complicated for television. Who's a good guy and who's a bad guy becomes hopelessly confused. I creep close to the screen, trying to understand, and a stray bullet flies out. I'm struck in the chest and knocked backwards onto the carpet.

I sit up to find Dad watching me from the couch. "You're dead," he says.

"No, I'm not," I reply.

"Are you hungry? If you're hungry, you're alive."

In fact, I am hungry. Ravenously hungry.

"Gonzalo dropped an olive around here somewhere. I wonder if we can find it," says my dad.

On the radio, the war is over. The speakers hiss. I look for Dad, but he's disappeared. Hercule is there. He holds out a silver hand.

My last day begins with me shutting off my alarm clock. I sit up tiredly in bed and swing my legs to the floor in the half darkness of the room.

"Good morning," says Hercule from by the window.

I stand and walk into the hall, Hercule following closely. As I move to shut the bathroom door, he's right there, halfway through. *"Really?"* I say. This hasn't been a problem before, but apparently it is now.

"If it's any consolation," says Hercule, "I will close my eyes."

Grumpily, I allow him in, and he stands by the wall as I pee.

"You have a powerful stream," he observes.

"Thank you," I say. I can't believe this is my first conversation of the last day of my life.

The sun has just risen as my parents, Hercule, and I walk to church. I observe my surroundings closely: the redbrick building across the street, newspaper boxes by the light pole, parallel-parked cars, light glancing from windows, grass blades creeping through cracks in the sidewalk . . .

We reach St. Mary's to find it decked soberly for Lent. Instead of taking our usual seats in the transept, we stand at the back of the nave, not wanting Hercule's presence to cause a stir. As it is, we get plenty of curious, stern, and fearful glances. The church is solemn and quiet. The congregation looks tired, and I know some people are fasting and keeping vigil during these days.

I've always liked Ash Wednesday. I imagine that this service alone is still like it was at the very beginning of Christianity. No matter where you live, or when, whether you're a modern person or a historic one, death is sad.

The service includes somber readings and singing. Father Ernesto gives a short homily. He's got more on his mind than the fact that I'm departing today, but his words seem meant for me. He speaks of preparations, of the repentant attitude that should be with us through Lent, and of the sorrow of our physical demise. Our spiritual immortality, he says, does not exempt us from the tragedy and pain of death. Indeed, in the Bible, Jesus weeps when Lazarus dies. But Father Ernesto can't help letting in a ray or two of light as well. How can you not, when you know Jesus will come back? Despite the awful, cold certainty of it all, the mind makes that leap of faith. To jump for a wild pass you can't possibly catch. *At least it is a fate, and not death.*

At the conclusion of the service, a line forms down the central avenue from the altar to the front doors, where several deacons stand with bowls of ashes. These they apply in the shape of a cross to the forehead of each person. Everyone leaves marked. When Hercule reaches the front of the line, the person making the crosses is speechless and afraid. Hercule says, "Don't worry if I'm too tall to reach."

We return to the apartment afterward, the sun shining brightly between buildings. It's going to be warm, probably the warmest day so far this year. Sarena, Iris, and Raahi are waiting for us on the front steps.

"Raahi!" I say.

"Still here!" he says cheerfully.

"Will you come to the Caballero tonight?" I ask.

"They'd have to drag me away," he says.

We walk up to the apartment. Mom tosses her purse on the kitchen counter and says, "Anyone hungry?"

"Kind of," I say. "Are there any leftovers from last night?"

"You want *leftovers?*" She laughs, and I do, too. I really do want leftovers, though. She goes into the kitchen to begin heating them up, and I turn to Sarena.

"Sarena, I wonder if I can show you something."

"Sure," she says.

We leave Iris and Raahi, and go to my room, followed by Hercule.

"I don't want those guys to know," I say. "Maybe it's silly, but . . . well, I wrote you some lyrics. For your song." I take the page from my desk. "I don't know if they're any good. They're probably not. But . . ." I hand it to her.

She reads, and I twist my fingers together.

After what seems an eternity, her eyes reach the bottom of the page. She smiles. "They're *great*," she says. She places the page on the desk and picks up a pencil. "It fits almost perfectly! I'll trim one line . . ." She starts scribbling in the margin. She looks over at me. "Gabriela, I'm going to perform this. The band already knows the tune."

"Perform it . . . *tonight?*" I say.

She folds the sheet, puts it in her pocket, and gives me a hug. "Thank you," she says.

snake lake

Mom heats up lunch, and we all eat together. With each bite, I'm aware of time passing. The leftovers disappear with distressing speed. *This is really it,* I think, *my last day.*

Mom and Dad take the plates into the kitchen and start loading the dishwasher. I look at my friends. "You guys," I blurt, "do you want to go for a drive?" Because that's what I want all of a sudden—to get out of town for a few hours.

"Where to?" asks Raahi.

"How about Snake Lake?" I say. "We'll come back in time to go to the Caballero."

I break the news to my parents, and they accept it though I can tell it grieves them to think of spending time apart from me today. It grieves me, too, but a few minutes later Iris, Sarena, Raahi, Hercule, and I pile into Raahi's car. Raahi and Sarena are in front, and Iris and I are in back with Hercule sandwiched between us. That first night, when we thought Hercule couldn't fit into this car? We just didn't try hard enough. He's crammed, shoulders between his knees, head jutting forward.

Though Raahi's car has no radio in it, we have Sarena, who's a human jukebox. As the car climbs out from town, she leads us through a hit parade of today's Billboard toppers. In about twenty minutes, we're entering the pines. At the Y that leads left to the Fields or right to the lake, we go right. The city falls picturesquely behind and below, cut by the blue ribbon of the Snake River. Its source is the lake we're heading for, Snake Lake, near the top of the foothills, a popular day trip with plenty of private nooks because of its circuitous shape.

"Hey, Gabriela, remember this one?" says Sarena, and she starts singing a song I'd almost forgotten:

> *Caro mio ben,*
> *credimi almen . . .*

"Did you hear that guy sing it?" I ask. "The Singing Man?"

"You just listen once, and you remember it forever?" says Raahi.

"I don't have an eraser when it comes to music," says Sarena, then continues, *"senza di te languisce il cor . . ."*

We enjoy our first glimpse of Snake Lake. It isn't particularly amazing, because you only see one bend at a time without ever seeing the whole thing, but what's visible at the moment—bright blue water reflecting the blue sky—satisfies me that I picked the right thing to do for the afternoon.

The first parking lot has cars in it already, so we drive to the next, and then to the third. At the fifth little lot, there's no one. We park and step into the sunshine. I stretch and turn my face skyward, eyes closed, thankful for this unseasonably warm day. Everyone follows suit except for Hercule.

"Hercule, doesn't the sun feel good?" says Iris.

"I don't feel heat," he says.

"You don't feel the sun?" I say.

"No."

"Can you get a sunburn?" says Iris.

"We can neither burn nor freeze."

We all fall silent at this. I can tell everyone feels it — just in case we were about to start looking at Hercule like he was a regular person, these little facts keep emerging. *We can neither burn nor freeze.*

The part of the lake we can see from our private waterfront is very nice, a long watery hall lined with boulders and protruding stumps. Snake Lake is an odd place — there are dead trees sticking out of it, as if they grew up through the depths. They're a hint that this lake is man-made. Decades ago, before my parents were born, there was no lake here — instead, there was a town called Andeola, a tiny spot with a few hundred residents.

The people living down in the valley decided they wanted electricity. One good way to get it was to dam the Snake River just below Andeola. So the valley bought out the town, over the course of about ten years, and all the residents relocated. Then the dam was built. The river swelled, and Snake Lake grew, swallowing Andeola. The town is still down there somewhere, abandoned, empty, and nearly forgotten. Every once in a while something breaks free from the bottom and floats up. Last year a toolshed appeared, with tools still in it. Because of some initials carved into the remarkably preserved handle of a rake, the Municipal Archives (with my dad's help) deduced the former owner and located the grandkids, now elderly men and women, who donated it all to the county museum.

Most of the time, though, you don't see anything. On a sunny day like this, with the water the color of bluebells and emeralds, it's strange to imagine the dark, silt-covered town below.

Because of the nature of the lake, there aren't sandy beaches here. The water's edge is composed of hillsides and boulders. The spot we've chosen today is one we've all been to before. We ascend a large boulder to its flat lookout. The rock is warm from the sun. We throw blankets onto the sunny sandstone and relax. Hercule wanders the top of the boulder, looking around a little — the tether between us, at the moment, is slack. Eventually he sits as well, first fussily dusting off a little landing zone for himself.

After reclining for a few moments, Sarena stands. She takes her wallet out of her jeans pocket. She takes off her watch, and her shoes and socks. Then she steps to the edge of the boulder, a cliff about fifteen feet above the surface of the lake. Her face shines in the sun streaming over the hilltops. We know what she is going to do.

She looks back at us and shouts, "Cannon-ball!" She leaps over the edge, and disappears. There's a brief silence, then a splash, and then a series of cold-inspired shrieks. We listen to her paddle to the base of the boulder. She climbs out and hurries back to the top, sending chilly drips onto everyone. She towels off, briskly rubbing her now-soaked clothes, and then flops down to start drying off. "Warm as bath water out there," she lies.

Raahi stands next. He takes off shoes and socks, and continues to strip down to his surprisingly flowery boxer shorts. I haven't seen him dressed to swim since we last came up to Snake Lake, last summer. He's changed a lot. There's hair on his chest that wasn't there before, and his body, which was bony and angular last year, has filled out. He looks graceful as he approaches the edge, surveys the drop briefly, then bends his knees. He leaps high and disappears in a graceful dive. "Wow!" I say as he goes. There's a quiet *snik* as he slices into the water.

"Fairly good," says Hercule, "though he overextends his arms."

A few moments later, Raahi returns to the top of the boulder, dripping.

"Where did you learn to do that?" says Iris.

Instead of replying, Raahi dives again. When he returns

this time, he says, "You guys have never seen me dive? That's weird. I used to be pretty good for my age group." He towels off. Maybe the lake really is as warm as bath water—it doesn't seem to have bothered him.

Iris takes off her shoes and socks, and then strips to her underwear—black bra and panties. She's always been the most mature of us, but like this, poised before a whitish blue sky in the brisk snap of the spring air, she looks like a model in a magazine with long, slender arms and strong legs. She jumps, taking a straightforward approach. A few moments after the splash, she climbs back up . . . and it's my turn.

I take off my shoes and socks. Following Iris's lead, I disrobe to my underwear. I step to the edge and look down. The water is glassy and clear in the shadow of the boulder, but all I can see through that clearness is the silt that stands suspended through it, a wafting field of greenish gray.

"Go, Gabriela!" says Sarena.

All of them are sitting behind, pushing at me with their eyes. *Go.*

I jump.

The journey from the rock to the surface of the lake is so brief that calling it a journey is an overstatement. It's an interval.

The lake and I collide, and the freezing water engulfs me—a tiny bit of nothing thoughtlessly swallowed. My eyes pop open and confront the fuzzed, steady wall of silt. Below me somewhere is the abandoned town of Andeola, held eternally among the shreds. Old fence posts. Empty kitchens.

Then the lake seems to say, *Not yet, Gabriela*. It pushes me upward, ejecting me into the sun accompanied by a shower of glittering droplets, to see my friends smiling down from above.

When I return to the top of the rock, Iris reaches out and puts her thumb on my forehead.

"What are you doing?" I say.

"Your cross is running," she replies.

"My cross?" I'm not sure what she means. Then I remember—the ash cross I got after Mass. I'd forgotten about it.

Sarena approaches with a handkerchief in one hand, and Raahi with his shirt. They all go to work, rubbing my forehead clean. Behind them, Hercule stands and watches. His long shadow falls over us.

always about to disappear

I don't know where the day goes, exactly. Where does life go? The questions are the same.

Iris, Sarena, Raahi, and I are all in my living room. We're dressed up. Iris wears a white shirt with a white knee-length skirt over green stockings (she looks like the flower she's named after). Raahi has on a blue shirt with a wide collar, and tan pants that reveal about an inch of his yellow socks. Sarena is in her suit — her uniform for the Washington Fifteen. I'm wearing my blue dress from last night (I can't help that it's my favorite). All four of us are sitting on the couch, Hercule on a chair across from us.

"Okay, we're ready!" I shout, and my parents emerge from the hall to take a slow turn. Mom's wearing a long green dress with a white cardigan, and Dad's in a light brown suit with a matching vest, which must have come from a spot in his closet he hadn't plumbed for years. His hair is loose over his shoulders.

"You guys look great!" I say. It's true, especially with the evening sun streaming through the windows, but I can tell by the way they stand together that they still haven't made proper amends. Maybe they're past such things now. Maybe at some point it's impossible. Nonetheless, they're making an effort, and I appreciate that.

"Should we take two cars?" I ask.

"I'll drive us all," says Dad.

"Your car?" I say, envisioning his old station wagon, filled to the ceiling with boxes.

It's parked at the curb right outside. And for the first time in my memory it isn't crammed with junk. Also, it's been washed and waxed. The wood paneling shines, and the hubcaps gleam.

"What did you do with all the . . . stuff?" I ask.

"The dump," he says.

Despite the incredible spaciousness of the emptied car, we're in close quarters: Mom and Dad in front; Iris, Raahi, and Sarena behind; and I and Hercule in the rear, in the seats that face backwards—it's the only place where Hercule can fit. As Dad begins to drive, Hercule and I watch where we've been.

Sarena's dad has been playing music at the Caballero for as long as I've known Sarena. His job as bandleader was the reason her family moved here. Although our city is small potatoes compared to Chicago, the Caballero is a nice hotel.

We enter through the large double front doors and walk past the lobby to the restaurant. It looks considerably different from when I was last here (at three in the morning). The stage at the front is set with risers and chairs, occupied already by the band's instruments. Before it, the smooth boards of the dance floor shine in the red and yellow stage lights. Ranged around this area is the restaurant seating, large circular tables. Because it's early, I don't expect to see many people, but a quick glance surprises me. There are lots of people here, and I think I know most of them. At one table I see Ms. Lime sitting with two pear-shaped children whom I take to be her sons. Near the dance floor, Wendy converses with some kids from school — Dawn Fuller and Meg Rhinehardt (both cheerleaders) and Milo Stathopoulos and Jeff Dounais (from the football team). It seems like word got around.

At another table I see Aunt Ana with Hector and the kids, all of them eating plates of spaghetti. Another group enters behind us — it's Iris's parents and Raahi's mother.

Dad tells the maitre d' the name for our reservation, and we're led toward our table, near the dance floor. I'm still gawking at how many people have showed up when suddenly I feel a tugging in my chest. It's like my insides are being yanked backwards. I press on, but the sensation increases. I turn around.

Behind me, Hercule has stopped walking. He's standing

stock-still at the edge of the dance floor, peering intensely across the restaurant at the far wall. I try again to move forward, and again am prevented—it's definitely Hercule, standing stiff and resisting the pull of me. He fixes me with a glance and says, commandingly, "Come here!"

I obey out of curiosity. He points to the far end of the restaurant. "There," he says, with a smug satisfaction that indicates he thinks he's proved something.

"What?" I say. I look out across the tables, full of friends and acquaintances.

"*There!*" he says again, shaking his pointing finger. "I know you see it."

"It?" I say.

"Yes, *it*," says Hercule. "My *chair*. From my *house*. You summoned it with me, and this restaurant has now stolen it."

Hercule wades in through the tables, me hustling to keep pace with his long, slow strides. He causes considerable commotion, people craning their necks or leaping from their seats as he passes.

We reach the chair, and I do remember it—low back and seat upholstered in sparkly gray, carved claw-foot legs. Hercule lifts it with some difficulty and drags it from the wall. We make our return journey to our table, my parents and friends all watching with great interest. When we reach them, Hercule says, "*My* chair," as he puts it down. He gives the maitre d' a challenging look, and the man holds up his hands and backs away. Hercule sits in his chair, and the rest of us sit in ours. We're informed of the specials, which I don't listen to — I'm still looking around. I see Mr. Hale. I see Father Ernesto and Father Salerno.

My long glance ends at the stage, where it encounters, above the risers on the back wall, a clock. It's nothing fancy — a round metal clock like in our classrooms at school, with bold black numbers. As soon as I see it, my gaze is pinned. It shows five after seven. It ticks insistently.

"Good to see all of you."

I pull my eyes from the clock when I hear Sarena's dad's voice. He's a large man, wider and taller than my dad, wearing a black suit with a trumpet lapel pin. I wonder if Sarena will eventually prove to have the same body type as her dad. It's kind of funny to imagine her as a giant forty-five-year-old. I glance across the table at Iris and Raahi. How will they look when they're our parents' age? Rounded, wrinkled. Happy, I hope.

Sarena's dad has always struck me as easygoing, though Sarena says he has a temper. But he loves his work, and if Sarena sticks with music, she'll have a career she loves, too. "Gabriela, it's especially nice to see you," he says.

"I'm looking forward to hearing you play," I say.

"Everything is on the house for this table tonight," he announces, "courtesy of the band." He gestures to the empty risers as if the band were there, tipping their hats to us. My eyes flick back to the clock above the stage. Two minutes have passed during this exchange. I feel cold.

Sarena and her dad depart backstage, and the rest of us study our menus, then place our orders. Dad requests a bottle each of house white and red for the table. I ask for the tuna tacos. Hercule requests an extra-rare rib-eye steak. "And when I say extra-rare," he explains to the waiter, "I'd like the chef to simply *consider* cooking it."

Soon the band enters the stage, everyone in suits. When Sarena steps out, our whole table shouts her name. The band members file onto the risers and take up their instruments — trumpets, saxophones, trombones, a bass guitar, and drums. There are fifteen people including Sarena's dad, who leans over a mike at the front and says, "I'm Clyde Washington, and we're the Washington Fifteen."

They begin to play. The music is up-tempo, the trumpets bright and fast. I glance at Hercule to see his reaction. He's leaning back in his chair, face tilted toward the ceiling. His eyes are closed, and he nods along. When I first met him, I couldn't have cared less what kind of time he'd have tonight, but I find myself glad he's enjoying it. Aggravating as he is, I guess he's growing on me.

An enthusiastic audience takes to the dance floor. Raahi stands next to my chair and offers me his arm. He knows I don't know how to dance, and I know he doesn't know how. We walk onto the gleaming floor as the band begins a slightly slower number. The people around us are doing some step I don't know — jitterbug? Foxtrot?

"Thanks for spending today with me," I say.

"I'm honored," says Raahi. "You're one of the best people I know, Gabriela. Everyone thinks so, actually."

"They do?" I say, raising a skeptical eyebrow.

"But you aren't conceited about it."

"Oh-kay," I say, grinning despite myself. Onstage, Sarena takes a solo. She isn't quite as polished as some of the other performers, but she's also less than half their age. I like seeing her up there.

"So," I say, moving the conversation away from my merits, "has anything happened? About, you know, not reporting for duty?"

"There was a call," says Raahi. "My mom took it. They asked where I was, and she said I was at home, and that I didn't intend to comply with the draft. They're sending MPs tomorrow. They'll arrest me, I think."

"Oh, my God," I say.

"I'm glad," he says. "Everything that's happened in the last week, everything with Sylvester, and Mr. Hale, and even you putting me on your Wrap-Up List . . . it all helped me. I know I made the right decision."

"How long will you go to jail for?"

"I guess a judge will decide," says Raahi. "I'm going to say I'm against the war. But I want you to know," he says firmly, "that I *owe* you . . . I probably owe you my life." When the song ends, we return to the table. The soup and wine arrive. I ordered lentil soup, and I see Hercule has the same. He brings a spoonful near his mouth and holds it by his gills. He takes a sip.

The band plays two more fast numbers, and the floor crowds. Dad serves wine, walking around the periphery of our table. He gives me a little more than everyone else. "How are you doing?" he asks, tousling my hair.

"I'm okay," I say.

Soon, distressingly soon, the main course is delivered, and the stage clock's hour hand continues its slow climb. Nine o' clock: I'm popular on the dance floor. My parents each ask me for a song, and Wendy comes over from her table and asks after that. Father Salerno even takes me for a turn — and he's an excellent dancer. He says he used to dance competitively. I'm not surprised. *I understand how things are now*, I think.

Ten o' clock: Dessert is served, and I eat a scoop of orange sorbet. Then, I sense Hercule standing next to me.

"I recall asking, early on," he says, "if you would save me a dance." He towers overhead, his grayish silver form spectral in the stage lights.

Then, from the side, Iris says, *"Smile!"*

Hercule and I turn to find her peering at us through the lens of her camera. The flash goes off.

"Me, just before my departure," I say.

"I'll title it 'Gabriela About to Disappear,'" says Iris. No sooner are the words out of her mouth than both of us gasp, astonished.

"The Hint!" we say in unison. It was right in front of my nose the whole time: the photo of Grandfather Gonzalo. On my desk. There he is, preserved a moment before he was lost forever — *always about to disappear.*

I turn to Dad, holding out one hand. *"Car keys!"* I command him. He takes them unquestioningly from his pocket and is about to give them to me when something quite unexpected occurs.

There's a couple standing nearby, an elderly man and woman. They've been here all evening, dressed in fine clothes — the man in a suit, and the woman in a long, black dress that curves over her hunched shoulders. I've seen them a few times, eating at a distant table. But now they are right here. They've approached us for some reason.

And when Dad sees them, his whole demeanor changes. His face goes pale, and in his eyes is a kind of rage that I've rarely seen him display — so intense that all of the good humor in him is burned up by it.

Then Mom is at his shoulder, placing one firm hand on his elbow.

"José," she says, using his first name calmingly.

But her tone does nothing to stanch the force of Dad's anger. *"You!"* he says loudly to the couple. He takes a step forward, aggressively. "How dare you!" He points at them and repeats, louder: *"How dare you?"*

I think he might actually take a swing at these people. My mind is reeling, and my desire for the car keys is forgotten.

"Get out of here!" Dad yells, waving his arms toward the doors. The old couple backs off, and Dad turns to Mom. "Did you *invite* them? Did you *bring* them here?" He's out of control. I've never seen anything like this before, and I stare, transfixed.

"I wanted them to see her," says Mom quietly. "And now they have. Now they'll leave."

Finally, I understand. These are the Mason-Hunts — Mom's parents. My grandparents.

The scene is a paralyzed tableau in which my grandparents haven't quite left, my dad hasn't quite attacked, and my mom hasn't quite calmed anyone down. But one person is not caught up in it — Iris. She darts forward, snatches the car keys dangling from Dad's fingers, turns, grabs me, and shoves me toward the exit. "No time!" she says. And then I'm running with her. I think I hear Hercule's voice yelling after me, but I'm moving too fast to listen.

first kisses

Outside, Iris and I jump into Dad's car. She gets behind the wheel (she's been taking Driver's Ed at school this quarter), and we roll into the street.

"What was that all about?" she says, accelerating through a yellow light, going kind of fast.

"My mom's parents," I say. "I've never seen them before."

Iris leans forward, her chin nearly touching the steering wheel as she speeds toward my apartment building. *"Faster,"* she whispers to the car.

In a few minutes, my block appears before us, the old square brick buildings forming walls to either side of the street.

Then, out of nowhere, I feel a sudden, violent pull in my gut—it's like someone's trying to rip me right out of myself. "Oo-*wowh!*" I say. The force of it yanks me backwards into my seat, and I'm pressed there, pinned as the car races on.

"What? What?" Iris shouts, swerving.

I can't speak. I feel like I'm being crushed by a hundred gravities. I've got one hand on my chest, the other on my abdomen, and they each seem to weigh a thousand pounds.

Iris hits the brakes and screeches to a halt in the middle of the street. "It's Hercule!" she says. "Your connection to him — we stretched it too far!"

My head is locked against the headrest. My feet are pulling backwards, wedged under the seat. *". . . get . . . the . . . picture . . ."* I whisper, though my tongue is straining back the way we came, and my lungs are wrapped around my shoulder blades.

Without another word, Iris opens her door. "The photo on your desk, right? Of Gonzalo?"

I can't reply, but I manage to creep my fingers into my purse and produce the keys to the front door.

Iris takes them and rushes down the block while I sit, paralyzed. The moment I'm alone, everything seems very quiet. There are no cars on the street. No people. I watch Iris climb the stairs of the apartment building and slip through the front doors. I look into the rearview mirror, back down the empty street. *Always about to disappear,* I think. I feel like I should make some important realization as I sit here with nothing to do, but I don't realize anything except that this really, really hurts.

Finally, Iris bursts back through the front doors and rushes to the car with the framed photo in her hands. She holds it before me. Turns it upside down. "What is it? What is it?" she says.

"Take it out of the frame," I whisper. I try to lift my hands to do it myself, but they're too heavy.

Iris releases the little catches around the edge and pulls the picture free. Together, we look at the back of it. There's writing on the old, yellowed photographic paper. Two lines, scrawled in an awkward cursive. In Spanish.

"What does it say?" says Iris.

"I don't know," I moan. "But . . . Dad can translate."

Iris starts the engine and executes a clumsy three-point turn. On the first point, the weird gravity that's pulling me toward Hercule slams me against the door. On the second point, I'm slammed against Iris, knocking her nearly out of her seat. She manages to get her hands back on the wheel and her feet on the pedals. I'm thrown forward against the dashboard as we speed back toward the restaurant. It's almost like my own body is pulling the car.

The pressures upon me lessen as we hurry on, and soon I'm sitting normally, freed — back within the bounds of an acceptable proximity to my Death. "Thank God," I say, breathing easily again, my tongue back in its regular place, my feet in theirs, and my organs in theirs.

"It's going away?" says Iris, looking worriedly over at me.

"*Stop! Stop!*" I yell, pointing ahead.

Iris slams on the brakes — as Hercule's giant and completely unexpected form looms up before us in the middle of the street. The car screeches to a halt.

I open the door and leap out. *"Hercule!"* I say. "What are you doing out here?"

He doesn't reply. His hair is a mess, floating in wild wisps. His smoking jacket is torn open, with the belt dangling, and his pants have holes in both knees, showing the silver flesh of his legs.

"I *distinctly recall*," he says, *"yelling* after you. But did you listen? Did you stop?"

I'm trying to piece this all together. Hercule's dress shirt is askew on him, bunched up to reveal an iridescent belly button. "I felt a tug," I say, "as we were driving . . ."

"I'm sure you did," says Hercule. "The tug of me *flying from my chair*. The tug of me pitched through the restaurant and into the street."

Iris's face lights up. She does not even try to disguise her fascinated delight at this.

I stifle a smile. "Well, would you like a lift back?"

We park half a block from the Caballero, and then walk. There's commotion around the entrance. Several employees are outside picking up some kind of rubble — bits of wood and glass. As we reach the fragments, I realize that they're pieces of the front doors, smithereens all over the sidewalk and street. The doorway is gaping open with just a few splinters of wood remaining at the edges, dangling from bent hinges.

"Was that . . . *you?*" I ask Hercule.

He doesn't reply. He rubs the back of his neck with one hand.

We enter the restaurant to find the whole place recovering from what looks like a tornado. Tables are overturned. Some guests are nursing twisted ankles or bumped heads. I hear several versions of the story breathlessly recounted. Some voices are raw—mostly, I note, from laughter. Several people point to Hercule, and his frown deepens.

My family's table is unscathed but for Hercule's single overturned chair (which is in one piece, on its side). Apparently he was jerked backwards from it and then catapulted through the restaurant, across the dance floor, and into the hotel lobby, where he obliterated the front doors before launching up the street after me.

As I survey the fracas, my eyes, almost by accident, find the clock above the stage. Fifteen minutes to midnight.

There's Dad, standing next to our table. I rush to him as the Washington Fifteen strikes up a slow waltz in an effort to restore some sense of normality.

"Dad," I say, "could you translate this?" I hold out the photo.

He takes it in hand, and looks. "'I'd forgotten this was written here," he says. He mumbles the words to himself in Spanish, and then says, "To my family. If I could give you life through my death, I would.'"

"What does it mean?" I say.

"It was from a prayer Gonzalo wrote," says my Aunt Ana, approaching us from the other side of the table. "I remember Mother reciting it. He wrote it before he left for the war."

Iris and I share a puzzled glance over what possible connection this prayer could have with Hercule's Noble Weakness. Onstage, Sarena approaches the microphone.

"Thank you, everyone," she says. "Sorry for all the commotion tonight, but we'll keep playing if you keep dancing. This next number is a new one for the band. It's my arrangement. With lyrics by my friend—Gabriela Rivera." She points to me.

Then, the whole population of the restaurant stands. They begin to applaud as the band strikes up the tune, and Sarena sings, her voice clear and strong—my words.

The day you held me close
In springtime showers . . .

As the tune grows, and the dance floor fills, something strange happens. A gentle breeze blows in, through the busted doors. It's fresh and cool, bathing everything.

And it is bursting with the scent of hyacinths, stronger than I've ever smelled it—stronger than I believed possible.

The air crackles with the bite, and drips with the sweetness. My nose itches. My eyes water. Suddenly, I sneeze—and then sneeze again. Around me, I hear other people sneezing, some uncontrollably. To my left, a man doubles over while his wife's eyes swell with allergic tears.

But the smell is too wonderful to resist. I breathe deeply, my whole body suffused with a tingling pleasure, my mind a mess of colliding infatuation even as my sinuses clog. It's more than intoxicating — it's deranging. It's the smell of everything about to begin, the whole of creation on the day of the first sunrise, and I'm filled with an intense, reckless desire — an agony of it. My hands grasp the air, hunting for something. Sylvester's phantom is before me, evoked from memory with a greed for detail I didn't think I possessed. If he were here, I would put my arms around him. Pull him to me. I would bite his lips. I would —

There's a commotion off to the side, and I turn to see through watering eyes something that I did not expect. It's Iris and Wendy, mere feet away. They're locked together in a passionate embrace. Iris has pulled Wendy to her. She's kissing her, both of them sneezing —

Then I see my own parents, at our table, making out like teenagers. Mom is sitting on Dad's lap. Dad's hands are everywhere, pulling Mom's dress from her shoulders. Mom is kissing the nape of his neck, tangling her fingers in his hair —

"Such strange powers — *ah-tchoo!*" Sarena sings, trying to continue as her eyes turn red and sneeze after sneeze possesses her, "in the smell of blooming flowers. Nothing mine — *ah-tchoo!* — and nothing — *ah-tchoo!* — yours — it all was ours . . ."

I turn to Hercule. He's sitting calmly in his special chair amid the uproar, looking about with a mildly amused expression. I take another breath of the narcotic air, and nearly swoon with desire. I can scarcely believe what's happening. It is bedlam! Milo Stathopoulos is holding hands with Jeff Dounais. There's Ms. Lime and . . . Mr. Hale? I turn away, blushing, and see my Mom's parents, the Mason-Hunts . . . they're . . . *goodness!*

"Hergyule!" I shout through my stuffed and running nose, "are you *baygig* dis *habbedh?"* I'm laughing and crying simultaneously as the passionate melee tumbles around us.

"I don't *make* things happen," says Hercule.

"Budh you *are* baygig dis habbedh!" I say, and sneeze twice into my sleeve.

Hercule nods.

I know what the last words of Sarena's song are, since I wrote them. But she doesn't quite get them out of her mouth. Just before she finishes, after an especially epic sneeze, someone leaps onto the stage—it's Raahi. He knocks the microphone off its stand. He grabs Sarena by the shoulders, but before he can kiss her, she kisses him, diving impatiently past his advances. The two of them stumble, then fall headlong from the stage onto the dance floor, oblivious, rolling over the boards.

As the ecstatically debilitated band plays the last few chords of the song (and I see one of the saxophone players inexplicably playing a trombone, and vice versa), Hercule stands slowly. His gray clothes waft up around him. He holds out his long arms, like the giant boughs of a tree, and a new wind washes in, slow and broad. It is crisp, clean, scentless. My racing pulse slows as the perfume clears from the restaurant, and I take a quick survey of the couplings joined in the past minutes. It seems everyone in the place is embracing tenderly, most in pairs but some in groups of three, four, or more. No one appears embarrassed. Even Ms. Lime and Mr. Hale are holding hands, Ms. Lime's two sons looking bemusedly at them.

Hercule raises his arms further, for attention. Everyone quietly gazes at him, awestruck and in love.

He gestures to the clock above the stage. It is midnight.

He motions to me to stand before him, and I approach. Around me, my friends and family converge, pressing gently forward, forming a ring. Hercule's clothes, though torn by his tumble in the street, are arranged correctly now, and his face is serious. "Are you ready, Gabriela?" he asks.

"No," I reply.

He extends his hand.

I reach out. I curl my fingers around his.

A chill races through me.

I take a surprised breath—

silver

I open my eyes without realizing I'd closed them. I see my parents first, then Iris, Sarena, and Raahi, all staring at me with a terrible awe on their faces.

I look down at myself, my clothes, my hands. Silver. A lock of my blanched hair floats up before me, coaxed by an unseen current. I lift my hand to brush it away and feel the very air resisting the motion, thick as water.

Hercule regards me coolly as I come to my senses.

"Hello, sir," I croak. "And . . . welcome . . . welcome to . . ." I'm trying to say what Gonzalo said to him, but I can't. I'm having trouble pushing the air through my lungs. I'm not breathing.

No sooner does this occur to me than I notice the strange, profound stillness of my body. My heart has stopped.

"Oh," I say.

"No hurry now," says Hercule.

"Gabriela?" says Iris. She steps forward. I grasp both her hands, and find them neither warm nor cold. Touching them is like touching a pair of gloves.

Friends and family around us, Hercule and I head out through the shattered front doors of the hotel. Soon we're all standing together on the sidewalk. I turn to Hercule.

"Yes, Gabriela?" he says. "What is it?"

With some difficulty, I push air through my lungs and speak. "Don't forget . . . your chair," I say.

"Oh! Yes, thanks." He disappears inside, emerging a moment later carrying the heavy thing with some difficulty.

"Dad?" I say, turning. Dad steps forward, his eyes scared, tears pouring down. "Would you . . . give us a lift?"

I help Hercule maneuver the chair onto the roof. Dad has some rope in the back, and we pass it through the rolled-down windows and tie it. Then we all cram into the car— Hercule and I again in the backwards seats way back—and begin to drive. Behind us, other cars file in, and a motorcade forms, snaking through town to the narrow road, the pine forest, and the fog. With the night, there's nothing to be seen beyond manifold red embers of taillights and the white beacons of headlights.

The procession enters the pitch-black parking lot. Most people leave their engines running and lights on, striping the public Fields with yellow. We untie Hercule's chair and walk slowly, finding our steps. Hercule leads the way. He struggles with the chair, which seems at every turn to confound his attempts to carry it, but he is remarkably sure-footed in the darkness.

"Can you see in the dark?" Iris asks him abruptly.

"I have a sense similar to that possessed by sharks," he replies. He gestures to the twin gill slits on either side of his nose.

"Sharks?" says Iris.

"We're related to hammerheads."

"How can you be related to *sharks?*" says Iris. "Deaths are supernatural."

"*Mostly* supernatural," says Hercule. "The rest is shark."

There are lots of people here to see me off; some of them had the foresight to bring flashlights, or lighters, or candles, which lend a spectral glow to the dark Fields, especially as we proceed to the rockier, more uneven ground farther from the parking lot. Sarena and Wendy approach a group of kids all dressed in their marching band uniforms. Someone hands Sarena her trumpet, and Wendy her flute, and the band strikes up, playing a slow version of one of the tunes they perform at football games. Sad "Tequila." The crowd gathers behind Hercule and me, following us onto the grass. Sarena leads her band alongside, instruments glittering.

As we cross the rougher field, each member of my immediate family stoops to pick up a stone. As a kid I wondered — if every family member who passes takes one stone to stack next to the boundary, and this has gone on basically forever, won't the field eventually run out? Yet there seems no shortage.

Finally, we reach the sign: DEPARTURE.

The turf to the edge is mowed and trampled. Beyond lies shadowy, waist-high grass. Ranged all along the edge are the cairns, in broad, sloping piles and neat stacks. Some appear recent. Others are half-swallowed by dirt and age.

Hercule and I face into the darkness, brushing the long grass with our fingers. The high field continues uphill out of sight. I find myself thinking back on my visit here with Sylvester — both of us kept out by the forces that now stand ready to admit me.

Hercule puts his chair down with a relieved sigh. He and I turn and face the crowd.

departure

My family stands off to one side — Mom and Dad;
Aunt Ana, Hector, and their kids; and Mom's parents — but
everyone else lines up before me. There's a standard script and
procedure here. It isn't required, but everyone knows it, and it
makes things easier. Ms. Lime is first, wearing an expression
that suggests she didn't plan this.

"Thank you for being my friend, Ms. Lime," I recite.

"Thank you for being mine, Gabriela," she says. We hug,
and she steps aside for the next person: Mr. Hale. He hands me
a bouquet of lotus flowers. As soon as he releases them into
my hands, they turn from red blooms on green stems to silver
blooms on gray stems.

"Thank you for being my friend, Mr. Hale," I say.

"Thank you for being mine, Gabriela," he says hoarsely.

"And thank you for being Raahi's," I say.

"Who?"

"You met him, at the wake. He's here now. He decided not to comply with the draft."

This strikes Mr. Hale deeply. "Thank you for telling me that," he says. Then, "Gabriela, if you *do* see Sylvester . . ."

"I'll remind him," I say.

Mr. Hale steps aside, and I hand the blooms to Hercule.

Father Ernesto is next. He's holding a glass chalice of blessed oil, which glows like liquid gold in the flashlight beams. He's here to administer Extreme Unction, a practice somewhat debated within the Church: considering that I'm technically dead now, theologians disagree about whether the destination of my soul can be affected by the sacraments. But the Pope said that those churches employing Extreme Unction during departures can continue — there's no harm.

"If you'd like, Gabriela," he says.

I know that Dad, watching off to the side, will be comforted, and I bow my head. Father Ernesto dips his fingers in the oil and recites, "Through this holy unction and His own most tender mercy, may the Lord pardon you whatever sins you have committed, by sight — " I close my eyes, and Father Ernesto smears oil on my lids — "by hearing" — he daubs oil on my ears — "by smell" — he anoints the tip of my nose — "by taste" — he touches my lips — "by touch" — I hold out my hands, and he puts oil in each palm — "or by walking." He kneels slowly on his bad old knees and puts a drop of oil on each of my gray shoes. He makes the sign of the cross in the air before me and delivers the benediction: "The Lord bless you and keep you, Gabriela. The Lord make His face shine upon you, and be gracious unto you. The Lord lift up His countenance upon you and give you peace."

"Thank you for being my friend, Jaime," I say.

"Thank you for being mine, Gabriela," he says. "And — thank you for the times we have disagreed."

"There will be more," I say.

Other faces proceed past — the very large Milo Stathopoulos, his eyes moist (he's as surprised as I am that he's upset) and several other acquaintances from school. Iris's parents arrive together, and Raahi's mom.

Next are Sarena and Raahi, together. They're holding hands, and they look at me solemnly.

"Thank you for being my friend, Sarena. Thank you, Raahi," I say.

"Thank you for being mine, Gabriela!" Sarena squeaks. We hug, and she shivers — I think I'm cold to the touch.

"Thank you for being mine, Gabriela," says Raahi. I hug him. He says, "I know you'll come back. You won't comply." He smiles.

There is one more person at the end of the line: Iris. She approaches me, tears shining in her eyes. She's holding something in one hand — fabric. She holds it up so I can see. It's a white dress. "For when you return," she says. She still believes it could happen. I think of Gonzalo's prayer — "If I could give you life through my death, I would." It's not too late. I can still figure it out.

I open my mouth to speak, but my throat is suddenly narrow. Iris can't speak either. I brush the tears from her cheeks with my cold fingers.

"I'll wait for you here," she says finally. She steps to the side to stand with the rest of the public, a few paces distant.

Now, it's my family's turn.

Dad's brown suit is rumpled, and Mom's cardigan doesn't seem nearly warm enough. They each hold a flashlight in one hand and a small stone in the other. Their eyes are bright with tears. Aunt Ana and Hector stand beside them, Ana holding Pia in her arms, Hector holding Juan's hand.

And my grandparents, the Mason-Hunts. They approach first, knowing, I suppose, that their goodbyes are a little less important to me than the rest. They're stooped and skinny. Their hair is white, their skin pale. They look almost like miniature Deaths themselves.

"Hello, Gabriela," says the old man. The woman nods to me. I take a breath and deliver the script that has, fortunately, been supplied, because I have no idea what else to say to these people, strangers to me for my whole life.

"Leave what you have come to leave," I recite.

"I leave a piece of my heart," says my grandfather, and he kneels with some difficulty and places a stone at my feet.

"A piece of my heart," says my grandmother, and she places her stone.

"A piece of my heart goes with you also," I say. But it doesn't—I'm honestly confused about their presence here, about why they would want to attend my death, having missed my life. "Did my mom ask you to come?" I say, as they begin to turn away.

"We wanted to meet you," says my grandfather.

"You've had plenty of opportunities before this," I say. "I thought you hated me."

"We don't hate you, Gabriela," says my grandmother.

"Well, after I get my Pardon, you should come over for dinner," I say.

My grandfather nods. I sound almost like when I chastised my parents. Why am I the one to teach all of these adults how to behave? These two, who resemble a sagging version of the imperious couple in the photo on my desk. They are tired, old, regretful. They step aside. "I'll see you later," I say.

My aunt and uncle and their kids approach next.

"Leave what you have come to leave," I recite.

"I leave a piece of my heart," says my aunt, and she kneels and places a stone at my feet. Pia drops the little pebble she's been given. Hector and Juan follow.

"A piece of my heart goes with you also," I say to them.

Finally, my parents. The three of us hug for a long time. Mom's arms nearly crush me. When we separate, she looks at me tenderly. "You're the best daughter I could imagine," she says. She kneels and places her stone. "I leave my heart here," she says, her voice suddenly slipping. Dad places his next to hers, leaned against it. His breath rattles. "Come back," he stutters. "That's . . . that's *final*."

They step away.

Hercule and I turn from the gathered, silent crowd. Sarena strikes up the band again, and they play, roughly, the song she sang at the Caballero. She begins the tune, and her voice is steady, ringing across the Fields.

Hercule lifts his chair, and we step across the boundary. I leave my life.

the oaks

I'm not sure how much time passes after that. One step follows another through the blackness, Hercule grunting under the weight of his chair.

Eventually, the brushing blades of the long grass diminish, and I find myself staring down at low turf, clarifying in a new, thin light. It seems like morning is coming, but that much time can't have passed already, can it? Small yellow flowers peek from scrubby green grass. Then—blue, purple, and white flowers emerge in clusters from thick stalks. I look around, wondering. The flowers are everywhere, continuing up the rise in dense multicolor groups. I take a deep breath, but I can't smell anything.

"Are these hyacinths?" I ask.

"Yes," says Hercule, laboring under his chair. "Quite abundant here." He places the chair roughly on the ground and leans against it.

"Why don't you let me carry that for a while?" I say.

"I thought you would never ask," he replies.

"Is it old?" I lay my hands on the low back.

"No. I've had it about five years."

"You sure were upset about losing it."

"It is my favorite chair."

I lift it and carry it sideways, by its back and one leg, and we start up the hill again. The hyacinths continue for a while but diminish in number as we near the top of the rise.

The light increases. The blue sky is textured with a fine tulle of stretched clouds. Soon, we crest the hill and stand at the start of a short plain, which leads to a sparse but healthy grove of old oaks straight ahead, a few green buds beginning at the tips of recently dormant branchlets, casting a net of shadow on a floor of rusting leaves. To the left a rough, rocky outcropping mounds up. Swallows fly here, swooping, looking for bugs or playing.

"The Oaks," I whisper. I've heard about them my whole life, and now here they are. The very end of everything. I'm about to say something more when I'm distracted by a startling revelation.

"My *clothes!*" I exclaim. I am totally naked.

"Yes, it happened at the top of the rise," says Hercule.

"But you still have yours," I say. It seems a little unfair.

"I am not dead."

Now that his chair is jouncing against my bare skin, it's even more uncomfortable to carry.

"Um, could we *share* this?" I say.

Hercule takes the legs, and I take the back, and we continue.

As we near the Oaks and the rock outcropping, I see we aren't alone. There are two figures ahead, at the edge of the trees. One is extremely tall, a Death. The other I don't recognize at first. He's an old man, fat and naked, the early light gleaming off his hairy shoulders, chest, and bald head. His pendulous stomach lolls, weightless before him. He waves to us when he sees us.

"The Singing Man!" I say. I wave back. "That's Gretchen next to him, isn't it?"

"Yes," says Hercule. Gretchen stands silently, tall as a willow and wearing a form-fitting gray-black dress. Her mass of dark gray hair swims smokelike around her head and shoulders.

"You don't sound pleased to see her," I observe.

"She's been giving me the silent treatment," says Hercule.

"You two know each other?"

"She is my wife."

I blink. *"Married?"* I say. "Has she been worried about you? Since we kidnapped you?"

"I expect it has been a nice vacation for her," says Hercule. He frowns. "I'm not the easiest person to get along with, some say."

"Hello!" the Singing Man calls as we arrive.

"I know you," I tell him. "I saw you outside our school. We called you the Singing Man."

"That's good!" he says pleasantly, with a slight accent. "My name is Alfeo. I see you've come prepared to sit awhile?"

"I'm Gabriela," I say. "This is Hercule."

"Nice to meet you," says Alfeo.

"My friends and I enjoyed your music," I say.

"That was my wrap-up," says Alfeo. "I loved to sing, but I was a salesman for all my life. I wanted finally to realize that dream, just a little. This is Gretchen, my Death," he says.

"Hello, Gretchen," I say. She doesn't reply.

"She won't speak to you," says Hercule icily, "because you're with me." He glares at her, and she glares back.

Hercule and I put the chair down between us.

"What are you still doing here?" I ask Alfeo. "You departed days and days ago."

"Yes, well, she gave me a week to guess her Noble Weakness. But no. Since then, I've been deciding — getting ready." He nods significantly toward the Oaks. "I've walked all around here," he says. "You know what? We don't have to sleep anymore, isn't that nice? Plenty of time, and I stop and talk to everyone."

"But you haven't crossed over," I say.

Alfeo clasps his hands before him, encircling his belly. "It's hard. Singing is one thing — *fah*, I could leave that. But my most sacred — my wife and daughter. I couldn't! Only after talking to other people who came by, I understood I don't have it so hard. I was sixty-seven, you know. Not too bad." He looks at me sadly; I'm an example, I guess, of someone who does have it kind of hard—someone who had less time.

"I saw you on your departure day," I say. "You sang a last song."

"Yes, a great song!" says Alfeo. "A triumphant song!" And he sings it, just as he did then.

Vittoria, vittoria, mio core!
Non lagrimar più,
È sciolta d'Amore
La vil servitù.
Nel duol, ne' tormenti
Io più non mi sfaccio
È rotto ogni laccio,
Sparito il timore!

"You speak Italian?" he asks.

"No, sorry," I say.

"Well, that song says, 'Victorious, my heart! Weep no more! You're no longer Love's servant. Grief and torment don't worry me. Every snare has broken. Fear has disappeared!'" He nods as he goes through the lines in English, approving of them. "I'm glad to have met you, Gabriela," he says. "Now . . ." He turns to Gretchen. "Thank you for your patience."

"I needed none," she replies. Her voice is low, a breathy wisp.

Without hesitation, Alfeo steps into the shadows of the Oaks, walking almost merrily. The air changes around him as he goes, silver, like mercury. He pushes forward, using his arms, wading into the waves of it, and he begins to fade. The ripples increase, roiling around him thick as ropes.

And he's gone. A shimmer remains, then nothing. The swallows chirp in the trees, flutter down to the leaves he just stepped on, and race away on the wing, as if he never passed.

Gretchen, likewise, is gone — disappeared.

"Finally," Hercule mutters.

"Where did Alfeo go?" I ask. "The afterlife?" I stare under the trees. "He couldn't guess her weakness," I say.

"Hers is impossible," says Hercule.

"You know it?"

"Of course." Hercule pauses, then says, "What did you think of that song? It seemed like a good choice, to declare victory."

"Maybe for him," I say. "How can I be victorious? I haven't even fought yet." I pause. "Hey, your *chair!*" I exclaim. It has disappeared from between us without a trace.

Hercule looks a little surprised. "Gretchen took it," he says. "That was nice of her."

I find myself upset that it's gone. My arms are still aching from having carried it all this way. And to have it just vanish . . .

Suddenly, I'm crying. It's funny, I haven't shed a single tear this whole time, but losing Hercule's chair has somehow set me off. He stands quietly next to me, saying nothing, while I weep. I put my face in my hands. Each breath, which I don't need anymore to live, is used for more tears. Then Hercule says, "Someone's coming."

I lift my head, wiping my cheeks.

There's a sound from our left, by the rock outcropping.

"This place is busy," says Hercule. "You'd think there was a war on."

"Sylvester!" I shout.

He's already seen me. When he arrives, we're both awkward, looking at each other's naked, silver bodies.

"You're beautiful," I say, speaking the words as I think them, which leaves me a bit embarrassed.

"You, too," he says.

"I saw your father," I say. "He told me to tell you he loves you." Sylvester is so gorgeous, it's not easy to let my eyes rest on him.

"I waited for you again," says Sylvester.

I'm a little startled as I recognize Hercule's Hint from Sylvester's list — "Wait for Gabriela." I still don't know why.

I look under the Oaks, at the dappled shadows there, which are growing more firm as the light around us grows stronger. Sunrise will come soon. I find myself thinking about Gonzalo's prayer. "If I could give you life through my death . . ."

And perhaps something starts to come together.

"Hercule," I say, "you told me my grandfather gave his Pardon to someone he was with."

"Did I?" says Hercule.

"Yes, you . . . Well, no. You never did quite say that." I turn to Sylvester. "Sylvester, I think I have something for you. I didn't know it until just now. It's unclaimed, isn't it, Hercule? *That's* why there was a blank next to it, in the archives. Gonzalo gave his Pardon to his family — to me. To give life through his death."

"That's correct, Gabriela," says Hercule. "But consider carefully. 'To my family,' he said. His intent was that it be passed to his descendants. It is *yours* to use."

I ponder this. "Hercule," I say, "what did you think of my grandparents, when you saw them today?"

"Eh? Who?" Hercule frowns.

"My mom's parents, the Mason-Hunts — they attended my departure."

"I suppose I thought nothing of them," he says.

"Did you know I'd never met them before?" I ask. "They disowned Mom when she and Dad married."

"For what reason?" Hercule asks.

"Because Dad is Mexican," I say. "And mom's parents, the Mason-Hunts, they're part of me — *that* kind of family is half of me. Family as a kind of . . . a kind of uniform. Family that divides everything into Us and Them. Maybe it's about skin color, or religion, or who you fall in love with . . . it's all Us and Them. But I can't accept that. Not after everything that's happened to me, to my parents — my friends. And I know that Gonzalo's gift had nothing to do with that. That's not who he was, and it's not who I am. He would have wanted me to reach out. To help someone in need, whoever they are."

"'Each of you should use whatever gift you have received to serve others,'" says Hercule.

"That's right!" I say, surprised to hear St. Mary's motto — the very verse that inspired my Wrap-Up List in the first place. "And you knew all along that I'd do it," I say, "even though you're pretending otherwise. Did I tell you that I saw Sylvester's Wrap-Up List? He'd asked you about signing up for the army, and your Hint said, 'Volunteer.'"

"That is the usual way of going about it."

"But he wasn't eighteen yet. He departed before his birthday, so the Hint didn't make sense. But now it does; he's old enough now." I pause. "This has been it all along. I have one last gift to give away."

Sylvester is watching the back-and-forth between us like a mouse watching an argument between cats.

"Are you sure then?" says Hercule.

"I'm sure," I say.

Hercule turns abruptly to Sylvester. "Young man," he says, "you are hereby granted the Pardon first earned by Gabriela's grandfather. It has been transferred to you. Return to your life, and live well."

Sylvester looks confused. "You're . . . letting me go?" he says.

Hercule continues: "Your father is out of town right now, visiting his sister. But he left the side door unlocked." He observes Sylvester strictly, trying to discern if anything is sinking in. "You listening?" he asks. "I will also point out, though Gabriela has already done so, that you are eighteen now."

"Eighteen," Sylvester echoes.

Hercule shakes his head. "A few steps down the hill may revive you," he says, gesturing back the way we came. Sylvester looks at me. He looks at his bare feet.

Then, he takes a step downhill.

He gasps.

Air fills his lungs, and his body wrests itself away from death. Color floods into his chest and down through his arms and legs. His hair falls, plastering his skull as if he's just been pulled from a dunk tank. He shudders, and then sobs. *"Gabriela . . ."* he croaks.

"Iris is waiting at the Departure point," I say. "She brought some extra clothes." I turn away from him. It's too hard to look. I lock my gaze under the Oaks.

"Thank you," he says, the words drenched in insufficiency.

He takes another step downhill, and then another. I listen as he retreats, straining my ears until there's nothing left.

the last dance

"That was foolish," says Hercule.

"But you knew I would do it," I say. "You told Sylvester to wait for me. You told him to volunteer."

Hercules shakes his head. "I can only encourage things —"

"That *might* happen, I know," I say.

"You're like your grandfather, Gabriela, in that way — generous to a fault," says Hercule.

"I'm glad to be like him," I say. "But I'm not dying under an olive tree."

"That's why I called you foolish." Hercule seems a little mystified by it all — he's calling me a fool, but he says it gently. "Anyway, it makes no difference to me. I already suffered my Abeyance."

"Is that when Deaths disappear after they grant Pardons?"

"Indeed."

"What is it?" I ask. "Is it bad?"

"Yes," says Hercule, "but you wouldn't understand."

"Well, is it a tragedy or just an inconvenience?" I ask.

"It is between the two," says Hercule. "In the case of your grandfather, I didn't suffer too badly." He looks at me soberly. "You know, Gabriela, much of what has happened here has been important for me. It's been a long time since I've enjoyed an opportunity to see through such a splendid wrap-up. Kisses — and each one important in a different way. It was quite ingenious."

"You're welcome," I reply. And I am glad, I really am. But it's not enough. "Hercule, why did you pick me?" I ask. "In school we always learn that it's random. But this wasn't random — it can't be."

"Anything can be random," said Hercule. "That's the nature of randomness." He pauses. "But no, it wasn't quite. A few days after I'd been attached to your friend Sylvester, your name came up — Felix was going to get it. I called in a favor he owed me, and he handed you over. It was nagging at me, I suppose, to have this unused Pardon floating around."

The triviality of this tale strikes me kind of hard. My whole story is reduced to Hercule feeling "nagged." I wish it could have been something more important. I look away down the hill. "What if I just ran off? Ran back home?" I say.

"You'll find you can't take even a single step," says Hercule. "The forces that prevent others from coming here will prevent you from leaving. But you can console yourself that you accomplished much of what you set out to do. A victory that might be quite freeing, as your friend Alfeo suggested."

"I'm barely sixteen."

"I know," says Hercule. "I'm sorry, Gabriela. I agree, you are young."

I look under the Oaks and imagine my grandfather, all those years before I was born, staring into the Tunisian olive grove.

"Hercule," I say, "you told me to save you a dance. But I don't really know how to dance." I step up to him, hugely tall before me.

He takes my small gray hands in his enormous silver ones. "A waltz," he says, and begins, setting the tempo with a tuneless little *tum-tee-tee, tum-tee-tee*. The two of us turn in a slow circle, at the very edge of everything. The predawn glow has increased around us, evaporating the mist hanging above the turf, turning the grass brilliant green. The tanned oak leaves shine with dew. The swallows flit across the field.

"Goodbye, Hercule," I say. "Thank you for being my friend."

"Thank you, Gabriela. I was proud to escort you."

I release his hands.

I look under the Oaks, observing as the shadows continue to sharpen with the approach of dawn.

Then I turn away from them. Downhill — toward home.

Hercule blanches, and an annoyed expression crosses his face. *"Gabriela,"* he says strictly, "don't embarrass yourself."

"You're right that my grandfather was noble and generous," I say. "But I think he was also kind of tricky."

I close my eyes.

I lift one bare foot, and take a step downhill.

No force prevents me.

As my heel sinks into the grass, a sudden clap of thunder cracks in my chest, and I gasp, inhaling. I look down to see my gray skin flood with color, starting at my belly and spilling through my arms and legs. Another crash reverberates. It's my heart beating.

My hair falls straight down, slapping my shoulders, soaking wet. The thick air around me evaporates, and I stumble.

"Stop!" Hercule yells. He holds out his long arms commandingly.

I turn to him, shivering and thrilled, breathless. *"I figured it out!"* I shout, laughing. "Your Noble Weakness is *giving away a Pardon!* That's what Iris found — everyone who ever earned a Pardon from you transferred it. They promised it to someone else, didn't they? Just like Gonzalo did — promising his to his descendants."

"But — but — " Hercule stutters.

"Only this time was different. This time — it was more complicated. The Pardon I gave away and the Pardon I earned weren't the same. I gave away Gonzalo's Pardon, to

Sylvester—and because of your Noble Weakness, that generous act earned me a new one. Which I'm using for *myself*."

Hercule's eyes are wide in startled shock as I explain.

Suddenly the sun breaks over the horizon, throwing my sharp, solid shadow far ahead of me down the slope. "I really meant it, by the way, Hercule—about you being a good friend. And I'm truly sorry to do this to you."

He stares at me silently, rage and confusion smoldering in his eyes.

"I hope this is an inconvenience, and not a tragedy. Um—will you be able to sit in your favorite chair during your Abeyance?" I know I'm needling him a little. I can't help it.

For a moment, it looks like he won't respond. Finally, he nods. "Yes," he says icily, "I will be able to sit in my favorite chair." And then he vanishes, blinking out as quickly as a slammed door, and I'm alone.

I glance under the Oaks, where the firm, dark shadows lie upon the rust leaves. My eyes linger for a moment, but there's nothing for me there. Not yet, anyway.

I turn downhill.

After two or three steps walking, I break into a run. The grass is wet, freezing on my bare feet, but it doesn't slow me. I'm rushing, my breath deep and strong. Up ahead, two figures come into view down by the departure point. I yell to them, and they see me and wave. Iris is there, with Sylvester next to her, wearing the white dress she brought for me. It fits him badly.

I pass the hyacinths, and their scent fills my lungs, tickling my nose. It's not the impossible soup that Hercule brought to the Caballero—it's just flowers, fresh, sweet, stinging, and alive.

I suddenly remember Hercule's Hint to me.

—*The Fields.*

I am ready to be kissed.

TRANSCRIPTION FROM OFFICIAL
DOCUMENTS
PROVIDED BY: ELLIS COUNTY DEPARTURE
AUTHORITY
Attending Death: Hercule
Site: Ellis Fields, Oak Grove
Departing Person: Gabriela Rivera. Citizenship: USA
Departure Status: *Pardon 1. Trns. from Gonzalo
Rivera; Re-Trns. to Sylvester Hale
Pardon 2. Granted and used

*See attached article for further information. Iris Van
Voorhees, "The Departure of Gabriela Rivera," *Journal of
the Association of Departure Science,* vol. 96, no. 7.

acknowledgments

The humble first draft I produced of this story had the wonderful fortune to benefit from the help of several first-rate minds. I'm particularly grateful to my agent, Jenni Ferrari-Adler, who had the patience to steer me through draft after draft of my strange affinity for wrong directions. I'd also like to thank Margaret Raymo at Houghton Mifflin for her solid advice throughout the editing process — it was wonderful to have such wise guidance at the moment the book gained its final shape. But most of all I'm indebted to my wife, Anne, for talking everything through with me again and again. Anne, you continue to be the greatest influence on the way I live and think. I count myself very lucky to have such help as I muddle through this life.